Jules Breton

# The Life of an Artist

Jules Breton

**The Life of an Artist**

ISBN/EAN: 9783337013882

Printed in Europe, USA, Canada, Australia, Japan

Cover: Foto ©Raphael Reischuk / pixelio.de

More available books at **www.hansebooks.com**

# THE LIFE OF AN ARTIST

## AN AUTOBIOGRAPHY

BY
JULES BRETON

TRANSLATED BY
MARY J. SERRANO

NEW YORK
D. APPLETON AND COMPANY
1890

MESSRS. D. APPLETON AND COMPANY, *New York*.

*Gentlemen*: It is with great pleasure that I authorize you to publish the translation of the Life of an Artist. The importance of your house, and the conscientious care which it gives to all its publications, are to me a sure guarantee of the attention which this book will receive from you. This history of my life is at the same time the genesis of my art. It offers also portraits of the painters who were my friends or contemporaries, and the history of the movement of art since 1848 of which I have been a part.

*The great favor with which this book has been received in France will find, I hope, its echo among American readers. I am deeply interested in their opinion, for I am full of gratitude for the constant success with which their noble and puissant country has been pleased to encourage my work as a painter.*

*Please receive, gentlemen, the assurance of my best wishes.*

JULES BRETON.

COURRIÈRES, *October 17, 1890.*

# INTRODUCTION.

WITH charming frankness and simplicity Jules Breton relates in this volume his memories of boyhood, the aspirations and struggles of youth, and the associations of those later years when Delacroix, Millet, Corot, Rousseau, Daubigny, and others of that memorable company still lived to the glory of the national art which Breton himself represents so worthily. Of his own great successes he speaks with becoming modesty, but we in America have learned long since to value Breton's best work wholly apart from the unthinking admiration aroused for the artist whose "Evening at Finistère" brought a price at the Seney sale in New York which was deemed phenomenal until, at the Morgan sale in 1886, his painting of "The First Communion" reached the astonishing price of $45,500. But neither the contention of millionaires for Breton's paintings nor their presence in most of our larger collections nor the exact rank of his art need concern the reader of this delightfully intimate autobiography, written not from the standpoint of the technician or craftsman, but from that of a man whose quick perceptions, fine sensibility, and command of literary as well as pictorial expression impart a rare value to his story of a life which has touched or included so many of the significant political, artistic, and literary movements of this century in France. It is always, however, as the man or the artist that Breton writes his recollections, and we can see that politics and social problems have rarely disturbed a life singularly serene and devoted to one purpose. The picture which he presents is a personal one, and in harmony with the dedication of the original to "my daughter Virginie, for whom alone the first chapters were written originally." A few Americans know Breton's poems, but in this autobiography we may justly claim the pleasure of presenting the famous painter to our public as an author whose hope that Americans will find something of interest in this story of his life will not, we think, be disappointed.

# THE LIFE OF AN ARTIST.

## I.

THE Garden of Delight, the cradle of Adam, we have all dwelt in it.

Those sudden bursts of joy whose source is unknown to us, mysterious smiles that without cause gladden our hearts, are but dim reminiscences of it. Thus does the eye preserve the image of the sun long after it has ceased to look at it.

We all treasure in our memories the splendors of a wondrous time, when the light was clearer, the dawn rosier, the air more vibrant, the skies deeper and more softly blue, than they are now.

Who does not remember this earliest spring-time, when the tender buds mingled their wild fragrance with the aroma of the earth ; when we felt the soft clay of the garden-paths, still moist from the winter snows and only partially hardened by the sun, yield under our tread ?

In those days joyous bushes bloomed with starlike flowers, rosy and white, and, forever in motion, buzzed with clouds of golden bees.

Where now are those trees that lived and sang? And how many animals were there that we no longer meet with in the gardens ? One of these was that little elephant, smaller than a mouse, that pushed its slender trunk through the crevices in the wall, watching me from the shadows with malignant glance, and quickly disappearing at my approach. Birds of a pale-green color, like that of our grasshoppers, sang among the corn.

I heard sounds around me as of the voice of one talking alone, and I was not afraid. It was the voice of God.

And the setting sun! How large it seemed on warm, stormy evenings ; how gloriously it shone among the golden clouds that took new and strange forms at every moment! I saw among them the figures of animals, of men, and sometimes of the Virgin. But my mother never appeared to me, and my eye sought for her in vain in those celestial processions; I missed her, for I had known her only for a short time on earth, and I knew she was there above.

The elderly cousin who came in the summer to cut the grass on our lawn—she had seen her! This woman and I understood each other, she was so old and I so little. She knew so many things ; she sang such beautiful songs in her drawling voice !

One very stormy day she had felt herself raised suddenly in the air and carried bodily to a distance, together with her bundle of grass ; and she had seen the lightning pass close by her under the form of a fiery cock, with swords instead of feathers in its tail.

I loved her dearly. She seemed venerable to me, especially when her figure grew indistinct in the twilight as she returned home in the evening.

I loved her on this account, and also on account of her sickle, which looked so like the crescent moon.

## II.

THAT my mother was in heaven I had no doubt, but I never knew just how she had left us.

I preserved a recollection of her at once vague and intense, which at occasional delightful hours was always present with me, revived by certain colors, odors, sounds, or states of the atmosphere.

Then I saw again her languid beauty, her sweet pale face, her mouth, expressing mingled melancholy and goodness, and her deep-set brown eyes, circled with dark shadows, that shone with so tender a light under their large white lids!

I fancied I could feel again her passionate embraces. Ah, I loved her well!

She had been ill a long, long time. I recalled her sitting in the corner of the wide chimney-place of our little kitchen, at times with her breast uncovered, to which horrible black reptiles clung, and there it was that she one day said to me, "I am going to die!" Did I understand her? Why did I weep? I recalled those words and others, very commonplace ones. When the period arrived at which I was to put off skirts and wear for the first time the dress of a boy, she saw through the window the tailor coming toward the house, and said to me, "Jules, here is your suit!"

Since I have grown up I have often shed tender tears thinking of my mother and repeating to myself those welcome words, "Jules, here is your suit!"

My mother! Again I see the straw hat trimmed with wild flowers, and the red and yellow shawl you wore in your languid walks in the garden, where you were soon to bid farewell to the flowers you loved, and that beheld you die!

I must have been bad indeed to have vexed you at such a time.

I had received that morning, from my godfather, my first sword. I fancied myself a rural guard ! And I went to the end of the village in search of some delinquent. I arrived very opportunely. A boy of about my own age was crossing the nearest cultivated field. I called to him to leave it, and, as he refused to do so, I made use of my weapon. The blow struck him full in the face, and the poor little fellow's nose began to bleed. At the sight of the blood I began to realize the wickedness of my conduct. I returned home ashamed of it. From the garden, where I had taken refuge, I soon heard angry cries filling the court-yard. On my account the mother of the injured child was abusing my poor mother.

Mamma called to me, and, as I did not answer, she hurried in search of me. Then, seeing myself on the point of being discovered, I slipped for safety into an asparagus-bed which had not yet been cut, and which was impenetrable to every one but me, and there awaited the cessation of the storm.

Soon the young invalid walked no longer in the garden. She kept her room, then her bed, and every evening before going to sleep my brother and I went up-stairs to kiss her.

After kissing us tenderly she gave us bonbons. And one day, when the bonbons were all exhausted, mamma went to Arras to buy some more. I did not understand then why she remained there. I did not understand, either, why she took us, before setting out, to the house of a relation who lived at a distance from us in the village, and why we spent the whole day there and received more caresses than usual. But on our return home I suspected that something strange had happened, for going into the empty room, I found Mlle. Rosalie there crying. She could cry then, this Mlle. Rosalie, who was so terrible when she punished the children with her long switch at the infants' school which we attended, and of which she was the mistress.

---

### III.

But let us leave Mlle. Rosalie.

I should like to go still further back into the past, to those first sensations which stand out faintly from the confused mist in which my memory, becoming fainter and fainter, finally loses itself—the dawn of the beginning, the light which dimly illuminates nothingness. There I see vague white shapes move about, and faces bend over me, of which all the features are indistinct, except the eyes that shine like stars, there I see smiles and eddying whirlpools.

When I begin to discern more clearly the forms of things, building was going on at our house. They were adding a new wing to the old part of the structure. Immense walls rose into the air, and on ladders which seemed to reach into infinity men were perpetually going up and down.

They had dug a hole for a pump, and the water they drew out of it at first was quite white. I thought it was milk—milk from the earth! I wanted to drink some of it.

On account of my mother's delicate health, I had been brought up by a nurse. Her name was Henriette. I called her *Mémère*. She was a young widow, a brunette, very active in her movements, and she loved me as she did her own children—an attachment which I reciprocated to the end.

Poor, and extremely neat, she lived in a room in a cottage in the neighborhood, which she divided by means of a curtain of cheap material, ornamented with blue flowers on a white ground. A single window, opening on to the street, lighted up an oaken wardrobe, kept scrupulously clean, surmounted by an *étagère* on which were a few pewter vessels, always bright, and some rustic earthenware. A high fireplace with white-washed, rough-cast walls, a black hearth covered with sticky soot, and a few straw chairs complete the picture.

When the curtain was raised a double alcove, so dark that one could scarcely distinguish the two beds in it, was revealed to view by the light of a small window set in the wall. There it was that Mémère often put me to sleep to the droning sound of some village lament.

When I was able to walk, I still went quite naturally to the house of Mémère to play with her two boys, both of them a little older than I. I preferred their coarse food to ours, and I always arrived at meal-times. Henriette would bring to the threshold of the open door the large black pot filled with steaming potatoes, their skins bursting open, and, seated on the floor around it, our hands for forks, we all would eat heartily.

One day, coming in hastily, I struck my foot against some obstacle which lay in the way, and fell with all my force against the edge of the pot, cutting myself severely under the lower lip. Henriette ran to me on hearing my cries and, frightened at the sight of the blood gushing forth, clasped me in her arms and carried me quickly to her little garden that opened out on the fields.

It was a beautiful sunny afternoon in spring.

The pain grew less; I restrained my tears and stammered: "Mémère, don't cry; 'tis nothing!" Suddenly I pointed with my finger to a large yellow mass at the end of the garden, so bright, so extraordinarily bright, that only to think of it dazzles me with an excess of splendor.

Henriette understood what my outbursts of delight and my extended arms meant, and carried me toward this marvel, which was nothing more than a field of colza in bloom. I have never seen another like it, but every other colza-field delights me because of that one.

My nurse plucked me a branch, and since then colza-flowers always smell sweet to me.

It was at about this time that I first knew what fear was.

Mémère brought me home one evening from a house at some distance from ours, where night had overtaken us. The streets were dark, the outlines of the roofs blended imperceptibly into the blackness of the sky, and everything appeared still darker from the lines of light that escaped through the cracks of the closed shutters, fiery arrows that all pointed in the darkness toward my eyes with a persistency that had something like sorcery in it. I buried my head in Henriette's bosom, and remained perfectly still. I had already been told of the horrors of hell, and the thought of them redoubled my terror. Suddenly at the turn of a street an extraordinary noise burst forth, and at the same time I heard a crowd of people, passing and repassing, close beside me. We were in the midst of the tumult—the harsh sound of rattles, the cracking of whips, the clashing of iron pots and pans. Frozen with terror I clung closer and closer to Henriette. I closed my eyes convulsively, shutting the lids tight, and yet I saw—I saw a legion of black devils, who pursued me, brandishing long bars of red-hot iron, and uttering ferocious chuckles and abominable cries.

When we reached the house I heard my nurse say, "They are blowing the horns for Zaguée."

To blow the horns for any one means, with us peasants, to give him a *charivari*.

They were blowing the horns then, for Zaguée, an old beggar-woman, who, with her owl's head and red eyes, looked more like a sorceress than an ordinary human being.

------

## IV.

I HAVE since seen many magnificent gardens, but never one that could make me forget the garden of my father—for me the first and only garden.

Surrounded by walls covered with espaliers, and crowned by vines with a verdant frieze, it was divided into squares by wide sanded walks, into which paths, bordered with sorrel, opened. At the various points where the paths met, pear-trees spread out their branches in the form of an arch.

A true French garden, with its beds of vegetables and its flower-borders.

At the entrance, between two grass-plots, a low marble pillar, surmounted by a sun-dial, rose from the midst of a clump of anemones.

But the wonder of the garden was the grotesque stone figures at its four corners, that gleamed in the sunshine, perched on high wooden columns painted green.

They represented the four seasons.

Spring, Summer, and Autumn, chubby-cheeked and plump, bore, one of them her basket of flowers, another her sheaf, and the third her vine-branch, laden with black grapes.

As for Winter, I do not know why it bore no resemblance to the other seasons. It was represented by the naked figure of a woman, of larger proportions than theirs, the head and shoulders only being covered with a kind of sackcloth.

Huddled up and crouching with the cold, this figure seemed to shiver, in spite of the brands that burned at its feet.

This want of harmony in the statues puzzled me. Doubtless this figure replaced a former *Winter*, broken by some accident, for it was newer than the others, and its outlines, more delicate than theirs, had not yet quite disappeared under the numerous coats of paint which, for a long time past, had renovated the figures each successive year.

Such was this garden, for me the garden of Eden!

Here, among the flowers and the insects, my first sensations, my first reveries, had birth.

Often, in the silent solitude, I would lie stretched on my back on the grass in the sunshine. Close to my face were the long blades of grass, seeming tall as trees, and I would let my fancy wander far away with the clouds floating past, while above me the branches of an immense poplar, which grew in our neighbor's garden, reached, quivering against the blue sky, into space.

At every breath of wind, every branch set in motion its flakes of cottony seeds that, becoming detached, fell softly at my feet; and, through the shadowy depths of the tree, occasional glimpses of the sky gleamed like blue stars. And the swallows darted past, flew round and round, hovered above me and then soared high into the air, diminishing in size, until they seemed no larger than the insects on the dandelions beside me.

Clumps of various flowers surrounded the grass-plot. Among the bees and insects that gleamed golden, purple, and emerald as they flew, the day-moth would suddenly appear like a flash of lightning, and, without pausing in its flight, would dart from flower to flower, hovering an instant above each with almost invisible wings, and plunging into its cup the slender proboscis that, lengthening itself out, wound round and round like a hunter's horn. And what delicate music accompanied these pure visions !

Buzzings, rustlings, murmurs, the sound of insects brushing against the rose-leaves, and of birds sharpening their bills.

Where find again the ineffable delights of these twilight hours when the red flowers were already black, while the blue ones still shone brightly !

The beetles whizzed blindly against my face, the night butterflies described indistinctly in the gathering darkness the abrupt zigzags of their flight, and from behind the trees the moon cast pale, trembling shadows on the walls. I experienced a certain pleasure in penetrating into the darkest places among the foliage, and feeling mysterious shudders run down my back at seeing some strange nocturnal animal, shrew-mouse or salamander, moving on the ground.

The profound silence was broken only by the movement of some bird concealed among the branches, and which I had awakened; or by the strange sound borne on the breeze from the distant marsh—the harsh croaking of the innumerable frogs making there their accustomed tumult, and by the shrill and ceaseless chirping of countless grasshoppers. On one of those evenings when I had been allowed to remain out later than usual, the idea occurred to me to shake a rose-bush at the end of one of the walks, for the purpose of bringing down some cockchafers, I think it was. But what fell out of the bush began to hop about in the flower-border. Cockchafers do not hop, frogs do not climb rose-bushes. Here there was some mystery which made me tremble at once with joy and terror. Yes, little living things were jumping and hopping about among the flowers.

I trembled, but I had the courage to put my hand on one of these strange little beings. O joy! I felt feathers! The rose-bush sheltered a bird's nest!

When I look far back into the mystery of the past, I find among the flowers of the garden a little girl, fair and rosy, with blue eyes. This was my sister Julie, who had come into the world two years before me, and who was so soon to leave it.

Important events make but slight impression on children, and I have no recollection of her death, which, they say, caused the death of my mother, who was inconsolable for her loss. But I remember that one day she was swinging from a ladder, her feet brushing the ground, and her charming head, from which the hair fell in a shower of golden curls, thrown back, while she sang in her sweet childish voice a couplet which I have never since heard, and of which the two following lines have remained in my memory:

> " Des souliers gris
> Pour aller au Paradis—"

I find, too, among the family relics, a curl of her hair, which seems still to keep a gleam of its former brightness.

---

## V.

EVERY year, as soon as the fine weather set in, the painter Fremy came, and his arrival was a great event.

I can see him now with his important air, his crooked nose, and his jacket of maroon-colored cloth, unpacking his painting implements and his color-pots.

The first time I saw this man, I said to myself, " I will be a painter ! "

He would glance at me severely whenever I touched his pencils or his book of gold-leaf.

He was very grave, and scarcely ever spoke. When he felt in the humor, however, he would talk to me about the various châteaux where he had worked.

He told me wonderful things about them, but I could not then imagine anything finer than the paternal house, especially after this same Fremy had repainted the wide plastered façade, with its pediment ornamented with a lyre of a bright rose-color, the large door yellow, and the shutters a cheerful green.

This most important part of the work being finished, the painter would descend to details, and now indeed my joy burst forth. I watched him as he took out the little pots that contained fine and brilliant colors, from his tin box. The first thing to be done was to retouch a painting of the setting sun on the ceiling above the staircase, and to renovate the *marchande d'amour* above the mirror on the parlor mantel-piece. Then the turn of the Chinese would come.

The court-yard of the house was in the form of a square, and was partly paved, partly sodded. It was inclosed on three sides by the main portion of the building, and two side wings, composed of the dining-room, the kitchens, the bake-house, and various sheds. This yard was separated from the back yard and the garden by a railing.

Overlooking the back yard was a square pigeon-house, resting on four pillars and terminating in a *chef-d'œuvre* of architecture.

This pointed roof consisted, in the first place, of a sort of small, round wooden temple, supported on an iron shaft, and surrounded by little columns, the bases of which, set in a circular flooring, remained in air. As the crowning glory of this diminutive temple of the sibyl, there hung over it a sort of extinguisher, ornamented with bells and terminating in a ball, through which passed the iron shaft on which turned an enormous weathercock— the famous Chinese, who sat in the midst of the landscape smoking his pipe. You may imagine the effect! All this took up fully a third of the pigeon-house, and did not frighten the pigeons. I remember that some years later, on a certain stormy night, we heard an ominous sound, and in the morning the temple was found lying broken to pieces on the ground, and the Chinese, all disjointed, beside it. But we must not anticipate events.

Fremy, assisted by a workman, set up his ladder and unfastened and took down the Chinese, who, with every step which Fremy took, seemed to grow larger, and soon I was able to look at him close by, and to measure the thickness of the flooring of the temple, which was strengthened by iron plates fastened with large nails.

But if I clapped my hands with delight when the painter brightened the jacket of the figure with a splendid chrome-yellow, what was my joy when I saw him, for the purpose of repainting its trousers, mixing blue with the yellow to obtain a most beautiful bright green!

After this, the " Four Seasons " were ranged around the shed, leaving their vacant pedestals and the deserted garden behind them.

And, indeed, they stood in great need of the painter's help, for they were covered all over with spots where the old paint had blistered and fallen off in scales. High up on their pedestals this was scarcely noticeable, but close by it was hideous. Fremy scraped them carefully, gave them a first coat of white paint, and then, like a veritable magician, restored to them the appearance of youth and life, touching their lips and chubby cheeks with carmine, and their fixed and squinting eyes with brown, while thousands of little insects settled giddily on the fresh paint, to remain fastened there by their wings till the following spring.

## VI.

I MADE the acquaintance of my uncle Boniface, whom at that time I called my Lille uncle, about 1830. My mother had not yet begun to keep her room, and still attended to the details of housekeeping.

No one around us suspected the influence my uncle was fated to have on our destinies. But one might fancy I had a presentiment of it, for, although I was then only three years old, I remember the minutest details preceding and accompanying his arrival.

The sun was shining. I was gay as a lark. I had promised to be very good; and I was the more disposed to be so, as I expected some handsome present from a man coming from a large city, and who must be of some importance, judging from the assiduous preparations I observed going on.

Ever since morning the house had worn an air of festivity and joyous anticipation, in which the masters, the servants, and even inanimate objects shared—the fresh flowers on the chimney-piece, the table glittering with its shining silver, and the antique bottles covered with a bluish cloud, iridescent with time, and of which the corks were beginning to crumble into dust. I remember with what respect and with how careful a touch my father set these bottles always in the same place on the console fastened to the parlor wall.

My mother walked to and fro, and my father stood with his eyes fixed on the newspaper, reading it half-aloud in an indistinct voice.

Taking up a sheet of paper I tried to imitate this odd way of reading, making my parents, who saw in this a mark of a precocious intelligence, laugh, when (my dear uncle, you were no ordinary man, since I can recall and recount with pleasure details so insignificant regarding you)—when the rolling of carriage - wheels was heard, first in the street, and then entering the court-yard.

We hurried out, uttering joyful cries of welcome, and for the first time I felt myself raised in the arms of the generous man to whom I owe everything. I shall speak at length of him later on. All that I could observe on this day was, that my uncle was a man of elegant bearing, that he wore a blue coat with gilt buttons, in the French fashion, light-colored trousers, and a wide white cravat ; that he held his head erect, and that his high and wide forehead was surmounted by a superb toupet, trimmed in the form of an arch, which must have been the object of special care.

I was not disappointed in my expectations from him : he brought me a bright hunting-horn. I loved him at once.

<hr>

## VII.

BESIDES the persons already mentioned, there were in the house my maternal grandmother, Scholastique Fumery, who had long been a widow, my grandfather, Dr. Platel, having died many years before ; Joseph Carpentier, an old soldier of the empire, and his wife, Phillipine. If we add to these the persons hired by the day

—the gardener, Buisine, nicknamed Frisé, often accompanied by his son; the *bueresses* (laundresses); the carpenter who split the firewood, a work that occupied a long time; a joiner, who for months and months hammered, planed, and smoked innumerable pipes in the unfinished parlor of the new building; and our little companions dressed up by their sisters, who came to play with us—it will be seen that there was no lack of animation in our house.

My father, the steward of the Duke de Duras, for whom he superintended important estates, among others the forest of Labroye, was compelled to be often absent from home.

Besides this, the functions he exercised as assistant of the justice of the peace often detained him at Carvin, and compelled him to take a part in many of the affairs of the canton. Thus it was that he was seldom at home, and when there he was always busy, scarcely ever leaving his desk, which was always covered with maps and books.

Before his marriage he had been a lawyer's clerk in the office of my uncle Platel, at Herim-Liétard.

He had been a member of the municipal band of that city, which explains the lyre on the façade of our house.

I have seen his abandoned buccina, which for a long time was thrown from one corner to another, and which was finally hung up in the dark passage behind the staircase. This snake, with its crocodile's head, its large, wide-open mouth, and its red eyes, often set me to thinking. Its head and neck still preserved, in the midst of the verdigris that overlaid them, a few scales of lacquer and gold.

My grandmother never left the house; I may even say that she never left the little kitchen, where she sat in her chair beside the window looking into the yard. This window was to the left of the large chimney-piece, in the style of Louis XV, of finely carved marble, which had belonged to a château that had been pulled down, and in which Fremy had been. She walked with difficulty on account of her age, her stoutness, and the shortness of her feet. Only on fine summer afternoons would she carry her chair to the grass-plot under the large cherry-tree in the yard. She spent whole hours there knitting, paring vegetables, or shelling peas.

Émile's nurse would come with her charge and sit beside her in the shade, while I played on the grass with my little brother Louis.

## VIII.

It will be seen that under these circumstances I must have enjoyed a liberty almost without limit, spoiled as I was by the servants and by those of my playmates who were in an inferior position to mine ; and that I easily escaped from the surveillance of a father who was often absent, of a mother who was dying, and of a grandmother who was almost helpless. I abused this liberty by running about the streets.

I brought home from there bands of little scapegraces who gave me lessons in boyish tricks by which I profited only too well. I went so far one day as to throw stones at the windows which opened into the garden, breaking all the glass, only to prove to the little rascals who applauded me that I was far above considering the expense.

Yet there was something good in me. I felt my heart filled with tenderness for my parents, and with compassion for the poor who, on Saturdays, crowded our court-yard.

I even felt an inward satisfaction in conquering the disgust caused me by their beggars' rags, and above all by the sight of physical deformities—a disgust which, in certain cases, became horror. I felt myself at times seized with a trembling when I held out the sou which I was charged by my grandmother to give to certain cripples. I shuddered only to hear the noise of their crutches on the pavement.

But the idiot, Bénési, inspired me with no repugnance, because he was always good and always clean, with his gray coat and his coarse shirt, whose collar cut his enormous ears, adorned with rings. I would scarcely even ridicule his stammering when it took him two minutes, in speaking to my uncle, to say, " Monsieur Biébiéeniface." He had a strange appearance, however, with his large nose, wide mouth, and head the size of one's fist, close-cropped, and streaked with furrows like a potato-field.

What solicitude, like that of a faithful dog, he manifested for his blind sister, whose guide and careful guard he always was !

Therefore it was that we protected Bénési, and defended him against the street boys who threw stones at him and made fun of his insane but harmless fits of anger.

My parents, seeing that I was beginning to grow wild, sought to put me under the care of a good woman of the neighborhood, who kept a school for little children. But, when we had reached the house, I rushed toward the door and clung to it so desperately, uttering furious and persistent cries the while, that they were obliged to take me home again. Some time afterward they had recourse to the terrible Mlle. Rosalie, an old maid, a for-

mer servant of the curé, who kept an infants' school. I
was more docile in allowing myself to be taken there:
in the first place, because my brother Louis, who was
now old enough to go to school, accompanied me; and,
in the next, because the little carriage which they had
ordered from the joiner of the large parlor, so long ago
that they had forgotten all about it, being at last finished, after the smoking of innumerable pipes, we had
the glory of being driven to school by Joseph in this
brilliant equipage.

Besides, the implacable switch of the schoolmistress
soon reduced me to good conduct. I fancy I can still
feel her blows, when, at the least sign of rebellion, she
would strike me heavily with it over the head.

---

## IX.

THERE we were in a little room without ventilation,
a crowd of children huddled closely together. Doubtless our parents were not long in perceiving the bad
effect of this *régime*, from a hygienic point of view, for
they took us away of their own accord from Mlle. Rosalie's school. Those few months of unhealthy bondage
made me better appreciate the joys of liberty.

We resumed once more our life in the open air with
our little playmates, and that was a happy time.

Each season brought its games and its festivals.

I shall have occasion enough to speak of summer. I
wish now to say a word about our winter pleasures, which
were worth all the others put together. Winter is not
always, as we personify it, a melancholy and trembling
old man, his beard hung with icicles; nor the freezing,
half-naked woman, her head covered with sackcloth,

who shivered, huddled up in the garden, notwithstanding the plaster flames which Fremy had caused to burn with so beautiful a red. Does not Winter rather resemble, at certain times, a cold and beautiful young girl, clad in robes of dazzling whiteness, whose blue eyes smile through her veil of mist starred with diamonds?

Ah! what delight when the first snow-flakes eddy through the air, like a cloud of white butterflies, and fall with velvety softness upon the ground, which is gradually covered with their cold and immaculate splendor!

How our cries of joy re-echoed sonorously in this vibrant silence! What an awakening for the morrow! The rosy sunlight falls slantingly on the white roofs. The sky, of an extraordinary purity, casts a blue shadow on the smooth white carpet of snow in the court-yard. Among the branches of the cherry-tree, capricious rays of light play in rosy hues among the myriad sparkles of the iridescent hoar-frost.

My eyes open wide with delight. They take in at a glance all this wonderful glory. All this white splendor reflects my soul, which grows white also. I rise quickly, impatient to press with my foot the unstained whiteness of the walks.

Like the joyous wren that hops, dazzled, from branch to branch, making a fine rain of white flakes fall at every bound, my heart beats in a tumult of unalloyed ecstasy.

How many surprises! Everything looks different. The Chinese, whose hat is now adorned with a garniture of plush, smokes snow as he sits, motionless and frozen in his temple. The walls of the pigeon-house, pink before, look as if they had been painted a brownish-red. Here comes Mylord, our spaniel, bounding toward me, flecking the snow joyously with his tail. But has he been rolling in the mud? How yellow and soiled his coat, generally so clean and white, looks now! The garden in its robe of hoar-frost looks gayer than in the spring-time.

I go into the kitchen, of which the floor, contrariwise to Mylord, is whiter than on other days. How bright it is! What mysterious embroidery has covered all the window-panes with flowers?

I think all the world ought to rejoice as I do, and I am very much surprised to hear my grandmother say:

"The snow has come. The poor are going to suffer now!"

For us, who thought only of our sports, the snow meant skating on the ponds, joyous combats with snow-balls, and bombardings of the pigeon-house, with occasional interruptions caused by the numbness and stiffness of our fingers from the cold, followed by sharp pain when we warm them at the fire.

Soon the snow grows softer and more yielding, and we learn to roll it up and heap it in enormous blocks that become hard and ugly and are pierced by little holes, and which it takes an eternity to melt.

How soiled and unsightly the garden then looks, with its dahlias and chrysanthemums, their leaves hanging sadly in blackened, shriveled shreds!

How those plants must have suffered!

* * *

## X.

IN the evenings Joseph takes us into the garden, which is all bathed in mist and blue moonlight. He holds his lantern high up toward the trees which he shakes. At times, a sparrow, suddenly awakened, flies terrified against the light, extinguishing it. But Joseph has already shut the lantern, taking the bird captive.

At other times it would be a hunt with *pactoires*. *Pactoires* we called a string attached to the end of a long pole and stretched on hoops by means of forked sticks. This was a surer and more formal way of trapping sparrows.

I was indeed excited when we set out at night, our *pactoires* on our shoulders. Nocturnal things took on a fantastic aspect. Here we were, five or six little boys, holding our breaths, we who were so noisy in the daytime. Joseph set down his lantern on the ground in our midst, and our shadows prolonged themselves indefinitely in the mist, like the dark spokes of an immense wheel. A pale light trembled on the walls of the barns under the old thatched roofs, whose outlines faded imperceptibly into the sky.

From time to time Joseph set the pavilion of the *pactoire*. Sparrows flew into it from all directions, dazed by the light, striking themselves against the hoops and uttering little cries of terror accompanied by that nocturnal sound of wings, unheard in the daytime. The captives struggled wildly to escape.

We remained dumb with mingled fear and delight.

At times the forked sticks became detached from the hoops, and it was a matter of some difficulty to set the *pactoire* upright again. We went along looking for the thatched roofs ; we crossed court-yards where Joseph was acquainted with the dogs. These would first bark at us and would then come toward us amicably wagging their tails. But sometimes we stumbled on a dung-hill which we did not see until it was too late, and into which we plunged up to the knees. We went on to the barns, where everything had a weird and unfamiliar aspect. But the grinning plowshares were less terrible than the impenetrable darkness of the corners.

---

## XI.

When the weather was bad, when the wind howled down the chimney, and the furious and storm-beaten figure grinned on the pigeon-house, Louis Mémère (the son of Henriette) would tell us stories.

He knew a great many that he had heard from his grandfather and from the brickmakers who employed him occasionally as a workman. These simple and fabulous tales struck our dawning imagination with wonder. Sorcerers, ogres, and demons were mixed up in them with God and the Virgin.

According as the rude plot of the story unfolded, I seemed to see pass before me living pictures. I saw the peasant who boiled his soup by the light of the sun, by means of a magic whistle. I saw Jean d'Arras, the shoemaker who hunted in the forest with only his tools for weapons.

What a skillful man must Jean d'Arras have been! With what skill he could strike a hare on the forehead with a bit of wax! It was not long before this hare ran against another, and behold the two fastened together, forehead to forehead, and unable to stir from the spot. How adroitly Jean d'Arras escaped from the wild-boar, that, rushing toward him one day, missed him and struck the trunk of a tree instead with his terrible tusk, piercing it through and through! How quickly Jean turned round, took his hammer, riveted the tusk, and killed the monster with a stroke of his knife!

But when, having lost himself far, far away in the

forest, urged by hunger, he entered a solitary house, I trembled with him at the thought that this house was inhabited by an ogre just about to dine, and whose wife was serving him with soup, a meager repast for a giant.

And scenting in advance the delicious supper he would make of him in the evening, what covetous looks he would cast at poor Jean, paralyzed with fear!

On the other hand, as he was polite, he invited our shoemaker to partake of his soup. But the unhappy man, whose teeth chattered with fear, could not eat even a spoonful of it; and, in order not to disoblige so amiable a host, he pretended to carry the spoon to his mouth, but poured the contents of it into the pocket of his leathern apron, casting meanwhile a glance of terror toward the half-open door.

At last, the ogre having gone out for an instant, Jean escaped. Oh, terror! It was not long before he heard behind him, close in pursuit, his ferocious enemy. Jean was a swift runner, but the confounded pocket, heavy with soup, struck against his stomach and retarded his progress. He seized his knife, made a large slit in the pocket, and all the soup ran out. Then the ogre cried out : " Ah, you knave, I understand your *ruse!* The soup I have drunk keeps me too from running ! " And with his long sword he rips his belly open, and falls dead.

One might fill a volume with the tales that Louis Mémère related to us. But we must not delay. It is plain that winter was indeed a pleasant season.

This was the case in those days white with hoar-frost, and since, when, enveloped in delightful mystery, the guardians of the joys of childhood descended from paradise, through openings in the blue sky.

St. Catharine was the first to come, bringing with her heart-shaped spiced cakes, in the center of which, above her wheel, was her likeness in starch, surrounded by arabesques made of little dots of colored sugar.

François L——, my father's secretary, generally met her on the eve of her festival, on the road from Carvin, when he was returning from the office of the justice of the peace.

He announced her coming to us, representing her under the form of a simple peasant, seated on an ass between two panniers. Once he even brought us bon-bons which he had taken from her after threatening her with his pitchfork, and tumbling her and her ass into a ditch by the wayside.

And, little ingrates that we were, we had not a word of blame for this unworthy proceeding, or in defense of the poor saint.

Afterward came St. Nicholas. He descended through the air and entered by the chimney to fill our shoes with chocolate May-bugs. It was in this way that he escaped François L——, who was never able to plunder him.

We regaled ourselves on his bonbons, without showing him for our parts, either, any very great gratitude.

But the child Jesus was the object of all our affection. A little boy like ourselves, although the Son of God! What admiration, what respect, what emotion he awakened in us!

Have you ever observed that those children, who are the boldest in the presence of grown-up persons, become timid and embarrassed in a *tête-à-tête* with other children who are strangers to them? This is what happened to us in the presence of this mysterious comrade, radiant with celestial glory.

What a fascination his image exercised over us! A rosy child enveloped in white, fleecy clouds and clad in gauze sprinkled with golden spangles, who smiled at us with his porcelain eyes! In those days they had not yet introduced into our villages the Christmas trees, that blaze with a thousand lights; and yet what a delighted awakening, when we found under our pillows those cakes of a familiar shape, called *coquilles*, and which inspired us with such veneration that we hesitated for a long time, between greediness and respect, before we could make up our minds to bite them!

And New-Year's-day! What a festival! At midnight we were awakened by the rolling of drums, the tumult of the big drum and the shrill sound of clarionet and flute. The band was serenading in their turns the members of the five or six companies of archers. They executed in unison the same music more than four hundred times in succession—an air which must have come down from the remotest antiquity, so strange and barbarous it was.

We could hear it at our house, at times faint as a murmur, at times loud as thunder, according as the musicians receded or approached, and when it sounded before the house all the windows shook and our beds trembled at the boum-boum of the big drum, while the shrill sound of the fife pierced our ears like an auger.

We could not sleep all night; but we did not mind this, in the first place because the music amused us, and in the next because it foretold to us handsome New-Year's gifts, sous and silver pieces, which the magnificent velvet purses made by our grandmother had been waiting for, for some days past.

When day dawned we jumped out of bed to run and kiss our parents.

How many people came to the house during the day! How radiant did every face look! The archers filed into our court-yard, their ensign floating in the breeze, women following them—and then there was dancing. The music of the night before began again with daybreak, and now we could see the musicians. One of these especially, old Gaspard, who played upon the flute, delighted us with his red face and hair, and his big blue eyes. A hard drinker and a large eater, he was soon to end his life at table, at the banquet of St. Sebastian, without having so much as finished his soup. As he remained there a long time without eating, his neighbor pushed him gently, saying to him, "Why don't you eat, Gaspard?" And the poor old man fell over dead.

But he did not now foresee this misfortune, and he played his flute with calm animation while we all went out to visit our neighbors and friends, tramping through the snow, our hands stretched out before us, holding open our large purses.

----

## XII.

THE recollection of these hours of childhood comes to me like the memory of some delightful dream. Ah, with what enchanting tenderness those far-off days were filled! What dazzling splendor they assume, seen in the midst of the cruel disenchantment of age! What aspirations we had toward heaven! And at the same time how we felt ourselves comrades of the flowers and the beloved animals! Ah, the days of our childhood!

To be one's self the dawn and to behold the dawn! Days of marvelous discoveries! To run about where we chose, as we chose, over roads which at times terminated abruptly, as if there were nothing beyond, as if that were the end of the world.

To be received, on our return home, with fond caresses by our grandmother.

And to express all these emotions, so delightful because they are infinite and inexpressible, I must make use of words which I was then ignorant of. But if one were to express one's self as a child does, one would say nothing. At that age it is enough to feel. There were fresh summer mornings in the garden, when the roses were wet with dew, and we plunged our noses into their hearts to breathe in the perfume, and at times the little insects, that made us sneeze.

But did it never rain in those days as it rains now? I can scarcely remember any bad weather. I search my memory in vain, I can recall only sunshine. I think this must be because the Chinese always turned his pipe in the direction whence fair weather came; because there was a sort of witchcraft about this figure, so that we could always tell beforehand whether we would have rain or fine weather by the position he condescended to take. Every one consulted him; even Joseph, who had seen so many things when he was in Russia! When his pipe was turned toward the dining-room, we could hear the "beast," pan, pan, pan!—pan, pan, pan! This cry would be repeated all day at regular intervals, with terrible and persistent monotony.

All we knew was that the "beast" was far off in the fields, and that it was called *Torgeos.*

But when the Chinese faced the back yard, this noise could not be heard, or was so faint that we had to put our ears to the ground in order to perceive a faint pan, pan, pan!—pan, pan, pan! And, enveloped as it thus was in mystery, this cry awoke within us a feeling that was almost awe.

This strange beast must have been gifted with a mysterious power, for I heard Joseph say at times: "We can hear the Torgeos more plainly now; it is going to rain."

But this must have happened very seldom ; for, as I said before, I can scarcely recall any but sunny days and feast-days.

When the first cherries began to redden at the time of the peonies and new rushes, how gay the Sundays were, with their snow-white chapels at the cross-roads and close by the hedges, all decked out for the procession !

How joyous we were ! How fine we were ! Everybody was in an ecstasy of delight over our beautiful caps and our new suits ! And we walked along, our hearts brimming over with happiness, holding ourselves erect, and clutching tightly the cuffs of our sleeves, which were too long.

The street was full of sunshine.

Pious women with reverent zeal fastened red and blue ribbons in zigzag fashion, bunches of flowers, and silver hearts, to the dazzlingly white bedclothes hung against the walls, near these improvised chapels.

Joseph, assisted by the gardener, carried our fine laurel-trees in their green boxes to the front of the house and set them down before our great door, covering the earth in the boxes with white napkins, while we sat there in chairs, somewhat ill at ease in our Sunday clothes, our hearts beating with expectancy.

When we grew tired waiting, we would go to the garden and put our ears to the ground to listen for the sound of the coming procession.

The bells pealed with all their might, and familiar sounds announced the distant chants. The procession was approaching. Then we would return to our chairs near the great door. Joseph would make haste to finish strewing on the ground the rushes, the tall grass, and the reeds that he had cut that morning in the marsh, mixed with flowers from the garden. The perfume of wild mint, peonies, and roses filled the air with fragrance.

The old men, sitting at the grating of their yards, would kneel down slowly and carefully. On either side of the procession boys walked, carrying on their shoulders the supports for the litters of the saints which were to be placed before the temporary altars, and which there had been a struggle to get possession of on account of the two sous paid for this service. They ran at a gallop, and deposited these supports before our chapel.

Then the saints themselves appeared under slender arches covered with leaves and flowers: St. Piat, our patron saint, clad in a silver robe; St. Roch, showing the wound in his thigh, his spaniel lying at his feet; St. Sebastian, scarcely two feet in height, but whose sides were pierced by arrows of the natural size, followed by the brothers of the order, their ensign, on which the death of the martyred saint was represented in silk embroidery, floating on the breeze; St. Catharine, with her wheel, and the Holy Virgin, supported by young girls dressed in white.

All these saints, strangely hideous, painted, gilded, and silvered by our painter Fremy, passed along triumphantly, shaking and jolting on the iron pedestals that rose from amid the peonies that covered the floors of the litters, and among which the simple bearers did not fail to deposit their rustic caps.

The defaced and ugly figures of all these saints inspired me with a vague fear, and I could never bring myself to laugh at them. At times even the clouds of incense and the flickering flame of the tapers seemed to transfigure them, and they appeared to live with a supernatural life, and from their holy mouths mystic psalms seemed to proceed, mingled with the bellowing of the chanters and the soft plaints of the ophicleide.

The curé now mounted the steps of our chapel, and while the children of the choir swung their censers and rang their bells, and the roses fell about in a shower, he blessed the humble peasants, and the rustic procession passed on again.

After the dais of the curé came the notables of the village, the municipal authorities in their midst. I knew them well. Their faces were indeed the same, and yet they seemed different, as if surrounded by a mystic aureole. These men had lost every trace of vulgarity.

They seemed to move in a divine atmosphere. And they walked gravely, with bent head, carrying reverently their large torches, the almost invisible flames of which flickered in the air, and which from time to time they held downward to pour out the melted wax, that it might not drop on their clothes.

They walked on, soon to be lost to view among the fields at the end of the village, as since then, alas! almost all the persons who composed that procession have one by one disappeared in the shadows of oblivion.

---

## XIII.

OTHERS, too, have passed into oblivion—all those friends of my father who, at the *Ducasse*, filled our house, and in three days devoured the mountain of viands that the butcher of Carvin had brought in his wagon on the eve of the feast.

I fancy I can see now the fillets, the calves' livers, the rounds, the cutlets, the sirloins, the sausages, the calves' heads, the legs of mutton, the sheep's feet, the hams, the smoked tongues, and I know not how many other things, as they were unpacked from the wagon.

The pantry was filled with them. I can still perceive the savory smell that came from the kitchen, and escaped by puffs into the street, to meet the guests whose hearts it gladdened. These arrived red and heated by their walk, but with sparkling eyes, mopping their foreheads with their handkerchiefs ; all eager, all happy, and—all present.

There were among them some curious and excellent types. The repast lasted all the afternoon.

Ah ! where has all this sprightly gayety gone?

---

## XIV.

RED epaulets—yellow epaulets—yellow as the *coucous* (primroses) that I gathered the other day in the meadows. The red I have seen before (the firemen of Carvin with their beautiful tricolored plumes, who were here recently, had red epaulets), but the yellow? I made this remark to myself as I stood watching countless soldiers defiling past our door. For a long time the red epaulets and the yellow had been passing, passing, following one another in endless succession, to say nothing of the epaulets shaped like a clover-leaf, and without fringe, of the soldiers who carried the drums. Could it be possible there were so many soldiers in the world ! At every moment I thought the last of them had passed, and it seemed as if the procession were only just beginning.

They wore large gray cloaks ; broad shakos, on which the copper chin-bands glittered ; and sabers that were very big, but not much longer than mine. From time to time, at the entrance to the village, clarions sounded.

These soldiers appeared tired. My eyes, too, were

tired from looking at this continual movement, but I could not take them away, for it was all very beautiful, and very amusing, especially the yellow epaulets, yellow as the *coucous* that Joseph, Louis, and I had gathered in the *Malaquis* meadows, that were all yellow and fragrant with them. We had brought home a large basketful. And what happiness it was in the evening after we had made them up into fine bouquets to which long strings were attached, to throw them after the bats, crying :

> " Katt' soris
> Rapasse par chi
> T'auras du pain musi
> Et de l'eau a boire
> Katt' sori tout noir ! "

At last the red epaulets and the yellow epaulets have all passed, and the last of them have stopped in the village square, where something to drink is distributed among them.

In the evening I was made very happy by seeing some soldiers come to the house, among them a superior officer, who had so much gold on his uniform that I took him for a king.

A sight so new to me had confused my head, and I dreamed of it all night, and in my dreams I saw again our brilliant officer. He had on, like the Charles X in the picture in my father's room, a large ermine mantle, and he wore a golden crown. He was seated gravely on Mlle. Rosalie's red arm-chair on the great stand over against the gable end of the town-hall; and beside him, in place of the scepter, rose the terrible switch. He was teaching the alphabet to the soldiers ranged in front of him, and his primer was nothing else than the varnished leather chin-band of my cap that I had lost some time ago.

But the evening advanced and the time for recreation arrived. The bats flew round and round in the air, and the soldiers threw their yellow epaulets at them, crying:

> " Katt' soris
> Rapasse par chi !"

---

## XV.

ON the. following day the troops departed, and I thought no more of them ; but for some time afterward I heard a phrase repeated continually which I had never heard before, "The Citadel of Antwerp." This must have had reference to some great event, I thought. Contrary to the habit of most children, I scarcely ever asked questions, preferring to find out for myself the explanation of things, either through laziness, or in order to keep my judgment unbiased.

But the great event of the day was when the little band that my father was organizing came to rehearse at our house. I now discovered that the words "Citadel of Antwerp" must be the title of the quickstep played by this embryo orchestra.

This band was to form a part of the company of firemen, recently organized also by my father, and in which he had refused to accept any grade, in order thus to elevate the position of simple fireman, and to stifle the germs of discord caused by disappointed ambition.

Every one's thoughts, then, were full of this band.

Some fifteen young men came to our yard, at first without instruments, to learn to march (one, two ; one, two) ; and, when they lost step, they would take a little skip on one foot to fall into it again.

This brought a number of people around our great door; and the Lhivers, our neighbors, would climb upon the wall which separated our back yard from their little farm.

Then, after two or three rehearsals of this kind, the bright copper instruments arrived, unknown, for the most part until then, in our village.

My father had chosen the piston, at that time a novelty. His buccina, however, that neglected hydra, which had so long kept guard over the staircase, made its reappearance in the light of day, on the shoulder of a rustic, after it had been so effectually cleaned that all the lacquer and gold had disappeared from it, leaving only a little red in the center of the eyes.

Then this orchestra came every Saturday evening to rehearse in our large, unfinished parlor, immediately under my room, and I found it delightful to go to sleep to the discordant sounds of "The Citadel of Antwerp."

That was a happy day when we saw the firemen and heard their music at the mass of the first St. Barbara.

They walked to the church in military fashion, holding tightly their guns, that gleamed like silver, followed by crowds of street boys and gaping girls.

They all wore military uniforms—the coat with its velvet plastron and gilt buttons. But what variety in this unity!

On one, the uniform, too tight across the waist, opened out its skirts like the petals of a flower; on another, too loose, its tails would hang down like the tail of a frightened dog. There were also a great variety of shakos. Some were of oil-cloth, shaped like a blunderbuss, the crown bordered by a velvet band, with flames and hatchets painted on it. Others, of felt, diminished in size toward the crown, and bore symbolic ornaments of real copper.

There was the same difference in the pompons:
some, thin and scraggy, hung down sadly; others spread
themselves out proudly, blooming like fresh peonies.

And no one dreamed of laughing!

## XVI.

This morning I awoke earlier than usual. Why?
And why this gladness that fills my heart? My mind,
still clouded by sleep, does not clearly perceive the
cause, but it is filled with joy at the confused recollection of some extraordinarily happy event. I allow myself to be lulled by this vague remembrance, and pretend to be still asleep, in order to prolong this state of
delicious torpor. My grandmother has risen, and I hear
her movements: the rustling of her petticoat; the noise
of her steps, slow and a little heavy, as she walks across
the floor which trembles at times; the splashing of the
water as she pours it out into her basin.

Outside, the cocks are crowing everywhere: those in
our back yard clear as a clarion; those of our old cousin
Catharine, those of the Lhivers, and those of Charles
Ambroise, our neighbors, somewhat less clearly, while
the crowing of the cocks farther away I perceive only
by a slight trembling of the air.

How pleasant it is to listen to all this in the soft
warmth of the bed!

I half open my eyes; a ray of light illumines a corner of the ceiling and the top of the wall, that, lower
down, is the color of the sky.

My eyes wander to the picture hanging on the wall
near the foot of the bed, a "Return from the Chase,"
where beautiful women are seen going to meet hand-

some men who carry guns, wear black gaiters, and are followed by servants bearing hares and partridges.

Then my grandmother comes to waken me with smiling caresses.

Ah! now I know, now I know why my heart is filled with gladness, why the sunlight dances on the wall. The newly risen sun looks me full in the face, pouring in through the window his glorious rays. I know why he raises himself above the roofs to smile on me thus. It is because this day which has just begun is to be marked by a memorable event—my first journey!

Last night my grandmother said to me, " To-morrow is St. Druon's day, and we must get up early, because it is a long distance from here to Epinoy, where we are going." A league! Only think! And I who until now have scarcely been outside of the village! Therefore it is that I spring quickly out of bed and let myself be dressed without making mischievous resistance ; without thrusting out my feet when my grandmother hands me my stockings, or burying my head in her bosom when she comes to put on my shirt.

A journey!

At first we passed familiar things : fragrant and dazzling colzas, on which millions of little black insects were gorging themselves; corn in the blade, from which flocks of larks soared up into the air, hovering above us, beating their wings and celebrating our departure by ever sweeter songs.

I saw the same golden blossoms, the same dandelions, the same butterflies, the same brilliant beetles that waddle on the road and exhale a disagreeable odor.

But as we crossed the wooden bridge over the little river, oh! first surprise! A wonderful bird darts from the bank, uttering a shrill and prolonged cry. Its breast is of fire, and its back of a splendid green, more brilliant than the stone of the bracelet that my mother forgot to wear when—"A kingfisher," my grandmother tells me.

Here the unexplored regions begin.

There is a river, a real river, three or four times as large as our little river, with real boats on it, that have pretty little houses with white windows and green chimneys. The river is like a wide strip of sky.

A little farther on we found ourselves face to face with mountains, almost as high as the walls of our garden, and as my grandmother sat down here to rest, I explored their summits, but without finding there anything remarkable. At last I utter a cry. I have discovered a new flower; a little white bell-flower, delicately shaped.

From this spot we could descry the chapel of St. Druon with its slender spire of shining slates.

"St. Druon," my grandmother tells me, "was a simple shepherd, who lived at Epinoy, and we are going presently to see his well, all that remains now of his farm. He had the gift of being in several places at the same time — in church, where he prayed, and in the fields, where he kept his sheep. He made miraculous cures, and this is why you see those people going now to his shrine."

In fact, at every moment we met groups on the road who quickly overtook and passed us. We could distinguish among them the gray figure of the idiot Bénési, leading his blind sister as usual.

Long after they had disappeared we could still hear his psalms, his strange stammering seeming augmented in the echo.

## XVII.

ONE of the places in the house of which I was fondest was the loft, which was large, and filled with a crowd of curious objects. I spent long hours there rummaging in the dusty corners.

This place seemed to me worthy of veneration because of the many old things, long out of use, and which seemed to me dead, as it were, that it contained. And then the light entered so solemn, so austere, through the little dormer-windows. The air was swallowed up in it visibly, like dust coming down from heaven to add to this earthly dust.

Alone in the somber silence I was seized by a delightful sensation of fear, and I could hear my heart beat, at times, like a hammer. I heightened this feeling of secret dread by plunging my arm into mysterious holes.

At the end of this loft there were two large worm-eaten boxes, the one full of unimportant scraps of paper that my father used for wiping his gun, and which I knew later to be *assignats*, that had once represented a small fortune ; the other containing very interesting books.

While the pigeons outside hopped noisily about on the tiles of the roof, I forgot to turn over the leaves of these large old books, yellow with age, whose red edges, heavy bindings, and copper corners inspired me with so much veneration.

What wonderful pictures these red books contained !

There were lambs, eagles, beautiful climbing plants, and the whole life of our Saviour, represented by great crowds of very expressive figures. There were groups of Jews, bristling with lances, with Jesus in their midst, his head sorrowfully bent—the innocent victim with flowing hair; old men with beards, wearing large turbans; cities, with massive towers and thick walls; terrified women and children; beggars covered with rags and horribly deformed; and all these moved about at every page, advanced, withdrew, or disappeared from view, to reappear in other situations.

Who had painted these pictures? This thought has since occurred to me, on seeing the pictures of Callot. They were for me the first manifestation of an art which was to be the passion of my life.

They could not at that time serve any direct purpose of instruction, as they were too complicated.

My first master was a stranger, who had drawn a portrait in crayon on the side of a barn in the village. The picture was full face, and in the mouth was a pipe, whose reversed bowl sent its spiral column of smoke downward.

I copied the picture and gave proof of originality by correcting the position of the pipe.

At the same time the old papers in the loft furnished me material for cutting out a thousand arabesques of my own invention, with a skill which filled my grandmother and the servants with admiration.

Later I covered the walls of the large unfinished parlor, which the joiner had by this time abandoned, with scrawls in charcoal.

In addition to the wonderful pictures in the loft, I saw, in the matter of works of art, the statues and sacred pictures in the church, covered with *ambus* and shells, among which a *Pieta* set me dreaming. It was placed very high above the altar. One could divine in it, with sadness, the emaciated features of the Christ, his blue lips, and the sorrowful eyes of his mother!

Peddlers sometimes passed through the village, selling pictures—the Wandering Jew, the Prodigal Son, the Holy Sacraments — painted against vermilion backgrounds. One of these corrected my mistaken idea in regard to " The Citadel of Antwerp "; it represented the siege of that city, and there I saw again the yellow epaulets, and in the sky a rain of red bullets that described wide, madder-colored curves as they fell.

## XVIII.

ABOUT this time an event occurred which excited my curiosity greatly. A wagon - load of books, the greater number of which were richly bound and which awakened my admiration, was unpacked in our court-yard.

These volumes, an entire library, had been sent on in advance by my uncle Boniface, who soon arrived himself.

In compliance with the last wishes of my mother, he had come to live with us, with the intention of remaining with us for the rest of his days.

He installed himself in our house in the character of severe reformer. Adieu now to all idling in the streets ! Adieu to the games of prison-bars in our court-yard, which fifty little scapegraces often filled at a time with their savage cries.

He chased away without pity all these brats, among whom a few big boys and girls often slipped in.

Louis Mémère, and our neighbors, the Lhivers, however, were excepted from these rigorous measures.

Very soon we were compelled to remain for whole hours in my uncle's study, our heads bent over our primers or over the uninteresting Lhomond.

This study occupied half the width of the house, on the floor above the great door.

It was lighted from the north, the side which faced the court and the garden, by a lozenge-shaped window of rich colored glass, on which was cut the date " 1830," and from the south by the large window opening into a balcony that extended its arch under the frontal.

Near this window stood my uncle's bureau, with its double row of drawers, on which were placed two spheres, a terrestrial and a celestial sphere, a petrified aquatic plant, and some little shells. Then came a porcelain stove, and then our bureau which was divided into three compartments, and was flanked by three tabourets covered with hair-cloth.

Near the lozenge-shaped window stood a large Barbary organ which formerly played the overture to " Jeune Henri," and which had lost almost all the keys of its upper register, so that its bass accompanied only a few scattered notes that sounded like a shrill plaint.

One side of the room was occupied by the bookcase, whose glass doors, covered with green silk, hid the books within from view.

Add to this my uncle's sofa, two or three chairs, often littered with newspapers and pamphlets, a stuffed fox, a small box containing a flageolet and a wooden bugle, a music-stand holding some pieces of music, a horn resting on the organ, and, hung around the walls, tables of the principal mountains and rivers, and two colored engravings, representing Vesuvius and Etna in eruption; and when I tell you that all these articles of furniture were made of cherry-wood and had been carefully thought out, measured, planed, put together, scraped, polished, and varnished, one by one, in the odd moments left him by his pipe, by the joiner of the large parlor, you will be able to form a complete idea of this study.

---

## XIX.

THERE it was, under the dreaded eye of the master, that we spent long hours working, and longer hours dreaming.

How often was my wandering attention punished by a sudden slap! For, if my body submitted to the rule of an iron hand, my spirit often rebelled, and, escaping from this body, immovable on its hair-cloth tabouret, flew, now through the beautiful panes of colored glass into the garden, now into the street, through the large window which my uncle, who loved the fresh air, almost always left open in summer.

We remained there for hours, that seemed each an eternity, sitting on those hard seats that made our bones ache, and during those long and enervating summer days we heard all the sounds of freedom—the joyous bursts of laughter of our old companions, playing marbles or spinning tops; the goodies of the village humming *can-cans ;* the wheels of the barrows, creaking as they rolled; the vender of dishes and *télettes* (hardware) alternately crying his wares and playing on a Pan-pipe, and whom we knew to be approaching or receding, as the noise made by his cart, as it rolled over the hard and uneven pavements, grew louder or died away ; and the vender of pigs, who cracked his whip so skillfully, and the gruntings of the little pigs, which grew hoarse at times with their shrill squeaking; and the drawling sweetness of the songs of the embroiderers, whom, in imagination, I saw down at the turn of the street, bending over their work.

Oh, how the sun poured down his rays, lighting up the pools and the dung-hill in the open yard of old Thasie, that I could see before me, in front of the balcony! How was it possible to avoid being interested in the abuse this gossip heaped upon her husband, the deaf Jeannot, a surprisingly ridiculous-looking personage with his diminutive figure, his shirt always unbuttoned, leaving his red and sunburned chest exposed to view; his face redder still, his bald forehead, his large, round nose, and his wide, close-shut mouth, that betrayed the confirmed drunkard? How was it possible to help listening to this plague of his life, who kept time to her words with her flail, as she thrashed the corn? How was it possible to help looking at this fantastic peasant (whose likeness Van Ostade will show me later on), when, to refresh himself, he would climb up into his cherry-tree, laden down with fruit that showed purple against the blue sky? How was it possible to help looking at the sunbeams as they played on the floor and the wall of the study, in which danced a cloud of motes, through which the blue fly which darted suddenly into the room flew, striking the window-panes and the white ceiling frantically with his head and back? And, above all, how was it possible not to writhe with impatience on the hair-cloth seat of my tabouret on the day on which I heard the soldiers marching into the village, returning from the siege of Antwerp?

But this time discipline was less severe, and, leaning against the balcony, I could look at my ease at the red epaulets and the yellow epaulets—passing, passing, passing.

———————

## XX.

So, then, we have soldiers again in the village.

We go to the square where rations are being distributed among them. There are there a number of bags on which Louis Mémère is just sitting down, when the bag becomes unfastened, and rice runs out of it all over the ground. Seeing this, the poor boy gets up frightened, for a furious soldier aims a vigorous blow at him, which he dodges adroitly by slipping aside and drawing in his head, tortoise-fashion. The arm strikes the air. It was very droll. But nothing amuses me to-day. I am sad. My brother Louis is not with us, because he is sick at home. They have brought his bed down into the little parlor, where godmother (as we call our grandmother) sits constantly beside him. This morning she was leaning over him, looking so sad.

He smiled at me, however. He is a beautiful boy, and we love each other dearly! I can not take a step without hearing him behind me.

They call him Mademoiselle Louise, because no girl could have more beautiful blue eyes or brighter or more curly hair than he has. This hair is the despair of my uncle, who can not succeed in brushing it straight over his forehead. In vain he pulls, twists, and wets it; it always returns in the end to its natural curl. Our neighbor, Lhiver, who is a barber and hairdresser, declares that this can never be done, because "*there is a nest in it.*"

Yesterday the clarionet-players, who lodge at our cousin Catharine's, knowing there was sickness at our house, asked if it would divert the invalid to hear some music. They came into our court-yard, ranged themselves in a circle, and played. Louis said this amused him, but I think he did so only through goodness of heart, and in order to please them, for he is even more good than he is beautiful.

This morning the sick child is no better. The clarionet-players came into the yard to play again. Louis whispered to me that it made his head ache. I went to beg them not to play, and they went away quite sad. Every one is sad—and papa away!

To-day no one works. Godmother does not laugh, she who is always laughing. My uncle walks to and fro in the house and wanders about from place to place— from the court-yard to the garden. Seeing me grieved, he says: "It will be nothing; come, let us walk to the marsh." From the windows of our school-room I have often looked out at the marsh, which, according to the color of the pane one looks through, appears red, yellow, violet, green, or blue.

## XXI.

On that day the spring sunshine looked pale and sickly. We walked along the Souchez, whose gray waters, level with its banks, rolling slowly along, reflected the grass, the dandelions, the soft gray sky, deepening to a pale blue toward the zenith. The first swallows streaked the air with dark lines, passing so close to the surface of the water, at times, as to wet in it the white feathers of their breasts.

We took the green path that runs through the wood. Alders, willows, and aspens grew there together in confusion, looking like a violet haze, their budding leaves covering them like a shower of green dust. At intervals the trenches traversing the wood flowed into pools at our feet, bordered by straight and motionless reeds.

Through their calm and limpid waters could be seen the mossy plants growing at the bottom, bearing beautiful, delicate white flowers, tinged with a rosy hue, and shaped like candelabra.

At every step we took, some frog, golden or bronze-colored, would plunge into the morass. In the midst of the tender foliage, green and fiery dragon-flies brushed the rushes in their rapid flight; and almost on the surface of the water swarmed a black mass, countless broods of young tadpoles, giddy with the spring sunshine, that kept up an incessant motion with their flame-like tails.

My heart was heavy.

I gathered handfuls of reeds to make *gayolles* (little cages) and branches of willow to turn into whistles, as boys do, after carefully peeling off the bark, having first beaten it for a long time with the handle of the knife.

At the edges of the trenches grew plants bearing tall purple tufts of bloom.

My heart was heavy.

My uncle did not speak.

We entered the wood where white and pale-violet anemones trembled as we passed.

Here my attention was attracted for the first time by those beautiful, fragrant yellow pompons that grow in tufts on the branches of a species of willow, which we call *paquet.* Swarms of bees buzzed around them, detaching from the flowers, as they rifled them of their sweets, a fragrant golden dust which clung to their feet, part of it rolling off like a diminutive avalanche of light. I threw away my reeds and whistles, and gathered a bunch of these brilliant yellow pompons, that suddenly brought into my sorrowful heart a gleam of joy.

I gathered this bouquet to take it to Louis. It seemed to me that the pleasure it would give him would soon make him well again.

My heart beat fast as we entered the house. But Louis did not seem to see my flowers, and I knew then that he was very ill.

Then I crept away to a corner of the garden, and my tears flowed there in silence.

--------------------

## XXII.

IN the mild April days nothing is more delightful to a child than to see the reawakening of plant life.

The gardens especially rejoice the heart with inexpressible gladness. On all sides the buds are bursting their shining sheaths, whence young leaves and blossoms emerge together, an indescribable faint red clothing their budding mysteries.

A thousand plants are rising through the humid soil, happy to see again the light of day ; while others, more precocious, unfold their blossoms in all the freshness and splendor of a first blooming.

The peonies have not yet done sending out their wine-colored shoots, curved like bishops' crosiers ; but the violets, the tulips, the pansies, the yellow narcissus, the imperial crowns in whose hearts tears are always welling, the fragrant pink and blue hyacinths and the primroses unfold their petals to the first white butterflies ; and the sensitive peach-trees in the shelter of the brick wall open their rosy stars, continually surrounded by swarms of buzzing honey-bees.

But what most delights my eyes to-day is the anemones that cluster around the shaft of the sun-dial.

With what a wonderful intensity, with what an exquisite softness, gleam the purple, crimson, vermilion, or white velvet petals of these flowers, with their hearts of black satin !

But always haughty, they are more haughty than ever to-day. And why ?

Because my brother is getting better. Would I have left him for the anemones if he were not at this moment resting in a sweet sleep ?

Yesterday he played on the bed with a cross-bow. Every time he shot the arrow I picked it up and brought it back to him.

This morning he got out of bed for a moment. He tried to walk on his thin legs, but they were still too weak. He has grown taller.

Joy reigns in the house.

My uncle plays on the horn up-stairs and I do not study, for it is a double holiday. It is Easter Sunday !

---

## XXIII.

Joy reigns in the house. The bell tinkles. Joseph brings me an enormous *Pâque*, fragrant and wet with dew, gathered in the neighborhood, for we have none so large in our garden.

Louis Mémère and François Lhiver came in their Sunday clothes, carrying puny, wretched-looking *Pâques* in their hands. They will have to hold them very high indeed when they stand on the bench, as the curé passes with his holy-water sprinkler. They might, it is true, dip them in the holy-water font as they go out, but this is forbidden.

The din-din gives the last peal.

We follow the faithful, who are going to church : the men dressed in short jackets, the cases of their pipes sticking out of their pockets ; the women in long, black or lilac cloaks with hoods—those of the richer ones trimmed with fur. The poor women wear squares of black stuff on their heads, that fall down over their backs in folds, with a single little ornament embroidered on them in colored silk—a cross or a holy sacrament.

We met some of our playmates proudly holding their *Pâques ;* the grown-up persons content themselves with a slender branch of box, held between the fingers.

The church is overflowing with people, and is filled with the odor of a thousand branches.

The curé makes the tour of the church with his holy-water sprinkler, and, as he passes, all the *Pâques* rise up like a thicket of box.

On the steps of the communion-bench, which runs across the church, closing in the choir and the side altars with its hedge of sculptured foliage, a long line of pupils, some bold and mischievous, some devout as saints, press forward and kneel or sit down.

There are among them heads of a great variety of shapes : some broad, some pointed, with ears sticking out more or less, and locks, for the most part of a reddish-blonde, sometimes fading into a yellowish-white, and so bristly that they remind one of the stubble in a field after harvest-time, and so rebellious that not even a thick coat of lard will make them lie straight.

Occasionally, a face covered with freckles, with turned-up nose, long, white teeth, and blue eyes, sparkling with mischief, will turn round. All this little crowd jostle one another with their elbows, move about restlessly and scratch themselves.

The curé leaves the church, followed by the choristers and the choir-boys; the door is closed in his face, and he must knock three times before it will be opened to him again. The ceremony amuses me. After the

*Ita missa est*, the street boys, dodging the blows of the master, throng to the holy-water font, in which they dip their *Pâques* and raise a storm that sets the water in motion and scatters it over the flags.

Three days afterward my brother Émile declares that, as he was with his nurse, he saw the bells passing through the sky on their long journey from Rome, while the creaking noise of the first rattles was sounding in the village.

----

## XXIV.

Bum, bem, boum!  Bum, bem, boum!  The bells are back again.  Quick!  To the garden!  We arrived there out of breath, crazy with childish delight, running hither and thither, and so eager to see, that we can see nothing.

At last we discover an egg—two, three, four!  How beautiful they are—red, violet, blue, and yellow!  They gleam like flowers among the green leaves.

We keep running about from flower-bed to flower-bed, separating the leaves with our hands.

Bum, bem, boum!  We find eggs among the imperial crowns, among the lilies, the primroses, the sorrel, among the grass on the lawn, among the chervil, everywhere. Some, with their shells broken, have remained hanging on the branches of the rose-bushes.

How generously the bells have laid!  Bum, bem, boum!

----

## XXV.

On the following day we assist at the solemn ceremonies of Easter.

The church is resplendent in all its wealth of ornament.

The silver candlesticks, freed from their covers, glitter on the altar, among the paper hollyhocks.

All the tapers are lighted, the largest of them detached from the walls to which they are ordinarily fastened, revealing to me (what is one to believe after this?) their simulated flames of painted tin, inside of which little candles are set. Stars of light blaze over the picture of the principal altar, and set the Jewish soldiers, who are guarding the tomb, trembling, with their flickering flames. Above this the soft " Pietà " grows softer still, seen through clouds of smoke.

I am sitting on the church-warden's bench, set against the great pillar near the choir.

The singing begins, slow and squeaking; I listen mechanically, absorbed in my dreams. My glances wander over the assemblage, that I look down upon from my seat, higher by two or three steps than the others. When they encounter a familiar face, my thoughts dwell upon it for a moment. The first I see is that of the terrible Mademoiselle Rosalie, with her hard glance, who pretends to be reading her prayer-book, but who is, in reality, watching her little flock. Oh, I am taking good care to behave well! She may look at me as often as she will from the corner of her pitiless eye—she will have nothing to tell my uncle.

Behind Mademoiselle Rosalie's little flock is the school of the larger girls. My thoughts often wander in that direction. I am certain to see her there in the front row! Who? Her—the girl I call in my thoughts my little *bueresse* (laundry-maid) because she resembles one of our laundresses. I love her, and I do not dare to ask any one what her name is. She has rosy cheeks, and she prays like an angel.

Farther on the old women mutter their *oremuses*, and under the portal, growing indistinct in the shadow, men with a brick-red complexion and bald, white heads, shine like porcelain figures. There Bénési prays, making pious grimaces. I allow myself to be gently lulled by the chants, accompanied by the soft ophicleide. With the harsh falsetto, the nasal base, and the gasping cries of the two singers, are mingled at times the dry and harsh notes, always out of tune, of the curé, whose voice sounds like a trombone. My ears have grown accustomed to this *charivari*.

The curé, tall and thin, with his prominent nose and chin, and his curly black hair, has put on his resplendent gold-embroidered cape.

Now and then he turns round brusquely, with an angry " Hush ! " addressed to the boys on the communion-bench.

The curé ! We are all afraid of him. At times his face is strangely convulsed. When he reads the sermon, one can hardly understand a word he says. The other day, however, he was very amiable. I went to the raisin-confession. This is what they call the confession of us children. I had taken a basketful of onions to the confessional for the curé, who, after he had heard my sins, gave me the customary package of raisins.

My godmother had selected the finest onions, and he had seemed pleased with them.

But they say he is possessed by the devil at times. We had a great fight a few days ago in the village on this account. People went about in the street asking one another if it was true that he was not anywhere to be found. They went to the church to look for him. Yes; he was still there, standing before the altar with rigid form and convulsed face; and he held on high the consecrated Host, which he could not carry to his mouth. This lasted three hours, the time spent in going to Carvin to look for the dean, who came and broke the spell.*

Among the three singers, two are worthy of mention, and are as different from each other in appearance as they are in voice.

The one who sings in falsetto is old, ugly, and cadaverous-looking. He sings only on great occasions, for he is an important personage. He wears a sort of wig of couch-grass; his skin is rough, like the bark of an old tree, with a few black plaster patches here and there; his eyebrows, resembling in form a circumflex accent, are set high above his eyes, whose lids stand out against the darkness of their sockets. The turned-up nose is also set high above the mouth, which is almost lipless; add to these a long chin; a white necktie; gold eye-glasses and ear-rings; a large collar; a yellow waistcoat with brown stripes, and a long gray coat with little buttons.

It makes me tremble to see how purple he grows when, between two fits of coughing, he throws back his head proudly and holds in his breath, to execute a trill in his harsh and childish voice.

The other, the one whose nose sings the base, is the usual singer.

Later, when my uncle bought an illustrated copy of Béranger, we were to be surprised by finding there his

---

* This overscrupulous priest, calmed by age, died a few years ago, having grown very tolerant and being greatly beloved by his people.

exact portrait. By a stroke of genius Grandville had divined him. This does honor to them both.

He had a square face, widening at the base, a very low forehead, thick wavy hair, straight eyebrows, almost touching the eyes, which were small, and whose blue color was intensified by the red of his complexion; an immense mouth with thick lips, that, unable to close completely, protruded in fleshy curves; a large head; a flat, drawn-in chest; a hollow for a belly—all this supported on knock-kneed legs, on which the trousers hung loosely, and which were terminated by ill-shaped feet with turned-in toes, that bent sidewise as he walked.

He is as pretentious as the other, but more amiable. He never says "yes" or "no"; he is one of those people who answer: "It is said"; "You say so"; "Such a thing has been known to happen"; "And even if that were so"; "But yet—"

In his capacity of drunkard, he consumes a great deal of gin, and, in the numerous taverns at which he just looks in, he has never asked for a glass of liquor. He says: "I want something"; "I have a sou here which I don't know what to do with"; then, "I have another sou here." And they understand him, and he empties his glass without having compromised himself in words.

One day, when he fell down in the choir, and was so drunk that he was unable to get up again, he said to the curé, who reprimanded him sharply, "Help me to my feet, and talk afterward." As a punishment for causing this scandal, he was forbidden to wear his surplice for a couple of months.

Such is the man who sends forth in the choir droning sounds in which the nose only takes part. Those strains are so monotonous, and the ophicleide accompanies them with such long-drawn, wailing notes, that I can scarcely keep my eyes open.

And then this mass is so long.

I grow weary like the captive sparrow who flies against the window-panes or perches on the little statues that project from the wall, forming tail-pieces under the arches of the ceiling. These statues have no longer any heads. The wicked people (as my grandmother has told me) cut them off during the Revolution. The old carpenter, P——, was one of these. Therefore he inspires me with the same terror as do the Jews who are striking Jesus in the picture on the altar.

The heavy odor of the incense makes me grow more and more sleepy, and I fall to dreaming, looking through half-closed lids at my little *bueresse*, who is so well-behaved, and who prays with such simple fervor.

---

## XXVI.

AFTER Easter was over, and Louis was well again, we resumed our usual occupations. Our little rooms adjoined the room of my uncle, which was at the extreme end of the new part of the house.

My uncle rose at five at all seasons of the year, and came to my room, which served him as a dressing-room, to shave. I fancy I can still hear the sound of the brush rubbing the soap into a lather, the gliding of the razor on the strop, and the rasping noise it made as he shaved his harsh beard.

Soon he uttered his invariable cry, "Children, get up!" and, rubbing our sleepy eyes, we would rise by the flickering light that cast dancing shadows on the bunches of daisies on the carpet.

As soon as we were dressed we would go and sit down on our hair-cloth tabourets with the pretense of

studying until half-past seven.   How many times have I
not wished to be ill that I might remain in bed !   Day
dawned slowly.   The light of the lamp grew paler, and
its yellow rays flickered on our lips in the blue light of
morning.

All the familiar sounds of rural existence began to be
heard again, one by one : in the stables the cows lowed ;
in the poultry-yards hens clucked.   The doors of the
barns creaked upon their hinges.

My uncle threw open the blinds.

When the dawn was further advanced and the sky
grew rosier and brighter in the east, he would call us
out to the balcony.   He spoke to us of Nature and her
charms.   He repeated to us the following lines from
some old opera :

> "Quand on fut toujours vertueux
> On aime à voir lever l'aurore."

Under the purple light of the sky the distant fields
stretched far away, still wrapped in the mists soon to be
dissipated by the glowing disk of the sun.

Against this clear and brilliant background the old
thatched roof of Jeannot stood out sharply like a square
of black velvet, bordered at the top by dark-red flames,
while in the gray light below the mist rose silently from
the pool in the yard.

. All was so peaceful, so sweet !

At half-past seven we went down-stairs to breakfast.
we dined at half-past twelve, and supped at about eight.

Although the street and the village surroundings
were forbidden to us, the house, the court-yard, the poultry-yard, the sheds, the barns, and, above all, the garden, offered a sufficiently wide field for our prolonged
recreations.

It would take too long to describe our daily intercourse with all the creatures that inhabited these various places.

Butterflies and birds, frogs and salamanders ; bees, drones, beetles with golden breasts ; cock-chafers that fell to the ground with the drops of dew from the rose-bushes in the morning; shrew-mice with pointed nose, and eyes like grains of powder, moles and field-mice, snails, and you, lady-bugs, asparagus-bugs bearing shutters on your backs ; and you, beautiful red insects that dwell in the heart of the lily and utter a wail like the cry of a little puppy when one holds you close to the ear ; and that insect with the terrible jaws, which raises its tail menacingly, and which we have not the courage to touch ; and that other one, of the color of dust, that holds itself rigid when one puts it on its back, and then— tic-tac—jumps away suddenly.

How many times have we been stung by the bees ! As for the drones, especially the *red-tails*, which are the strongest, we would catch them with our handkerchief, extract their sting with our nails, and make them draw little wagons to which we harness them by tying threads to their feet.

Sometimes, to our amusement, they would fly away with their thread, borne down by the weight of which they would fall back again, when scarcely a foot from the ground, into the border of the grass-plot—poor prisoners dragging along their chains !

At other times we would exhaust the patience of the necrophores by pushing still deeper into the ground the moles they had almost finished burying.

How often have I listened for hours at a time to the grasshoppers chirping among the bushes, holding my breath, for the least noise silences them, and straining my ear, first on one side and then on another, without ever being able to discover the precise spot whence the cry proceeded. The same mystery surrounded the croaking of the little green frogs that frequented the vines.

But the toads filled me with horror, alike when, slimy and moist, they dragged themselves along the ground after a storm, and when, in dry weather, they moved about upon the earth like living clods, distinguishable from it only by the shining of their golden eyes. All these creatures whirred, fluttered, buzzed, whistled, sang; and, far away, far away, at the end of unexplored fields, was that mysterious noise which made our hearts quake with a terror full of charm, the cry of the "Beast," of the Torgeos, pan, pan, pan !—pan, pan, pan !

There was also the sorrowful plaint of the fauvet whose nest we had robbed, that flew from tree to tree, uttering its wailing cry like a tormented spirit seeking rest from its anguish but finding none.

<hr>

## XXVII.

WHEN the animals failed us, we fell back upon the gardener. I have already spoken of Buisine, nicknamed Frisé, a venerable old man of patriarchal aspect, with a fresh complexion, wondering blue eyes, and a forehead covered with a thick forest of wavy gray hair.

When he was stooping over his work, we would often jump, two or three of us at a time, upon his back and cling to his blouse, kicking our feet mischievously. He would get angry. "He would go complain to our uncle." "We kept him from his work." "We were always pulling him to pieces." "We were unendurable."

But, as his mild eyes were incapable of expressing anger, we only laughed at him. At last he would laugh himself, threatening us playfully with his pruning-hook ; or he would give us *la barb*—that is, he would rub his chin, with bristles sharp as the spikes on the cylinder of a bird organ, against our cheeks. And Frisé gave us bird-organ music too, old ditties with never-ending refrains. Among others he sang one called "Joseph sold by his Brethren," consisting of a hundred and one couplets, whose droning sounds he accompanied with the monotonous movement of his rake as he cleaned the paths, or the click of his pruning-shears as he clipped the branches:

> "O Joseph, mon fils aimable,
> Mon fils affable,
> Les bêtes t'ont dévoré."

As my uncle had had the patience one day to listen to him till he had sung the ditty to the end and then praised his good memory, and told him that such was really the history of Joseph, Frisé, delighted with the compliment, sought every opportunity to repeat his song, and when he had succeeded in making my uncle listen to a few verses, he would say gravely, "You know, M. Breton, that is history."

This phrase amused us, and he made use of it to plague little Émile, who would grow as angry as a young sparrow, when we followed him about, droning the ditty into his ears ; and when he would turn round, furious and shoot arrows at us, happily harmless ones, from his little bow, we would say to him mockingly, "You see, M. Breton, that is history."

We amused ourselves also with the gardener, by hiding his tools, of which he was very fond, and the handles of which his rough hands had polished and worn, or his large cap, which exhaled a peculiar odor.

Many years later it happened that my father brought home from one of his journeys a pineapple, a fruit until then unknown to us. When he was cutting it, a strange perfume diffused itself through the room, and my father, who was very fond of good eating, made us notice how exquisite the odor was. Yes, the perfume was exquisite, the more so as it awakened in us a vague recollection. Somewhere we had smelled something like it. But what, and where?

We were all trying to remember, when Émile, his face lighting up, suddenly cried, "Frisé's cap!" Yes, it was indeed that.

We had an affection for one corner of the garden especially—the dampest and the least clean. It was there that the hole had been dug into which Frisé threw weeds, useless plants, and dead vegetables, after their seeds had been gathered.

A brick wall, low enough to look over, surrounded the hole; from this wall we could see over the whole garden, with its rows of painted posts surmounted by white balls. Oh, what a lovely night butterfly I discovered one morning, asleep on the damp moss that covered this heap! How brightly it gleamed, with its wings of black velvet, streaked with yellow, and its purple back, and its under wings of a superb red, dotted with brown spots!

From the top of this wall we could see the Château de Courrières, the former dwelling-place of the lords of the village, the last of whom, before the Revolution, was the Baron de St. Victor. Of this château, built in the style of Louis XV, the ugly old man we have seen on Easter Sunday, standing at the music-desk in the choir, had been at one time the steward. My father, who had been early left an orphan, had been confided to the care of this man, and had spent part of his childhood at the château. He did not preserve a very agreeable recollection of it.

It happened one day that they locked him into a room, and as he grew impatient at the length of his captivity, my father, at the risk of breaking his neck, escaped from his prison by lowering himself to the ground by his hands, grasping the moldings of the façade, and then ran and hid himself in the depths of a wood, where he remained for three days, a playmate supplying him with food.

Long abandoned, this silent château, this prison of my father, with its barred windows, its deserted steps, overgrown with thistles; its tall chimneys, from which smoke never issued; its dilapidated roof, from which the tiles were being carried away one by one by the wind, was associated much more closely in my mind with the tales heard from my companions than with the realities of daily life. It affected my imagination powerfully. Those closed shutters, I thought, must conceal behind them some strange mystery.

This Specter of the Past stood there silent in the midst of the golden harvests of the old park surrounded by its moat. It was inhabited now only by the owls, but I could never disassociate from it, in my thoughts, the image of the ugly tyrant who had once inhabited it.

For the most part, then, our hours of recreation were passed in the garden, which we quitted only when night fell.

Ah! what happy summer evenings I have spent there!

Hazy shadows hung in every corner, while the tops of the pear-trees, trimmed in the form of a distaff, were gilded by the splendors of the setting sun. A light breeze sprang up from time to time, setting in motion the warm vapors that hung heavy over the earth.

The sky was darkened by clouds of buzzing insects and shadowy gleams of red light that floated away, far into the depths of space, where the white stars were appearing one by one.

Amid the sound of fluttering wings and rustling leaves, the sparrows came, one by one, to hide themselves under the leafy garlands that crowned the garden wall.

At times the night-moth darted past, swift as an arrow, making the drowsy silence quiver.  Other moths circled giddily around clumps of *volubilis-pâlis*.

The twilight lent a sweet and peaceful charm to all these objects, lighted up only here and there by a ray of dying light.  Nature sank gently among the gathering shadows into a sleep that was disturbed from time to time by the noise made by some nocturnal prowler.  A pure and intense poetic spell hung over everything.

---

## XXVIII.

My father, however, was laying out a second garden, which was to be three or four times as large as the other, and which, as we children thought, was going to be a marvel.

The site chosen for it was on the banks of the Souchez, in the *lower marsh*, six or seven minutes' walk distant from the house.

We spent there part of our hours of recreation, and I assure you that nothing could have amused us more than to see all those men, almost naked, covered with mud, their trousers tucked half-way up the thigh, digging hollows and raising hills, passing and repassing, with their muddy barrows over the planks that, seesaw-like, would sometimes rise up into the air and then fall noisily down again.

My father had laid out the plans for the garden, making the most of the shrubs that grew in it, and utilizing the ponds and trenches. He planned various surprises. For instance, the gate was to open into a simple kitchen-garden, terminating in an ordinary orchard. But, arriving there, you found yourself suddenly before a fountain surrounded by thuyas, laburnums, and lilacs, whose jet, which rose from a natural spring, fell with a delightful murmur into the basin, the chosen haunt of the frogs.

They had found this spring scarcely two feet underground without any difficulty, while a châtelaine of the neighborhood had spent fabulous sums in fruitless boring. Providence must have guided them.*

Then there were to be bridges spanning the trenches ; three little ponds starred with water-lilies, where the gold-fish leaped about, flashing in the sunlight ; leafy bowers for archery, the cross-bow, and bowls; a pavilion ; circular lawns bordered with rose-bushes ; a dark grove with a labyrinthine walk ; a little bathing-house with a terrace ; and another fountain, this latter artificial.

On the other side of the Souchez was to be a larger pond, bordered by sunflowers, hollyhocks, and various tall, broad-leaved plants bearing large flowers, in which was to be a wooded island, in the shape of a pear, the most retired spot of the garden, and to be reached by a small boat.

Thanks to the former plantations, which had been preserved, and to the fertility of the soil, this garden soon became what was in those days called an *enchanting retreat*.

---

* These borings were not altogether useless, since they resulted in the discovery of veins of coal, the beginning of the coal-beds of Pas-de-Calais.

My uncle was passionately fond of it, and spent there a part of every day.

During the Ducasse* lovers walked in it in the morning, as if it were a public garden. Sometimes my father would hire musicians who played on the platform of the bathing-pavilion, while couples danced on the grass, as they do in the engravings, after Teniers, which adorn my godfather's parlor. What bursts of laughter, what songs, and what cries of joy, to which a thousand birds, concealed among the branches, responded! What boating excursions, what careless, happy hours!

Some townspeople of Lille, old friends of my uncle, shaking off for a time the cares of their somber dwellings, would occasionally visit us with their wives, and intoxicate themselves with the delights of country life, the greenery, and the summer sunshine, and sport like children among the flowers, beside themselves with joy.

On the pond the boatmen would make the boat rock in order to frighten " the ladies," who would utter cries of terror, followed by the delicate pleasantries of the time.

One day, one of these citizens of Lille, a man of mature age, married to a young wife, affected by the general gayety, behaved so well on the boat that he lost his balance and fell into the water. They dragged him out, covered with aquatic plants that clung to his clothes, from whieh the water poured in a stream, and looking very serious. Madame, seized with a violent attack of hysterics, heaped abuse upon him, interrupted from time to time by her spasms. They went to the house for dry clothes, while the gentleman, enveloped in a rug, which he wore like a toga, walked about in the sunshine

---

* A local festival.

drying himself and, madame being appeased, declaiming, "Of him, the greatest Roman of them all," etc.

I remember, too, those delightful summer evenings, when we would linger after nightfall with my uncle on the terrace of the bathing-pavilion, to sing nocturnes in the midst of the silence and the solitude, to the accompaniment of the croaking of the frogs:

> "Berger, cours à la belle
> Jurer flamme éternelle
> L'étoile du soir luit!"

And there, indeed, above the dark foliage of the wood, the evening star was shining.

The *Carperie* enjoyed the distinguished privilege of being sung in pompous alexandrines. The Abbé D——, the vicar of Courrières, wrote in honor of it a poem consisting of five or six cantos.

This ecclesiastic, a devotee of the Muses and of the pleasures of the table, in order to embellish our garden, drew upon his mythological reminiscences; and Flora, Pomona, Ceres, the nymphs, the satyrs, the naïads, and innumerable zephyrs, came to people, in his verses, our parterres, our orchards, our ponds, and our groves.

Venus herself did not disdain to come down and take up her abode on the island of Cytherea, as the little pear-shaped, wooded island emerging from the bosom of our pond was called. Naturally he made this island the abode of a hermit.

This hermit was none other than my uncle, probably represented by the fancy of the poet under the guise of an all-powerful Jupiter. And, indeed, the title of hermit suited him very well; for, although he lived only for others, he had lived almost always alone.

As for me, I confess I never discovered any mythological deity in the *Carperie*, not even the fairies, who were the most familiar to us; but I saw there one day, the idiot Bénési, who, with his shirt over his coat, was singing vesper hymns in the laburnum bower, that he doubtless took for an oratory.

Thousands of yellow blossoms hung in clusters from the leafy trellis, and the sunlight, filtering through the branches, lighted them up here and there in the midst of the surrounding shadow, making them look like the lights in a chapel.

----

## XXIX.

ABOUT this time great preparations were going on at our house. Fremy washed and revarnished his paintings; Joseph hurried to pluck the smallest blade of grass that showed itself among the pebbles in the yard; Phillipine rubbed, scrubbed, and polished, and, when she was not doing this, danced on her waxing-brush over the floors, making them shine like a mirror.

Everybody was in a hurry.

The gardener's rake moved about so quickly in the walks that " Joseph and his Brethren " passed from an *andante* to an *allegro*. (We had begun music.)

One thought filled the mind of everybody.

Soon cries of distress from the chickens, the ducks, and the turkeys that were being killed, resounded in the back yard.

Articles hitherto unknown there made their appearance in the house.

All this delighted me greatly, the more so as, in the midst of the feverish agitation that prevailed, we were able to neglect our studies with impunity.

In brief, we were expecting a visit from one of the

greatest noblemen of the kingdom, the Duke of Durfort de Duras.

I knew him from his portrait, painted in the costume of a peer of France, that formed a companion piece to the portrait of Charles X.

He was represented in it as young, dignified, and handsome.

When the long-expected day arrived, every house was hung with garlands of leaves and flowers. Groups gathered at every corner. We were all at our front door, which stood wide open.

At last the noise of wheels was heard at the bend of the road, which was enveloped in a cloud of dust ; men and women rushed forward toward a post-chaise drawn by four horses that came galloping up the street, amid the cries of " Vive monseigneur ! "

The postilions wore red trousers, high boots, braided jackets, and oil-cloth-covered caps. I thought them magnificent. But I was greatly disappointed when I saw the duke, who, alas ! bore scarcely any resemblance to his portrait.

He descended from the chaise with the help of a chair which they brought him. He looked to me old; his cheeks were flabby, his complexion highly colored, his nose too big. He had a mole on the left temple, I think it was, and wore a cloth cap over a silk one, from beneath which straggled a few white hairs.

I, who had expected regal magnificence, stood there, my eyes wide open with amazement, to see an old man differing so little from other old men.

His face was lighted up, however, by a look of benevolence.

He embraced us affectionately and made inquiries, not only concerning our health, but our little occupations. He even went into the kitchen in the afternoon, and seated himself in the corner of the Louis Quinze fireplace, beside my grandmother, with whom he chatted for a long time.

I recollect that after dinner my uncle spoke to him of his ancestors, of some of his illustrious friends, and of the romances of the duchess, his first wife.

The duke, charmed to find so lettered a man and one who was so well acquainted with his history among country people, complimented him on his knowledge in courteous and even friendly terms.

As for us, we soon found a comrade in the person of his valet, M. Michel, a Pole, a man about forty years old, very quick in his movements and who stuttered frightfully, which at times made him appear in a very comical light.

He was very tall (at least six feet high). I have heard my father say that he carried his devotion to his master so far as to add, out of his own pocket, to the gratuities of which the latter made him the disburser. Where do we see a valet now who would sacrifice his savings to protect a great nobleman's reputation?

Michel loved children, and after the first day we amused ourselves by plaguing him as if he were of no greater consequence than Frisé himself.

St John's day arrived.

At this time all the women and young girls assemble at the cross-roads of the village and dance and sing roundelays in the twilight, often prolonging these festivities far into the night.

Those who lived in our street came to sing under the windows of the duke, who had retired early. He slept on a mattress, which was not horizontal, but sloped a little toward the feet, a peculiarity that had seemed to me odd.

These rounds and village lays at first amused the

duke, but at the end of a quarter of an hour he was tired of them. Not wishing to offend these villagers, however, who devoted themselves so heartily to the task of amusing him, he sent Michel to them, after he had thanked them, giving him orders to take them to the village inn and offer them refreshments.

The jovial valet, according to his custom, supplemented his master's generosity with attentions of his own; not content with regaling the women at the inn, he took them from wine-shop to wine-shop, recruiting their numbers on the way by members of other bands, so that these feminine heads soon became heated with wine, and by midnight the excited troop were running through the streets of Courrières, crying, "Vive Monsieur Michel! Vive Monsieur de Duras!"

This was not the duke's only visit to Courrières. He came a second time, accompanied by the duchess, a tall Spanish woman with long features, who wore a little green veil. We saw again our friend Michel. We neglected him a little, however, for the *femme de chambre* of the duchess, a young and pretty brunette with lively manners, who rolled us on the grass of the lawn, kissed us, and tickled us, much to our delight. And when we shot our arrows into the air she would cry, with a look of surprise, "See, how high!" There was in the neighborhood a company of little archers, whose ages ranged from ten to fifteen, whose *berceau* (target) was set up at the end of a dry ditch that bordered the road leading to the village.

The joyous exclamations of these boys reached us in our house, and attracted the attention of the great lady, who, wishing to see the sport near by, caused herself to be carried in a chair to the edge of the ditch. The sport, interrupted for an instant, began again gayly. It occurred to the duchess to give two sous to the boy who should succeed in hitting the red circle around the bull's-eye.  This redoubled the ardor of the contestants, who accomplished prodigies of skill.

A little sick boy, muffled up to the eyes in a cap of woolen cloth, was an object of special interest.

The shots which hit the circle, however, became so frequent that they were at last rewarded by only one sou.

This was another piece of economy which Michel would not have practiced.

------

## XXX.

IDEAS present themselves to the mind of the child under the form of images.  Before we reason, we imagine.  Imagination!  I know not why it is that this marvelous faculty, instead of becoming stronger as the reasoning powers develop, declines with their growth. They stifle it, and this is to be greatly regretted.

There is nothing more delightful than to yield one's self up to this creative power, which can evoke to being, under our closed eyelids, so many strange and beautiful forms, impalpable and yet plain to the inner sight, and illuminated, as it were, by supernatural splendors.

How I longed for the moment when, cuddled in my warm bed, the light extinguished, I prepared to witness this diurnal spectacle.

At first pale twilight gleams, mingled with dark, floating shadows, moved before my closed eyes, eddying in a formless chaos—an image of creation, where points of light, like stars, soon sparkled.

Then forms began to take shape, massed themselves together, gradually grew clearer and then changed into other forms; all this absolutely without effort of the will on my part, and accompanied by ever-new surprises.

The pictures followed one another, beautiful, fantastic, wild, or horrible, according to the mood I was in.

I looked at them all with curiosity and delight, and without fear.

At times I saw wide plains the color of blood, wrapped in shadow, where hideous serpents, stiff as posts, crawled with a jerking movement that kept time to the beating of my heart. And then all this grew luminous; the serpents stretched themselves out into garlands of flowers; marvelous birds flew back and forth; the sails of windmills turned round and round against the background of the sky, and then all soared upward in a dizzy whirl, in which I felt myself borne, with my bed, dazzled and intoxicated. Oh, how beautiful it all was!

This picture would vanish. Then I saw the sea as I had heard it described, like an immense piece of cloth, furling and unfurling itself. I felt myself caught up and rocked delightfully in its folds. Then it was the sky; nothing was to be seen but the sky, hung with glorious golden clouds on which walked St. Nicholas, St. Catharine, the Virgin, and the infant Jesus, and where hovered groups of joyous, blue-winged angels.

At other times I saw dark rooms filled with strange implements like those in our barn, and vast kitchens where burned immense fires, before which the devil turned the spit. Or, the room would be filled with showers of many-colored rockets, like those I have since seen in displays of fire-works.

At times I saw animated toys, marching by themselves in procession—guns, Punch-and-Judies, Pan-flutes, trumpets; and also sights that were more natural, the real procession in which the curé, the choir-singers, Mademoiselle Rosalie, and Bénési took part, One day

—oh, joy!—my mother rose suddenly before me and clasped me in her arms.

And, as I have said before, all these pictures appeared before me without effort of the will on my part, really visible to the inner sight, and not those vague images that later haunt the brain—images so slow to take the final shapes in which we clothe them.

I think many children possess this gift of inner sight. My brothers and I described these visions to one another, sometimes from one room to another at the moment of their appearance.

## XXXI.

My uncle had a great affection for Lille, where he had spent the best part of his youth.

He often spoke to us of that city, of its theatre, its concerts, its houses with their richly decorated rooms and resplendent windows.

I could form to myself no idea of all this, and in my nocturnal visions Lille appeared to me like a vague splendor, a crowd of people and of carriages with fine postilions and, heaped on the roofs of houses dazzlingly white and of immense size, gold and precious stones like those of fairy-land. These fantastic images haunted me particularly on the night preceding our journey to Lille.

We set out early in the morning, my uncle, Louis, and I. We were to take the Carvin-Lille coach, a line established by Maximilian Robespierre, a member of the family of the Robespierre of the Convention, who was a native of Carvin.*

---

* On seeing a cast of the tribune, later, I was struck by its resemblance to the Robespierre I knew.

The coach was already full, which did not prevent them, however, not only from crowding all three of us into it, but from heaping up there besides the numerous packages which the driver, Maximilian himself, took up on the way.  And yet there are still people who execrate railroads.

It took us three hours and a half to travel five leagues, for Maximilian practiced the worship of the Genevan god and made frequent libations at his shrine.  The thought of the wonders I was going to see, however, made me bear this long torture with patience.

At last we arrived at Lille.

The Porte-de-Paris, with its massive architecture, in the style of Louis XIV, impressed me somewhat.

I was also struck by the immense number of windmills, that, like a cloud of gigantic cock-chafers, agitated their wings in the air.  But how describe what I felt, when, having reached the inn (Moulin de l'Arbrisseau) where the coach stopped, after having stretched ourselves and recovered to some extent from the effects of the cramped position we had maintained in the coach (one may fancy the state in which people must be who for three leagues had not been able to move even so much as the tip of their fingers)—when, I say, I could contemplate at my ease the promised marvels !

There they are, the houses of my dreams, those yellow houses, grimy and hideous.

Behind those mean-looking fronts it is that stream the splendors of gilded *salons*.

We were given no opportunity, however, on this occasion, of seeing these gilded *salons*.  In the house at which we stopped we were shown into a large room filled with ugly objects—high porcelain stoves, and parcels of various shapes and sizes.

There gentlemen with black or red side-whiskers

glanced up at us and then went on with their writing. Then one of them, his quill pen sticking behind his ear, went to look for the landlord. The latter came to us with noisy protestations of friendship; led us through long passages full of windows, but none the less dark on that account; and showed us, at the end of a little court, which the sun never visited, into a pretty pavilion built in a style of architecture like that of the little temple on the roof of our pigeon-house, and my uncle and his companion chatted and laughed incessantly, recalling a thousand past events in which we had had no part, while we remained there yawning, our eyes fixed alternately on an alabaster clock and a porcelain figure of Napoleon, who from the column on which he stood directed an imaginary battle.

And when we came out my uncle said to us, "There is a happy man, who has plenty of money."

In the hotel at which we put up we found the same dark passages, the same dark and narrow yard, the same commonplace porcelain ornaments. And everywhere the same thing was repeated; and my uncle, at every new sight, would nod his head with an expression which seemed to say, "Well, my child, what do you think of that?" And, in order not to offend him, of course we were obliged to pretend to admire everything.

We dined at the house of some friends, where, at least, we found children; but, just as we thought we were going to be rewarded for our past disappointments by some entertaining game, we discovered that we were among good boys, who shortly opened their History of France, where we were obliged to look at endless likenesses of the Merovingians in the traditional oval. And, indeed, whenever those pale city-bred boys chanced to move their elbows a little too quickly, their mother, with glare and severe glance, would immediately reprimand them for it.

This gave me enough of the Merovingians!

But I must bear witness to the prodigious learning of these babies, beside whom we felt ourselves to be only village donkeys.

After the champagne we were allowed to stretch ourselves a little in the low kitchen where these young gentlemen kept their playthings.

Oh! what a gloomy room—with its dark windows, through which the light scarcely ever penetrated—light that came down from an invisible sky between walls of grimy brick, at whose feet a narrow stream dragged along its muddy waters in shiny eddies formed by the heaps of broken bottles and bits of crockery and other countless objects that encumbered its bed!

At night everything wore a different aspect. The city was then lighted up, and I experienced a genuine pleasure in the long walk we took between the rows of booths erected for the fair in the great square. A pleasant odor of spice-cake, oranges, and perfumery mingled, diffused itself through these improvised walks that resounded with the cries of the venders. How many beautiful objects were there displayed, transfigured in the floods of light which the lamps and the candles shed around in profusion: ingenious toys, tempting bonbons, weapons, carved walking-sticks, knives of every shape, curious snuff-boxes, and magnificent gilded clocks, with figures of pretty shepherdesses or naked savages!

I saw there also strange fruits which a Turk, like one of those in the *Magasin Pittoresque* (the new periodical which amused us so greatly), was selling.

What was my surprise to see this Turk shake hands with my uncle and enter into friendly conversation with him ! How proud I was of having an uncle who was on such familiar terms with a Turk !

I was not so proud of my brother Louis though, who, notwithstanding my repeated remonstrances, hobbled along in full view of everybody, the poor boy having burned his foot a few days before by upsetting the coffee-pot as it stood on the kitchen fire.

He had begged so hard to be taken with us that my uncle had brought him, a slipper covering his burned foot. I felt on this account a foolish mortification.

We visited the museum.

I thought all those large paintings, dark and smoky-looking, very fine indeed, but, I must confess, not very amusing. Louis frankly avowed that he preferred the cabinet of natural history, where were a large whale and some pretty birds of various colors. I would have been of his opinion also had this not been unworthy the dignity of a future painter.

As yet Fremy was more within my comprehension than Rubens. Happily, I was able to admire sincerely a little picture of the Flemish school, in which two old men were represented reading in a large book by the light of a lamp. The light of this lamp was perfect. The slender flame passed so naturally from blue to yellow, and then to a smoky red. The only fault was, that the light cast on the figures was too red.

In the evening my uncle took us to the theatre, where they were playing *The Dumb Girl of Portici*. We were the first of the audience to arrive. The hall was still empty, and was dimly illuminated by the bluish light that came from the ceiling. Then they lowered the chandelier, which an attendant turned round, lighting each of the lamps in succession.

Soon the hall was brilliant with light, but its splendor fell far short of that of my nocturnal visions. The orchestra played a prelude. From time to time fingers were thrust through little holes in the curtain, through which, at other times, eyes shone. I was again made proud by seeing my uncle make a friendly gesture to the first horn, his old teacher, and an incomparable musician, whose face bore so strong a likeness to that of the chrysalis of the butterfly known as *Vulcan* that, as his name was Laoust, we called those chrysalids ever after Monsieur Laousts.

The opera began, but there was too much singing in it. I could not understand a word. I amused myself by looking at the costumes and the decorations of the theatre.

In the last act I saw the Vesuvius of our school-room represented on the stage. Here a new disillusion awaited me. I discovered immediately the cords fastened to the stones used in the eruption, and then the dumb girl threw herself, without any attempt at deception, not into the crater, but beside it.

As for my uncle, he bounded from his seat at every moment, with such bursts of enthusiasm as to draw upon him the ridicule of our neighbors.

---

## XXXII.

" Le reverrai-je, enfant qui traversas mon rêve,
Le temps que met l'étoile à passer dans la nuit ! . . .
C'était un jour de mai tranquille où pour tout bruit
Aux branches ou croyait ouïe monter la sève."

WHEN she arrived with her father it seemed as if a ray of paradise had entered the house, so heavenly was the light that shone in her blue eyes ; so bright was her golden hair, and so dazzling the rosy whiteness of her skin.

Whence did she come? Where has she gone? I know not. Nothing remains in my memory but the name of her father—vague, also, Dubois, a name so common that it can scarcely be said to indicate any particular individual. And whence came the charm that attracted us all the moment we saw her, at the same time that it kept us at a distance, for from the very beginning we were bashful and shy in her presence?

Other little girls did not produce this effect upon us. Why did we forget our toys? I can see her now, walking down along the garden, without once turning round to look at us.

We watched her from a distance in silence. Then, with assumed boldness, we jostled each other noisily, laughing loudly to attract her attention. We could not think how to make the first advances.

But in the evening, before we were put to bed, when godmother had arrayed her in her little muslin night-dress, and imprisoned her curls under a cap, she appeared to us more like one of ourselves, and we kissed her and I fell in love with her at once.

And the following day! Oh, what a happy day it was, brightened by her presence! How joyously the rosy light played on the ceiling in my room when I opened my eyes in the morning—rosy as the little girl's frock!

At dinner they put her chair beside mine.

From that moment we were friends.

We shared each other's dessert. We had drunk some champagne and our tongues were loosened. Oh, there was no more timidity after that!

She followed us out on the lawn. There we sported like mad creatures, turning around with outstretched arms like windmills, until we grew dizzy and fell, one on top of another, on the grass. We got up again staggering. The earth seemed to rise with us, then sink away from under our feet. The walls of the garden continued to turn around. Blissful intoxication! And she cried and laughed at the same time. Her teeth and her eyes glistened with an adorable charm.

When we had calmed down a little, we showed her the sights of the poultry-yard, where the magnificent peacock (a recent arrival also) strutted about proudly in the sunshine, spreading out its tail starred with eyes like a fan.

My uncle calls us. They are going to the *carperie*. "And what is the *carperie?*" "You shall see." We set out. We walk across the fields. I point out to her the corn, the oats, the colzas, the pinks—for of all this the little town-bred girl knew nothing. We pass the château, walking by the side of its dry moat, where thistles, nettles, and dandelions are growing. At last we reach the *Carperie*, verdant and blooming with flowers. We bury ourselves in the tall grass in the orchard, where she is lost to sight among the daisies.

The murmur of the fountain attracts us. The green frogs hop in the basin where the clean water bubbles in the sunshine, for the apparatus which sends the jet upward is not placed directly over the opening of the spring. We walk among the clumps of rose-bushes, meadow-sweet, and snow-balls, and we watch the carps sporting in the ponds. My father sets playing the fountain of the bathing-pavilion, the one that rises so high in the air—a fresh delight for my little friend.

Cries are heard at the grating, where a dozen of our little playfellows ask permission to enter. I open the gate for them, and we get up a party of hide-and-seek. We run into the dark woods, where the sun, now near his decline, darts his fiery arrows almost horizontally through the branches. We hide in all sorts of places, among the branches of the leafy nut-trees ; in the sheds where are kept the cross-bows and archery sets ; among the rose-bushes. There we are silent ; we keep quite still, scarcely daring to breathe when we hear the seekers passing by. Oh, how delightful it was to be hidden there so safely with a single companion, and to look at each other with wide-open eyes, a little frightened at the thought of being caught.

We are discovered. We jump about like goats, uttering crazy shouts, and flights of birds, frightened at the sound, fly away, fluttering their wings, to hide among the branches.

In the play she and I had remained for a long time undiscovered behind the laburnum-bower, where I had heard Bénési a little while before singing his vesper hymns. In this retreat we lay crouched among the grass, whose intense green made her cheeks, rosy with childish excitement, seem redder by contrast. Here we were completely hidden from view by the luxuriant foliage. Beside us was a trench whose clear, still waters abounded with tangled masses of vegetation. Before us, on the opposite bank, large aquatic plants, with broad serrated leaves of a pale-green color, displayed their flowers, also of a pale green, that sprang from long, pointed sheaths. Tall umbelliferous plants, a species of vegetation extraordinarily long-lived and of exquisite delicacy, raised high their parasol-like flowers.

There we were, our hearts palpitating in the midst of this exuberance of life. As she had been running, her face was suffused with a light moisture. I could hear the beating of her heart. Whenever the danger of being discovered appeared most imminent, we would draw more closely together.

We looked at each other with frightened glances, in which there was a mixture of tenderness.

No; we had not been discovered! The steps and the voices withdrew, then returned. I can not tell how long this delightful silence lasted.

Suddenly, with a quick gesture she pointed out to me, close beside the water, not two steps away, and half hidden among the leaves, a bird's nest—a bird's nest made of moss and twigs gracefully curved. The mother, with half-spread wings and little nervous movements, protecting with her body her brood of fledglings, watched us with eyes fixed with terror.

My little friend, trembling with delight, gets up and leans over to obtain a better view, but her movement has betrayed us.

The mad band run toward us, shouting : " Here they are ! here they are ! " and we spring from our hiding-place, while the bird darts away among the reeds, uttering little cries of terror.

———

## XXXIII.

SHE has gone—leaving an indescribably dreary void behind her. Gone—taking with her the brightest rays of the sun, that now shines with a pale and melancholy light on the drooping petals of the flowers. Even little Émile cried this morning, for, for the past two days we have all been under her spell, taking pleasure in nothing in which she had no part.

We must now go back to our lessons and our copy-books, sitting on those odious hair-cloth tabourets and be content, for sole amusement, to watch Thasie's chickens scratching in the dung-hill, and her pig wallowing in the mire.

Happily, since the planting of the *Carperie*, my

uncle, who is often called in that direction, makes frequent absences, and we are left much more to ourselves than formerly.

About ten in the morning, after he has heard our lessons and mended our pens, he puts on his yellow cap, ornamented with spiral stripes, and goes down-stairs. We can hear him in the yard giving some directions to Joseph or Phillipine, then he walks across the garden with firm and rapid steps.

We watch him with patient glance through the panes of colored glass to which our foreheads are already pressed. At the end of the walk, that terminates in a clematis-bower, he opens the door which leads out into the fields and disappears from our sight.

The wall hides him from view for a minute or two. Then we see again the yellow cap make its appearance, and move swiftly along among the corn and oats beside the moat of the château.

This is the signal of release.

Émile, who is only just learning his letters, is the first to run away. Louis and I, who have our copies to write, hurriedly scrawl a few words for form's sake, and then blunt the points of our pens which refuse to write, so of course we can not go on.

Louis darts off in his turn. And I remain behind to give myself up to the fascinating occupation of rummaging in forbidden corners.

Under the book-case there are five or six drawers, which it would be delightful to rummage. There are there strange-looking instruments in leathern boxes; rolls of maps; medals; parchments with red waxen seals; shells; spy-glasses; lenses; and, what interests me more than all the rest, color-boxes for painting in water colors, and even bladders containing oil-colors; flasks of varnish with an odor more exquisite than that of flowers; and, finally, specimens of lithochromy—an art which my uncle, who wanted to learn a little of everything, had practiced.

My heart beating, and straining my ear for every sound, with what agitation of mind did I rummage among all these curiosities!

My uncle might have permitted me to look at some of these things, but I had never dared ask him, so sacred and precious did they seem to me. I almost felt as if I were committing a sacrilege in touching them; as if I divined the multitude of arts of which they were the humblest emblems. But curiosity soon got the better of respect. I carried my daring so far as to handle some of the objects. I tried at first, on the back of my hand, all the cakes of paint, one after another. Then I painted the lid of the box, so that my uncle could not open it again, as the slide would not work. And in his innocent simplicity he suspected nothing!

I would also prick the bladders with the point of my penknife, and once, one of them bursting open in my hands, covered my fingers with Prussian blue, some of which fell on the carpet. How frightened I was!

What if my uncle were to return unexpectedly? I hurried to the bake-house to wash my hands with sand, telling Phillipine that I had stained them with her washing-blue, and then, by dint of sponging the carpet with soap and water, I succeeded at last in effacing the stain.

If my uncle returned before the hour of recreation, we would hear his key turning in the lock of the garden gate, and in the twinkling of an eye we would run to seat ourselves at our desks and open our books. He would come in and look at our copy-books. Then we would show him the pens.

Then, before going away again, he would mend five or six more, and then each of us had to write his page. We would hurry and scrawl it anyway. We had orders to remain in the school-room till half-past eleven in the morning and till four in the afternoon. The signal of release, long awaited, came from a tall clock behind the staircase. By leaning over the banisters I could touch its case.

But it happened that this clock, which had always kept very regular time, would occasionally hurry forward wildly. The watchmaker came to set it right a dozen times, and declared at last that it was beyond his skill. The more he worked at it, the faster it went.

Oh, my innocent relatives! They never once suspected that it was I, who, contrariwise to Joshua, hastened the march of the hours, so as not to be found fault with, if my uncle were to return unexpectedly.

---

## XXXIV.

ANOTHER of the forbidden pleasures which I used to enjoy with my heart beating at the sound of every step on the stairs, was, also during my uncle's absence, to turn over the leaves of the books concealed behind the green silk-lined doors of the book-case, but from which their owner, in his unsuspecting trust, had neglected to withdraw the keys. The five or six compartments contained rows of very handsome volumes, all bound in calf. There were in these books a number of fine engravings, some steel engravings even, so fine that it was necessary to look at them very closely to distinguish the strokes. The illustrations by the younger Moreau of Voltaire's romances, those of *La Pucelle*, for instance, awoke in me strange emotions, and plunged me into profound reveries.

I soon had more leisure to devote to these stolen pleasures, for my uncle, who still continued his walks to the garden on the marsh, spent a good deal of his time also in the unfinished parlor, where, for several weeks, he had been giving singing-lessons to some young girls. He taught them canticles, first for the planting of a Calvary which my father was going to erect in a corner of the cemetery, and afterward for other occasions.

I could hear these songs distinctly, as the large parlor was directly under our school-room.

Those fresh voices coming from below had an inexpressible charm for me.

In my mind there was a mysterious association between them and the figures in the engravings, which seemed animated by a supernatural life. This fantastic idea produced a delightful agitation in me.

One of these pictures initiated me into the cruelties of which men were capable, and opened before my mind a vista of anguish hitherto unknown. It represented a row of negro slaves bound and fastened together by a sort of ladder, which rested heavily on their shoulders, and between the rungs of which their heads passed.

They walked, thus impeded, bending beneath its weight, and groaning under the pitiless lash of their overseer. It was horrible!

When I heard the languishing voices of the young girls in the room below, it seemed to me that those poor negroes uttered wails and moved their legs automatically; or I would fancy I heard the supplications of angels imploring Heaven to end their torment. My heart was filled with boundless pity. From contemplation I passed into a state of ecstasy. The unhappy slaves writhed with ever-increasing anguish, and I could hear their groans in monotonous cadence with the voices of the singers below:

> "Venez divin Messie,
> Sauvez nos jours infortunés! . . .
> Venez! venez! venez!"

## XXXV.

I OFTEN went to visit Cousin Catharine, the old woman with the sickle, whom you already know.

Her little farm adjoined our grounds.

I admired the rustic simplicity of the old dwelling: its narrow yard, where lay about various articles pertaining to agriculture; the majestic appearance of the tall gate of the barn, which only opened, with prolonged creaking, at the time of the harvest.

I loved the mystery of this dark barn; the pungent vapors that issued from the stable when the bright sunlight entered it, while the cows rested peacefully in the shadow lighted up by golden gleams.

I loved the kitchen with its wide, dark fireplace, where the broth for the animals boiled, diffusing an odor of herbs through the whole house; its window with its little panes of greenish glass; and its clock, with its high oaken case and its monotonous tick, tick; and finally its dresser, studded with shining brass nails, where were displayed all the modest crockery and brass pots of the household.

But, above all, I loved old Catharine herself, the good genius of this peaceful retreat.

I have only a faint recollection of Cousin Zidore, her husband, one of the few men I had seen wearing the queue, knee-breeches, and shoes with silver buckles. His head covered with a white cotton cap, a tranquil smile upon his face, he spent almost all his time dozing in his straw arm-chair. During his brief waking moments he plaited *clachoires* (whips) for me. This is all I can remember of him, except that he was wrinkled with age.

One day godmother said to me : "Your Cousin Zidore is dead; he will make no more *clachoires* for you." And I pictured him to myself like the little birds I found lying on the ground, stiff and motionless, eaten up by the ants.

This event made me feel a sort of terror, and especially their putting him into a hole in the earth while the bells tolled.

Cousin Catharine, small and still active, although she was bent double by age and by the rude labors of the fields, was always singing and smiling.

She was all love, the good old woman !

When she looked at you, her gray eyes sparkled with tenderness beneath her gray eyebrows and the rebellious locks of her gray hair that escaped from under her cap of dazzling whiteness. What a kind expression rested on her face, seamed with wrinkles, the mouth protruding, as if to kiss and be kissed, for time, which had worn her teeth without causing them to drop out, had brought her nose and chin close together, without making her lips, which curved outward, recede. Her knotty, square-nailed fingers clasped mine with a friendly pressure. She was always gay, and yet she had known hard times.

In fine weather she spent whole hours seated at her front door knitting, or at the threshold of the kitchen, spinning. I think I can still hear the sound of her wheel. On stormy evenings she and I would watch the clouds, as they formed themselves into fantastic shapes of animals and human beings, which would change the next moment into other shapes. These eternal images of the sky, among which Catharine had once seen my mother, caused me an indescribable emotion.*

---

* The peasants, in their picturesque speech, call these flaming clouds *storm-flowers*.

I went too, occasionally, a little farther on, to the farm of Jean L——, at the end of the village.

Jean L—— and his wife Augustine, a childless couple, were farmers who enjoyed an honest competence, and who remained to the end faithful friends of my family.

They were both at this time nearing forty. The wife was a little older than the husband, a thing which is not rare in our village.

They resembled each other as much as if they were brother and sister. The faces of both were round, like the full moon, the husband's was always smiling ; the wife's always laughing. The one was always gay and sprightly, the other always serene.

Jean L—— spoke slowly, never raising his voice on any occasion whatsoever. The peasants said of him, "He is a man who thinks slowly."

His conversation was not wanting, however, in a certain amusing charm. He told of his fits of anger, which no one had ever witnessed except himself, in the same tone in which he would have spoken of his gentlest emotions.

His picturesque turns of speech were strangely comical, from the contrast between the vigor of the words he used and the calmness with which he pronounced them.

In no wise inquisitive, he was never surprised at anything.

Madame Jean L—— it was who first took me to see the *Torgeos*.

Having occasion to speak to the miller, she took me one day with her, for the famous beast was a windmill, a fulling-mill—Pan, pan, pan !—pan, pan, pan ! This I discovered in my journey to Lille.

How many *Torgeos* I had heard there !

The vague feeling of terror with which it inspired me still clung to me, however, and I could not approach it without strong emotion.

We went there through the fields along a little path winding among the hay-stacks. This walk has remained in my memory as one of the most romantic excursions of my childhood, like the journey to St. Druon. There I made closer acquaintance with the pretty blue beetles that flew against my face in the garden when I was very small, and which I picked up from the ground where they had fallen, to play with.

Fie! What filthy habits I discovered in them! I was disgusted with them forever afterward.

But was not this *Torgeos* indeed an animal? Was it not an immense beetle with its four half-transparent, half-opaque wings? With what a terrifying sound they creaked in the wind!

And then how loud sounded this noise close by, that I had before heard only from a distance—Pan, pan, pan! pan, pan, pan!

It was always Jean L——, who drove us in his rustic vehicle to the Ducasse at F——.

Early in the morning, from my uncle's balcony, we could see Madame Jean L—— getting the vehicle ready. She spread fresh straw on the floor, placed seats for us, and arranged over hoops the white cloth that was to protect us from the sun.

We followed with happy glances these preparations which promised us a day of unusual pleasure.

Jean L—— harnessed the gray mare—"the carriage-horse "—and the colt, " the farm-horse," and we took our seats on the chairs and settled our feet among the straw.

Then the equipage, swaying from side to side, was started with some difficulty (the roads at that time were not very smooth), and set off at an easy pace, in harmony with the character of the phlegmatic driver.

One by one the houses of the village were left behind, and then the long rows of hay-stacks from which the mist was slowly rising under the influence of the morning sun.

Through this mist appeared, far in the distance, other villages—Hénin, Dourges, Noyelles, Harnes, Fouquières.

Above the thatched roofs and red tiles could be seen the shining slate and glazed tiled roofs of the houses of the wealthier inhabitants.

We were told the names of these, and learned how their fortunes had been made.

The road stretched far away in the distance, seeming endless. We drove on and on.

At last F—— appears in sight.

Leaving the high-road we enter an alley bordered by tall poplars and soon reach the farm-house of Monsieur D——, our host, a real farm-house, whose two high pigeon-houses we had for some time past perceived rising above the trees. These stood side by side with the belfry tower with which they struggled for pre-eminence, the one emerging from the leafy trees of the orchard, the others from among the broad roofs of the barns.

On our arrival the gate was opened admitting us into a large, light yard, where the sun shone golden on the dung-hills, and swarming with poultry—turkeys with mottled feathers, proud peacocks, hens, cocks, and guinea-hens.

Pigeons flocked upon the roof, circling around the pigeon-houses, and dropping showers of their feathers into the puddle.

Geese, noisy and threatening-looking, came up to us and plucked at our trousers.

More hospitable than these their master stood with a friendly smile upon his countenance, waiting to receive us on the threshold, surrounded by his wife and sons.  Embraces were exchanged.  We then went to the dining-room, the walls of which were hung with views of Lyons and of the wharves of the Rhône and Seine, crowded with boats and people.  We found some of the guests there, who had arrived before us.  Others came later on in cars, covered like ours, in coaches and in cabriolets.  They were a mixed company—some wealthy farmers, a doctor, two elegant young men from Douai, friends of D——'s sons, a veterinary surgeon, an unfrocked priest who swore like a trooper, and, finally, the curé of F——, the Rabelais of the village, who published stupid and indecent pamphlets against his church, possessing none of the genius of his master's works, but surpassing them in grossness.

The repast, consisting as with us of fifteen or eighteen dishes, lasted from two o'clock until evening.

But as soon as we children had satisfied our appetites we left the table, to which we returned only for a moment when the champagne made its appearance.

While the grown people ate and drank, we ran delightedly from corner to corner of the farm, where no one was at the time to be seen; we jumped on the heaps of grain in the barns, where we found the stable-boys sleeping off the effects of their gin.

We went to the orchard to shake down the ripe mulberries, at times staining our clean shirts with their juice. We ran after the peacocks, to pluck feathers from their tails, which we hid under the straw of our car.

When we went into the parlor at twilight the guests were excited with wine, and noisy discussions were going on.  The unfrocked priest was swearing more loudly than ever.  The sons of D—— were quarreling among themselves, while their father preserved, amid all this confusion, his patriarchal gravity, for he was a little old man with white hair, who never lost his dignity, although like Abraham he had married his servant—whom, however, he had not sent away.

As for our friend Jean L——, the man who "thought slowly," he appeared as tranquil as when we had set out in the morning, only, when he went to the kitchen to light his pipe at the chafing-dish, we noticed that his gait was a little unsteady.

We returned home in the evening. My father and my uncle exchanged their impressions of the visit, while we children, tired with running about all day, leaned back in our seats, thinking dreamily of our beautiful pea-cocks' feathers, and watching, with sleepy eyes, the tall poplars that stood like phantoms at either side of the road, disappearing one by one in the darkness.

## XXXVI.

THE day for the planting of the Calvary arrived. The crucifix was waiting ready in our house. We were struck by the beauty of the countenance, which formed a contrast to the defaced and ugly features of the saints in the church. A painter had come from Lille to color it—a pale man with long hair, who caused Fremy to descend considerably in my estimation. And then, instead of painting the flesh of a uniform red color, he was able to variegate it with blue veins, and to blend the tints in it with finished skill.

From the wound in the side he had made three drops of water and three drops of blood gush forth. My uncle reminded him that the blood and the water should be mixed together. He made the necessary change, praising my uncle's perspicacity. All great artists are modest! It was a slow business, this erection of the Calvary, and one which was not carried through without some difficulty.

In the village, indeed, no one could carry out any undertaking without having obstacles thrown in his way.

First, the question of the costume of the girls who were to sing was discussed. The white frock was unanimously accepted; but when my uncle proposed, in addition, a black sash, because the ceremony should be given something of a mourning character, a lively opposition was raised by the feminine flock. They all wanted a blue sash. My uncle held his ground, and insisted upon the black. This resulted in a great many secessions from the choir. The prettiest girl, and also the one who was most coquettish, left, and never returned. Then there was another annoyance. One of the female singers had a voice like that of a man, which, in the opinion of her companions, spoiled the singing. She was excluded. Thence sprang pangs of wounded vanity, which extended to the lovers and relations of the principal parties concerned.

The whole village took up the quarrel.

The. effects of all this were soon apparent. Thus the band of the firemen, who were to play some funeral marches at the ceremony, stirred up by the lover of the pretty coquette who had withdrawn from the choir, rebelled and refused to play. This insignificant occurrence was the source of innumerable vexations to my family later on.

And all because of their solicitude for the public good.

From this time forward, there did not pass a single day

in which I did not hear them complain of the ignorance, the stupidity, and the base envy of some one or other of the villagers.

I must hasten to add, however, that the great majority always showed their appreciation of them.

---

## XXXVII.

I WAS about eight years old when my father took me with him in one of his journeys to Regnauville, a little village in the neighborhood of Hesdin, situated on the borders of the forest of Labroye.

This forest, a vast and magnificent domain, belonged to the Duke of Duras, whose manager and steward my father was, as I have already said. The recollection of this visit remains in my mind like a distant dream of a long and sunny holiday

At Sens we visited my grand-aunt Platel, the widow of a notary of that name, my mother's uncle. The impression she gave me was that of a great lady, very old and very dignified.

The only other recollection I retain of my visit is that of a very talkative parrot with a red tail, which must still be living ; and three terra-cotta figures, painted after nature, which stood at the end of a long garden—two beggars, a woman carrying a basket on her back, and a man with a crust of bread in the pocket of his coat ; and a hunter eternally taking aim at a hare which he never hit.

The house, too, was old, and all the trees in the garden were old.

I was standing with my father in my aunt's little yard, when I perceived at the window of one of the rooms a man of immense height, almost a giant, who wore a green uniform with silver buttons, ornamented with silver braid. He laughed down at me from where he stood a good-natured, noisy laugh, stretching his mouth from ear to ear, and showing all his teeth.

"Have no fear," my father said to me; "he is a faithful servant, who will love you dearly, and you will sleep at his house while at Regnauville. He is my chief forester. His name is Bonaventure."

I do not know why he had come to meet us.

We set out in the stage-coach at a quick pace, the horses shaking their manes.

Oh, how buoyant the air was! And what a long and delightful drive!

What ever-fresh transports, as the massive wheels rolled along, across vast plains, over white and dusty roads, that every instant seemed to stop short at the sky, as if the earth came to an end there! Soon we passed mountain after mountain, village after village, these latter seeming in the distance like groves, so completely hidden were their mossy roofs and slated spires among trees on whose dark foliage the light and shadow played.

Beggars came to meet us at the entrance to every village where we stopped, holding out their ragged felt hats, and asking alms in a whining tone. We changed horses, with loud clanking of chains, at inns like farmhouses, where we dined hastily, surrounded by chickens, who picked up the crumbs as they fell from the bare table. We saw things we had never seen before: wonderful sign-boards, strange deformities, and sunshine—sunshine everywhere—burning up the meadows, filtering through the branches, clinging to the roofs, casting on the streets great splashes of light, gliding, glowing, disappearing, and shining, reflected back from every pool with dazzling brightness.

Large pigeon-houses of brick and white stone, like enormous bee-hives, around which pigeons fluttered incessantly, raised their heavy square masses into the air, and were reflected, with their spotted tiles and grimacing weathercocks, in the dark puddles, into which the feathers fluttered in a shower, and where innumerable ducks paddled about.

Inhabited by poor wood-cutters, Regnauville was at that time a very small and unpretentious village, situated near the high-road, and consisting of a few rows of straw-thatched houses shaded by fruit-trees whose roots were hidden in the grass. Scarcely taller than these cabins, the sort of pigeon-house or barn which served at once as church and belfry, was also covered by an old, dark-thatched roof, dotted with green moss, and blooming with spreading plants.

As humble as these buildings was the little cemetery that surrounded them.

The parsonage behind, shaded by a clump of elms, did not disturb this rustic harmony. There was nothing to distinguish it from the thatched cottages around.

In it three old men passed their peaceful existence : the curé ; his brother, formerly a Professor of Philosophy ; and their servant, whose name, it is needless to say, was Marie.

Bonaventure's house, the last in the village, a pretty little farm-house, very white and very neat, roofed, unlike the other houses with red tiles, from its gable window commanded a view of the tall forest that, like a straight, dark curtain, stretched, six or eight hundred yards away, across the horizon.

In front of the house was a square building, a dependence of the domain of Labroye, which contained a rather large hall for the sale of the wood, and my father's office and bedroom. Yellow roses covered its walls. It was separated from the street by a railing, back of which was a garden opening into the fields.

When she welcomed us on our arrival, I observed that Madame Bonaventure was a woman of enormous size, about fifty years old, but very active, and that her frank, bright eyes lighted up a large face with massive features.

The Bonaventures had no children, but my glance fell with pleasure on a young niece who lived with them. She was called Antoinette.

She took me by the hand, led me up a short, steep, narrow staircase, opened a door, and said to me: "This is your room; I am to take charge of you; if you need anything during the night, call me. I shall be close by."

The arrival of my father at Regnauville was always an event. The house was soon filled with people— wood-cutters, wood-venders, guards, people who came to make complaints and beg indulgence.

Fatigued with the journey, we went to bed early. Antoinette tucked me up in the bedclothes, kissed me, and I soon fell sound asleep.

---

## XXXVIII.

On the following morning, when I opened my eyes, still heavy with sleep, I felt a sort of languor, which was a reminder, rather than a remnant of fatigue, just sufficient to make me appreciate the better the rest which I was then enjoying.

In this state of semi-consciousness, which I made no effort to shake off, confused ideas, having no connection with the events of the day before, floated through my brain.

I thought myself still at home, and I expected to hear at any moment the sound of my uncle's step in the room, and the noise of his razor and his soap, but he did not come. Was it because he was lazy, like me?

But the silence was more profound than usual, and the noises by which it was interrupted were unfamiliar. The cocks, heard at rare intervals, crowed a little differently. I opened my eyes. I was surprised not to see the bunches of daisies on the carpet. Then I remembered everything.

I recalled with delight the incidents of the journey. I tasted in anticipation the new delights that awaited me.

My first glance fell on the muslin curtains of my bed, curtains of a lilac color and with a pattern in which two scenes repeated each other alternately; the one an old curé mounted on a donkey, to whom a maidservant was handing a cup of milk; the other the same curé for whom the same servant was placing a chair to enable him to dismount from his saddle.

In places the folds of the curtains gave these figures a curiously grotesque appearance, compressing or distorting them.

The little room was all white, with whitewashed walls, and, although the window was a very small one, extremely bright. A shower of sunbeams streamed in, falling on the lower part of the door and on the floor, brushing my pillow and dancing on the walls—a shower of sunbeams so glorious that they seemed to know that they were lighting a Sunday and the Ducasse of Regnauville.

But a quick, light step mounts the stairs, and Antoinette knocks at my door, calling out, "Lazy little fellow!"

She opens the door, and I behold the young girl, her teeth glistening and her hair and face reddened by the light, in which her eyes, like those of a bird, sparkle mischievously.

She leans over me and begins to tickle me vigorously, with merry bursts of laughter, while I leap on the bed like a trout, drawing with me in my struggles, the curé, the donkey, and the servant, who dance about with every movement of the curtain.

And she devours me with kisses, like a joyous young mother, while she continues to tickle me.

Then she straightens herself up in the sunlight, and her red hair seems on fire, like a flaming distaff.

Then, when she has put on my stockings, I jump out of bed, dress myself, and run to join my father in his room, where the yellow roses seem to shine with redoubled brightness. I find him very happy; here he is completely in his element.

On my way to church, where we went after breakfast, 1 could observe at my leisure the humble cottages which I had only been able to catch a glimpse of on the day before, as we drove along the road.

The church seemed to me very small, gloomy, and bare. With the exception of two chairs, placed for us beside the choir, it contained nothing but wooden benches.

The curé, a feeble little old man whose delicate face was surmounted by white locks, under which his black eyes appeared still blacker, greeted us with a friendly smile.

We were to dine at his house.

The sermon which he preached to his parishioners was in substance as follows :

" My dear children, I shall not detain you long. Today is the Ducasse, and each one of you should have his

Ducassier.* I have mine, Monsieur Breton, whom you love because, as you know, he is the friend of the poor. Enjoy yourselves. God does not prohibit innocent pleasure. Dance as much as you please. I shall go to the ball to see you ; but do not forget that God disapproves of couples wandering away alone into the forest, especially at night."

The dinner at the curé's was very gay and friendly. Poor as the parsonage looked, it was not bare of everything. An ancient wine-cellar, which was opened only on great occasions, contained an onion-wine almost as old as its owner.

My father had an inexhaustible fund of anecdotes, which he related with an animation and naturalness that made the old man laugh until the tears came. They discussed the affairs of the place. Things were going badly in the household of the mayor, and my father would do well to set them straight. Monsieur So-and-so and Monsieur So-and-so were at daggers drawn on account of a certain hedge, and the like.

The curé was a simple, easy man, enlightened and tolerant in his views. His brother under his cotton cap concealed solid learning and an independence of judgment formed, according to what my uncle said, by reading the philosophers of the eighteenth century.

We took coffee in the garden, which Frisé would have thought greatly neglected. Everything there grew as Nature willed, and the wild eglantine climbed unhindered up the unpruned pear-trees. Innumerable plants grew together in confusion in the flower-beds. Secular box-trees spread themselves out in gigantic *pâques*, and the sun streamed through the glass roofs of the beehives upon the swarming bees within.

---

* Patron of the festival.

In the afternoon my father gave audience to a great many people in his office, while I chatted with Antoinette, who took me to see the cow, the horse, and the pig, to which latter she spoke as if it were a human being.

In the distance could be heard the sounds of the violin and the clarionet playing for the dancers, among whom, after what he had said, I saw in imagination the curé.

From Bonaventure's door I perceived to the left the village *en fête*, bathed in a clear white light, while to the right, somber and impenetrable, stretched the curtain of the silent and mysterious forest.

----

### XXXIX.

ON the following day the same awakening, the same excess of sunshine in my little chamber, the same rosy apparition of the young girl, the same merry sport.

We breakfasted hastily and were soon on our way to the forest, my father chatting with Bonaventure, and I running and jumping over the pebbles that lay in heaps beside the graveled path.

My father explained to me their use, and profited by this occasion to speak to me of the stone hatchets employed, before iron was known, by our ancestors, who dwelt in forests such as that which I am going to see.

The forest! There it was, seeming to rise from the confused shrubbery on its borders higher and higher into the sky with every step we took. All at once its vast, shadowy naves, lighted up by sudden flashes, opened before us—a sublime and awe-inspiring sight to a child who had hitherto seen only the tender verdure of willow and alder groves.

The coolness, like that of a church, the strange odors, the night-like silence, the obscurity, through which, at times, flashed dazzling gleams of light, and the solemn and mysterious sense of awe inspired by all this, as if one felt here the invisible presence of the Deity, filled me with a poignant pleasure mingled with a secret fear.

At regular intervals a sort of wail reached us, the notes of a distant cuckoo, uttering its melancholy plaint.

Close beside us, from the high tops of the cherry-trees, a silvery voice responded, so clear, so sweet, so pure, that it seemed to come through the waters of a limpid fountain. I recognized the voice of an old friend, the goldfinch ; but the song which resounded plaintively through our meadows had not the brilliancy of this.

The cuckoo took up the strain. Then followed a silence like that of a church, and our footsteps rustled through the short grass and brambles with an unfamiliar sound, while through the high, dark arches overhead glimpses of the sky shone like stars.

And the giant beech-trees raised their white trunks spotted with velvety black patches, and the oaks twisted their wrinkled branches.

At times I shut my eyes, dazzled by the green fulgurations of the sun darting over tufts of heather and fern that glowed like red and black flames among the turf, striped like the skin of a wild-cat.

Ivy grew along the ground and climbed to the summits of the trees, clasping them in its thousand arms.

Now and then a light breeze sighed among the masses of dark foliage, swaying them gently, and among the masses of transparent verdure that glowed with a brilliant light.

But I can find no words in which to describe the impression I then received, which was one of the strongest of my childhood.

The child, who is all feeling, has no means of expressing his thoughts. He does not analyze his sensations, and, in order to describe what I then felt, I must use words that I would not at the time have understood. This presents a difficulty.

My father, radiant with enthusiasm, appeared to me under a new aspect ; he seemed to me handsome. Ah! the child who, at the risk of his life, had escaped from the prison of the château and hidden himself in the depths of the wood, this child still survived in him!

Later on it will be seen that his passion for forests brought about his ruin.

Every part of the forest, however, was not clothed with this wild majesty.

We traversed clearings where only puny trees and heaps of fagots were to be seen, and openings into which the sun streamed, where flights of butterflies that seemed made of mother-of-pearl and fire soared in zig-zag flight.

And I felt happier in these luminous places than among the lofty trees.

But by-and-by I felt very lonely, and I began to think of those at home and of the more familiar and cheerful scenery amid which they lived, of my god-mother, who at this season never failed to prepare for us three pots of different kinds of cooling draughts. I missed even my uncle, who, in spite of his occasional severity, manifested great affection for us, and who had so strong a sentiment of justice that he would beg our pardon, with tears in his eyes, when it chanced that he had punished us undeservingly. Then the holly, with its hard and thorny foliage, and the rough brambles, recalled to my mind by the contrast they formed to it, our vegetation, so tender in comparison. Oh! the colzas, the pinks, the blue flax!

In short, I grew tired of the forest, because I felt, when I was there, as if I were lost in it; and then it was always the same.

So that one day I begged papa to let me stay in the house under pretext of writing some copies, but in reality to be with Antoinette, whose petting began to please me.

In fact, she was the only person who could console me for the absence of all I had left at home.

And many a happy hour we passed at the little farm-house—she, the animals, and I.

When the morning of our departure arrived she came to awaken me, and essayed in vain to play her accustomed pranks. The moment she kissed me she burst into tears.

------

## XL.

WHEN we set out I thought the horses moved more slowly than they had ever moved before, so impatient was I to see my family and my home. I would have liked to fly there!

How I envied the swallow that skimmed so swiftly along the ditches by the roadside! My thoughts flew on before me, and, huddled in a corner of the stage-coach, my eyes close shut, I fancied I could hear, amid the noise of its jolting and the rolling of the wheels, the refrains of my native place; my uncle's songs and the ditties of Henriette and Frisé, and the rattling of the window-panes brought to me, like a joyous echo, the cries that my brothers, excited by their sports, were at that moment uttering.

And again I saw before me my father's house and the dear ones there.

I recalled again those long evenings when Joseph would describe to me, while he was polishing the shoes, his campaign and the retreat from Moscow. He had slept upon the ground in the snow, wrapped in the skins of the horses whose flesh he had eaten. Once he had carried on his back for hours one of his comrades who had become insensible from the cold, and had thus saved his life. And he made no merit of this action. What other man in his place would have been equally modest?

The dreadful hardships he then endured had left him with rheumatism, from which he suffered greatly, and an inextinguishable thirst, which compelled him to stop at every gin-shop he passed for drink, for which he never paid. But in every other respect what a fine fellow he was! What blind devotion, like that of a faithful dog for its master, did he show for my family! I can see him now, when he was sawing wood one day in the unfinished parlor, and the loud voice reached us, of a man speaking to my father at the front door, strain his ear to listen, and then start up trembling with anger, throw down his saw, and, at one bound, quick as lightning, leap through the window into the yard. I recalled to mind also an incident that occurred a year or two before (in 1834) at the time of the cholera, of which every one was in such terror and which I too was a little afraid of, on account of the table covered with black cloth and supporting a crucifix, that stood before the door of every house in which lay a dead person. My father fell suddenly ill, and as the doctor ordered a medicine which was to be given to him at once, Joseph started in the middle of the night to bring it from Carvin, for then, as now, there was no apothecary at Courrières. He set out, as I said, and lo! he found the ferry-boat turned round.

He tried in vain to waken the sleeping toll-keeper, who made no response either to his cries or to his blows against the closed shutters. What was to be done! Throw himself into the water, dressed as he was, and swim across the river. And this is what Joseph did!

By what strange contradiction of character was it that this man, who was so good at heart, had so peevish a disposition, and why was he always quarreling with his wife Phillipine, who was also a model of goodness?

My thoughts dwelt on all this while the trees and the houses flew past us on either side of the road, and the apple-trees in the meadows whirled past dizzily, keeping time to the noise of the coach-wheels, and I said to myself, "What happiness it will be to embrace this faithful follower to-morrow, notwithstanding his rough skin pitted with small-pox, his large nose covered with pimples, and his woolly hair like that of a savage!"

I thought too of my uncle.

A proof that he was not always severe is the fact that in the evening he often recited plays to us, and that then, in his own words, he became a child again to amuse children. At times we would sit on his foot and cling to his leg while he would pretend to be making desperate efforts to raise our light weight. At other times he would take a candle in his hand, I would seize the border of his dressing-gown, Louis would take hold of the tails of his coat, Émile would place himself last, and we would tramp along, one behind the other, keeping time with our feet as we sang:

> " J'ai perdu tout mon bonheur,
> J'ai perdu mon serviteur,
> Colin me délaisse. . . ."

But I was moved to tears as I thought of my old godmother. And, indeed, we never had occasion to remember that we had no mother; so devoted was she to us in every way. Even her wrinkles made her all the dearer to us. We made haste to give her proofs of our affection, as if we felt that she would be the first to depart.

How many times have we fallen asleep in her lap, while murmuring the prayer she taught us, resting our heads against her bosom, that rose and fell with her breathing, tranquil as her conscience!

How many sleepless hours had she spent bending over us in our childish illnesses! She often told us the dreams these constant anxieties would produce. At times we would be attacked by ferocious dogs, and she would throw herself upon them and tear them to pieces. Then it was a man who pushed against little Louis, who was blowing a whistle, and knocked the whistle down his throat. She would fall upon the man and strangle him in her arms.

And the vehicle rolled on, and beyond the plains the slender slated spires of belfry towers pierced here and there through the somber shadows of the woods.

And as we were to stop at Calonne on our way to visit my granduncle, Henry Fumery, my godmother's brother, who still dwelt in the paternal farm-house, the thought came to me that godmother had once been as young as I was, and that she had made her first communion, a white veil over her fair rosy face, a white taper in her hand, and had returned from church between the yoke-elm hedges of a village like the villages we were driving through.

.     .     .     .     .     .     .

I have forgotten where we slept that night.

On the following morning the sunshine played no longer in the little room, and I might have waited long in vain for Antoinette to come. I saw in imagination the young girl, with her golden hair, standing there yonder, looking at my empty bed, as I had often looked into empty nests robbed of the young birds.

----

## XLI.

When I entered my granduncle Henry's farm-house I recognized it by the glowing descriptions of it with which my grandmother had interspersed the stories she used to tell us of her youthful days.

And, indeed, nothing had changed there since the time of my great-grandfather, the magistrate.

I recognized the pastures and the ditches, bridged with planks over which my grandmother had many a time walked with careful step, as she returned at night from some sick-bed, carrying her lantern in her hand, undisturbed by the fears of witches ; the muddy roads, paved with stones, so far apart that one had to walk in a series of jumps ; and the shady paths crossing the sunny meadows.

And here, at last, is the bowery, tranquil village, with its little church roofed with green moss-covered slates.

Here it is that godmother spent her youthful days— days full of affection, courage, and piety.

I had these qualities of hers in my mind when depicting the character of Angèle in my poem " Jeanne." Let me recall here a few of the events of her life.

This dates back as far as the Reign of Terror, when the ferocious Le Bon, commissioner of the republic at Arras, brought dishonor, as, alas ! did so many others of our countrymen, on the justest of causes.

In his ignorant simplicity, believing what his father

before him had believed, Scolastique Fumery did not divine the benefits that were to result from the Revolution, and saw in it only the crimes, the recital of which filled the farm-house with indignation and terror.

The storm was approaching.

Bands of wicked men (as godmother called them) went through the country, desecrating the churches and decapitating the sacred statues.

The pious young girl concealed the patron saint of the village under her mattress; and when the wicked men came, placing herself at the head of the most courageous women of the village, she led them to the church, which these men had entered, and, rushing toward them, threw in their faces sand and ashes which they had brought with them in their aprons.

Betrayed and denounced, after a search which resulted in the discovery of the hidden saint, godmother was thrown into prison in Arras, where she daily expected to be led to execution, for I know not how long.

She emerged from prison when the death of Robespierre brought about that of Le Bon.

They came and told her she was free, and, as she was unable to communicate with her relatives, she found herself, outside the prison-gate, friendless and without knowing where to turn.

There she learned that among the prisoners liberated with her was Doctor Platel, of Lestrem, a village not far from her own. She knew him by reputation. She went to him.

They returned to the village together, recounting their sufferings to each other, mingling their tears of joy, uniting their hopes, so that the journey must have been a happy one, filled with tender emotions; and Cupid, who doubtless lay in wait for them, with drawn bow, in some corner of the yoke-elm hedge, did not miss his aim, for they were soon married.

During this time my paternal grandfather Lambert Breton was fighting in Belgium, under the command of General Vandamme.

Let me here say a few words in relation to his history.

The religious old books, with their wonderful pictures, which had excited my admiration in the loft at home, will be remembered, but I forgot to say that, in the same trunk which contained them, I had also found a sword, the hilt of which terminated in a Phrygian cap. I broke the blade of it one day, plunging it into the earth to clean the rust from it, and this was one of the deepest of my childish griefs, for I had a veneration for this sword which had belonged to my grandfather.

These books and this weapon symbolize two phases of his life.

When the Revolution broke out he was studying theology at the Abbey of Anchin at Douai. He had dedicated himself to the priesthood. The irresistible pressure of events, the new ideas which circulated in the air, turned him aside from this project.

He quitted the abbey and returned to Courrières. He did not long remain tranquil there.

Denounced by an aristocrat, he too was arrested by order of the same Le Bon, and conducted to the prison at Arras. At this moment France called all her children to the defense of her threatened frontiers. The inhabitants of Courrières formed a company, chose my grandfather for their captain, and marched to Arras to demand his release, which they obtained.

As I have before said, they set out for the seat of war in Belgium.

We keep among our family archives letters of Captain Lambert Breton that breathe an ardent patriotism, for he had yielded to the contagion of the movement that drew with it all hearts.

As soon as the campaign ended, he married.

It will be seen that, but for the Revolution, I would never have been born.

---

## XLII.

I WAS to quit this dear spot, to bid adieu to the paternal mansion and to those scenes where every one and everything, the animals, and even the trees, had been so closely intermingled with my existence. The days spent in the freedom of the open air were past. I was about to leave my Eden for a gloomy school.

My uncle wished to place me in the college of Douai, but my father preferred a small seminary about twenty leagues distant from Courrières, where some of our friends had placed their sons.

On the day of my departure my brothers wept in corners. Godmother and Phillipine wept—everybody wept. I was scarcely ten, and I was going to be deprived of the sweet indulgences of home.

On the journey my cheerfulness returned : I saw new objects ; and then my father and my uncle were with me.

When they left me and I found myself alone among this crowd of school-boys whose faces were strange to me, the recollection of all I had left, of all that I loved, filled my swelling heart with poignant grief and I broke into sobs.

I wandered about the large, gloomy court-yard, the butt of the jeers of my new school-fellows, whom I began to hate with the unreasoning hatred of the exile for everything belonging to the place of his banishment, thinking them, with a few exceptions, ugly and rude.

And instead of the vast horizons, the trees and flowers, an immense building, bare as a barrack, the Military Hospital, rose above the court-yard wall.

I remained there three weary years—years that the bright intervals of the vacations only served to render all the more gloomy. I gradually became accustomed to this narrow existence, in which everything was uncongenial, in which an organized system of espionage existed among the pupils, and in which I search my memory in vain for the face of a friend, for friendship was prohibited and punished. Thus, when it was observed that I preferred the company of some of the boys to that of the others, I was forbidden to associate with them, and I was forced to choose my companions from a list of a dozen of the pupils most repellent to me.

I was unable to conquer the repugnance with which these boys inspired me, and for a long time I preferred to remain alone. I became dreamy and absent-minded, and spent my time idly gazing into vacancy.

From these degrading surroundings, however, there was, for some natures, a refuge in mysticism.

Wounded in my tenderest affections, I fell into a state of spiritual languor in which I abandoned myself to celestial raptures. I heard the torments of hell, the terrors of purgatory, and the dazzling splendors of paradise, continually talked of.

Religious ceremonies were frequent, and were celebrated with comparative splendor.

I had been brought up by an uncle who was a Christian philosopher. I did not believe all that was taught in the seminary, but I had a thirst for emotions, and I gave myself up to mystic reveries. Among the masters and the pupils, although there were some hypocrites, with languishing eyes, gaping mouths, and pious grimaces, there were many who were sincerely devout. I was touched by the ardent piety of some of these, especially of little L——, whose fair face, framed in curls, wore a truly angelic expression when, motionless and lost in prayer, his soul soared heavenward.

I loved him and would have liked to make him my friend, but, even if he had shared this feeling, all intimacy was prohibited, and I did not approach him.

There was another of the pupils, also, who was sincere in his devotion, E—— C——, the son of a friend of my father, a *bon-vivant*, whose character presented a strange contrast to the spirituality of his son.

How retiring he was! What a melancholy expression in his eyes! Older than I, and my monitor of study, he would reprove me gently for my faults, which he never reported.

He was thin and puny-looking. He would spend whole hours in a state of ecstasy in the chapel. He soon afterward decided to study for the priesthood, and went to the large seminary. What storm shook his soul I never knew. But one day we learned that he had thrown off his cassock. He returned to the village, to fall ill and die. Poor friend!

Oh, how long and weary were the ceremonies in the chapel, especially at vespers, when, in the warm and languorous summer afternoons, I would give myself up to meditation, while the sun streamed through the high windows, with their bright-red blinds, darting into every corner of the little temple rays red as blood! I felt as if I were among the fires of hell; while at the end of the chapel the altar, starred with light, shone like a glimpse of paradise through the smoke of the incense, whose odor at times made me faint. Ah, what celestial ravishment I experienced the first time I saw my young companions make their first communion !

But what I took for divine love was, my confessor explained to me, only a trap set by the evil one for my pride !   It is evident that I was far from being orthodox in my reveries.   This confessor rated me soundly for it.

I was not allowed to make my first communion, which grieved me greatly, for I had looked upon this act as the acme of felicity.   Every year there were two or three weeks of retreat, during which we abandoned all play, all work, all profane study, in order to practice religious exercises.   Then Jesuit fathers came to hold conferences in the chapel and in the study-room.

This was an occasion of special graces and plenary indulgences.   It was also a good opportunity to enlighten the hesitating and confound the proud.   Well, during those retreats I was sent to the infirmary, along with some *esprits forts* among the pupils, to continue our usual studies, with the pretext that we would not profit by those graces, and that our hearts, not being prepared to receive the divine seed, the devil would avail himself of the occasion to sow there his tares.

All this helped to cure me of my mysticism.

The following year, although I was at the head of the class in the catechism, my first communion was again postponed.   But I had now grown more indifferent, and when, in 1840, at the age of thirteen, I was at last permitted to make it, my strongest feeling was one of mortification, caused by finding myself overtopping by a head my happy little companions.

Ah, how much more enlightened and liberal did my uncle's teachings seem !

In our walks, however, I enjoyed once more a little real sunshine and healthy pleasure.

We would play foot-ball, and eat cherries that we bought from an old woman, in sunny meadows surrounded by vast uncultivated heaths, growing on heights bathed in a purer atmosphere, whence could be seen the hill of Cassel, whose windmills and houses seemed to quiver in the distant light.

The masters would take off their cassocks, and, in their shirt-sleeves, join in the sports of the boys.

I think this sort of *camaraderie* was one of the secrets of their influence, and I regret that it is not practiced in secular institutions.

Even at play-time, however, I often remained alone. The unruly city boys scorned my rustic simplicity, and, in fact, I felt myself, when among them, awkward and weighed down by a timidity that was fostered by my lonely habits.

Amid these deteriorating surroundings one passion saved me—the love of art.

To become a painter! This had been my dream ever since the time when Fremy used to paint the figures in our garden. My father allowed me to take the drawing-course, directed by an easy, good old man, whom I regarded as a great artist, because I had seen a lithograph of his representing the ruins of the Abbey of St. Bertin in the stationer's window.

The first time I entered this class I was seized with a lively emotion at the sight of the copies hanging over the desks. With what delightful thrills I penetrated, little by little, into the agitating mysteries of the stump and charcoal! What happy hours of forgetfulness I spent copying figures of Moses, of Mordecai, of Scipio, and, above all, Raphaelesque, wearing handkerchiefs twisted around the head like turbans, and fastened underneath the chin!

Ah, to be able to follow the delicate and graceful outlines of those foreheads, of those regular noses, those rounded cheeks, those exquisitely flexible necks !

O Raphael ! O sublime genius ! You consoled me for the disturbance in my uneasy mysticism.

During the drawing-hour some of the pupils took lessons in music, in an adjoining room, and nothing could be more delightful than to hear, as I drew, the silvery sighs of the flute—mingling the pleasures of sound with those of sight—vibrating in unison with the raptures of my growing passion, and their melodious expression, as it were. We drew in the evening by lamplight.

At times we could perceive—O mar-joy !—the severe countenance of the Superior, looking in at us through the window-panes, as he prowled around in the dark courtyard, for we were everywhere under surveillance.

I liked geography. This, too, was a species of art. Certain countries charmed me by their shape ; others displeased me. That of France seemed to me the best proportioned, the best balanced. South America attracted me by its *svelte* elegance of form, and Terra del Fuego, which terminates it, plunged me into mysterious reveries.

But to color my maps I had only very poor paints. It was necessary to soak them in water for a long time to obtain even a pale tint ; and I remember a red and a green, very beautiful in the cake, from which I could extract nothing, while the boy whose desk was in front of mine had superb paints, three or four times as large as mine, and I wondered at the ease with which he blended them and filled the brush with their splendid colors.

I would never have dared to ask my father for paints like those, so much beyond his means did they seem to me.

This treasure kindled in me the consuming flames of

covetousness. I experienced the tortures caused by a fixed idea and by the pangs of envy. A demon whispered ceaselessly in my ear, "Take them! take them!" I lay awake for hours thinking of carmine, emerald green, gamboge—oh! above all, of gamboge—and in my sleep I dreamed of them.

One night, unable to resist the temptation any longer, I got up and went to the study-room, my heart palpitating with guilty terrors; my teeth chattered; my legs bent under me; and I trembled in every limb.

By a singular coincidence, of which I never knew the cause, at the moment when I opened the desk, a school-fellow suddenly came into the room and asked me what I was doing there.

I thought I should die with fright, and, as in a case like this, one is always stupid, I answered, "I am looking at the butterflies!" (The owner of the paints was a collector of butterflies.)

I had thrust the box hastily into my pocket, and, as I hurried up-stairs, my heart beating so violently that it caused me 'pain, my companion, who was close behind, noticed the noise that sounded from my pocket—accusing noise, produced at every step I took, by the shaking of the paints in the pine-wood box.

I did not sleep all night, agitated between remorse and the happiness of possessing the object so ardently coveted, and which I kept closely clasped to my breast. With the first ray of daylight I tried on the back of my hand the wonderful colors.

I was not to possess them long, however. My escapade became known to their legitimate owner. He was an excellent boy, named D'Halluin. He deserves that I should mention his name, for he was very generous. All he said was, "Give them back to me—I will say nothing about them." And he kept his word.

## XLIII.

MY passion for drawing led me into another disagreeable adventure which left a feeling of rancor in my heart.

In the school there was a large black wolf-hound, which answered to the name of Coco.

I took a fancy, one day, to draw this dog standing on his hind legs, clad in a cassock, and holding between his fore paws a book. I wrote underneath, "The Abbé Coco reading his Breviary."

This innocent sketch made the tour of the schoolroom, passing from hand to hand, provoking the mirth of some, the disapprobation of others, when it was noticed by the master, who ran and seized it. "Who has been guilty of this wickedness?" he asked. I was immediately denounced.

The master pulled my ears, made me kneel down in the middle of the hall, and sent my poor caricature to the sub-director.

A few moments afterward the bell rang for supper, and all the boys went to the refectory. I was about to follow them, when he said to me, "Stay where you are!"

And there I stayed, asking myself anxiously what they were going to do to me.

I had not long to wait. I was soon aroused from the torpor into which I had sunk by a formidable blow from behind, and I knew then that those who told me they had seen in similar cases, thirty-six candles, had not spoken figuratively, for it seemed as if a shower of fireworks had exploded in my brain. Half stunned, I felt myself lifted from the floor and dragged in an iron grasp down the whole length of the stairs, my feet bumping against every step.

When I reached the room of the sub-director, he threw me on the ground, and looked at me in silence with pale and implacable countenance.

I was terrified. When he saw that I had to some extent recovered my senses, the monster put me this pitiless question :

"Was it to ridicule your professor, or was it from irreverence, that you made that infamous scrawl ?"

To ridicule a professor seeming to me the graver of the two faults, I responded :

" From irreverence ! from irreverence ! "

He immediately took off his cassock, seized a cat-o'-nine-tails lying ready on his desk, and then followed a long and terrible struggle, in which I rolled among the chairs and under the table, striking myself against every corner, and writhing under every stroke of the lash. The sub-director was a tall and powerful man, of a very pale complexion, with broad, square shoulders, and arms of which he was in the mood to make me feel the full strength.

It is needless to add that during this rain of blows he exhausted the vocabulary of epithets usually applied to the greatest criminals.

Strange to say, this barbarous punishment did not enrage me at the time as much as the recollection of it does now. It was convincing. I regarded myself as a hardened sinner, a species of reprobate.

In my imagination, excited by the blows of the whip, my executioner assumed supernatural proportions, and, seen through a cloud of dust, whirling the thong, he appeared terrible and beautiful, and surrounded by a halo like an avenging archangel ; and the next time I went to the cathedral I thought of him when I looked up at the St. Michel of Ziegler over the principal altar, shining in his golden armor. I was certain then that I was foredoomed to hell ; but, as I had no positive knowledge regarding the location of that place, I suffered less from fear of its tortures, than from a feeling of self-contempt. Though at times, indeed, I saw again in imagination those devils, armed with bars of red-hot iron, whom I had imagined I had seen pursuing me when I was in my nurse's arms on the evening of the *charivari* given to Zaguée.

I had not yet seen the last of my humiliations.  One day, when I had thrown mud against one of the window-panes of the class-room, they dressed me in servant's clothes, tied a blue apron around my waist, gave me a basin of water and a sponge, and, mounting me on a table, made me wash the window in the presence of all the boys.

This brought me into ridicule, and did not tend to elevate me either in the estimation of my companions or in my own.

Regarded by my school-fellows and by myself as a black sheep, I continued to wander about in the gloomy court-yard, more lonely than ever.

When I received letters or presents from my native place, I fancied for an instant that I saw again my home, and I shed tears of poignant anguish.

Often during the night, lying with wakeful eyes, I saw my father's house, the gardens, the wide plain dotted with fields of grain, and again I saw the dear ones there, and, like the swift winged butterfly, that, without paus-ing in its flight, hovers, now over this flower, now over that, my imagination spread its wings and flew swiftly from my father and my uncle to my brothers, from the servants to my playfellows, from the animals to the trees, from one familiar spot to another, rushing through the alleys, skimming along the ponds, and meeting with a smiling welcome everywhere, from the kindly eyes that lighted up the wrinkled face of my grandmother, to the motionless faces of the figures in the kitchen garden.

But how swiftly the illusion vanished, when, in the morning light, I saw, through the little window of my room, the stone flames of the Military Hospital, and, a little beyond, the two towers of the ancient church of the Jesuits!

About this time a trunk was sent me from Courrières, containing articles which I needed. I opened it, and it seemed as if a breath from my native place was wafted to me, bringing with it at once all the love and tenderness and all the familiar scents of home. At the sight of the order with which those articles were arranged—the white shirt, among which loving hands had concealed bonbons, folded in a particular fashion—I felt myself shaken with quick sobs, and tears of grateful affection streamed from my eyes. When I got to the bottom of the trunk, I found there in a corner a scrap of paper, folded. It contained a liard,* and bore these words, in little Émile's handwriting: " Jules, *je te çaule!* " †

---

## XLIV.

But how quickly all my griefs and mortifications were forgotten when, on the first morning of the vacation, a ray of country sunshine came to waken me in my white bed, with its sheets feeling a little stiff with the fresh starch—when I heard again all the familiar sounds of home!

How small the house appeared to me, that I had thought so large!

---

* A coin equal in value to the fourth part of a cent.
† Equivalent to "Jules, I send you my love."

With what transports of affection I kissed all the beloved faces! How impatient I was to visit every corner of the house! What good bread! What delicious coffee! Even the hair-cloth tabourets in the schoolroom appeared soft to me. As soon as I had seen everything, I chose for my special retreat an unfrequented spot, a little room lighted by a single window that opened on the garden—the same window of which, some years before, I had broken the panes.

When I entered this room a strong odor greeted my nostrils—an odor composed of divers smells, for it was in this place that our gardener kept his flower and vegetable seeds. But this mixture of smells, among which those of celery, shallot, and carrot predominated, inspired me with no repugnance.

Here I established my atelier, and amused myself by carving figures of peasants in soft stone, or by painting on wood with the juice of flowers and berries, such as the scabious and the mulberry.

One day, I received a visit from a woman named Marie, who lived in our village and who earned a livelihood by painting weeping-willows on monumental urns, crosses for the cemetery, and ornamental sign-boards for taverns.

On this occasion she had received an order for a sign-board, of which the decoration was to be of so complicated a character as to be beyond her skill, and she came to ask my assistance, which I promised her without hesitation, proud of this mark of confidence.

While I cleared a space to work in, by pushing into the corners the gardening implements and the bundles of willow and osier with which Frisé's room was encumbered, Marie went to bring the board—a large panel rounded at the top—and her brushes and color-pots.

We placed the panel on a table, resting it against the

cases of the herbal, and I soon discovered that the artist stood, indeed, in great need of assistance.

She had begun, by writing around the top of the panel the title of the subject, " The Society of Associated Friends."

As these friends were a society, it followed that they were associated. I drew her attention to this pleonasm in the first place.

In addition to this it was difficult to distinguish the friends in Marie's confused daub. One could make out a blue sky with white clouds shaped like corkscrews in it, and a column supporting a vase of flowers, flanked by two aloes, but the figures of the friends bore no likeness to anything whatever.

I rubbed out all this mess, and asked Marie to go away and leave me to my inspiration.

I was filled with emotion. These little pots of chrome, vermilion, and Prussian blue, transported me with joy.

But how set about the composition of the picture? I thought for a long time in vain. Then I had recourse to the *Magasin Pittoresque.* My uncle had been a subscriber to it ever since its establishment, and, after the engravings in the loft, nothing had contributed more to inspire me with a love for art than this periodical, founded by Eduard Charton, to whom I have since had occasion to manifest my gratitude.

I chose a scene after Giraud, representing some jolly French Guards, and I copied the composition of it, changing the costume of the figures for that of our peasants.

Marie was satisfied with my work.

This must have still smacked somewhat of the school of Fremy. A certain peasant in knee-breeches of chrome-yellow and an apple-green coat, might, so far as coloring was concerned, contest the palm with the Chinese of the pigeon-house.

The poor Chinese! Let me say here, before leaving him forever, that he had fallen greatly from his former splendor.

The catastrophe I have before spoken of had already happened. The plainest rules of common sense forbade the restoration to their former position of his airy temple, his extinguisher hung with bells, or his ball. Even the landscape had suffered considerably.

The figure itself, however, continued to smoke its long pipe as philosophically as before, and showed as much zeal as ever in pointing out the quarter from which the wind blew.

As for my sign, I never saw it again. My brothers came across it one day, in one of their excursions, hanging over the door of a wine-shop in a village whose name I have forgotten. But the sun, the frost, and the rain had greatly softened its barbarous realism.

Such was my first picture.

And the next? This had its existence only in my imagination. I have often seen it, always the same, in my dreams, hanging in the shadows of some village sacristy, full of a spirit of simple devotion.

It is a triptych, the Holy Trinity in the center, the Virgin and angels at the sides.

Which of these angels is it who has led me a hundred times in sleep into that dusty sacristy, where thou, picture of my dreams, a dream thyself, reposest? And I tremble with joy when I see thee always in the same place, always radiant with divine love!

## XLV.

It was in 1840, during one of my vacations, that we took dancing-lessons in the large, unfinished parlor which I have so often mentioned.

My uncle, who desired to neglect nothing that might contribute to form our manners, had found a skillful professor for us—a retired soldier who, in the intervals of leisure left him by his military duties, had caused himself to be initiated into the mysteries of Terpsichore.

His household was established on a very simple footing, and he himself carried in a wheelbarrow the manure with which he enriched his bit of land.  He stopped at our house during the expeditions necessitated by the requirements of his modest gardening.

And I can assure you that on these occasions he did not exhale the perfume of the rose.  I can still see his large feet in their heavy shoes dropping manure with every step he took, and his legs covered by linen trousers stained with suspicious-looking patches, executing their pigeon-wings and capers.

Ah! simple days!  His wheelbarrow, with the cask containing the manure, would remain standing before our front door until the lesson was ended, without any fear of its being stolen.

I do not know whether this manner of learning dancing has contributed to the feeling, but from that time I have always entertained a profound indifference for that graceful art.

I remember also that during this same vacation, finding myself alone one day in my uncle's study, and ransacking his book-case as in former times, I opened the portfolio in which he was accustomed to keep copies of his own and other letters which were of any importance.

What was my astonishment in turning over one of the leaves to find—guess what? I might give you a hundred chances, and you would never guess it—to find the Abbé Coco!—the Abbé Coco, carefully fastened there with a pin.

I felt as if I had fallen from the clouds! For nothing in the world would I have dared to speak to my uncle of this abominable piece of irreverence and he knew all about it, and he had never said a word to me! And he preserved among his interesting papers the impious caricature that had drawn upon me the thunders of the clergy!

Counting on the indulgence of my father and uncle, I resolved to relate the whole incident to them at dinner. Scarcely had I pronounced the name of the Abbé Coco, when they both burst into a loud laugh, but their merriment changed to indignation when I reached the end of the story.

"Why did you not tell us of this before?" they said. "Do you think we would have left you a moment longer in that abominable place?" And then I made a general confession. I told them of my mortification, my isolation, my troubles, the incessant espionage from which I had suffered, without forgetting to mention the rare moments of unalloyed delight in the drawing-class.

My father and uncle decided at once to place me in the College of Douai. I need not say with what joy I heard of this resolution. I was to pass at Douai three comparatively happy years. My entrance to the college was not a brilliant one. My rustic appearance and the manners I had acquired in the seminary, of which I had not yet been able to rid myself completely, made me the subject of many a jest. I thought for a moment that my troubles were all going to begin over again, but quite another spirit reigned here. Here was no espionage.

Freedom of action was not interfered with, and liberty in the choice of friends was allowed.

When I had exchanged a few vigorous blows with the most quarrelsome of the boys, I had no longer anything to fear. I loved my companions and they loved me. The yard here was larger and a part of it was planted with trees ; and the buildings, less elevated than those around the seminary, allowed the sunshine freer entrance ; while in place of the Military Hospital the museum presented to us its wide high gable to send our balls against.

And the uniform, with its shining brass buttons, and the boots, and the strapped trousers, and the towns-people looking at us with admiring glance as we passed by in line, our steps resounding on the pavement ; and the band of music ; and the lyre which I proudly displayed embroidered in gold on the collar of my coat !—and the loud-sounding drum, in place of the plaintive bell ; and, above all, Art !

We occupied the ancient building of the Abbey d'Anchin. Like a cuckoo bringing up its fledglings in a ring-dove's nest, the state had there established its college. The chapel, formerly as large as a church, had been divided. One part of it was still devoted to worship, and the other to profane uses—some of the dormitories and the hall of design being there.

This vast hall, with its thick walls and heavy pillars, was well calculated to inspire respect. I experienced a profound emotion whenever I entered it.

There, as in the seminary, were displayed eyes, noses, and mouths, small, medium-sized and large faces ; academic figures. There I beheld you again, Moses, Mordecai, and Scipio, and you also, young Raphaelesque girls, with your ravishing faces. But my ambition went further than this now—as far as the hall of casts, that could be seen beyond, smaller than this one, and silent as a sanctuary. I walked straight thither with a resolute step.

When I entered it I was seized with a sort of religious awe, and I began to tremble in every limb. I found myself in the presence of Euripides, of Solon, of Plato, of Homer; of the Laocoon, writhing forever in the serpent's folds; and of Niobe, forever sending up to heaven from her sightless eyes looks of inconsolable grief.

A moment afterward the drawing-master entered the room. He was a short, robust old man, brusque and frank in his manner. He looked at me with amazement. "What are you doing here, Baptist?" he said to me. "You are a new-comer. Go sit down yonder before the eyes and the noses."

I had been told beforehand how I must address him, and I stammered, "I beg of you, papa, to let me practice here." "Have you drawn from the cast?" "No, but I have made the portraits of some of my schoolfellows." "Very well; sit down there; we shall see." And he placed before me the head of one of the sons of Laocoon. The trial resulted favorably, and I remained in the class.

This may be thought a strange specimen of conversation between pupil and professor, and yet I have given it word for word as it took place. This excellent old man addressed all his pupils in the second person, singular, called them all alike "Baptist," and all the pupils addressed him in the second person, singular, and called him "papa."

My fellow-pupils and the inhabitants of Douai of my time will remember Father Wallet.

We loved him dearly, and the familiarity of which I have given an example detracted nothing from the respect with which he inspired us. At times he pretended to be terribly angry, and dealt about blows right and left, which never hit any one.

I think he was not without some genius, which he made but little use of. He was at once a disciple of David and of the Romantic School of Art. He organized a historical *fête* which was much talked of in the place, the entrance to Douai of Philip the Good. These celebrations of historical events were then in fashion. My father and my uncle, a year later, represented in our village the visit of Philip II, King of Spain, to Jean de Montmorenci, the Lord of Courrières, who sleeps with folded hands on his tomb in the church there. This celebration was a complete success. The brilliant and well-drilled procession which traversed the streets of our poor commune called forth the acclamations of the numerous citizens of Douai, Lille, and Arras, who had come there to laugh at it.

Father Wallet watched it from one of the windows of our house, and Philip II was very proud of earning his applause.

As for me, I was unable, much to my regret, to see this cavalcade, the strict rules of the college not permitting it. I consoled myself, however, by playing with my school-fellows.

A word in regard to these latter.

Some of them, among others General Cary, General Cornat, General Delbecque, and René Goblet, one of our most learned statesmen, now occupy brilliant positions; but how many names are missing from the roll! The estimable Eduard Blavier, who died Inspector-General of Telegraphs; Louis Duhem, a tender soul meant by nature for a poet, and whom chance made a custom-house officer; and Louis Bauchet, whom I met in Paris, where he had entered on a brilliant career, soon alas! to be cut short by death. Already distinguished as a surgeon, he died a victim to duty, at the age of thirty-nine, from the results of a wound received at the dissecting-table. At his funeral I saw Velpeau, who loved him like a son, weeping unrestrainedly. He had married a young girl of Lower Brittany, connected by marriage with my family, who has consecrated her life to the worship of his memory.

----

## XLVI.

IT was about this time that I began to acquire a taste for poetry.

I was then reading Racine and La Fontaine. I remember a line of Athalie that to many people may seem to possess no special merit, but which enchanted me:

> " Et du temple déjà l'aube blanchit le faîte."

It captivated my ear by its melody and called up before my mind a charming twilight scene bathed in a soft and tender light.

Then I made an attempt at rhyming.

One day I hurried carelessly through my Latin verses, and then wrote below a translation of them into French verse.

The professor seemed amused at first; he read aloud to the class my unfortunate attempt at poetry, accentuating comically every false rhyme, and ended by imposing on me a double punishment for the faults in my Latin composition.

Later on, fancying myself in love, I gave expression to my sentimental sorrows in verse.

At fifteen my verses were despairing and pessimistic, and shortly afterward I sang the loss of all my illusions.

Have I the right, then, to smile at the young poets of twenty whom we see springing up on all sides around us ?

My father, after the death of the Duke of Duras and the sale of the forest of Labroye, entered into partnership with two natives of Lille, for the purpose of buying the forest of the Amerois at Muno, in the Belgian Ardennes.  He had been unable to conquer his passion for forests.

He lodged, while there, at the house of some excellent people, for whom he soon conceived a friendship.

One day he brought back with him to Courrières one of the sons, named Hippolite.  This boy, about my own age, but quicker and more precocious in some respects than I was, spent with us the vacation preceding my admission to the College of Douai.

He often spoke to me of his native place and of a friend whom he had known from childhood, named Florentine, and whom he loved like a sister.  The name of this young girl, continually sounding in my ears, gave rise to many a vague revery.  " You shall see how pretty she is.  You must fall in love with her," he would constantly say to me.

And, without my ever having seen her, she filled my thoughts.  Whenever Hippolite wanted to ask a favor from me, he asked it in Florentine's name, and I was sure to grant it.

As for him, he was in love with a young lady who wore velvet bodices and who rode on horseback.

Nearly two years had passed since that time, however.  Hippolite had gone back to Muno, and I had quite forgotten this romantic fancy.

During my vacation in 1842 (I was then fifteen) it was arranged that we were all to spend a month at Muno.

We went there accordingly.

The parents of Hippolite lived about three quarters of a mile distant from the city, in a house standing by itself by the roadside, whose front windows looked out on green fields, through which ran a clear brook shaded by willows and frequented by trout and crabs. The house was sheltered at the back by the Monti, a hill covered with brush-wood and pink and white heather. To the left was a kitchen-garden. In front were a leafy bower and a row of hollyhocks. This sylvan and attractive abode was called "The Hermitage."

The first person to meet us on our arrival was Mademoiselle Elisa, the eldest sister of Hippolite. She was a tall, slender girl of twenty-two, with a queenly air. She was very dark, with pale-blue eyes, and hair black as the raven's wing, falling down her cheeks in the English fashion. Her father, a native of Provence, had given her her southern beauty, while her eyes were as blue as the periwinkles of the Ardennes.

It was the eve of the Kermesse of Muno. Hearing us coming, Elisa had left the bakehouse, where she was making tarts, and a bit of the dough had remained clinging to her eyebrow.

Let me say here that a noble and tender heart beat under her broad breast. She is now old, her jet-black locks are white with the snows of age, and profound respect has taken the place of the admiration she then excited.

This noble woman has never wished to marry, so that she might be able to dedicate her life to the children of her brothers and sisters, with an unselfish devotion of which she alone seems to be unconscious.

We were fatigued with our journey, and went to bed immediately after supper.

In the morning, when I saw from my window the sun

brightening the Monti, and lighting up the white mists that hung along its sides, I got out of bed quickly.

I went down to the kitchen and was chatting with Elisa, who was occupied in some household task, when the door at the foot of the staircase opened and a young girl made her appearance.

"Good-morning, Florentine," said Elisa.

Florentine!  It was she!

I can not describe the happiness that filled my heart when I heard this name, that had formed the subject of so many dreams.

The evening before, after we had retired, she and her mother had come from Carignan, where they lived, and she had slept in the room adjoining mine.

She did not possess the brilliant beauty of Elisa. She was about sixteen, and was short and slender, with bright chestnut hair, brown eyes, and a pale, clear complexion, like a tea-rose.

But by a sort of hallucination she appeared to me clothed with supernatural splendor.

Elisa, taking a basket, said to her, "Let us go gather some heather for the chimney-piece and the dinner-table."

Behold us then, crossing the Monti, which was wrapped in white mists produced by the evaporation of the dew—silvery mists that the sun, darting his rays through the forest trees, pierced with a thousand fiery arrows.

Elisa was a charming picture, seen in the softened brilliancy of the morning light, with her black hair, pearly with dew, her yellow handkerchief, and her gay spirits, to which she gave vent in snatches of merry songs.

But I had eyes only for Florentine, whose blue robe gleamed in the sunshine that lingered on its hem, while her bright hair was surrounded by an aureole of gold; and the zenith sent down its pure light to caress her pearly neck, charmingly shaded by the down on the nape.

She went along gathering the heather, and I followed enraptured, and I thought myself desperately in love.

One may be in love without knowing it. With me the contrary was the case. I mistook for love the first ardors of an impatient imagination.

This fancy was to vanish like the golden clouds of dawn, bright harbingers of the sun that is soon to rise, but it has left with me a passion for pink and white heather, and their innumerable little bells seem to me since then to vibrate with a thrill of love.

## XLVII.

One evening, during the same vacation, my brothers and I were seated around the lamp in the dining-room, when a stranger entered, bringing a letter of introduction from M. D——, the notary, of whom I have spoken.

He was enveloped in a large black cloak, and wore a long thick beard, something which we had never before seen. He had strongly marked features, the nose straight and slightly turned up at the end, the arch of the brow very prominent, and heavy eyebrows, raised toward the temples, shading deep-blue eyes. His handsome face was browned by the sun.

This sudden apparition strongly awakened our curiosity.

At first sight, our visitor was not unlike the picture I had formed in my mind of a bandit-chief. D——'s letter informed us that this gentleman was M. Félix de

Vigne, a painter, and a professor in the Academy in Ghent. A learned archæologist, he had just published his "Painter's Vade Mecum," a collection of the costumes and weapons of the middle ages, and was now preparing a work on the trade corporations of Flanders.

He had heard that my uncle possessed a work on French costumes of divers epochs, and he had come to request his permission to examine it.

My uncle went to fetch the four volumes of which this work consisted.

We thought these books superb. We had often looked at their beautiful colored plates, resplendent with gold and silver, and had not a doubt of the admiration they were going to awaken in our visitor's mind.

De Vigne opened the first volume at random, and his glance fell on a picture of Charlemagne in the costume of the fifteenth century.

He smiled, closed the book, and after a short conversation, excused himself and took his leave.

A painter! He was a painter! Ah! if I had only dared to go up to him, and tell him of my passion for art, perhaps he might have tried to influence my father and my uncle. But a stupid bashfulness had kept my mouth closed.

And he was gone!

I returned sorrowfully to the college, where Florentine and De Vigne's visit were the subject of my reveries. The figure of the painter presented itself to my romantic imagination clothed with ideal attributes, and grew more and more somber as time passed on.

I forgot my sadness for the time in the drawing-class, when I saw again the Laocoons, the Caracallar, and the Niobes, those old friends with their sightless eyes.

During the vacation of 1843, my uncle, returning from a journey to Lille, found himself by chance seated beside De Vigne in the famous coach of Maximilian Robespierre, whom we already know.

They had here an opportunity to become better acquainted with each other. My uncle spoke of me to the painter, and to attract him to our house he gave him an order for a likeness of himself.

De Vigne came accordingly, one day, with his box of colors and his canvas, and it may easily be imagined what an event this was for us. There were perfumed essences, delicate oils gleaming in the light, and beautiful little bladders filled with paints of various colors.

With what devout attention I followed the different stages of his work—the outlining, the rough draught in red crayon, the sketch that changed with every stroke of the brush !

And the painter himself, too, who, when I first saw him, had realized my idea of a bandit, was wonderfully transformed by the light of day.

He grew almost genial, and, notwithstanding his terrible beard, was much less imposing in appearance than were the figures in the garden after Fremy had repainted them.

I showed my sketches to De Vigne. He was not greatly pleased with my drawings from the cast, although they had taken the first prize in the college.

He was more interested in my portraits in pencil and my landscapes copied from nature.

He proposed to my father and uncle to send me to him on trial, promising to give a definite opinion regarding me after I had studied three months under his instructions.

Oh, joy ! my uncle and my father consented !

I went to my room, and, seizing my class-books, threw

them up to the ceiling twenty times in succession, until the oldest of them fell in tatters.

Then I threw into the fire the task assigned me for the vacation, and which I had scarcely begun. This *auto-da-fé* was hardly accomplished, when I received a letter from a school-fellow asking me to lend him this task in order to copy it.

In what triumphant terms I answered him that henceforth the college and I had no connection with each other, and that I was going to enter the Royal Academy at Ghent!

I arrived in that city on the 15th of October, 1843.

---

## XLVIII.

THERE are many humble painters who might have become great artists if Fate had placed them in circumstances more favorable to the development of their natural gifts, but who die unknown to the general public, their merits recognized only by a limited circle.

High-minded and conscientious in the performance of their obligations, seeing themselves in the necessity of providing for the wants of the family, and devoted to their domestic duties, they are not free to enter the arena where alone fame is to be won.

Their first pictures have had some success; the beginning was full of promise. They had had their dreams of a glorious future.

But they had neglected to take into account the noble weaknesses of their nature.

Obstacles placed there by their affections are to detain them on the road to fame at every step.

And in the unselfishness of their hearts they will see

their rivals attain fame and fortune without a pang of envy, while they still continue to persevere in their humble labors.

Their efforts, however, are not altogether fruitless. With comparatively easy means, hours of leisure come.

The nest is built. The new house has a more sunny outlook. A broader stream of light illumines the studio, larger than the other one.

The talents which had caused their first paintings to be admired, stifled for a time, reappear in works produced in a more vivifying atmosphere, and the artist begins to attract attention.

A ray of fame may even fall upon his brow.

He is able to give himself up to studies long interrupted. Real progress, surprising at his age, leads to fresh successes. He has still a long future before him.

It will be only a dream. All those emotions, all this ardor, like the warmth of a St. Martin's summer, only serve to shatter still more an organization enfeebled by long-continued vigils, and the artist breaks down while apparently in the full enjoyment of health.

Such might have been the history of Félix de Vigne.

---

## XLIX.

Narrow and deep, with its gable dating from the sixteenth century, and its long corridor leading to the different apartments, to the small yard, and to the garden, the house in which De Vigne lived in 1843, number 8, Rue de la Line, was situated in one of the quietest quarters of the city.

I was cordially received there.

Ghent impressed me greatly. I had not at that time

seen Paris. In a journey I had made the preceding year I had caught a hasty glimpse of the principal cities of Belgium—Liége, Louvain, Antwerp, Ostend, and Brussels—where, for the first time, I visited an exhibition of paintings, for me the most glorious of sights.

I can still see all the beautiful colors, more beautiful even than those of Nature itself, of those lovely complexions so smooth and rosy ; of those heavenly blue eyes, of those military epaulets so brilliant that it was almost a miracle that they could have been made to shine so brightly ; and those large oxen that look at you with their melancholy eyes, and those well-combed sheep, and those horseshoes that looked so real, hidden in the corners of the pictures ; and those drops of water that tremble on the thistles ; and, in fine, of all those beautiful yellows, brilliant greens, and flaming reds. How dingy the pictures of Rubens, which I had seen at Antwerp, notwithstanding the profound admiration I entertained for them, appeared to me beside these marvels !

The city of Ghent seemed to me magnificent. I felt proud and happy to be able to walk at will through the streets of this Flemish Venice, with its innumerable bridges, its old wharves crowded with merchandise, its ancient houses, some of which look down upon you from the middle ages, and whose trembling images are reflected from the waters of the canals, where glide countless boats.

I never tired of looking at all these sights. I loved its monuments, its Hôtel de Ville, in the flamboyant style, its court-house, and its Gothic churches, with their chapels, in the style of the Renaissance, where, surrounded by the somber grandeur of the Spaniards, are old pictures of the early Flemish school, at once sensual and devout.

The school of Ghent, which prides itself on having

given to the world the brothers Van Eyck, the Gaspards de Crayer, and the Rooses, had greatly declined since the time in which De Vigne had attained his first success.

A pupil of Paclinck, who had followed at Brussels, in consonance with the bent of his genius, in the steps of his master David, whose fame was then on the wane, De Vigne had spent some time in Paris whence he returned to his native city, his mind confused by contradictory teachings. On the one hand, he had learned to strive after a grace of form like that of the Apollo Belvedere, the Diana, and the Venus di Medicis, while he was fascinated by the brilliancy of coloring of the Romantic school on the other.

The two currents of opinion which divided Paris, flowing in opposite directions, the one toward Ingres, the other toward Delacroix, united in Belgium in a bastard school of art, formed of an expressionless eclecticism.

Louis Gallait himself, the best painter of this school, was a compound of Deveria, Paul Delaroche, and Robert-Fleury.

The bitter dissension which caused these visions, concerned, for the most part, insignificant details. I have never seen mediocrity arouse more acrimonious disputes.

Antwerp believed that the glorious days of Rubens had returned.

They thought they had rediscovered the coloring of the ancients, while uniting with it a grace of form copied from the antique.

They imitated the painters of the old Flemish school, thinking they were free from their heaviness of style, and had improved, by exaggerating it, the splendor of their coloring.

They sought inspiration in the inferior works of Rubens, those most resembling porcelain, as being the most beautiful, and finding there glowing tints, they learned to mix the smooth with the rough style of painting to obtain transparency in the flesh-tints, so that all the faces had the appearance of being flayed on one side.   A horrible sight !

Add to this, in the case of the historical painters, a sort of insipid sentimentalism, which showed itself in their pictures in tearful eyes and gaping mouths, and, in the case of those who drew their inspiration from the old Dutch painters, a sort of peurile jocoseness.  The public flocked to the exhibitions without knowing anything about art.

They went into raptures over the childish tricks of still-life deception.

They spoke only of "skillfulness of execution," "transparency," and " warm tones."

The landscape-painters had a regular system of degrading their backgrounds which they threw back, mechanically, painting them in bluer and bluer tones, until they at last faded into the sky.  I have seen a landscape-painter work during a whole sitting at a little bit of his picture, while the rest of the canvas was covered with a curtain, in order to protect it from the dust. Why consider the general effect of the picture ?

What they failed to study was the sunlight, with its solemn splendors and its thousand caprices ; the relation of the parts to the whole, and variety of effect and execution, according to the sentiment of the subject.

I hope the Belgians, and especially the people of Ghent, will forgive me for the frankness of these words. They have made great progress since that time, and their enlightened painters and connoisseurs, far from being offended by them, share my opinions.

## L.

WHEN I arrived in Ghent, I found it still affected by the impression produced by the Grand Triennial Exhibition of the Fine Arts, which had taken place there the preceding year, and in which Verboeckhoven had won laurels from the artists and connoisseurs of Ghent.

Louis Gallait had exhibited there his large painting, "The Abdication of Charles V." Universally admired, he was even thought by many to be the equal of Rubens.

Immediately after him, in the estimation of the public, came Wappers and De Keyser. These were the trinity that presided over the Belgian school of art.

Opinions were divided, however, regarding the comparative merit of these two latter artists, and the slight differences between them were made the subject of bitter disputes. "What boldness, what admirable coloring in the paintings of Wappers!" the partisans of the former would say; to which those of the latter would respond, "What delicacy of form, what feeling, in the paintings of De Keyser!"

Alas! hardly any one ever mentions the name of either of them now.

At this same exhibition De Vigne had attained a comparative success with a triptych, "The Three Ages of Woman," a picture afterward purchased by the king.

The Society of Fine Arts also held a small exhibition every year, of the works of local artists, where I had an opportunity of seeing specimens of the crude style of art. I must confess that I admired some among them that I would now think detestable.

How charming some of those pictures seemed to my

simple and ignorant eyes! I occasionally meet with pictures like them now, in walking through the museums of small towns. They repose there, antiquated, mediocre, dingy, sticky, dull, and cracked in curves, as happens, why I know not, to provincial pictures.

How have you fallen in my estimation, O painters who then enchanted me—Gernaert, Van Maldeghem, and you, Van Schendel, who lighted up with such vivid flames the ruddy countenances of women selling vegetables, in dark and musty markets, where a workman would occasionally be seen wheeling his barrow, his face illuminated by a wonderful ray of moonlight, reflected from the shining peak of his cap!

Such was the environment in which De Vigne lived.

One of the first pictures which I saw him paint was the portrait of some great lady visiting Hemmling to dress the shrine of St. Ursula. She was represented wearing the *hennin*, pointed shoes, and a robe of cloth-of-gold.

De Vigne was remarkable for the graceful folds of his draperies and the skill with which he painted the lights reflected from precious stones and the gleam of gold.

He painted this picture by fits and starts, constantly interrupted by his lessons, and having to take off and put on again continually his green-and-black Scotch plaid dressing-gown, a style of garment which De Winne and I had also adopted for our working hours.

This is the first time I have had occasion to mention Liévin de Winne, an artist who was to occupy, later, a conspicuous place among the painters of the Belgian school, and whom I was soon to love like a brother. Nothing at this time foretold the brilliant future that awaited him.

For the student of those days was far from being the

great artist whose gayety of spirits made him, later on, so delightful a companion.

He did not then wear his blonde hair in those long locks that he has since adopted, and which he throws back with the gesture so familiar to his friends ; his face was not then, as later, rosy and lighted up by an expression that made it seem beautiful, vaguely recalling that of Van Dyck. No, his face was thin, his air melancholy, his head bent. With his long nose and short, reddish hair, he seemed almost ugly. He was shy in the extreme, disposed to gloom, painting in silence, and at times sensitively morbid.

For, although grateful and affectionate by nature, his pride caused him to suffer keenly ; he had, too, met with many disappointments in his affections.

Brought up in easy circumstances, after seeing his father and two lovely young sisters die, he had witnessed the ruin of his family.

At twenty years of age he found himself penniless and under the necessity of providing for two other sisters, who were then in the convent completing their education.

The eldest of his brothers had gone away, no one knew where ; another was earning a livelihood in Paris. His family, at one time consisting of eleven members, had been dispersed by misfortune or death. His mother had been a woman of great piety, and his elder sisters had died, it was said, like saints. Their names, Theresa and Monica, seemed to predestine them to mysticism.

Such was the situation of the unfortunate Liévin.

Félix de Vigne, who for some time had aided him with his advice, profoundly touched by these unmerited misfortunes, received him into the bosom of his family, taught him his art, and was henceforward a second father to him.

On my entrance to the studio, my attention was immediately attracted by one of the students, whose impassive countenance, adorned by a red beard, was surmounted by a high black woolen cap. I watched him while he painted. He tried all the tints on his palette, which was covered with a countless number of little hillocks of paint. He turned round at my entrance and said to me, "Painting is a work that requires patience." He gave good proof of this.

The picture on which he was working represented the painter Breughel, the elder, who was accustomed to keep count of the lies his servant told him by cutting a notch in a stick, for every lie making one of these notches.

The legend says that he had promised to marry her if, at the end of a certain time, the stick were not completely covered with notches! What was the end of the story?

The pendent to this picture, sketched in chalk, on the opposite wall, answered the question. It represented Breughel imitating the example of Abraham with regard to Hagar, and sending away the unhappy servant, who was drying her tears in the corner of her apron. He is pointing angrily to the stick, completely covered with notches.

There worked with us also a young French girl, Mademoiselle I. T——. She had agreeable manners, was somewhat of a coquette, and had a frank and careless disposition. She was the daughter of a retired soldier of the Empire, who lived in Ghent.

She had but little talent for painting, and we augured an obscure future for her. She was destined, however, to an unhappy celebrity. Fifteen or sixteen years later the public was to hear of her, when in the judicial records these terrible words appeared: "In a bottle on the table of the prætorium are the entrails of the victim!" for she was the unfortunate Madame de Pauw, who was poisoned by a well-known physician, condemned to expiate his crime on the scaffold.

Poor De Winne, melancholy enough already, having committed the folly of falling in love with Mademoiselle T——, grew so gloomy that we called him "Cousin Brouillard," * the name of one of Paul de Kock's characters.

I can still hear him sighing.

I had already begun to like my new fellow-student, and I did my best to console him for his sorrows.

He received my friendly attempts at consolation with gratitude. It was in vain that I tried to make him share in my amusements, however, which were somewhat expensive; it was in vain that I talked to him of my raptures at the theatre on Sundays, where Albert,† the wonderful tenor, was singing to applauding crowds. I could never prevail upon him to accompany me.

The only diversions he permitted himself were our excursions into the country.

Now that you are no more, friend Liévin, I can not recall those excursions without deep emotion.

We would turn our canvases toward the wall, clean our palettes and our brushes, and set off in the sunny afternoon—sunny with the sunshine of youth, that will shine for us never again!

We would walk on, admiring every new sight, and talking of those nothings that make the tears start when we recall them later on, until we came to the city gate, where, under the blue sky, the plain stretched far away before us.

On we walked. In the tea-gardens, under leafy bowers, stood tables of worm-eaten wood. Hunger, the

---

* Fog.    † This tenor is still well remembered in Belgium.

pleasant hunger of youth, soon made itself felt. Oh, the savory repasts, washed down with Flemish beer!

We confided all the tender secrets of our hearts to each other; the melancholy Liévin grew gay for a moment. And, returning, we would watch the sun sink, large and red, behind the grassy plains.

Next day we would resume our painting.

Liévin ground his colors himself, and would paint some banner for a procession, or some Oriental picture for the convent where his sisters were, or some weeping Virgin dressed in a white satin robe, with a mantle of Prussian blue showing against the eternal yellow background we knew so well; for he had a number of pious patrons. And then he would paint little pictures whose subjects alone are sufficient evidence of their innocent character — An Old Man Skinning an Eel, An Old Woman Grinding her Coffee, A Jew Selling Trinkets, Rose and Violet, The First Communion Postponed.

Who would have divined, in these puerile creations, the touch of the artist, at once vigorous and tender, who was one day to depict with so much skill every emotion of the human countenance?

Meanwhile, we rallied him on his melancholy, and tried to enliven him a little.

Sometimes he would whistle while he painted, and whistle discordantly—not because he had no ear for music, but through absent-mindedness, habit making him always return to his favorite airs, "The Little Flower of the Meadows," and "Yes, Monsieur," a silly song then in vogue.

As for Félix De Vigne, he sang agreeably, accompanying himself on the guitar. Moved by the sounds of this sentimental instrument, De Winne would cast more languishing glances than ever at Mademoiselle T——, and redouble his sighs.

## LI.

In the evening we went to the Academy.

A new director was endeavoring to raise it from the state of decadence into which his predecessors, men without either energy or talent, had allowed it to fall.

His name was Vanderhaert, and he was the brother-in-law of our great sculptor, Rude.

A mediocre painter, but a skillful draughtsman, he threw a vast amount of energy into his teaching. He explained with great clearness the play of the muscles, the planes and the different angles on which forms, even the most rounded, are constructed.

He had an enthusiastic admiration for the best works of the old masters, and his ardor, which was contagious, had a very beneficial effect upon us.

De Vigne was also a professor in the Academy, but, as he was very modest, one of the lower classes was assigned to him; and in this way he was often imposed upon. He taught also at the Athenæum, and gave private lessons besides. What time remained for his art? But he must live, and he had his children to bring up.

Notwithstanding all this, he was cheerful.

He sometimes worked until midnight on the plates for his works, which he himself engraved.

In 1849, when the grand historical *fête*, which we have mentioned, took place in Ghent—a *fête* still remembered in the country—and which outshone everything of the kind ever attempted before, he was the real organizer of the pageant. He not only organized it, but he designed all the costumes and planned the effects himself. For whole weeks his studio was transformed into a sewing-room. When he sent the account of the expense incurred to the authorities of the city, he was too modest to include the fee for his own services. It was not perceived, but he never mentioned the matter to any one outside his family.

The life at this household was mildly austere. Each one pursued his occupation in silence. Every evening Elodie, Edmond, Jules, and later on Georges, before going to bed would come and ask their father's blessing, which he would bestow upon them in the episcopal fashion, making the sign of the cross on their foreheads with his thumb.

A recent loss, the death of two charming children, Eléonore and Félix, both about four years old, made this household still more gloomy.

Their mother, an estimable woman, was the daughter of Philippe Ave, who had gained the first prize for the violin at the Conservatory of Paris.

He was a native of Hondscott in France, and his death took place in Ghent, where he had established himself shortly after his marriage.

In this house I felt as if I were among my own family, and I had a strong attachment for the children, who reciprocated my affection.

The eldest, Elodie, was a gentle child, in whose blue eyes, shaded by long, silken lashes, there already shone a mysterious charm. She went about the house silently, gliding rather than walking. She held her fragile figure thrown slightly backward, and her delicately outlined face, resembling that of one of the angels in a Gothic cathedral, inclined forward, as if bending under the weight of a prematurely thoughtful brow. She seemed a child of the middle ages, of which her father had made so profound a study. She was about seven years old, and I danced her on my knees.

Her sweet, childish caresses inspired me with a feeling that was almost paternal.

Félix de Vigne, born on the 16th of March, 1806, was the eldest of six children—four boys and two girls.

The second son, Pierre, and the third, Edouard, the one a sculptor, the other a landscape-painter, had each gained the *Prix de Rome.* Alexandre, the youngest of the boys, was a musician. Five or six of their cousins were also musicians.

Truly a family of artists!

It is unnecessary for me to mention here the place now occupied among Belgian sculptors by Paul de Vigne, the son of Pierre, who, at our Great Exposition in 1889, obtained a grand prize of honor

Félix had begun to earn a reputation for himself by pictures of an order somewhat more elevated than the childish productions I have mentioned. The first painting which brought him into note represents Mary of Burgundy imploring the pardon of Hugonnet and Ambercourt, in the public square of Ghent, the Marché du Vendredi. An excited crowd surround the scaffold, which the condemned men are ascending, and on which the executioner, clad in red, and holding his axe in his hand, is standing.

The figure of Mary of Burgundy, who is represented kneeling, and clad in a black robe embroidered with silver, and a long mantle of cloth-of-gold, the head, covered with the *hennin,* thrown backward, displaying the youthful countenance to view, and the hands outstretched in supplication, seemed to me very touching.

This picture was destroyed in a fire.

## LII.

WHEN I left Ghent, in 1846, before proceeding to Paris, I went to Antwerp, and remained there five or six weeks.

I put up at the Hôtel Rubens, in the *Place Verte*, directly below the cathedral.

I have a remembrance of sleepless nights spent in cursing the deafening noise of its chime of bells, which recommenced every quarter of an hour.

In the daytime, however, nothing could be more cheerful than their showers of clear and silvery notes, especially on Sundays, which were also *fête*-days, when banners and pennants floated on the breeze.

I entered my name at the Academy, directed by the illustrious Wappers.

He was a stout man, with brusque and familiar manners, which those who have known our painter Couture can easily picture to themselves.

He wore ostentatiously the honors of a reputation which was beyond his merits.

At bottom, however, he was a very worthy man.

His teaching was not as valuable as that of Vanderhaert. He limited himself to showing how to obtain by measurement the proportions of the figure, and to enunciating aphorisms like the following : " An artist, who makes his tones too dark in drawing will always make them too gray in painting." He taught the students who were learning painting to work in the grounds and the tones with touches as distinct as those of a mosaic, and to paint the flesh-tints in bright lakes, the half-tints of a greenish-gray, and the lights in yellow and pink, to give a lifelike expression. It will be seen that our impressionists have invented nothing new.

I soon quitted the Academy attracted by the great painter with whose name Antwerp resounds.

I went to the museum to study Rubens.

I there copied the "Christ on the Straw."

It will be seen by this that I was at that time attracted more by the faults of the painter than by his beauties.  Naturally, I exaggerated in my copies the carnations, making them still brighter and more porcelain-like than they were in the original.

I never suspected that the greatest work of Rubens was at Ghent, for the painting was at that time hung in so bad a light, between two windows in the cathedral, that it could scarcely be seen.  The picture I refer to is the "Calling of St. Bavon."

But I was not always painting in the museum at Antwerp, and my hours of idleness were more profitable than my so-called working hours.

In this unpretending gallery, with its austere light, and its plain and simple arrangements, are to be found some masterpieces, in the midst of the crowd of labored and dull canvases of the Contortionist period, from Breughel to Pourbus, that here display their smooth and puffy flesh and distorted anatomy, depicted with the cold realism of the dissecting-table.

What a simple and intense life do the Memlings, the Van Eycks, the Quentin-Matsys, and, above all, the portraits and the "Seven Sacraments" of Roger Vander Weyden, breathe in the midst of the limbo of the Flemish Renaissance, dispelled by the triumphant splendors of Rubens !

And I imbibed, without knowing it, the chaste sentiment of Gothic art.

The "Dead Christ" of Van Dyck also made a profound impression upon me.

After leaving the museum I delighted to wander

about this devout city whose picturesque streets display at every corner Virgins, gorgeous in the midst of their golden clouds, or to plunge into mystic reveries at the hour of evening prayers, seated in Nôtre Dame when the celestrial strains of the organ rose in swelling waves to the lofty vaulted roof, then returned to mingle softly, like seraphic echoes, with the voices of the long procession of white-robed virgins, moving with downcast eyes among the gleaming lights of tapers and the clouds of the incense. These chants, this religious pomp, intoxicated my senses, and I felt stir within me something of the pure joy I had felt the first time I saw my little companions of St. Bertin kneeling to receive their first communion.

## LIII.

The close of this year was gloomy indeed.

On leaving Antwerp I contracted a cold on the chest, which developed into chronic bronchitis.

My father came to take me home with him, and I learned afterward that when we were gone my worthy friends had shed tears, thinking they would never see me again. De Vigne had painted my portrait some days previously, that he might have a souvenir of me.

I thought myself doomed. To add to my inquietude, I found my father greatly changed. For a year past his formerly robust health had been declining day by day. Seeing him constantly, no one had noticed this at first. He did not complain. Some of our friends, alarmed at the change in his appearance, drew the attention of the family to it. He would not hear of calling in a physician, but it was necessary to have recourse to one at last. My father went from bad to worse, notwithstanding the remedies he took. His complexion turned very yellow. Instead of sending him to Vichy—fatal error!—they had bled him.

Anxious about each other, as we were, the journey from Ghent to Courrières was a very sad one.

It was now the end of autumn.

The winter was glorious. I have a remembrance of cold, bright days, when everything sparkled with hoar-frost. Kind Nature thus threw a little brightness over our sad household, formerly so full of life!

My brother Émile was still at school, and Louis was learning the art of brewing beer, in Ghent.

Here, then, were my father and I, both ill; and my uncle, although he concealed his uneasiness, could not conceal his sadness.

My grandmother, who loved us all, was visibly declining. She was now seventy-nine years old. She still laughed, however, from habit. She never now stirred from her chair, which, as you know, stood near the Louis Quinze chimney-piece, in the little kitchen.

But youth does not long give way to despair. I began to take an interest in life again. New blossoms sprang up in my heart.

I profited by my sleepless nights to compose strophes that formed themselves in my brain, without conscious effort on my part.

These were the first verses I had made since I had left college.

I began to regain my strength; my father, also, began to grow a little better—when, without warning, a sudden illness put an end to my poor godmother's existence.

On the 13th of February, 1847, she sank to rest, with a serenity befitting her pure and simple soul. You have read the history of my childhood ; you have seen how devotedly this good woman watched over us; you will understand my grief.

--------

## LIV.

At this time I felt myself strongly attracted to Paris.

In the year 1845 I had spent nearly three weeks there with my father, who, at the time, was having published in the Rue Foin Saint-Jacques a Forester's Guide, of which not a single copy is now to be met with.

Through the influence of L. D——, a doorkeeper at the Louvre, I had obtained a card of admission to the museums for the purpose of working there.

I remember that I was more struck by the facile graces of the decadence than by the masterpieces there.  I made some sketches after Spada, Guido, the Carracci, and some Flemish and Dutch painters.

At the Luxembourg, the paintings of Leopold Robert filled me with admiration, while the paintings of Delacroix, with the exception of the Massacre of Scio, appeared to me hideous.

The faulty drawing of this painter aroused my indignation.

I fancied to myself the furious reproaches Vanderhaërt would have hurled at me if I had drawn hands and feet as distorted as some of those in the " Algerian Women," and the " Jewish Wedding."

As for his coloring, filled as my mind still was with the transparent lights of the pictures of the Flemish school, I thought them dull and muddy, although at the same time they impressed me strangely.

Besides attending to our business, both my father

and I had made good use of our time 'in other ways. Like all good provincials of those days (one might think they were two hundred years ago), we had sent the *Wonders of the Capital*, without forgetting the Vault of the Blind, the silver scales of Vero-Dodat, the glass staircase, and the pipe which was worth a thousand francs.

We had made the round of the theatres, applauded Duprez, Madame Stolz, Rubini, Mario, Lablache, Rachel, and the Ravels, the Bouffés, the Lepeintres, the Vernets, the Arnals, the Grassots, and many others.

We had passed whole nights scratching ourselves, and writhing among the bedclothes that smelled of chlorine, mingled with other perfumes, devoured by the bed-bugs, in a small hotel of the Rue Saint-Honoré, whose name—Hôtel des Ambassadeurs—might, however, have led one to expect something better.

I had seen Versailles! I find in the rough draft of a letter, addressed at this time to a school-fellow who was still at college, this pompous phrase : " Versailles, where are to be seen the giant progeny of the grandest genius of the age—I refer to the great paintings of Horace Vernet ! " And to think that the illusions of still-life painting could mislead me to this extent ! for it was not the beauties of this painter that I chiefly admired, but his little tricks to catch the vulgar—the skillful foreshortening of a gun, the gloss on hair moist with perspiration, the exactitude of the details, the deceptions of still-life. And yet, O fellow-painters of the present day, thus it is that we are appreciated at our exhibitions by a multitude of people, who still judge art in this fashion l

I was not, then, altogether a stranger in Paris, when, in 1847, I took up my abode there in a little room, on the third floor, at No. 5 Rue du Dragon.

I had a good many acquaintances in Paris, Courriè-res and its surroundings having sent there a part of its surplus population. We visited them all, so as not to create jealousy—from M. Delbecque, head clerk in the office of the Minister of Public Instruction, to Louis Mémère, the son of my nurse, who, as you will remember, used to tell us stories in our childhood as we sat around the fire.

My father, who was good-nature itself, was of course intrusted with some message for each one of them.

Many of these compatriots of ours served as waiters in *cafés*. I was struck by the Parisian accent and the affected manners of these youths, whom I had known as rude peasants.

Some of them smiled at my simple and provincial air, and waited on me in a way that savored more of mockery than respect. I must say that I have no complaint of this kind to make of Louis Mémère, although he was one of the most accomplished waiters of the Café de Mulhouse, and, later, of the Café des Mille Colonnes.

The desire to use fine language made them at times commit singular mistakes ; thus, because the letters *an* are pronounced in the provincial dialect like *in*, they pronounced the letters *in* in every word like *an*. In this way they pronounced *vin* (wine) *van*, because in the provincial dialect *vent* (wind) is pronounced as if it were written *vint*. And when my father and I went again to visit our compatriot, L. I——, the doorkeeper of the Louvre, whom I have before mentioned, to ask his opinion regarding the studio I ought to enter, he responded gravely: " It is indispensable that Jules should enter the studio of a member of the *Anstitute ;* there are Messieurs Cognet, Picot, Delaroche, *Angres*, and *Drollang*, to choose from."

After reflecting for a moment, he advised us to choose Drolling, because a former beadle of the studio was a friend of his.

When, carrying my portfolio under my arm, and accompanied by my father, I knocked timidly at the door of his studio, it was Drolling himself, his palette in his hand, who opened the door for us.

He wore a knitted woolen jacket and a red Greek cap, as he is represented in the portrait painted of him by his pupil Biennourry.

His frank and simple manners, somewhat brusque, and his long white mustache, gave him the air rather of a retired officer than of an artist.

Under this exterior I divined an excellent nature, and I gathered courage.

I opened my portfolio, which contained, along with some drawings and still-life studies in my own style, a torso painted by one of the shining lights among the students of the Academy of Antwerp, after the method which I have before mentioned. This gaudy torso, which resembled an omelet with jam, shocked at the very beginning my future master. "Look at that! It is horrible!" he cried.

Happily I could tell him that it was not my work. I then showed him a still-life study which I had painted while in the studio of De Vigne, to which I attached but little importance, and which I should never have dared to compare to the gaudy picture of the Academy of Antwerp.

His expression immediately changed. "This yours?" he said to me. "Why, it is divinely painted!"

Divinely painted! With what sweetness these words fell on the good ear of my father, who, like me now, was deaf in one ear!

My father was very ill at this time, dying within a

II

year.  He was not permitted, alas! to witness any of my successes, and of my paintings he saw only one—" St. Piat preaching to the Gauls "—my first picture, executed while I was at Ghent, and which we so proudly hung over one of the side altars of the church of Courrières.

This praise from the lips of a man whom we considered a great painter moved him profoundly.

When we again found ourselves alone on the landing, after Drolling had closed the door of the studio, my father clasped me in his arms, repeating, "You paint divinely!"  Then, as we went down-stairs, he added: "Hey! what if you, too, should one day become a member of the Institute?"

Blessed be your memory, O good Drolling, for by your words you justified in the mind of a father, soon to die, his confidence in his son's future—his supreme consolation!

---

## LV.

My father soon returned home, leaving me alone in the whirl of Paris, that desert full of unknown faces.

For the first few days I was like one dazed, without knowing which way to turn—wandering aimlessly on, losing myself a dozen times, and finding myself again in the same street, when I had thought myself miles away.

O solitude in the midst of the crowd—solitude without peace, how heavily you weighed upon me at first!

I had indeed, at the beginning, on Sundays, the society of some of my compatriots, the waiters; but their fine language and their endless conversation about the great men who frequented their restaurants, and of whom they spoke as if they were their intimate friends, possessed but little interest for me.

I was not familiar with either the names or the histories of the celebrities of the day.

I had a liking for Louis Mémère, however, at the same time that I could not help smiling at his pretensions.

We often walked together in the outskirts of the city, and it was wonderful to me, who blushed up to the eyes whenever I was obliged to address one of the waiters in a restaurant, to see with what self-possession and ease he spoke to everybody. He knew how to make himself served, glaring at the waiter, and threatening to complain to the head of the establishment if the slightest delay were made in serving him, or if the merest trifle had been forgotten. "Have you no lemons here? Go bring the landlord!"

These despotic ways embarrassed me a little, indeed, but when the lemon had been obtained, and the bill paid, I loved to continue our walk farther on into the corn-fields. This recalled our childhood to me, and we spoke of our native place with emotion—of my father, my uncle, my younger brothers, and of Mémère Henriette, who had nursed us, and who was beginning to grow old, and of grandfather Colas, who was still living, the one from whom he had heard so many tales, and of a thousand nothings—of the brown salamanders that prowled at night in the flower-beds in the garden, and of the gooseberries he ate there so greedily, while the grasshoppers chirped in the gathering twilight. And those nothings would make my bosom swell with an intense longing to be once more in my native place.

———————

## LVI.

My entrance to the Drolling studio was not unattended by some disagreeable incidents. The moment I put my foot inside the door a deafening tumult greeted my ears, and I saw myself surrounded by faces whose expressions, bantering, menacing, or strange, absolutely terrified me. I felt myself at the same time pulled about from one side to another, while I received on my head the blows of the cushions of the tabourets, that rained upon me from all parts of the room.

It was in this way that new pupils were greeted in those days.

Quiet being restored, one of the tallest of the students, who, better dressed and more distinguished-looking than the others, appeared to me to be of a superior station, approached me and asked me very politely:

"Where are you from, monsieur?" I answered in a tone that I tried to render as amiable as possible, "From Pas-de-Calais." "Oh, that is easily seen," he said, without moving a muscle of his countenance.

This polite young man was called Timbal.

Then the oldest of the group, Deligne, a young man from Cambrai, near my native place, came up to me and said: "See, my boy, there are seven or eight among the students whom I am going to point out to you, and whom it would be well for you to make friends with. As for the others, you may snap your fingers at them." And then, raising his voice, he said to the students: "This new pupil is a compatriot of mine; I shall take him under my protection, and let him who dare touch him!"

From this time forth I was left in peace. I was assigned the task, in accordance with the custom of the time, of taking care of the fire and going on certain errands; and the first time I took my hat from the nail to go on one of these, I saw that they had drawn on it with chalk the cockade and aigrette of a lackey.

At the height of the *mêlée*, through the dust raised by the blows of the cushions and the stamping of the feet of the boys, among whom Ulman, nicknamed " Horse's Head," was one of the wildest, I had caught a glimpse of a young man, of quiet demeanor, who was looking at me less mockingly than the others.

His countenance at once arrested my attention. He was short, thick-set, very dark, with hair the color of the raven's wing, that rose abruptly from the head and then fell down in a twisted lock over the straight forehead. His eyes, which were deep-set and very black, shone from beneath overhanging brows. A budding mustache shaded his short upper lip, and his mouth, notwithstanding the proximity of the square jaw and the prominent chin, denoting self-will, had a sweet and melancholy expression. It was the face of an eagle touched with feeling.

His name was Paul Baudry.

What struck me most in the work of the students here was the cold, dull coloring of the greater number of the paintings.

They were very different from the glowing canvases of Antwerp, but the drawing was more correct. I thought some of them skillfully executed, but wanting in life. The faces of Baudry, however, with proportions that were often incorrect, had a singularly lifelike expression.

The master visited the studio twice a week, limiting himself on these occasions to pointing out arms that were too long, or legs that were too short, and never finding the necks flexible enough. He advised us to make sketches, a great many sketches, from the antique, and from Poussin. Sometimes he would say: " More light ! Light is a fine thing ! " Alas ! it was easier to give the advice than to follow it.

Baudry was already regarded as destined to become famous. If his genius had been divined, however, that of Henner was still unrecognized. The latter worked silently, painting his figure conscientiously and with even touch, without himself suspecting the brilliant future that awaited him. Timbal gave no greater promise than Henner, but he was very noisy, speaking in a loud tone of voice, and singing in the same manner.

He sought after *esprit*.

One day he said, " Nature, who never makes a mistake, knowing that I was born for noise, called me Timbal." *

There were others, too, who sang unceasingly—Merson, Pouttier, Langlois, and the worthy Roy, now living in Rennes, and with whom I still keep up an intimacy.

Merson, who is also still my friend, has, as we know, given up painting for literature, leaving to a son the task of covering the family name with glory in the field of art. Maillot sought after style, which he occasionally found, and in the rare intervals, of silence he would tell witty anecdotes with a grave air, speaking in a monotonous tone that lulled the ear agreeably, and separating each syllable, with a simplicity of manner that had something very comical in it.

The presence of Bertinot scarcely made itself felt. He was in poor health, and rarely stirred from his chair, digging away industriously at his work; nor, that of the poor Roguet, a handsome young man, and who was twice to obtain the *Prix de Rome*, and also the prize offered by the state, in 1848, for a statue of the Republic.

---

* A kettle-drum.

We all thought a glorious future awaited him. Alas! he was soon to die at Rome from the consequences of a fall from his horse, like Géricault.

It was here, too, that I became acquainted with the worthy Léon Moricourt for whom I still entertain an affection, and the excellent and intelligent Émile Sintain.

But, although it is true, I had now made some acquaintances, I had not yet found a real friend.

Habituated to the quietude of a retired life, I felt myself, in the whirl of Paris, dazed and out of my element.

My work suffered from this confusion.

I no longer *painted divinely*. I received no prize, and in the School of Fine Arts I was placed in the supplementary class.

At the competition especially I made a botch of my drawings, tearing the paper by dint of digging at it. I always grew disgusted with my figure before it was finished, and either threw it aside or continued to work obstinately at the same part, making it worse than it was before.

I became discouraged.

Drolling, who did not believe in the sincerity of my fruitless efforts, regarded me as a rebellious pupil, and took a dislike to me. Every Saturday, at the sketch-class, I was the subject of some sharp reprimand. "What do you call that? Now we have a specimen of Diaz and Delacroix!" There was something of prejudice in this, perhaps, as he always placed me lowest, even when I painted "The Death of Epaminondas," which Baudry had considered good.

One day I took my revenge. We had the "Death of Antony" given us as a subject, and I made two different compositions of it. He recognized my touch in the first of these which his eye fell upon, rated me sharply, and, as usual, put me at the tail. Then, when his examination was almost finished, he saw the second sketch, in which I had purposely disguised my style, and, before knowing whom it was by, he praised it so highly that he was compelled to give it the first place.

Thus it was that at the same competition I was both first and last.

This slight success was only a faint gleam of light in the midst of the many annoyances and mortifications I endured, especially as I had no one to whom I could unburden my full heart. I missed the sweet scent of the clover. I missed, too, Flanders, and the simple life there, the rustic villages around Ghent, with their green fields so near the city; and the tea-gardens, where we went in a boat, and where for a few sous one could get a glass of excellent beer, and cold eels, dressed with sorrel. I missed, in a word, the comfort which was there to be had at little cost, and which was not to be found here. The theatres were too expensive, and what tenor in Paris, even Dupré himself, could be compared with the famous Albert? He was afterward the teacher of Lauwers, one of the most admired singers of Paris— ask him what he thinks of Albert! Ask any of my contemporaries in Ghent if they have ever heard an artist who was comparable to him? What storms of applause greeted certain airs, when the bravos interrupted the performance for minutes at a time! Often I would return home from the theatre, striding along the street gesticulating, intoxicated with enthusiasm, as on the occasion, for instance, when, lost in these raptures, and not seeing whither I was going, I stepped between the loose bars of a cellar-grating, and thought myself fortunate on drawing my foot out, and seeing the large rent in my trousers, to find that my leg was not broken.

How beautiful the city looked on winter nights, as I

returned from the theatre, the light from the street lamps falling palely on the snow, while from the slated roofs and spires the cold rays of the moon were reflected brightly!

How far I was from all this and from those pretty girls whom in summer I would meet on my Sunday walks, and whom I looked at boldly in the distance, toward whom I walked with courageous step, to blush from bashfulness like an imbecile, while my knees bent under me, as I passed them by!

And the bare room which De Winne and I shared, with its book-shelf that, supported only by a single nail, fell down on the same day with the bell-tower of Valenciennes. How we had laughed at this coincidence, saying that the shock produced by the fall of the shelf had caused that of the bell-tower!

And I recalled all these trifles with sadness, and, above all, I recalled the little friend whose delicately outlined face, like that of one of the angels in the Gothic cathedrals, vanished from my sight the moment I sought to fix it on canvas.

How many sorrows did you witness, O little room in the Rue du Dragon!

How all my dreams of glory had vanished! How direct my course in this labyrinth? How make my way through this busy crowd that jostle and hinder one another at every step?

Ah! weariness!

I remember dark, rainy days, when I wandered alone through the muddy streets, sick at heart, walking on and on aimlessly, without pausing, perspiring under the hood of my coat, and splashed to the waist, while the rain fell ceaselessly, seeking consolation, not in the gayety, but in the desolation around me.

One day, when I had been again placed among the

last in the sketch-class, I felt so profound a sense of dissatisfaction with myself that, wishing to see misery still greater than mine, I yielded to the irresistible impulse that drew me to contemplate the horrible sights in the morgue.

---

## LVII.

FORTUNATELY, it was not long before my brother Émile came to live with me.

My excellent father, who wished before his death to assure the future of his children, had built a factory for him, and now sent him to Paris to take lessons in chemistry.

But, in place of devoting himself to the sciences, Émile spent his days regularly at the Louvre or the Luxembourg, although he did not yet comprehend the vocation that attracted him to art.

His presence chased away the evil dreams that had haunted my solitude.

He was now sixteen. I was astonished to discover in him all at once a turn for art that we had never before suspected. I scolded him for wasting his time, but without effect.

One afternoon, returning to our room, I found upon the table a rough sketch in. water-colors, exquisite in tone, and I was astonished to learn that this was the first attempt of my young brother.

From that time I ceased to oppose him. In other respects we were not in accord in our views regarding art. He admired neither Ingres nor Leopold Robert, while he adored Delacroix.

The *Salon* of 1847—the first held since I had been in Paris—was soon opened.

The hall was reached from the corner of the Place du Carrousel by a massive staircase, no longer used.

How this place has changed since then! Starting from the Rue de Rivoli, various alleys, narrow and dirty, in which twilight always reigned, encroached upon it. These alleys terminated near the little Arc de la Victoire, in a few scattered and forbidding-looking houses. In the middle, standing alone, was the Hôtel de Nantes, and near by rose a small monument erected to a student killed in July, 1830. In the approaches to the Louvre were crowded together a number of wooden barracks, occupied by venders of birds that filled the air with their cries, and by venders of old books and engravings, soiled maps, tattered pamphlets, grimy paintings, and dusty *bric-à-brac*, among which thin fingers were always rummaging, and long, yellow noses diving inquisitively.

The whole place, even the court of the Louvre, was unpaved, as far as the rising ground on which stood the statue of the Duke of Orleans by Marochetti, replaced by the equestrian statue of Francis I by Clisinger, called the *Sire de Framboisi*.

The pictures of the Exhibition were displayed in the Square Hall and in the Grand Gallery, much longer then than now, against wooden partitions which, for three months in the year, hid from view the Old Masters that hung, deprived of light and air, behind them.

Another gallery of unplaned boards, a permanent one, supported on rough beams, ran the length of the Carrousel.

Great as had been my eagerness to see it, I did not experience when there the same emotion as I had felt at Brussels five years before. My eyes were no longer unpracticed. I had penetrated behind the scenes in art, and vivid coloring had lost its fascination for me. I now looked for harmony.

I enter the Square Hall. In place of the Veronese that had hung there before, I see the grand success of the day, "The Roman Orgy," of Thomas Couture.

I stand before this picture, undecided whether to admire it or not. At first it gives me the impression of something faded, like one of Boucher's legs of beef. I am struck by the decorative part of the picture, the beautiful architecture and the wide-mouthed vases dropping their faded flowers on the floor.

The coloring of the picture seems to me confused, as if seen through a greenish-gray fog. I admire the figures of the philosophers, the mastery of the grouping, but I am little struck by the character of this orgy, that I should prefer to be either wilder or more moderate. Here are *bourgeois* diverting themselves, vulgar debauchers. Neither can I reconcile myself to this eighteenth-century art, these Roman costumes and architecture, with these men and women of the time of Louis Philippe.

I have said that I made but little progress at the studio ; but spring, whose mild airs caused the magnificent chestnut-trees, since dead, of the Garden of the Luxembourg to send forth their shining buds—spring, which sifted its pale sunshine through their spreading green branches on the ladies, and the nurses and their little charges seated at their feet—spring chased away my fits of gloom, and cheered and revived my heart, in which a new joy had sprung up.

For I had just begun, in my little room, a sunlight sketch from nature of a scene in this delightful garden.

I must confess that I was not dissatisfied with this painting, the first in which I drew my inspiration direct from nature. I saw a new world, as it were, open before me, a world of new harmonies of color.

This feeling of pride, for which there was so little foundation, it was that made me so severe toward Couture and the other exhibitors at the *Salon* of 1847.  I had not yet acquired the experience which gives modesty.

I did not lay down my arms even before Delacroix, whose Lance-Thrust seemed to me heavy from its excessive elaboration.  The recollection of the pictures of the middle ages, at Brussels, for which I cherished so profound an admiration, prevented my doing justice to the sentiment of this work.

I anticipated a keen pleasure in seeing the pictures of Horace Vernet, whom I had so ardently admired scarcely a year before, and I was greatly surprised to find his " Royal Family " and his " Judith " both a little dull and commonplace.

In exchange, with some slight reservations, I admired Diaz.  I found reproduced in part in his paintings my impressions of the Garden of the Luxembourg and of the Forest of Labroye—these latter received so long ago.

I was charmed by his shimmering draperies, his pearly, transparent flesh-tints, and his bursts of sunshine darting through the branches and lighting up with dazzling gleams the trunks of the trees of the tall hedges.  I also found real sunlight in the May Dance of Muller.

Corot enchanted me.  There was a silvery pool of his that reflected back the sky and the trees wet with morning dew that recalled to my mind hours spent in childhood wandering along the borders of the ponds in our *Carperie*.

----

## LVIII.

THE circle of my friends, meantime, had widened. I had met again some of the former students of the college, and among them Ernest Delalleau, a young architect and a pupil of Labrouste,

This Delalleau was a strange-looking young man. He had an animated face, extremely mobile and intelligent, with light-green eyes shot with yellow, and set close together like those of a monkey. The head of a Roman, covered with stiff and rebellious locks; a straight forehead; eyebrows ascending toward the temples; a *retroussé* nose; very thin lips, always wearing a mocking expression; strong, square jaws; a large and prominent chin, on which grew a short, ill-kept bristly beard; a very long neck, with the glottis extremely prominent; the neck set firmly on the shoulders—such were the parts that went to complete the picture, odd rather than ugly, and singularly remarkable, of this young man.

I met him for the first time, in the year 1838, at the little seminary of St. Bertin. He was then about twelve years old.

We were in the refectory when he entered for the first time—the only first appearance of a student among us which I remember, although I have witnessed many. Why? Why, because it was he, and the world could never contain two Delalleaus.

He wore a jacket of green lasting, bound with braid, like many of the other boys; trousers plaited on the hips, like all of them. His hat only, of a somewhat peculiar fashion, seemed to have made any demands upon the imagination. It resembled a cardinal's hat from its shape, as well as from the silk tassel that floated at the end of a complicated gimp ornament.

But what most struck me, as I said, was himself: the nose like a trumpet, the mouth with its receding lips, the bristling locks, and, above all, his expression like that of a frightened squirrel, as if he had suddenly fallen down among us from some tree in the forest of Hesden, his native place.

The first thing he did was to draw the attention of his neighbor to the flies walking on the ceiling.

Fate willed that we should pursue the same paths. I met him again at the College of Douai, where we first became intimate on account of the similarity in our tastes. He drew, and made verses which he sent to his simple-hearted father. The latter was enchanted with his son's genius, and sent back the same verses to him, recopied in his own neater handwriting.

Delalleau was my chief rival in the competition for the prize for drawing from the cast, in which I came out victorious.

He soon showed that he had plenty of intelligence, but a lack of connection in his thoughts.

He might have accomplished a great deal, if he had been able to fix his attention on any one subject.

He would have made a first-rate actor.

He had fits of enthusiasm which changed like the wind.

The censor of the college, a Gascon, laying his large hand one day on the head of Delalleau, said, "And when are they going to put a leaden cap on this head?" No one could make more absurd accusations, or defend with greater eloquence the side he took up, than he His sallies were never-ending. But all this bore no fruit. The leaden cap, alas! was wanting.

I met him a third time in Paris, on which occasion we saw each other daily.

I soon observed that the same contradictions existed in his moral as in his intellectual nature. He was at once bold and timid, generous and avaricious, domineering and affectionate, proud and tender. He always gave evidence of a strong sense of justice, however.

The events of 1848 were approaching. Various incidents, unnecessary to relate here, had served to fan the flame of party animosity.

Paris had become irritable and feverish. Odillon Barrot, in the *National*, and Ledru-Rollin, in the *Reforme*, were especially furious in their attacks on the party in power.

These journals were eagerly devoured by the people, and passed from hand to hand.

The excitement extended to the provinces, and was especially intense in certain large cities where the speeches of the Reform banquets found an echo.

My uncle, always enthusiastic and an assiduous reader and blind believer in the doctrines of the *Democratié Pacifique*, was very proud of having fraternized at Lille with the great tribune Ledru-Rollin.

My father, calmer by nature, and ill at the time, besides, had not been present at any of those banquets, although a democrat in theory and in practice. He had for many years, indeed, thought himself a legitimist, on account of his long connection with the Duke of Duras, who had presented him at a *soirée* at the court of Charles X.

But he was even then at heart, as he afterward said, a republican without knowing it.

As for me I felt but little interest in politics, never reading the papers, and always engrossed in my affections and my art.

Delalleau, on the contrary, enthusiastic by nature, and a great admirer of the Robespierres and the Dantons of history, his mind crammed with the declamatory phrases of the press, went about preaching revolutionary ideas. He said "the Rrrrevolution!" He came to stir me up in my peaceful retreat, calling the state of *quasi*-indifference I maintained with regard to the burning questions of the day monstrous selfishness.

But it sprang rather from ignorance on my part.

He enlightened me regarding public affairs.

He had no difficulty in proving to me that Louis Philippe, whom I had not hitherto regarded as a bad man, was more cruel than Tiberius or Nero.

He took me to the lectures of Michelet, whose eloquence drew me along with almost all the young men of Paris into the popular current.

People began to grow excited.

Ah! and how touchy they became!

The king, in his speech, had dared to talk of "*blind or hostile passions!*"

You should have seen with what flashing eyes Delalleau repeated this phrase, "*Blind or hostile passions!*"

Was he addressing a free people, or were we slaves? It was monstrous, unheard of!

Truly we were returning to the times of the cage of Cardinal de la Balue.

Not Camille Desmoulins himself had exercised a more magnetic influence on those who heard him than did Delalleau, when, on the occasion of Michelet's next lecture, he rose in his seat before the arrival of the illustrious professor, and with quivering nostrils, his hair and beard bristling with indignation, his yellow eyes flashing, read in a thundering voice the famous Discourse from the Throne.

His *retroussé* nose quivered with rage as he shouted the words "*Blind or hostile passions!*"

With what indignation he cast from him this document, of a past age; with what rage he stamped upon it afterward!

Thus did Delalleau offer himself a willing victim to the vengeance of the tyrant.

He was not molested; but the lectures of Michelet were stopped.

This piece of bravado had a pitiable sequel.

A few days afterward I was at the house of Delalleau, when his porter brought him his paper, the *Reforme*.

He opened it, and his glance fell on a letter of Michelet's.  It referred without doubt to the famous incident !

He read—he read—what ?

But no, it could not be possible !

At the end of the letter he read this sentence : "Besides, it was easy to see, from the fantastic appearance and dress of the individual who read the king's speech, that he was an emissary of the secret police."

---

## LIX.

MEANTIME Émile had returned to Courrières, having learned more from the Louvre than from his teacher.  I saw him depart with keen regret, although in future I should be less lonely than formerly, having now made some friends.

Among these I will mention Feyen-Perrin, who had just been admitted to the studio Drolling.

He was about nineteen.

Careless in regard to his dress, he had a great deal of natural distinction of manner, and was beautiful as a Greek youth, with his dark, flowing locks and his regular and expressive features overspread with a bronze pallor that redoubled their charm.  His glance was at once veiled and ardent, and he had a melancholy mouth, slightly disdainful in expression, shaded by a growing beard, shaped like that we see in the pictures of Christ.

It was now 1848.

The revolutionary spirit, which was destined to overturn the existing order of society, was paving the way, at the same time, for radical changes in art and literature.

The pupils in the studios as well as in the colleges, irrespective of station or political opinion, felt the attraction of a movement as popular if not as violent as that of 1830.

The one was the result of new aspirations, more or less chimerical, the other the revolt of reason against the brilliant fancies of Romanticism.

If this latter movement drew some artists toward the lowlands of art, it impelled others to those heights where spring its living sources. I remember what a strange new restlessness agitated my companions and myself.

Soon to the ferment of ideas were added the emotions of active life.

We were about to pass through one of the great social crises which, throwing men out of the beaten paths, excite their imaginations and sharpen their creative faculties, as storms plowing up the earth fertilize certain parts of the soil barren before, and stimulate the growth of new vegetation.

---

## LX.

I HAD been ill. I had been confined to my room for several days in consequence of a return of my old bronchitis.

It is the 22d of February.

I have just awakened, finding a proof of returning health in the joyous feeling of well-being I experience. I luxuriate in the soft repose of the bed, and in that poetic egoism of convalescence which makes joy spring up, with health, in the heart, especially when one is young.

I hear the accustomed sounds, the cries of the buyers of old clothes and rags, and the shrill screams of the brush-vender, that reach me while he is still in the Rue des Saints-Pères.

I am about to take my chocolate, when a heavy blow from the butt-end of a musket shakes my door, and my crazy friend Delalleau, in the uniform of the National Guard, bursts in, and, leaning on his musket with one hand and placing the other theatrically on his hip, cries :

"We are making a Rrrrevolution !!!"

"As usual," I answer, shrugging my shoulders.

He goes off to join his company.

I left the house a moment afterward.

The day was fine. The sun shone brightly in the Rue Taranne, where groups of soldiers were stationed near their stands of arms.

To this unusual sight I attached little importance.

Besides, no one seemed to regard the disturbance as anything more than a simple riot. Great events, however, were about to take place.

The following is the account I gave my uncle of the scenes I witnessed on the 23d of February, in a letter dated the morning of the 24th :

"Yesterday, Wednesday, there was a sharp struggle between the people and the Municipal Guard, and blood flowed in the Rues St. Honoré, St. Martin, St. Denis, and Montorgueil. In the evening things were quieting down, when the news spread that the ministry had resigned. From eight to ten in the evening Paris was *en fête.* The principal streets of the city, which were illuminated, were filled with crowds of joyous and excited people crying : '*Vive la Réforme!* Down with Guizot !'

"The National Guard sang the Marsellaise. I walked through the streets with Monsieur Broquise, a law student, who lodges in the same house with me. After crossing the Rue St. Denis, which presented a magnificent spectacle, we walked along the Boulevard. The people seemed to have only peaceful intentions, and we were walking on quietly when, at about forty paces distant from the residence of the Minister of Foreign Affairs, we suddenly heard the sound of musketry. Without stopping to learn the cause, we took the first street we came to, and ran away at full speed."

.     .     .     .     .     .     .

Next day, the 26th, I go to the studio. I find there only a few of the students, who, greatly agitated, are discussing the stormy events of the day before.

The insurgents had carried the victims of the fusillade on wagons through the streets, by torch-light, uttering cries of " Vengeance ! "

Numerous barricades had been erected. There was a little fighting on the other side of the river.

Under such circumstances no one thought of working.

The students went away one by one, until only Fey-en-Perrin and I remained.

Neither of us could resist the temptation of going to see what was taking place on the right bank of the river.

In our quarter nothing extraordinary was going on. There were few people in the streets, and these were gathered about here and there in agitated groups.

We continued on our way and soon reached the seat of action.

After crossing the silent Louvre, the deserted Rue de Coq and the Rue St. Honoré, whose barricades were deserted, we suddenly found ourselves in the Place du Palais Royal, surrounded by armed men who had come from we knew not where, and between the insurgents, who from their ramparts of paving-stones were already pointing their guns, on the one side, and on the other the soldiers who occupied the post which then stood in front of the palace.

This crowd seemed to have sprung up from the ground, while, thoughtful and agitated, we had been looking at the soldiers supporting their arms, an angry and dejected expression on their pale countenances.

We sprang on the barricade, seeking to make our way out of the tumult, which we succeeded in doing after some difficulty, and arrived at the Rue de Valois, where, happily, on our left, was the Café du Nord, in which we took refuge.

Hardly were we inside, when a volley of musketry burst forth.

From the window where we stood we saw an immense crowd rushing toward the barricade.

Those haggard faces with unkempt beards; those men armed with pistols, halberds, and even custom-house officers' probes; the ceaseless firing; the gloomy and livid light, dimly illuminating the street, silent but alive with motion; the sudden flashes seen from time to time in the midst of the smoke; the noise of the musketry suddenly breaking through the silence; the wounded men whom they brought to the Café du Nord where we were; the fury of the ragged populace—all breathed a tragic horror.

How long did this terrible scene last?  We did not know.

Suddenly we see, through the windows overlooking the yard, men running over the roofs of the Palais Royal.  The firing slackens, then ceases.

The Revolution is accomplished!

We proceed on our way.  In the Rue de Valois the

air is filled with a cloud of feathers from the ripped mattresses which grotesque figures are shaking out of the windows of the Palais Royal. Hundreds of books and engravings which have been thrown out of the windows of the library lie heaped in the gutter.

Behind the blood-stained barricade, in the guard-house, which is on fire, the unfortunate soldiers are roasting alive!

What were then our feelings? It would be difficult for me to define them.

If I remember aright, I think I discover in the first place a great sadness, a profound disgust at the blood which has been shed, an overwhelming pity for the victims, but at the same time an indescribable, all-pervading thrill, an intensity of life, that redoubled the power of the senses, sharpening the vision ard causing us to receive a more vivid and rapid impression of the acts, the shouts, and the faces of this delirious crowd rushing through the streets singing patriotic hymns.

In this flood of emotion we felt ourselves better artists as well as better citizens, and, behind the dark clouds of the smoke of the revolution, we could see shining the bright sun of the future.

We walked toward the Tuileries along the quays, after having retraced our steps through the Louvre. On the Pont des Arts we saw a young man, an officer of the National Guard, with his head bound in a bloody handkerchief. They were carrying him on a stretcher, but he did not seem to feel his wound, and was triumphantly brandishing a branch of laurel, while he sang the *Air des Girondins*.

The Pavilion of Flora had been invaded by a crowd intoxicated with victory, who were giving full sway to their destructive instincts.

Mingled with the *débris* thrown from the windows,

wine flowed along the gutters, and, as every dramatic situation must have its comic side, a wag had put on the red livery of the valets of the king and strutted about on the balcony, haranguing the groups who danced on the quay.

From a letter written on the evening of the same day to my uncle I copy the following passage :

"The Rue St. Honoré presents a horrifying spectacle.  The houses are riddled by bullets ; the pavement has been torn up for almost the entire length of the street, which is in places covered with blood.  This evening almost all the guard-houses are on fire.  The emotions I have to-day experienced are so numerous and so varied that it would be impossible for me to describe them.  In them horror and enthusiasm are confusedly mingled together."

Once masters of the city, however, the people will prove themselves capable of self-government, respecting the rights of the individual and of property, and themselves shooting down the pillagers.

---

## LXI.

THE causes that led to this revolution and the consequences that resulted from it exerted a powerful influence, as I have said, on my mind, and on that of every other artist, as well as on the general movement of art and literature.  In every department new experiments were tried.

"The new social stratum," as Gambetta called it later on, together with its natural environment, became a subject of study.  There was a deeper interest in the life of the street and of the fields.  The tastes and the feelings of the poor were taken into account, and art conferred honors upon them, formerly reserved for the gods and for the great.

If 1830 had brought back feudalism, 1848 will broaden the popular field. Living nature, the nature that laughs, labors, and weeps, as well as the nature which we do wrong to call inanimate, will be more closely studied. For this nature, too, thrills with life, with its fields, its skies, its waters and its verdure, its winds, its rains, its snows, and its sunshine—always vibrant, always varied.

This movement had nothing in common with the experiments that it was right and necessary to make in the absolute negation of what had been accomplished in the past in the arts. Tradition, that beacon from the past which serves as a light to guide the future, was respected.

Genius met with consideration, and Delacroix was admired none the less because pointed shoes, top-boots, and all the old-fashioned wardrobe of Romanticism were hung up in the closet, together with the Nanterre cap which, up to that time, had served to represent the costume of the Greeks and Romans.

The ancients were studied.

Almost every school of art, even the Neo-Greek, Hamon and his rivals, profited by this movement toward the True.

The landscape-painters had led the way—Rousseau, Corot, Cabat, Diaz, and Troyon, who was beginning to win a name.

At first there was a return to the Dutch school. In his early pictures, Rousseau, in more than one of his characteristics, recalls Hobbema.

I think the influence of the English school has been exaggerated. I recognize its influence, indeed, through Bonington, on Delacroix, the Deverias, and their school.

But I recognize scarcely a trace of it among our newer landscape-painters, with the exception of Paul Huet, whose part, however, has been an unimportant one.

Turner is a painter of the Romantic school, full of genial fancy, when he does not draw his inspiration from Claude Lorraine.

Constable, like Rousseau, has occasionally shown the influence of the Dutch school.

In reality, the Ruysdaels and the Hobbemas are the real fathers of our modern landscape-painting. They have penetrated deeply into the secrets of Nature, and their somewhat conventicnal execution does not prevent them being in the main simple and true to Nature.

Rousseau had studied their works for a long time. Then he went to Fontainebleau, and in gravel-pits and wild thickets clothed in the gorgeous tints of autumn, he found again, in part, the tones and harmonies of his favorite masters. For a time he saw with their eyes, and then, retiring to the forest, and giving himself up to the study of Nature, he formed an original style. He painted some masterpieces.

But he confined himself to his own inspiration too long, forgot his early teachers, and declined lamentably in his style ; for it is never well to fall back too much upon one's self.

Corot, on his side, derived his inspiration from Poussin and Claude Lorraine. Italy attracted him. The beautiful Campagna of Rome, and, above all, the tender beauty of the Lake of Nemi, filled his soul with enthusiasm. He formed under this influence an original style, at once sublime and simple. He gave shape to the chaste visions of an imagination, where up to old age will bloom an eternal spring.

Rousseau gives us rugged gullies with steep, rocky sides and impenetrable thickets, gnarled oaks shading motionless pools ; his springs are cold, his autumns red ; Corot depicts the gentler emotions of Nature, her virgin charms, her enchanting mysteries, her serene grandeur, her flowers laden with dew. Daubigny, the humblest and the most natural of painters, depicts in all their freshness the simple pleasures of country life ; Fromentin is subtle ; Français, elegant ; the solitary Jules Dupré adopts a style between Rousseau and Troyon.

But however great may be the originality of their productions, all these painters—and I insist upon this point—derive their inspiration from the Old Masters, and found their art upon the rules observed in their greatest works.

Courbet comes in 1849 with the intention of overthrowing past art and constructing it anew.

One day, when we were traveling together in Belgium, he mentioned the works of Raphayel (thus it was that he pronounced Raphael) disparagingly, and I said to him, "You deny his right to fame, then ?"

"No," he replied, "I speak of him, therefore I acknowledge it."

In the same way he spoke of Titian, and other painters like him, with an air of patronage.

And we know that no one had less right than he to do this.

While he assumed these disdainful airs in speaking of the Old Masters, he studied them in the shelter of the obscurity which enveloped his name, soon to resound through the world of art.

And what is the result ? While, with the sly secrecy of the peasant, he speaks only of realism, of which he proclaims himself the messiah, his pictures show preeminently those qualities which are learned in the museums. His admirable compositions, run in one piece, so to say, the beauty of his somber coloring, his harmony of style, he owes in great part to those Old Masters, whose title to fame he deigns to *acknowledge*.

His masterpiece, " After the Banquet at Ornans," in the museum of Lille, even to the costume, might be the work of a pupil of Rembrandt.

His fine painting, " The Man with the Pipe," recalls Correggio. " The Man with the Leathern Girdle " looks as if it might have been hanging for centuries in the Louvre; and, however startling his Interment may be, and although he has crowded it with grotesque details, it is in nowise realistic, since the sun does not shine in it, and it looks more dingy than a Ribera.

Finally, he paints few open-air scenes. He frequently copies the patina of the Old Masters, and while rendering full justice to the genuine though limited gifts he has received from Nature, may it not be said of him that, like the wag who clothed himself in the livery of the Tuilieries to preach his revolutionary doctrines, he has borrowed the livery of the Louvre to preach his pretended discoveries ?

I may add, besides, that if on the one hand by his vigor he may have served to stimulate art, on the other hand he has propagated the most detestable of abuses— the use of the palette-knife, which may be attended with the most serious dangers.

In contrast with him, our glorious Meissonier, who does more than *acknowledge* the title to fame of the Dutch artists, gives striking and triumphant proof of his qualities of observation, absolute conscientiousness, and marvelous clearness of vision.

I will speak later on of the great Millet. At this time he was quite unknown, and his first exhibition in the next *Salon* was an Œdipus, a strange picture in which the coloring is sticky, and which is at once fantastic, odd, tame, and heavy, but through which may be divined a blind force seeking to free itself from powerful influences—a genuine but confused originality of style that halts between Michel Angelo and Subleyras.

This picture, which attracted but little attention from the public, produced in the minds of his fellow-painters the emotion that told them they stood in the presence of dawning genius.

This movement of art toward truth to Nature had, so far as form and modeling are concerned, a powerful leader in Ingres, who is still called *Monsieur Ingres*, as Thiers will always be called *Monsieur Thiers*, because each of them had a *bourgeois* side.

He was a great and remarkable figure, this painter, whom Praeult wittily called a "Chinese, strayed into Athens."

In his person, as in his style, there were surprising anomalies.

Physically he has something sacerdotal in his appearance.

Is he a dignitary of the Church or a parish beadle? One can hardly tell.

His proportions are almost grotesque. He has very short legs, a large abdomen, arms extraordinarily long; the lower part of the face is wanting in dignity; the nose is ordinary, as they say in the passports; the chin is round and receding, the cheeks are large and flabby, the mouth is sensual, though not wanting in character: this is the beadle side. But the eyes and the forehead are extremely beautiful. The dark pupils seem to flash fire under the eyebrows, which indicate strong self-will, modified by the descending line toward the temple, indicating piety. Here we seem to see the highest dignitary in the World of Art.

The same contradiction exists in his talent.

In the beginning a disciple of David, he fell, later on,

under the influence of Raphael.  He soon had flashes of sentiment, which revealed to him marvelous accents of nature.

In an inspiration of genius he recognized the sentiment of Phidias.  Of Phidias!  The divinest incarnation of the living ideal!  Then Ingres, like another Polyeuctus, dethrones the false gods.  Down with you, Venus de' Medici and Apollo Belvedere, whom our fathers and David himself have worshiped!  Your progeny, with their insipid beauty, their cold eyes, their limbs rounded like architectural moldings, is already numerous enough.  Down with you!  And, indeed, in some admirable compositions he attains to ideality of form, expressive and beautiful without being insipid, graceful delineation, firm and flexible modeling, richness and variety of composition.

As I have said, he attains this by flashes, for he places side by side beauties of the highest order, and defects that are ridiculous at times, making limbs which seem to have no joints, twisting the bones, spoiling noble conceptions by childish blunders or *bourgeois* vulgarity.

David, in whom the influences of the *pretty* antiques of the Decadence has stifled so many natural gifts—David, too, in his hours of freedom, had felt the powerful spell of Nature, as had Gros, whose heroic genius, however, took bolder flights, and the valiant Géricault, and the tender and dramatic Prudhon ; but in the French school no one before Ingres had realized the formula of lifelike and varied composition.

There is no doubt that, counting among its members the painters I have mentioned, the French school was in advance of every contemporary school.

But there was something it had not yet even sought to attain—the relations between the human figure and inanimate nature.  It had not yet succeeded in associating fully animate and inanimate life, in making the figures respond to the life around them, in making them participate in all the phenomena of the heavens and the earth, in making them breathe their natural element, air.

The " Battle of Eylau " is a singularly moving drama, the work of a great painter, and one of our finest pictures ; but the figures are neither under the sky nor, *in their values*, on the snow.  The " Shipwreck of the Medusa " is a noble and heroic composition, full of boldness and technical power, but the black and bituminous shadows are out of place, the composition is too complicated, the whole is wanting in atmosphere.  The " Massacre of Scio," the " Bark of Dante," and several others of the paintings of Delacroix, have the elements proper to them.  The atmosphere, tragic and at times sublime, that surrounds them, is a pure creation of the genius of the master.  So, too, is his design, wonderful for its wild beauties, as well as for its fascinating blemishes.  Although forming his style on Rubens, Tintoretto, and the English school, Delacroix, whose head looked like a sick lion's, is a genius who must always remain alone.  Woe to the painter who seeks to approach him !  He is not one of the leaders of the movement of 1848, like Rousseau and Corot.

And were there other precursors of the contemporary school ?

And when I say contemporary art, I do not mean that which only seeks after what is called the *modern spirit*, a high-sounding name, which too often only means the *mode*.

Art concerns itself only with eternal laws, not with ephemeral caprices.

A serious attempt toward the new movement had also been made by an artist greatly disparaged at present.  There is not a dauber who does not heap sarcasms upon him, and I must be careful how I mention his name.  It can not be helped if I should be considered a *bourgeois*, a "philistine," as Gautier says.  I will conquer all false shame, and confess that I mean poor Leopold Robert.  Whatever the errand-boys of the studios may say, I prefer his pictures to those curiosities in yellow and violet of artists who seem to think they have a monopoly of atmosphere.

Ah! they may heap insult upon him, but they can never be as cruel to him as he was to himself, as his suicide proves.

Yes; he is theatrical, affected, hard, thin, and discordant, but he had a clearness of vision peculiarly his own; he was consumed by a love of the beautiful!  He was the first to make a serious study of the peasant, whom he loved with the ardor and sensibility of his poetic nature.

His energy was great, his sincerity absolute, and the result, in truth, was not contemptible.  He has caught the glow, the sun-browned hue, the fine, harmonious lines.

I find in his brick-red carnations certain flashes of blue which make them like Nature's self, and of which the painters who preceded him had scarcely any knowledge.  He has not reached the goal, indeed, but he has pointed the way.

One must read his letters to understand the dissatisfaction with which he regarded his pictures, so far short did they fall of his visions.

And yet how enthusiastically admired he was by men like Lamartine, De Musset, and Heine!

And why is it, notwithstanding all that has been said against him, that he is not forgotten; that people go to look at his pictures and to copy them?

It is because the work of an artist lives in proportion to what he has put into it of himself!

He has imitators who are his superiors in technical skill, it may be, but posterity will forget them.  Why?  Is it solely because they were imitators?  The originals they copied from might disappear, yet their work would survive none the longer for it.  They die because being imitators and having nothing of their own to express, they have been unable to impregnate their productions with that elusive quality which is the soul of the artist—his passion, his love, his suffering, his life.

---

## LXII.

DELALLEAU soon quitted architecture and returned to the Drolling studio.

Every day, more and more absorbed in politics, and always placing himself on the side of the most advanced opinions, he accused me of being a reactionary, and did not cease to lecture me.  He went beyond the truth; I felt myself, on the contrary, strongly drawn toward the Republican party.

We considered it a duty, as Republicans, to give the Royalists a piece of our mind whenever the occasion offered, and to take our beefsteak smelling of burned fat, in the restaurants of friends and brothers whose sign-boards bore an equilateral triangle, and where, when we asked for a *beignet-montaguard* (fritter with gooseberry jam), the waiter answered, "Here it is, citizen."

We attended the clubs, sometimes taking our places among the audience, again as members of the committee, and at times even remaining in the little sentry-box

13

at the entrance to receive the ten centimes which each citizen contributed to the emancipation of the people. All this conferred some importance upon us, but, to speak the truth, we were somewhat in the position of the fly on the coach-wheel.

But it was not long before I returned to Courrières, whither I was called by the alarming state of my father's health, and my longing for home.

----

## LXIII.

I should like to throw a veil over this sojourn at Courrières—a time which has left me so many gloomy memories. Courrières, too, had had its little revolution.

My father and my uncle, who had always taken a great interest in public affairs, and were very popular, had long been at war with the former authorities of the village, who were animated, for the most part, by a spirit of selfishness and routine.

My father had sustained the struggle with calmness, but my uncle, who was of a more ardent temperament, and who had long before given utterance to his republican sentiments, notably in his History of Courrières, and in the letters which he published later under the title of *Misères Morales*, had given a rude shock to the self-willed obstinacy, the vanity, and at times the bad faith of our municipal functionaries.

At the first news of the events in Paris, the people of the village had flocked to the house of my father, who was then ill, and, insisting on having him for their mayor, had carried him in triumph to the town-hall with such demonstrations of enthusiasm, that, moved to tears, he cried out: "Thanks, my children, enough ; you will make me die of joy!"

Alas! this joy was of short duration. He found himself involved in a thousand difficulties in his private affairs. He had sold fine estates which brought a regular income, in order to buy a part of the forest of the Armerois in the Belgian Ardennes. (His passion for forests will be remembered.) He had gone to great expense in making roads and other improvements, and just as he was about to reap the benefit of this outlay, he felt that his end was drawing near (he never confided his troubles to any one), and he at that time resolved to establish my brother Louis in the brewery, and Émile in another factory, which he had caused to be built at great cost.

The Revolution having destroyed credit, he was forced to sell the forest, which he did under disastrous conditions.

Little by little we felt the embarrassments occasioned by diminished resources, but all we thought of was the illness of my father, who soon quitted us, leaving my uncle to bear the whole burden. He died on the 11th of May, 1848, from an affection of the liver, complicated with heart-disease.

The grief caused by this loss rendered my brothers and myself almost insensible to the ruin which threatened soon to overwhelm us. I will say nothing of this grief, nor of the tears shed by the worthy peasants, at the interment of this good man.

The law permitted us to accept our inheritance without making ourselves responsible for the payment of the debts of the estate beyond the amount of the assets. We refused to cast this insult on my father's venerated memory. We accepted our inheritance with all its responsibilities.

We were rewarded for this. The creditors, too, were grateful to us, for having given up our mother's property which we had the right to claim. The consideration enjoyed by our family suffered in no way from this reverse of fortune, although our ruin brought with it that of my uncle also. Notwithstanding this, he was unanimously elected mayor, in place of his brother, and afterward he was elected councilor of the district.

My father was born in 1796, and my uncle in 1798. They were the sons of Lambert Breton and Catharine Hottin. I have already related a part of the life of my grandfather. The brothers Breton were still very young when they lost their parents. My father was brought up at Courrières in the house of his guardian, Isidore Lecocq, the husband of the Cousin Catherine, with whom you are already acquainted. You know the rest.

My uncle, then a child in arms, was carried to Wawaghies, to the house of his Grandmother Hottin, and there he grew up in the sylvan solitude of the woods. He ran among the hedges, wild as a little savage, spending his time in childish sports with little playmates as wild as himself.

This education, or, rather this absence of education, inspired him with a profound love for sylvan nature, at whose vivifying springs he had early drunk.

How many poetic descriptions he has given me of those long-past days, descriptions which have contributed to develop in me a passion for the beauties of nature!

At the age of twelve he returned to Courrières to attend the village school, where a master more pretentious than learned gave him the only instruction he ever received.

He surrounded himself with books, which he read with avidity; he labored indefatigably to store his mind with knowledge, taking notes from every book he read, digested this medley as best he could, and when he went to Lille, at the age of eighteen, to enter business, he surprised everybody by the extent of his learning. He was employed in various banking and business houses, his employers all entertaining a strong friendship for him, and having implicit confidence in him.

He spent all his savings in adding to his stock of books and knowledge, studying in his leisure hours ; he filled many copy-books with notes, dipped into various sciences, and learned music. In the evenings he would go to the theatre or to some party.

His visit to our house during my mother's lifetime will be remembered. You know how, after her death, he came to live with us in order to devote himself to our education. I need say no more. This tells what he was.

His mind was a veritable encyclopædia. Lack of method, however, always prevented him from systematizing his knowledge.

With all this, he was simple-hearted in the extreme and devoted to us beyond measure.

What would we have been without him ?

If grief for my father's death and the indifference to material interests natural to youth made us view our approaching ruin with comparative indifference, such was not the case with my uncle, who regarded our future as blighted.

He displayed an indefatigable activity, leaving no stone unturned to avert the impending catastrophe.

He had moments of keen anguish.

One day when he was going to Lille to try to avert the disgrace of a protested note, he arrived too late for the train at the station of Libercourt.

He was thus obliged, with despair in his soul, to wait two or three hours for another train.

Distressed in mind as he was, he found it impossible to remain in a state of inaction.

In front of the station the woods of Libercourt and Wawaghies, where he had spent his happy childhood, began. He plunged into them, walking on at random. He saw again the paths his childish feet had trod, and which still bore, so to speak, traces of the sports of his youthful days. Here he had played cricket. There he had shot with the bow and arrow, and he remembered how once, when he had hit the bull's-eye, his little playmates had carried him in triumph.

He thinks he hears again their clear and joyous shouts, he breathes again the perfume of the lily of the valley, the pungent aroma of the oaks. A thousand recollections rend his soul, making his anguish keener, and the temptation to end his life begins to assail him. He walks on. He arrives at an opening where two roads meet. Here an old oak rises up before him.

Close to the trunk of this tree is a little chapel of worm-eaten wood, wreathed with hawthorn and withered flowers. He recognizes it ; it was there when he was a child. This sends his thoughts back to the past. He dreams.

On leaving Wawaghies, at the age of twelve, he had been accompanied thus far by the little Hélène, a gentle child, who soon afterward died. They were only simple children, but they loved each other. Their parting was full of sorrow. They knelt down before the Virgin of the little chapel and repeated a pure prayer which must have moved to pity the birds flying past. And my uncle remembered all this, and he, the philosopher, the disciple of Fourier, the pupil of Voltaire and Rousseau, threw himself on his knees and prayed to this Madonna hidden in the heart of the forest.

His courage revived ; he went to Lille and made his

situation known to a true friend, who came to his assistance.

I shall dwell no longer on our misfortunes.  Some
time afterward we settled our affairs under the disastrous conditions which those who passed through the
crisis of 1848 will remember.  Nothing brought at the
sale a fourth of its value.  All was lost save honor.

And we returned to our occupations with sixty or
eighty thousand francs of debts before us.  Little by
little we paid them all off.

The brewery was our plank of safety.  A friend had
bought it, rented it to us, and afterward sold it to us.
It was bid for eagerly for the same reasons that made
us desire to keep it.  Louis continued to manage it.

Émile enlisted in the Sixty-sixth of the line, and set
out for Toulouse, where that regiment then was.

My uncle and I remained for some time longer in
the empty house now bereft of its master.

All the furniture had been sold, as well as the fine
wines so highly esteemed by our friends, and the figures
painted by Fremy.

A little white wooden table supporting a common
wash-basin replaced the former furniture of my room.
I saw this bareness without grief.  I need not say with
what my sad thoughts were occupied.

And when more tranquil hours came, when new
blossoms of happiness opened in my heart—flowers suddenly springing into bloom amid ruins, joys that I reproached myself with, regarding them as the rebellious
protest of selfishness, but which were the more irresistible as being the secret agencies of the immutable
laws of compensation and reaction—then I found an indescribable charm in this modest wooden table, which
seemed to symbolize rural simplicity, and in thinking
that henceforward I was to be poor.

It was something like a relief to be rid of so many artificial and useless objects, and I felt a stronger sentiment of fraternity than before with the peasants whom I had always loved, and whom I began to regard with stronger affection in the lull succeeding so much anguish and so many misfortunes.

Like them, we began to wear the blouse; we mingled more intimately with them in their reunions and amusements, and we have never found them to fail in respect toward us, or to presume on our familiarity.

Thus it was that there grew up in my artist-heart a stronger affection for the nature, the obscure acts of heroism, and the beauty of the lives of the peasantry fostered by the pure joy and the fruitful peace which the spectacle of the immensity of the plains receding into silence and infinity produces in the soul.

----

## LXIV.

But, if it be true that I had never felt more strongly than now this peace, this joy that is to be found in nature, I did not yet understand its value from an artistic point of view.

I had, in reality, never tried to paint nature. My ideal was still to be found exclusively in the museums.

And in the works of the great masters I was much more impressed by external form, imposed upon them by the circumstances of their surroundings, than by the essential qualities of their pictures, those qualities that, developed by a profound study of natural laws, constitute their eternal essence. I thought them beautiful chiefly because of their subjects, beautiful in themselves, the expression of which they had succeeded in realizing, and which I believed to be no longer in existence, and to be sought for only in the history of the past.

"Happy the painters," I thought, "who had only to open their eyes to see marvels." I never suspected that these marvels are everywhere around us.

I should never have insulted Phidias by supposing that that little gleaner bending yonder over the stubble could for a single moment attract his attention.

I did not comprehend Phidias sufficiently, or rather I knew too little of nature to be aware that the immutable laws which governed the creations of the great sculptor manifest themselves also in the attitude and the forms of this humble peasant, with her rags floating in the breeze.

I had not yet sought inspiration in the recollections of my childhood, that mysterious world that in mature years seems clothed in light. I had not yet found (for though it be true that there is nothing new under the sun, we must discover everything anew, or else be copyists) that what is best is what we have unconsciously felt at the outset of life when we first opened our eyes to the light, and that what is most beautiful in the world is to be met with everywhere. A truth too evident to be at once accepted as such.

Ignorance admires only what is not simple, and is affected or labored in expressing itself.

An epoch must pass through a stage of affectation, artificiality, and false refinement before it returns to a comprehension of the simple in art.

This ignorance, and the sympathy I felt for the disinherited of fortune, turned me at first toward melodramatic subjects taken from the life of the people. I was impelled to this by my recollection, still vivid, of the scenes of the Revolution, which passed continually be-

fore my mind.   I thought to attain  great results by violent means.

I had tried in vain  to make  some use of  my sketch
in  the garden of  the Luxembourg.   In  the painting I
made from it, the  first impression was wanting.   The
result was pitiable.   Then I painted a " Susannah in the
Bath," according to the rules learned in the studio ; but
this little picture, which I keep for my punishment, is so
bad  that  if  a student  of  twenty were  to  bring  me  one
like it I should say, " Go, and become a bricklayer ! "

When  it  happens  now  that I am hurt by a criticism
which I  think unjust, I  say to myself by way of consolation :  " Do not forget that you  painted a ' Susannah in
the Bath,' and that you  could  not then dream of  ever
obtaining a quarter of  the  success  you  have since obtained ! "

In  this  state  of  discouragement I had  a vision  one
night, when I was unable to sleep, of a lugubrious composition.

I saw a garret.   A woman was lying there on a miserable pallet.   Her face was livid, her cheeks hollow,
her eyes red with weeping, her clothes in  tatters.   Half
rising out of the sinister shadow, she clasped to her withered breast, with her  emaciated arm, an infant with
frightful agony depicted  on  its countenance, while with
her other thin  and  bony hand she clutched the blouse
of her husband, who was breaking from her in a paroxysm of desperation.

Arrested  for  a  moment  in  his  course,  he  turns
toward her, but he is inflexible ; he grasps his musket,
with the purpose of  going  to the barricade that is seen
through the window, in the frame of which is a bullet-
hole that lets the light enter, and it is in vain  that the
crucifix suspended  to the wall  under  a branch of box,
seems to plead for pity.

With the purpose of painting this picture, I started at once for Ghent, after I had given the last touches to a little portrait of my mother which I had painted from a poor pastel made by an itinerant artist who had passed through our village in 1829  This pastel, which possessed no merit as a work of art, has since been lost. What would I not give to recover it ! Little merit as it had, at least it was painted from nature.  Perhaps now, with greater experience, I might be able to disentangle from it what the simple artist saw, and unite with his rude observation my still vivid remembrance of that sacred shade who mingled her life forever with mine in the effusion of her first caresses.

---

## LXV.

DE VIGNE no longer lived in the Rue de la Line. He had built a pretty house, the first fruits of his savings, in the Rue Charles V, a handsome street recently created among the fields.

My friends were shocked at the horrible nature of my subject, and at my intention of painting it life-size. This experiment had, in fact, scarcely any precedent. Courbet had not yet revealed himself.

And then was I capable of executing it ?

Evidently not !

What need to undertake so horrible a subject ?

No matter.  I put on a bold face.  Why should I take the sentimentalism of the vulgar into consideration ?

Was I not one of the people ?  Had we not just overthrown all tyranny ?

I set to work on my picture, then, with ardor, with-

out listening to the remonstrances of my friends.   In
vain De Vigne made me observe that I was exaggerating the expression, that my coloring, through my efforts
to make it dramatic, was coarse and muddy; in vain
the artists of the place said among themselves that it
was painted all *with one color*.   I put the last touch to it,
and then bravely signed my name.

Strange power of contrast; while my imagination
was plunged among these tenebrous shadows, the gentle
daughter of the house would often glide to my side with
frightened eyes whenever any errand chanced to call
her to her father's studio.

She passed silently and seriously.   There was no
more dancing her on my knees.

She was now twelve years old.   Strange and mysterious emotions were agitating her.   At times she would
burst into fits of laughter which she could not control,
and which ended in a torrent of apparently causeless
tears.

She was the first in her class in all her studies, and
would tell charming little stories full of unconscious
drolleries.   She was still a child of the Middle Ages.
Her first words on returning from school at midday
were always, " I am so hungry! "   The hunger-pang
of a little growing angel.

## LXVI.

I BECAME more intimate with Delalleau every day.
In the spring of 1849 we hired together a studio and
two little rooms under the roof, at No. 53 Rue Notre-
Dame-des-Champs.   I saw recently, with regret, that
this house had been rebuilt.

The moderateness of the price—350 francs—and the neighborhood of the Luxembourg, had decided our choice.

I was alone there in the beginning. Delalleau was in the Pas-de-Calais, taking sketches in the neighborhood of Hesdin, his native place. He wrote me letters from there that were every day more and more enthusiastic, in which politics were mingled with the raptures produced in his mind by the beautiful scenery of Artois.

My picture, which I called "Want and Despair," was at the Tuileries, where the exhibition was to be held.

I had learned with inexpressible delight, through an indiscretion on the part of L. D——, my door-keeper of the Louvre, at this time attached to the service of the *Salon*, that it had been accepted. He acquainted me with all that passed there. My picture was hung in the Orangery, on the wall fronting the quay. I went to see from the outside the precise spot where it must be hanging.

As to the effect it produced, I could not form to myself any exact idea. While I was painting it, it had appeared to me every day under a different aspect, according to the weather or my mood.

What I saw oftenest in it was my vision of the night. Surely it must express what I had so clearly seen. And then the good D—— had prophesied wonders in regard to it.

This state of anxious suspense lasted six entire weeks!

And when I say that during all this time I did not sleep, it is not a figure of speech. I did not sleep for a single instant. I tried in vain baths, opium, and various other remedies recommended by friends of mine who were students at the School of Medicine.

This state of things had disordered my stomach. I felt some symptoms which alarmed me for a time, for around me, as in every other quarter of Paris, cholera was raging. The thought of the plague did not serve to enliven my hours of sleeplessness. What if I should have the misfortune to fall a victim to it before the opening of the *Salon !*

It came at last, this long-wished for day! Delalleau had returned. We hurried to the Orangery. From the moment of our entrance, I perceived from afar those wretched figures, melancholy and gray, too well-known, though so different from those I had seen in my vision. In vain Delalleau declared that the painting was full of energy, that the vigor of its coloring and design made the pictures around seem weak. I saw that my tragic vision of the night would have done better to wait for a less inexpert interpreter.

Later on, this picture was rolled up and hidden away in a damp corner of the studio. When I went to unroll it, it fell to pieces. In fine, five or six newspapers had mentioned it, and I was not altogether dissatisfied with my *début.*

This was not the last of my attempts, however, in this lugubrious line. I thought of a composition more hor-rible still—"Hunger." This latter picture was exhib-ited at Paris in 1850, and afterward at Ghent and Brus-sels, where it obtained some degree of success.

It still exists, but in a deplorable condition. It is the common fate of all large first paintings to be rolled up, and put away in some corner to make room for others. Mine had already suffered in consequence of this treat-ment when I presented it to the Museum of Arras, where an ignorant picture-restorer finished the work of destruction by repairing the canvas in such a manner that it seems to have as many waves in it as a sea in a storm.

## LXVII.

WERE it not for the dark track left by the cholera this year, 1849, would have been a happy one, especially in comparison with my recent misfortunes. I painted with ardor, and, however imperfect my works might be, I created. And creation is happiness.

The painting "Want and Despair," still hanging on the wall, and that of "Hunger," resting on the easel, did not tend, it is true, to give a cheerful air to the studio, somewhat gloomy in itself, and where some rough sketches brought back by Delalleau from Artois were the only cheerful notes.

But when we emerged from its gray light in our hours of rest, the sun seemed to shine all the more brightly in the Garden of Marie de Medicis, a few steps away, where he darted his arrows among the foliage of the beautiful chestnut trees, and lighted up with vivid flames the pomegranate blossoms. How beautiful this garden was then and how happy we were in it, our somber visions locked safely in behind our studio door.

For Delalleau, who was so gay, also painted gloomy pictures.

Notwithstanding his rage for politics, he astonished us by the rapid progress he made. He was now engaged on a picture which Théophile Gautier, in the next *Salon*, praised highly, "A Convoy of Hungarian Prisoners" crossing the steppes under the conduct of some Austrian soldiers.

It showed deep feeling, some originality, and a true dramatic sense. I do not know where this picture, his first and best one, now is.

It was at this time that we began to give our attention to painting the figure in the open air.

Yes, it was in the hard and cold light of this gloomy studio that we dreamed of the dazzling splendors of diffused light.

The germ of this idea was due to a new acquaintance who had lately become an habitual visitor to our studio—Eugene Gluck.

I had become acquainted with him at the restaurant where I dined; he always sat at the same table, one near mine, and one day we entered into conversation, *à propos* of a street organ which was playing the air of Gastibelza outside the door in so dismal a *tremolo* that I fancied I could see the quivering lips of Ribera's wonderful " St. Bartholomew " flayed alive, which was then in our Spanish gallery, where there were also many other remarkable paintings of which our younger artists have no knowledge.

I could not help telling my neighbor of this absurd fancy, in which he recognized the painter. He acknowledged that he was a painter himself, and with that absolute trustfulness which is the charm of youth, we soon became friends.

He had had in the Exhibition, also in the Orangery, and facing " Want and Despair," a little picture, " A Roman Battle," in the style of Guignet. We must have seen each other, therefore, since, unluckily, we had both watched our pictures there.

He often came to our studio.

His thoughts were greatly occupied by certain grand effects of local color without shade, which he had observed in some old tapesteries, in certain specimens of Gothic art, and even in the works of Paul Veronese.

He had observed, too, that objects in the street are also lighted in this broad, clear, simple manner, and he had remarked, besides, how favorable this lighting, that no vexatious accident can interfere with, is to the sum of the values, and also what style and charm the character of the face receives from this unity.

And Gluck was the first to call this *outdoor* painting.

---

## LXVIII.

I DINED at the restaurant of a wine merchant named Comeau. This was a house that stood alone, in the middle of the Place St.-Germain-des-Prés, facing the church.

Baudry lived on the sixth floor of this house exposed to all the winds of heaven.

In front of it stood a very tall pole, which towered above the roofs of the neighboring houses, and which served as a beacon and point of observation for the opening of the Rue Bonaparte, a work which had just begun.

A new-comer in Drolling's studio had been made believe that this pole had been erected in Baudry's honor, because he had taken the second *Prix de Rome*.

I went every day, then, to Comeau's, to spend there the eighteen or twenty sous which my dinner usually cost me.

The summer of 1849 was a magnificent one, and it was under the light of a brilliant and unclouded sun that I saw the long line of hearses, constantly swelled by fresh victims to the terrible scourge, filing through the streets.

Sometimes there were not hearses enough to supply the demand, and carts were employed in the lugubrious service of carrying the dead.

In the end people grew accustomed to this, and ceased to take any notice of it. But an indefinable gloom filled the soul, and seemed to darken the rays of the sun, as if they came through a black crape veil. The recollection of this time comes back to me like a time of eclipse, where I see the red faces of the undertaker's men, unfailingly gay, flash out laughing.

In the streets one felt, as on a battle-field, always in danger of being struck down without warning, as if there were more safety to be found within the walls of a house.

On one of those days, as I was walking at noon to the restaurant, my eyes fixed absently on Baudry's pole, my thoughts lost in revery, I suddenly cried " Louis! " and we rushed into each other's arms.

Louis, whom I had thought at Courrières, was there before me in the Place St.-Germain-des-Prés ! It was indeed his sunny blonde head. (Those who remember him at the age of twenty know that he resembled the Apollo in the " Olympus " of Rubens.)  It was he.

I took him with me into Comeau's, praising the excellence of the haricot to be had there, and we sat down to dine.

My brother said he thought this famous ragout too greasy, and ate nothing but an artichoke *à la vinaigrette*. In reality, the pleasure of our meeting had taken away his appetite.

As for me, I swallowed, without knowing what I was eating, artichoke and haricot together, talking all the time with my mouth full, asking and answering questions.

The cholera had been appalling down there too—I had not heard it.  Now it was nearly over; hardly any serious cases.  The sweating-sickness—oh, yes ! plenty of cases of that—such a one was dead, and such another. And such another.  Some one else had been so much afraid that he had remained the whole time in bed, although he was not sick.  My uncle had been terribly distressed at so much misery; they had gone together every day to see that the sick wanted for nothing—to encourage them—to restore their confidence—to prevent people flying from the place.  In the village everything is noticed; every one knows every one.

Then, having satisfied our curiosity, having talked about Émile, our dear little *pioupiou*, then in garrison at Romans, who had just been made a corporal, we gave ourselves up to the pleasure of being together, letting our thoughts wander where they would.

We went for a walk in the streets, turning our steps wherever chance directed, talking ceaselessly, without stopping to think whether our words were silly or not. We called this "talking our little nonsense."  Indeed, it was nonsense without head or tail.  We rattled on in this way, as the birds twitter because they must give utterance to their happiness in some form, nothing more.  But as this happiness has something of delirium in it, it would be illogical to follow the rules of common sense in giving expression to it.

It was, on a small scale, the fine disorder of the ode, including every measure, mixing *patois* and French, affected conceits and foolish solemn phrases, heroic declamations, pious and earnest aspirations, puns in prose and verse, scraps of crazy sentences, all of which, nonsensical or droll, expressed the joy of having near one a beloved being, of knowing that all that either possesses belongs to the other also, that neither has a feeling which does not find an echo in the other's heart, of being conscious, in short, that the hearts of both are lightened by this exchange of tenderness; and is it not this that makes the birds twitter?

And meantime, what of the cholera?  We had forgotten all about it.

Next day we went to Meudon, Paris not being in

harmony with the state of our feelings.  We found this place also too noisy for us.

It was the *fête*-day of the village.

When we arrived there we saw a cruel thing.  Some peasants, the greater number of them under the influence of wine, were gathered in animated groups around a goose suspended from a sort of osier basket, out of which hung his neck and head like the mouth-piece of a clarionet.  One of the rustics, blindfolded and with a sword in his hand, was describing circles in the air with his arms, and, feeling his way with all sorts of precautions, which he tried to make as comical as possible, was advancing toward the feathered victim.

When he thought himself near the desired spot, he gave a violent blow in the air with the sword, which made him stagger, and loud bursts of laughter followed.

We left those people to their amusement, and took an ascending road to our left, walking straight on.

The ascent was a little steep, and the sun burned our necks, but the air was so pure, and the verdure so fresh !

We entered a wood.

Soon we felt the pangs of hunger.  We came very opportunely across a keeper's lodge, which on *fête*-days was transformed into a restaurant for straggling excursionists.  We espied a leafy bower with benches and a worm-eaten table inside.

Ah ! how pleasant it was sitting there !

On the rising ground before us was the pretty wood of Meudon.  Our chatter, which we left off for a moment to take breath, began again with more animation than ever, this time accompanied by real birds' notes.

They served us, under the name of veal *au petit pois*, the best dish I have ever eaten in my life.

And not you, Romanée Conti, nor you, Vannes or ·

Chambertin, once the pride of the paternal cellar, could equal the thin wine we drank here.

We drank a little too much of it.

After the coffee and a good pipe, we plunged into the wood, where brilliant bursts of sunshine streamed through the branches of the trees, lighting up a little path, capricious as the bounds of a goat. What an intensity of life we felt!

But what is that we see yonder—that dark pink and blue object? We draw near. Oh, ravishing sight!

On a knoll a young girl lay sleeping, like a rustic Antiope. She lay there, looking cool under the furtive caresses of the sun, with closed eyes and parted lips, while the sunlight, sifting through the waving branches of an oak, flickered on her face. The play of the light and shade gave an appearance of motion to her immovable form. A thousand pearly tints trembled on the sun-lighted face where the effulgence of the azure sky blended with the golden and rosy gleams cast by the glowing herbage.

Less bold than the satyrs of Coreggio or Titian, we admired her from a respectful distance.

Then with dazzled eyes we took the road leading to Meudon and continued our chatter.

We sat down by the wayside, near the station. Night was approaching.

The setting sun shot his fiery arrows, spreading out like a fan, through the branches of the acacias. Laden with perfume, the peaceful breath of sleeping Nature came to us through the blossom-laden boughs.

———————

## LXIX.

The Exhibition of 1851 was held in the Palais-Royal, in the court-yard of which a large wooden building had been erected.

My picture was hung in the Square Hall, so high that it could scarcely be seen.

Courbet, who had not been much noticed at the preceding *Salon*, attracted a great deal of attention on this occasion with his " Interment at Ornans."

The singular power manifested in this half-tragic, half-grotesque picture, gave rise to the liveliest discussions. It was bitterly criticised; the red faces of the beadles especially were almost universally found fault with. But it was impossible to deny that here was a painter who showed, along with his contempt for public opinion, a rare force of expression. This picture seemed to breathe a funereal horror that was Shakespearian in its power.

At this same Exhibition appeared " The Sower," of Millet, his first effort in the rural *genre*. This picture, which was hung too high, was scarcely noticed by the general public, but the connoisseurs in art were much struck by it. They found in it a fullness of action and a broadness of conception, which made it stand out in bold relief from the pictures around it. When I say *rural genre*, however, in speaking of this composition, I do not mean to say that we have here a page from nature ; it is a sort of allegorical representation of agriculture. Millet has seen this peasant through the medium of his epic visions, still influenced by his recollections of the classic school. The sower has, himself, the consciousness of the majesty of his attitude ; he is declamatory.

The effect of the picture is black. Millet has not yet

found the mysterious charm, acquired later on in his silent walks through the fields, which will bestow a beauty even on ugliness.

---

## LXX.

AFTER the Exhibition I went again to Ghent, for the purpose of painting a picture for the church of Courrières—a "Baptism of Christ."

I had longed to find myself again in the midst of the pleasant Flemish life, of which I cherished so many tender recollections.

I found De Vigne painting a "Marriage in the Middle Ages," and De Winne who, like ourselves, had taken up subjects of a not very amusing nature, working at a "Monk Consoling a Dying Woman."

I exhibited my picture "Hunger" at a small exhibition, and I must say that it produced so powerful an impression on some pretty women who were looking at it as to draw tears from them, a thing which touched me greatly.

I was happy to find myself once more among my excellent friends, and I set to work on my picture with confidence. If I had thought it an easy task, I soon found myself greatly mistaken. I sought in vain after the harmony I had dreamed of, and found it impossible to fix on canvas the face which, in my imagination, was so beautiful. I began it all over again twenty times. I became disheartened.

Was this solely because of my humiliating failure, or was there some other cause for it? A moral disquietude took possession of me.

I had dark fits of spleen, during which I wandered about alone. I chose for these solitary walks the deserted streets of the suburbs. I think the weather had something to do with my sadness, for I have a recollection of a leaden sun, and a high wind whirling about clouds of dust that blinded the eyes. I have since experienced weather as disagreeable, however, without feeling the same discomfort.

At about eleven o'clock, before dinner, I would leave the studio and go down to the parlor, where my little favorite was practicing her pieces for the conservatory, with abrupt movements of the head at the difficult passages, the elbows sticking out a little, the shoulderblades slightly projecting.

She was now fourteen, but she still wore short dresses. Age of bewitching awkwardness, when the rounded curves of the child are lengthening out into the sharp angles of growing girlhood!

Her dark eyes, full of a serious candor, but with something mysterious in their depths, no longer sent forth those flashes of gentle gayety which had so often rejoiced my heart in the long past days when she would clasp her little arms around my neck as I danced her on my knees.

I took an unflagging interest in her studies, and besieged her with my counsels. My earnestness frightened her; she had responded to it by marks of impatience that I had misinterpreted, taking them for aversion. I had thereupon scolded the little ingrate. She had melted into tears, but her attitude had not changed.

But after all, what rights had I over her?

Why was I displeased when I saw that she was more familiar with De Winne, whom she called simply "Winne," than with me whom she called "Monsieur Jules"? She had an unquestionable right to prefer him to me. And then what reason had I to suppose that she hated me?

In a trip that we had just made, accompanied by her mother, to Antwerp, had she not been gay and playful with me?

And was it not very disagreeable of me to be forever preaching to her?

And when I brought her home flowers, or other trifles, from my Sunday walks, she accepted them amiably.

One day I went to the conservatory to hear her play; she played well, and, in my haste to congratulate her, I went to the staircase landing to meet her.

She soon made her appearance, accompanied by her little friends. I advanced toward her, but seeing me thus unexpectedly, she turned her head aside, and walked on in silence, looking pale and confused.

"Decidedly," I said to myself, "that girl has no heart!"

A few days later, however, I saw her returning from the school after the distribution of the prizes. She had seven or eight wreaths in her hands, and as many more handsome gilt books; and, far from being gay, she was weeping bitterly. She had just bade farewell to her teachers, whom she was leaving forever. She had a heart for others, then! And when I left Ghent I took with me a counter-drawing, taken secretly from a portrait I had made of her charming face.

My picture had made scarcely any progress during all this time—this impracticable head of Christ that I was always beginning over again! Delalleau, whom I neglected, overwhelmed me with reproaches in letters eight pages long, in which he vaunted his own valor, and in which such phrases as the following were thrown at me: "Yesterday I went to Versailles, and I thought of you as I looked at the leaden turtles, which are good for nothing but to serve as water-spouts."

At last I departed, leaving my unfinished " Baptism
of Christ " and the dream, full of mysterious uncertain-
ties, that haunted me for the following year.

---

## LXXI.

IT was now 1852.   De Winne, having received a
small pension from the Government, had come to Paris
to pay me a visit.

We occupied together a rather large apartment, formerly used as a bookseller's shop, at No. 85 Boulevard de Montparnasse.   We divided it, by means of a
large curtain of lutestring, into a studio and a bedroom.
Two small iron bedsteads, costing eight francs, and a
few tabourets and easels comprised all the furniture.
Gluck shared the studio with us.   Our windows opened
on a little garden planted with trees where (and this
will serve to give some idea of its solitude) we one day
caught a snake.

The whole cost us two hundred francs a year.   We
managed ourselves our housekeeping, disorderly enough,
as may be imagined.   Our abode was at once humble
and gay.   A house of the time of Louis XVI, with a
pediment, of a single story, verdure in the court, verdure
in the street.

We soon found congenial companions in the neighborhood.   Brion, the family of Auguste Fauvel, Tabar,
Traviès, Dock, Bartholdi, Schutzemberger, and later,
Nazon, Gérôme, and Toulmouche.   We worked hard,
and our four walls were soon covered with verdant
sketches.   No more lugubrious subjects !

For we were digging away at outdoor painting.

The station of Montparnasse was close at hand.   In

the morning we set out for Clamart, Meudon, or Chaville, carrying our panels, our boxes, and our umbrellas, joyous and bold, as if we were going to conquer the world. They might have talked to us in vain of the studio and the school.  From the outside of our coach we saw the houses and the monuments of Paris fly past, and it was not unwittily that I compared the small, smooth dome of the observatory to the bald head of a member of the Institute.  Each day Nature revealed new secrets to us, and our eyes, eager to search into her mysteries, found ever new delights.

How many harmonies, long vaguely dreamed of, did our work suddenly reveal to us!

There were slopes of green and pink heather, landslips of red earth, lighted by the beams of the setting sun, while from dazzling breaks in the sky showers of light poured into the dark solitude of the underwood covered with dead leaves, giving it the dappled appearance of a deer-skin.  There were, too, interminable white walls, on which the lights and shadows danced capriciously, running zigzag along the forest through pleasant vegetation, their base hidden among the thick leaves of the nettles, and, shaded by leafy oaks, were sunny meadows starred with yellow and blue flowers, where at times a donkey grazed peacefully, while his cart, its shafts raised in the air, rested by the roadside, and finally, far away in the blue distance, like an ocean crowded with motionless vessels, were the broad zones, pierced with a thousand gleaming points, of the great city.

Enchanting suburbs of Paris, we thought there was nothing in the world to equal you!  Ah! if my poor Courrières had only contained a quarter of your marvels!

It was still the suburbs, but with a mixture of rusticity, that we found at St. Nom la Bretèche, where we spent some time, and where I conceived my first " Return of the Harvesters." Delalleau came to join us here. These where the last hours that we were to spend in community. The difference in our characters, growing more marked every day, rendered life in common difficult. I saw him again occasionally at the exhibitions, in which he took part several times, but without ever again meeting the semi-success obtained by his " Hungarians." He had the baffled expression characteristic of men who have been disappointed in their ambitions. He had been so confident of success !  He could never recover from the painful surprise with which he found he had been left behind on the road.  This is what one of our comrades, the now celebrated Vandremer, said to me, not long since.

Delalleau made an imprudent marriage and retired to a little village of Artois, named Lumbres.  He died there in obscurity, in 1865, at the age of thirty-nine, after a long and painful illness, of a malady induced perhaps, by secret chagrins.

Poor friend !  He sleeps there under the shadow of a weeping ash, and so utterly forgotten that the mildew of the lichens corroding the stone  has effaced his name. This was the end of so many dreams of fame !

---

## LXXII.

Unhappily it was impossible for me to execute my picture " The Return of the Harvesters " in the country with real peasants for models.  I had no study except at Paris.  I was obliged to be satisfied, therefore, with professional models.

Besides, I could stay no longer in the inn of *Père la Joie* at La Bretèche, for the exclusive diet of pork, to which we had been confined for the last six weeks, and which we had at every meal and under every form, had kindled a veritable fire in my digestive apparatus. I was for a long time ill from a chronic inflammation, augmented by the anxieties of a task beyond my strength and the absolute neglect of hygienic rules. The first half of the winter was exceedingly rainy, and I remember that I would arrive at our little cook-shop in the Barrier Du Main with my shoes running water.

Notwithstanding all this, I painted away desperately at my picture, now wildly hopeful of success, now utterly discouraged.

Completely exhausted, I was obliged at last to interrupt my work and go to Courrières to recuperate. I came back a month before the time for sending my picture to the *Salon*, with somewhat restored health. I resumed my task with fresh ardor, succeeded by the same alternations of satisfaction and disgust. Artists know how enervating this is.

The picture is finished. My comrades come to see it. Naturally, they think it superb. Tabar himself, the best artist among my friends, admires it warmly. "I see your picture already in a corner of the '*Salon* of Honor.'" De Winne, who thought my picture a masterpiece, said to me : "At times its warm sunset lights seemed to me, too, real light. Courage ! Let us hope for a success."

We hurry to the *Salon*.

Yes, I may hope for a good place. And then, the excellent Merlé, the director of the orchestra at the Opéra Comique, a native of Ghent and a compatriot of De Winne, had brought one of the inspectors who had charge of the hanging to see my picture, and he had praised it highly.

The exhibition was held in the Faubourg Poissonnière.

We reach the hall. I look for my picture. Impossible to find it. I find my inspector engaged in a violent dispute with Philippe Rousseau. This is not the time to choose to speak to him.

Artists, anxious as myself, are running hither and thither.

Animated groups are gathered before "The Young Village Girls" and "The Bather" of Courbet ("Look at the bather! What a figure!"); before Hamon's "My Lost Sister," "The Malaria" of Hebert, "The Skaters" of my friend Brion ("Bravo, Brion!"), "The Peasants" of Millet ("Very peculiar, that Millet").

But where is my "Harvesters"? De Winne has found his picture—"Ruth and Naomi" ("Not bad, a little pale").

Rousseau has released my inspector. I approach the latter. He is not in a good humor.

"My faith," he says, "I have done all I could; but you know there are so many *protégés!*"

And he points out to me my poor "Harvesters," hung under the ceiling. Impossible to recognize in this melancholy group, looking still more melancholy hanging up there, the gay peasants I had pictured to myself with that sunset flush that now seems to me a flush of shame.

I think I was scarcely more good-tempered than Philippe Rousseau, for my inspector gets rid of me in a sufficiently brutal fashion.

"Very well!" I say. "I know whom I shall appeal to."

And I went to the Champs Élysées to the house of the Count de Morny, to whom our deputy had recommended me.

"Can I see M. de Morny?" I asked the *concierge*.

"Have you a card of audience?"

"No."

"Then, monsieur, the count will not receive you!"

I was horribly disappointed. If any one had just then been able to prove to me that my picture was bad, I should have at once grown calm. But I had seen so many daubs paraded on the line! Oh, what injustice! Then base thoughts entered my mind. Returning home I stopped at the house of a man whom I occasionally met, but for whom I did not entertain any great sympathy. He was insincere. I recounted my discomfiture to him.

"Ah, you do not know the Belgians," he said to me with a chuckle. "Merlé and De Winne have played you this trick, my dear fellow. I know them, these Belgians!"

And in his bad French—he was a Fleming—he added:

"I can see peeping out of them the cloven foot!"

I ought at once to have given this odious person his answer. But no! I had hell in my heart, and I began to suspect the good, the generous De Winne, whom, until then, I had regarded as a brother! I had just reached home, my mind agitated by these vile suspicions, when this excellent friend came in.

"What have you been doing with yourself since morning?" he said to me.

I did not answer.

"Why, what is the matter with you," he said, with an anxious expression in his eyes.

"Forgive me, Liévin!" I cried, "I have done you an injustice!"

And I threw myself into his arms, and begged his pardon with tears in my eyes.

## LXXIII.

IN this *Salon* of 1853 there was an admirable picture of Daubigny, representing the margin of a cool, clear pond.

There was also a little landscape of Français, full of poetic feeling—an Italian meadow with a straight ditch and a black cow beside it. I stood for a long time, plunged in a profound reverie, before this gem. The time of day was so well expressed in it that, as it was the hour at which I was accustomed to breakfast, I felt (and this is literally true) a sensation of hunger take possession of me, while I refreshed my eyes with the sight of this beautiful still water, lighted by the sun shining through the reeds.

Millet made his appearance for the first time with real peasants, painted from nature, and not from the imagination, like the too solemn " Sower."

His picture represented a group of peasants in the field, whose dinner has just been brought to them. I have never again seen this picture, which was not included in the exhibition of the works of this painter.

It was wonderful. It produced a singular impression upon me.

This painting, baked in the sun, so to say, austere and earthy, expressed with marvelous effect the overpowering heat that burns the fields in the dog-days, a dull glow where breathe, stifle, and sweat horny-handed beings with knotty joints, thick lips, eyes vaguely defined in their sockets, outlines as simple as those of Egyptian art, and wearing clothes like sheaths, with baggy elbows and knees — beings of a stupid and savagely solemn aspect.

His enemies saw in it the glorification of stupidity.

It was indeed a singular picture, at first view. The gray tone of the wheat seemed to diffuse itself through the red atmosphere that, growing thicker in the distance, enveloped everything in its monochromatic waves, under the livid light of the leaden sky.

Was it sublime, or was it horrible? The public were startled by it, and waited, as usual, for the recognized critics to give the watchword. It was true they were not charmed by the picture, but they did not give way to the hilarity they had not hesitated to express before some recent disgraceful specimens of art. They felt the influence of a power, they felt themselves in the presence of a great creation, of a strange vision of an almost prehistoric character.

This feeling of absolute oneness with the soil is not at all that of our peasants of the north, but it is occasionally to be met with among those of La Beauce.

Millet has since given us many works of a higher style of art, in which he attains character and sentiment even with ugliness. Every one knows them. He has gradually added to his pictures an element wanting in them in the beginning—depth of atmosphere.

With a plow standing in a rugged field where a few slender thistles are growing, two or three tones and an execution awkward and woolly, he can stir the depths of the soul and interpret the infinite.

A solitary, at times a sublime genius, he has made of a sheepfold lighted by the rays of the rising Moon, mysterious as the eternal problem she presents, a little picture life-like and pure as a work of Phidias, unfathomable as a Rembrandt, but let others beware how they imitate it!

Because Millet has created masterpieces, depicting man degraded by poverty even to the effacement of his individuality, we have not therefore the right to

15

deny the exalted, the divine beauty of these master-pieces.

The wretched beings depicted by Millet touch us profoundly because he loved them profoundly, and because he has raised them to the higher regions inhabited by his genius, which has invested them with its own dignity.

But they have nothing in common with vulgar ugliness. Beauty will always remain the highest aim of art.

Admiration should not degenerate into fetichism, and those who best comprehend the genius of Millet, will take good care how they counsel others to imitate him.

In the first place, is it in truth ugliness that Millet has depicted? Is even that "Man with the Hoe" so ugly, who awakens our sympathy by something inexpressibly mysterious and venerable?

Many of his works prove that his harsh and austere ideal did not disdain the softened expression of a more serene art.

I had occasion to discuss this question with an artist with whom chance brought me into contact at the grand distribution of prizes of the International Exposition of 1867.

We spoke of the intolerance of certain short-sighted art critics who refuse the artist the right to give himself up to the inspirations of his originality, or who, judging every work of art by one common standard, would like to make them all conform to their favorite type, as if the types of nature were not as diversified as the forms of its interpreter, art. "Why should not painters have the right to choose," said this artist, "one, the rough potato, the other, the morning-glory that twines itself among the corn?" He went on to develop this doctrine in a clearer and more forcible manner than I can do justice to.

*This artist was François Millet.*

## LXXIV.

I QUITTED Paris in a state of extreme depression caused by my anxiety regarding my picture and by the state of my health, which still continued bad.

I had a longing for rest and retirement.

My excellent uncle who, with Louis's help, provided for the wants of the family, had built a little studio for me, at my desire, in the garden of the brewery.

I returned to Courrières, then, with the intention of working there.

I began a picture.

A study made at Ghent of the ruins of the Abbey of St. Bavon served as a motive for a "Gypsy Camp" that I composed.  A remnant of romanticism still remained with me.

I worked at this picture in a somewhat desultory manner, my attention distracted by my surroundings, by the beauty of rustic nature, that began to awaken in my heart a thousand recollections of my childhood.

All the earliest sensations of this dawn of existence were renewed in me, producing a delicious intoxication of the senses refreshed by the free pure air.

I lived again in memory those days when I was awakened by the song of the birds in the morning when the sunrise lighted up the room with a rosy flame that grew paler and paler in the light of an opal sky, while the lowing of the cows, the grating of the barn doors on their hinges, and the crowing of the cocks, coming softened through the morning mist, announced that rural life had recommenced.

Again I stretched myself, overpowered by a sweet languor, on the grass in the cool shade where the very air was luminous, where the profound silence of noon seemed deeper from the buzzing of the insects that flew swiftly past unseen in the midday glare.

Intoxicated by the perfumes and the harmonies of nature, I gave myself up to reverie, spending all my time in aimless sauntering.

Away with the studio with its livid stream of light falling from overhead, dull and leaden, through the dazzling glass of the skylight, on those poor pallid gypsies grouped in their dark ruin around the witch stirring their broth over the fire, to the sound of her muttered incantations. I have not the courage even to look at them again.

I had sketched them, however, with some spirit, from little clay manikins that I had draped in secret, showing them to no one, not even to my brothers, who had come occasionally to look through the keyhole to get a glimpse of them. The day on which I had opened the studio door to my brothers, however, judging the picture sufficiently far advanced to show to them, I was disappointed to see how slight an impression it produced.

After that the poor gypsies had languished on the neglected easel.

But the most delightful moment of the day was when in the evening, after supper, we smoked our pipes, sitting in our chairs tipped back against the wall, and let our gaze wander out into the road, where the evening mists were rising, wavering in the still heated air.

Everything floated in a white transparent mist, out of which rose, one by one, the sunburned faces of the peasants returning slowly from the fields, walking with heavy step, or mounted on top of the heaps of wheat or the bundles of grass in their spring-carts.

The somber landscape, where a few rays of light still lingered, stood out with wonderful effect against the saffron sky irradiated by the crimson flames fading into darkness behind the thatched roofs of the cottages.

Tall dark peasant girls passed by, upon whose tangled locks the last sunset rays lingered like an aureole, their shadowy figures outlined in light. In the somber and mysterious gloom of twilight, they seemed more beautiful and more dignified, carrying their sickles, on which the cold light of the upper sky gleamed like moonlight.

A gentle breeze at times set their well-worn garments in motion.

And I felt my heart melt within me in delightful transports of tender emotion.

Oh, joy! Joy of the eyes, joy of the soul! Reconciliation of the individual with himself in the out-pouring of universal love! I luxuriated in all the effluence of life—of nature—the effervescent life of plants wet with the morning dew, the waving of the grain in the morning breeze, the rapturous song of the larks heralding the dawn; flaming poppies, modest corn-flowers, mysterious distances fading into the peaceful sky, odors that waken ecstatic thrills, intoxicating emanations, radiance of the free pure light, splendor of rays filtering through the trees and shooting with gold the gray transparence of the sleeping waters! And the intensity of the silence, through which burst from time to time sonorous voices, through which thrilled rustling murmurs. Oh, joy! Joy of nature! joy of existence! Oh, divine charm! Oh, all-bountiful God, revealing thyself to the heart through so many ineffable blessings!

Often I would rise before the first rays of dawn had wakened the dark and sleeping fields.

The streets were silent. Here and there, however, some house would show signs of life; a young woman would open the window, her eyes heavy with sleep, her hair in disorder, half-dressed—delightful glimpses into other lives.  Further on was a child crying, or an old woman scolding.

And I would walk far into the fields, where the manure-heaps smoked beside the herbage wet with dew. The bending wheat sprinkled me with dew as I walked along the narrow foot-path.  Among the mists the willows dropped their tears, while their gray tops caught the light overhead.  Then I re-entered the village, now all bright and awake, where rose, at times, with the blue wreaths of smoke from the chimneys, the sweet, monotonous songs of the young embroiderers.

I returned to the fields to look at the gleaners. There yonder, defined against the sky, was the busy flock, overtopped by the guard.

I watched them as they worked, now running in joyous bands carrying sheaves of golden grain ; now bending over the stubble, closely crowded together.

When I went among them they stopped their work to look at me, smiling and confused, in the graceful freedom of their scanty and ill-assorted garments.

Ah !  I no longer regretted either Clamart or Meudon, and I loved the simple beauty of my native place, that offered itself to me, as Ruth offered herself to Boaz. Yes, I became one with you, O land where my first joys were felt, and thou didst infuse into my soul the tender beauty of thy carnations, the majesty of thy wheat fields, and the mystery of thy marsh, with its motionless waters shaded by ashes swarming with cantharides.  O land of my childhood, to thee have I given my heart, to thee have I dedicated my life !

## LXXV.

ONE day I made a little gleaner pose for me, standing on a flowery bank beside a field of wheat. Her bent face was in shadow, while the sunlight fell on her cap and her shoulders. As I painted her I felt a secret joy.

I can not express the feeling of rapture caused me by the harmony of this dark face, strongly defined against the golden grain among which ran lilac morning-glories, by the warm glow of the earth, the violet reflections of the blue sky, the flowers and the shrubs. All this enchanted me.

I had already sent my "Gypsies" to the Exhibition at Brussels, when one day my brother Louis, coming across this little "Gleaner" in the corner where it had lain forgotten said to me, "Why do you not send this too to the Exhibition?" "That?" I replied, "It is not worth while." And then I had no frame.

My brother persisted, and in the end discovered in the barn an old, tarnished frame that had once inclosed a poor portrait. It was near the expiration of the time of grace allowed in sending pictures. I sent it off at once.

What was my astonishment when, a few days afterward, arriving in Brussels, I found my "Gypsies" badly hung and my "Little Gleaner" on the line in the center of a panel, where it attracted general attention.

---

## LXXVI.

I WAS not completely happy, however ; I suffered in secret. A hidden sentiment often carried me in thought to Ghent, where unconfessed torments held me bound.

I had resolved not to look again at the counter-drawing of the delicate face, and yet how many times did I take it with a trembling hand from the bottom of my drawer !

When, on the 22d of August, 1853, she came to Courrières with her father.

She was now a young lady. I was surprised at the change that had taken place in her countenance. It no longer wore a severe expression. She was so happy to see us !

She expressed herself naïvely. " The nearer we approached," she said, " the more violently did my heart beat."

What tenderness did her ingenuous glance reveal !

Next day she came to me as I was sitting alone, and said these simple words : " I must have often caused you pain; I am very sorry for it. Will you forgive me ? " I kissed her.

Two days afterward we were engaged.

It had come about very simply. I was painting her portrait in the little studio, and when I came to the eyes I stopped, overcome by my emotion, and said to her : " Have you understood me ? " She nodded affirmatively. " Will you be my wife ? " She made the same affirmative sign.

------

## LXXVII.

THE success of my " Little Gleaner " had put me in the humor for work. I thought of a composition which should contain a number of these poor women and little girls and boys who look like flocks of sparrows as they bend over the stubble.

These moving groups that dotted the sun-burned

plain, defined in dark shadow against the sky as they bent in varied attitudes over the earth gathering the ears of grain, filled me with admiration.  Nothing could be more Biblical than this human flock—the sunlight clinging to their floating rags, burning their necks, lighting up the ears of wheat, luminously outlining dark profiles, tracing on the tawny gold of the earth flickering shadows shot with blue reflections from the zenith.

As I looked at this scene full of simple grandeur I thought myself transported to the times of the patriarchs.  And, indeed, is not a scene like this always grand, always beautiful !

I came away feeling as if I had emerged from a bath of light, of which the splendors still pursued me during the night in dazzling visions.

But the more sublime I felt this scene to be the more strongly did I feel my own weakness and my inability to do justice to it.

Was I not like those foolish grasshoppers, also drunk with light, and whose frantic exertions are only the heroism of weakness !  Poor brains, through which, too, flash at night luminous visions.

I began, then, full of ardor, but also without illusion, my first picture of " The Gleaners."

Did I think I was attempting a new thing ?  Not at all.  I even thought that this subject, as old as the poem of Ruth, must have already been handled by many artists.

I was greatly astonished, therefore, when I was afterward told that I had been the first to treat it.  My first picture of " The Gleaners " was painted in 1854 ; the " Gleaners " of Millet was painted in 1857.

I also painted at this time a group of three young girls, and a scene representing men drinking (" The Day after St. Sebastian "), suggested by the customs of the Archers.

I took these three pictures to Paris, and sent them to the building in the Avenue Montagne, where the International Exhibition of 1855 took place.

I confess that I trembled at the thought of this ambitious attempt.

I can see myself standing now, nervous and restless, in the vestibule where the names of the pictures were entered.

I waited for my turn, looking furtively at my poor pictures hanging against the wall in a frightful light, and before which such resplendent pictures were being carried past by porters.

How insignificant they appeared to me, this flock of girls, of whom the guard smoking his pipe seemed to be the melancholy shepherd!

A gentleman draws near, however; a gentleman wearing the ribbon of the Legion of Honor. He leans toward them, he draws back, he approaches them again. Is he interested in them, then?

He sees by my confused air that I must be the painter of the picture, comes to me and says, "Is that yours, young man?" I make an affirmative gesture.

He stretches out his hand to me and says, "It is very good."

And I look gratefully at this stranger whose frank expression makes my heart warm to him.

"And you think, monsieur, that—that my picture will be received?"

"Received! Why, it will have a success, a great success!"

Then somewhat reassured I added, "May I know, monsieur, to whom I have the honor—"

"My name is Alfred Arago."

He was the son of the great Arago! When we parted he already called me "my friend," and six

months later we were to say thee and thou to each
other.

My uncle was exceedingly proud and delighted when,
on my return to Courrières, I related this interview to
him, for he cherished a warm admiration for the name
rendered illustrious by the brothers Arago in literature
and science as well as in the annals of patriotism.

But at the end of a few days, having heard nothing
further of my picture, my apprehensions returned, so impossible did it seem to me that I should succeed in obtaining a place in that great exhibition.

At last I received a letter from the worthy door-
keeper of the Louvre, whom you know, and who was
again attached to the Exhibition.

It contained these simple words (oh, the power of a
few words !) that delighted my eyes more than a Parnas-
sian strophe would have done : "Your pictures have
been received, and have been greatly admired. The
picture of ' *The Gleaners* ' *especially has dazzled the jury.*"

---

## LXXVIII.

I OBTAINED the predicted success at the International Exposition ; my pictures were awarded medals
and were sold.

My little studio at the brewery had been only provisional. My uncle had it pulled down, and caused
another, of large proportions, to be built for me, for, full
of confidence, I had conceived a more important composition than "The Gleaners," "The Blessing of the
Wheat."

At the same time that I painted this picture I painted another also, called "Setting out for the Fields."

At this epoch exhibitions took place every two years.

While these pictures were at the studio in the Boulevard Montparnasse, where Gluck still worked, many persons had come to see them.

Among these were some celebrated artists—Gérôme, Corot, Belly, and others. One morning a man of tall stature, with a somewhat rustic air, knocked at the door of the studio. " I am Troyon," he said. " I have heard about your picture and I would like to see it."

It may be imagined with what haste I drew forward a chair and asked him to be seated.

He looked for a long, long time at the canvas without uttering a word. This silence disquieted me and I ventured to ask his opinion. He rose abruptly, grasped my hand, and expressed his satisfaction to me warmly.

And when I urged him to point out the faults of the picture for my future guidance, he answered : " Yes, it has faults, but they are faults that you will correct yourself of soon enough, and perhaps it would be all the better if you did not."

I awaited, then, with confidence, the opening of the *Salon.*

But when the day arrived, my friends had to look for the picture which they had thought was to occupy so prominent a place.

I had myself some trouble in discovering it, hung as it was, ten or twelve feet from the ground, above a rather large picture of Belly. A few dark silhouettes indicated the figures, and an indistinct patch of yellow the background. I was dismayed.

This was the great success that my fellow-artists had predicted.

In a state of nervousness that overcame all timidity, I hurried to Count Nieuwerkerke, whose tall figure I caught sight of towering above the crowd. "Count," I cried, "they have hung my picture shamefully!"

He answered me very gently: "I can do nothing in the matter; I have had no part in the hanging. I am sorry for this, for your sake, but you know how it is— every one can not be on the line."

He turned away, then paused a moment as if in thought, and returning said, "Where is your picture?"

I conducted the handsome and amiable superintendent to the place where my picture hung.

"Ah, it is that procession," he said, giving me his hand. "I know it, I know it." And calling the chief of the wardens, he said to him: "How is it that this picture is hung so high, when it was on the line yesterday?" "It is because Prince Napoleon wanted that place for a *protégé*." "Well, let it be taken down the next time there is a change made in the hanging."

Then he addressed me again in these terms: "Will you sell me your procession? I will give you five thousand francs for it; it is not much, but it is for the Luxembourg."

What happiness!

I thanked the superintendent warmly, and, descending the grand staircase four steps at a time, ran to the Café Durand (which has since witnessed the transports of many another conqueror) to write this amazing news to my good uncle.

I have never been either at the Tuileries or at Compiègne, nor have I ever been intimate with M. de Nieuwerkerke, but I must here say that he was a true gentleman. He knew, too, how to rid himself of the crowd, eager for notoriety, who too often obstruct the paths of official life.

I had another proof of his goodness after the distribution of prizes in 1867, when I expressed my surprise to him at my promotion to the grade of officer, which had been unsolicited—which I myself had never thought of asking for, and of which he had not even spoken to me at the beginning of the session.

All he said was : "But you are pleased, are you not ? "

At the general rehanging my " Blessing of the Wheat " was lowered, and the later visitors at the *Salon* saw it in a good light ; but the newspapers had, for the most part, finished their notices, and I was not really conscious of the success of my picture until the next *Salon*, in 1859, when the press accorded unanimous praise to my paintings there exhibited.

<hr>

## LXXIX.

WHILE my " Blessing of the Wheat " was waiting to be done justice to at the next rehanging, Paul Baudry triumphed over all the line with five or six pictures of greater or less importance—" Fortune and the Child," " The Punishment of a Vestal," " Primavera," " Leda," and some portraits.

His success was brilliant.

Edmond About, also at that time in the dawn of his fame, dedicated to him the volume which he published on the *Salon* of 1857.  They had contracted a friendship at Rome close as that between two brothers, confiding to each other their youthful enthusiasm and their dreams of glory.  At the first page of this extended review, About affectionately addresses the painter thus : " Pauliccio mio ! "

But, however merited his success, Baudry disappointed somewhat those of us who were his old fellow-students at the Studio Drolling. Our dear Baudry had changed.

He was no longer the little Vendean, rude as the wild trees of his native forests, who, without grace, but with a singular robustness and a virile simplicity of tone, painted faces and figures, boldly and firmly designed, at a heat; whom we had seen when he lived on the sixth story of the isolated house of the Place St.-Germain-des-Prés, drawing on the cloth with which he had hung the walls of his apartment barbarously savage Chouan scenes; whom we had seen execute, also at the competition of the school—a daring attempt—the " Vitellius " so true to life, in which he had dramatically depicted the stupid terror of that master of the world as he rolls from the throne which had become a sink of corruption, the victim of the ungovernable fury of the populace.

Was he indeed the same Baudry?

True, we still thought him a delightful painter.

His " Primavera " especially seemed to me an exquisite inspiration in which elegant figures are grouped with enchanting art, like the clear soft harmonies of a delightful melody.

But we had counted on a powerful innovator of the true French school, and he comes back to us Italianized and with a leaning to the tender in painting.

He had rounded his angles and softened his expression by contact with the suave Coreggio, he had borrowed the glowing colors of Titian. And the little Leda, lovely in her sacred grove, thrilled with pleasure at the gentle caresses of the divine swan, still more tender under the caressing touch of the brush, and " Fortune " betrayed the inspiration of Titian while attempting to smile *a la* Leonardo.

Yes, frankly, we expected, if not something better, at least something different from this savage son of a

Vendean shoemaker, from this young man on the way to become a great painter, who, in his humble cradle, had imbibed the primitive sap which makes leaders of epochs.

We found again the trace of these early impressions in his painting " The Punishment of a Vestal," with its faces tangled together like briars, its rugose frames with knotty muscles, where a vein runs here and there like a bramble, side by side with blooming young girls and children with the grace and freshness of the wild rose.

One feels that there are here reminiscences of hours when, escaping from the paternal dwelling, he would plunge into the woods, inhaling the aroma of the pines and oaks and following with inquisitive gaze the fantastic forms and twisted arabesques of the roots and branches of the trees, and at the same time, with a feeling for the beautiful, silently contemplating a flower, then break through the clearings, tearing his clothes among the brambles, to chase a butterfly whose colors already awaken his curiosity.

In 1857 Baudry came back from Rome; I met him at the *Salon*, and we embraced each other like old friends.  I went to his studio, situated at that time in the Rue des Beaux-Arts.

We were delighted to meet each other again and interchange our experiences during the years we had spent so far apart and in so different a manner.

I found him more correct as to his attire, but otherwise little changed.

He was still the same dark young man with aquiline profile whose pale-olive complexion harmonized so well with the intense black of his hair and of his eyes that had not lost their fascinating expression.  His lip was shaded by a light mustache, which in moments of absent-mindedness he twisted with a gesture that was habitual to him. There was a tinge of melancholy in his expression, and he enjoyed silently and apparently unmoved his success, at which, with becoming modesty, he confessed himself a little surprised. He recognized that he had allowed himself to fall too much under Italian influence, and he made an effort to recover his originality. But he vacillated, and, in my opinion, again went astray in the "Toilet of Venus," which he then had on his easel, and whose affectedness savors a little of the Pompadour school.

He finished also the "Madeleine," fine in tone, and full of tender feeling, although the figure, with its weak and awkward joints, is wanting in equilibrium.

These pictures made their appearance at the *Salon* of 1859 at the same time with my "Planting of the Calvary," my "Gleaners of the Luxembourg," and my "Monday" (a drinking scene).

The *Salon* of 1861 treated both of us well. Baudry exhibited "The Little St. John the Baptist," standing, bright and modern looking, his very remarkable portrait of Guizot, and his "Charlotte Corday."

I had in the Exhibition "The Weeders," "The Fire," "Evening," and "The Colza."

We both received the cross of the Legion of Honor.

I think I can now see Baudry descending the steps of the platform where he had just received the cross in the midst of a salvo of bravos, pale and trembling with emotion, his brow lighted by some mysterious aureole, the cynosure of our admiring eyes.

And as he passed behind me to regain his place, which was near mine, he put his hand, trembling with happiness, on my shoulder, and whispered in my ear: "All the same, standing there so long is enough to break one's legs."

But Baudry's greatest success was "The Pearl and

the Wave." What a delightful personification of the sea, pure and blue, and fringed with foam! How marvelous that warm and pearly figure, that ravishing head thrown back in ecstasy, absorbed in its vision of light! What a voluptuous, yet chaste charm it breathes! And how original the style, though different, indeed, from that of which the artist gave promise in his earlier paintings.

Why, after painting this picture, did he return to the Italian Renaissance in his " Diana chasing Love," a picture he recommenced three or four times before he could succeed in satisfying himself? Because he went to Rome to prepare for his great work on the Opera House.

I think he would have done better if he had composed and executed in Paris his great decorative paintings for this theatre. It was a fine opportunity to regain entire freedom.

He is haunted by dreams of supreme grandeur of vast epic compositions ; and, instead of giving himself up freely to his inspiration, he turns his eyes again toward Italy.

He goes to bow down humbly before the awful god of the Sistine Chapel.

He there erects a scaffolding from which he will not descend until he shall have imitated the grandeur of execution of Michael Angelo, a heroic and fruitless labor in which he will exhaust his health.

Far be it from me to deny the tremendous amount of talent expended by Baudry on the *foyer* of the Opera House, but when I think of all the ravishing creations of which this overwhelming labor has deprived us, when I think of the healthful joy which the artist would have had in painting them, when I look again at " The Pearl and the Wave," I can not help deploring the fact that he should have exhausted his physical strength and his genius in this undertaking, how heroic soever it may have been.

I deplore this fact all the more because this work is at so great a height that it is almost lost to view.

Ah, he has paid dearly for a fame which he would have attained more naturally by following the path sowed with recollections of his childhood passed at La Roche-sur-Yon, where Fortune came one day to find the little Paul, not on the brink of a well, but on the ill-joined planks of a rustic platform, playing on the violin for the peasants to dance.

Happily there are to be found traces of his original manner in many of his paintings, notably in his portraits. For his excessive elegance was of no avail ; in his painting, as in his person, there is something of the rudeness of the people, the harshness of his first impression ; in his Vendean *sabots* he still keeps a little hay.

His "Glorification of the Law" was the occasion of an indisputable triumph.

Baudry died at the height of his fame, and yet he died a saddened man. Even before his illness he was dejected. Was this because he felt within him something sublime to which he had not been able to give complete expression, always diverted from the task by the admiration of others.

Ah, why was he not permitted to live a few years longer ? Why was he not permitted to execute the " Jeanne d'Arc " of which he had so long dreamed, and which, by the power of love, would have reconquered for him his true country, France ?

He leaves behind him one of the greatest names of our school—a name, however, which, in my opinion, would have been still greater if he had never left France.

I have insisted strongly on this point.

By the preceding pages it may be seen how great is my veneration for the old masters. I have counseled young artists not to throw themselves into the unknown without leaning upon them in the beginning and returning frequently to consult them, but this is on condition that they shall retain their own individuality.

In fact, the greatest of the historical painters of our French school seems to have been laboring to prove that those who preach the doctrine of absolute independence are in the right.

We have seen David renounce his powerful and brilliant original qualities in order to imitate feebly the Greeks of the Decadence ; we have seen Ingres striving desperately to keep up with Raphael, letting drop his own most precious gifts by the way; we have seen Delacroix entangle his powerful and sublime dramatic sentiment in the magnificent harmonies of Rubens and the inflations of Tintoretto ; and now Baudry also seems too often to disdain his own strong qualities derived from the natal soil in order to seek inspiration at foreign sources.

---

## LXXX.

At this period I occasionally went to visit Baudry. Sometimes we breakfasted together, and I had an opportunity to appreciate all the tenderness of his heart and the fineness of his wit. He adored his brother Ambrose, and was devoted to his parents.

At first glance, he seemed extremely reserved, and even a little disdainful, but he had a strong affection for his friends, which he manifested to them in a thousand ways.

I have tried to describe the man and the artist; the friend was in no way their inferior.

He was ambitious, like all artists, but not at all vain ; it might be said of him that he was modestly proud, but nothing can better describe him than the charming letters which he wrote to his friends, and which have been given to the public.

He hesitated long before exhibiting his pictures; he feared criticism. He said, speaking of certain malevolent critics of the *Salon:* "Am I not the first to suffer for my faults, and do I not strive to correct them? Why, then, do they take a malignant pleasure in castigating me in public?" And he would add : "Bah ! I will exhibit no more pictures ; there is nothing but hard knocks to be got by it."

He carried his passion for his art to rapture, but it caused him keen suffering also. I think the struggle killed him before his time.

When he had finished his grand decorative paintings, and wished to return to his easel, he perceived that he had lost his former admirable power of execution.

The fine, even coloring of his earlier pictures had crumbled into sharp, dry hatchings. His imagination had never been fresher or more brilliant, but a sort of weakness of touch prevented him from defining with precision the images he saw. The charm endured, for it was derived from deeper, more mysterious sources, but his painting, properly speaking, was on the decline.

I compared him, at the time, to Michael Angelo, who by dint of contemplating the vaulted dome of the Sistine Chapel, where the heaven of his sublime visions unrolled itself before him, was no longer able, when he descended from his scaffolding, to bend his head to contemplate the earth.

Poor Baudry felt that he was ill, and struggled

against his malady—so successfully, that he produced
several other exquisite works, among them "The Rape
of Psyche," his swan's song.

---

## LXXXI.

I SPENT a part of the summer of 1857 at Marlotte,
on the borders of the Forest of Fontainebleau.

I lodged at Father Antony's.

At this inn, of more than doubtful cleanliness, there
were at this time Desjobert, Appian, Daubigny, some
other artists, and Theodore de Banville, who had just
published his " Odes Funambulesques."

I worked at first with a good deal of ardor in the
forest, whose austere grandeur impressed me.  But soon,
as was the case when I was a child at Labroye, I felt
myself seized with a sort of spleen, a gloom blacker than
the blackest haunts of vipers.

The first impression I had received was one of keen
delight, but this soon changed to a poignant melancholy.

So that, returning to the inn, on emerging from the
wood, I welcomed with a sense of deliverance the sight
of the little paths running along the wheat fields bordered with willows with drooping foliage.

I then studied the rustic side of the country, wilder
than Courrières, and more in Millet's style.

I cherish a pleasing recollection of the hours of hard
work spent among those clever artists.

Daubigny, like his style of art, was delightfully frank
and simple.

Our favorite haunt was Montigny, situated on the
banks of the Loing, where grew thick-leaved plants and

flowering reeds. What a charming study he made there one day of a simple belfry and a few little houses with terraced gardens reflecting their images in the water!

And in the evening we would return to the inn, famished with hunger, and seated in Father Antony's arbor, with what keen relish would we devour the *sautéd* rabbits, or the carps dressed with wine, washed down with the thin wine of the country!

Our studies were taken from the packing-cases and hung up on the walls of the inn. And every morning we set out to make the conquest of some new motive, and our umbrellas were to be seen like a crop of gigantic mushrooms, dotting the field in the sunshine.

There is nothing more delightful than the sense of physical well-being and mental exhilaration which the artist feels in outdoor study; he enjoys at the same time the pleasures of art and of nature; he breathes the perfumes of the wood and of the new-mown hay; he forgets the anxieties of daily life; he has the delighted satisfaction of seeing the image of what he admires take shape and perfect itself under his pencil. How many exquisite pleasures does he experience at once!

What rapture to penetrate little by little into the secrets of effect, to discover its infallible laws!

Is not each page of nature a visible symphony whose wonderful harmonies reveal themselves to the charmed eye that can perceive them?

And this symphony he sees gradually emerge on a simple canvas from the chaos of the first touches; formless and discordant at first, little by little it grows clear and harmonious, and the artist feels his soul exalted in a sort of delightful intoxication, and his hand works swiftly and at the same time unerringly, guided by the impulse of his clear and rapid perception.

And like flights of magical birds in the midst of this

work which might be thought so absorbing a thousand delightful souvenirs cross the mind, reminiscences awakened by a tone or a harmony, that gleam with a thousand colors as they fly past, like the soap-bubbles which children send into the air.

When several painters are working together, this state of happy excitement provokes a thousand exclamations of wild gayety and sparkling sallies of wit.

How quickly would we hurry to our room, on our return, to judge the effect of the *study,* for the light out of doors is even more unfavorable to painting than was the blue-flowered paper of the inn.

----

## LXXXII.

I RETURNED to Courrières, taking with me vivid impressions from my sojourn at Marlotte.

I immediately set to work at "Calling the Gleaners" and the "Planting of Calvary."

I had witnessed this ceremony long before in a village near Courrières, a spectacle which had awakened in my mind the remembrance of that first planting of a Calvary which I have mentioned in narrating the events of my childhood.

Felix de Vigne came to spend his vacation at Courrières, accompanied by my young *fiancée.*

He profited by the presence of my models to make some studies which astonished us by the remarkable progress they denoted in this artist who was now in his fiftieth year. It was as if a second youth had renewed his powers. His color grew clearer, his touch more flexible. It was indeed light that sprung from the touch of his pencil. Adieu to the influence of his master Paclinck!

My young *fiancée* posed for me for the Calvary as one of the three young girls in white bearing the symbols of the passion, the girl who carries the crown of thorns.

It was a happy time, happy as it was possible for it to be although our affairs were still embarrassed, financially speaking, and consequently we were not in the enjoyment of complete independence, but, thanks to the good management and the unselfish devotion of my uncle and the consideration which he enjoyed, our pecuniary position improved every day, and allowed us to catch a glimpse of this independence in the distance.

We all remained at the brewery, now enlarged and brightened by the presence of a young woman, my sister-in-law, Constance Charlon, whom Louis had married, and who was in complete harmony with us.

She was the sympathetic confidante of the secrets of my heart during the long period which, owing to our pecuniary embarrassments, of necessity elapsed before my marriage, so ardently desired, took place.

The house was enlivened also by the sports and the prattle of their first two children whom we adored, and whose death later on caused us such bitter grief.

Émile, who had returned from his regiment, after having tried several business enterprises in every way uncongenial to him, began to be discontented at not being able to employ his energies in a way suited to his natural aptitudes.

As he used to do in Paris, he would occasionally take my palette and begin painting imaginary landscapes (he who had never made even the simplest study), which astonished us by their spirit and truth to nature.

Where had he learned to see and interpret nature thus?

But he attached no importance to these attempts.

Could he be a painter? This was in his eyes a dream impossible of realization. Besides, our uncle would never lend a favorable ear to such a project.

As for me, I did not dare to advise him.

It was De Winne who, astonished at my brother's attempts, decided us to put him in the path where he was soon to make such rapid progress.

My uncle had a studio fitted up for him, and he set himself assiduously to work.

Louis, who managed the brewery, painted also at times in his leisure moments. He even once exhibited one of his studies under the pseudonym of Noterb. He also had a natural aptitude for poetry, and amused himself in making verses that were incorrect, indeed, but not without grace.

Mayor and councilor of the district, my uncle was as much of an enthusiast as ever, although he was approaching his sixtieth year. He continued his solitary walks through the fields, always turning over in his mind some new improvement for the place—a town hall, an asylum, schools for girls and for boys, a bridge across the Deule, the restoration of the church—works which were all afterward carried to a successful termination with the aid of the Government. He was always engaged in some new plan, always in correspondence with the prefect, the sub-prefect, the engineer, the architect, the road surveyor, inviting them to dine with us whenever their business chanced to bring them to our place.

In no case, on the arrival of the mail, did he open his private letters before having first opened those which concerned public business.

Shall I speak of the domestic or conjugal dissensions in which he was called to play the part of peace-maker?

Or could he neglect to relieve worthy cases of distress, he who was still embarrassed in his own affairs?

He began, it is true, by scolding the petitioners, who quietly let the storm pass by, knowing very well that this manifestation of ill-humor was already a proof of compassion.

I remember one day when annoyed at being disturbed during dinner, he said impatiently to his troublesome visitor: "Do you not dine, then?" "Thanks, Monsieur le Maire," replied the other, "I dined before coming."

I married Élodie de Vigne on the 29th of April, 1858. On the 26th of July, 1859, was born our daughter Virginie, who was to be the source of so much happiness to us.

Émile also had married. The phalanstery of the brewery became too small. Each family had to have its own home.

We took up our abode in a house built for a vicarage by my father in his prosperous days.

It was in this dwelling, with its little front yard concealed from view by a wall, and its peaceful and modest garden, that we passed our existence. Here it was that Virginie grew up. Here it was when three years old, as soon as she was able to hold a pencil in her hand, that she began to make scrawls of peasants, in which we could soon begin to see some meaning. When about seven years old she made compositions, representing, for the most part, children at play, remarkable for their action and their foreshortening.

But, if I shall still speak of my impressions as an artist, and of our trips to Brittany and the South, henceforth, like our modest house, I must place a wall between the public and my life. I should have to depict emotions of too private and personal a nature.

I shall speak henceforth only of art and of nature, and will only permit myself some necrological details regarding persons mentioned in these recollections and in whom the reader may have become interested.

For, alas! the hour of mourning will soon strike again!

---

## LXXXIII.

BUT, however profitable my sojourn at Courrières might be, it was not long before I felt the need of seeking new inspirations elsewhere.

The too prolonged sight of the same objects in the end dulls the emotions. The mind constantly revolving in the same circle of observation loses its elasticity.

The peasants no longer inspired me as formerly, and my imagination exhausted itself in chimerical dreams.

Finding everything commonplace and unworthy of reproduction, I grew extremely indolent. I felt it an effort to look for models, and the finest of these did not please me when they were in the studio—not even the tall Augustine of the " Turkey Keeper " and the " Day's Work Done."

Even the very sunshine seemed sad in this insignificant country!

And I caught glimpses, in my dreams, of distant shores flooded with light—sublime scenes, peopled by beings of extraordinary beauty.

I had never traveled, and these visions of light impelled me to the south of France. I did not yet dare to dream of Italy.

By a happy coincidence at this critical moment, Count Duchâtel, who had bought my " Weeders," desiring a companion-piece to that picture, invited me to Medoc to witness the vintage of his estate of Château-

Lagrange. He had given me this motive as the subject of his order.

The occasion was found. I would return by the south.

And I became more and more absorbed every day in my glowing dreams.

One city, especially, attracted me—Arles. Arles the Greek! Written, this name dazzled me ; spoken, it ravished my ear by its indescribable sweetness. Arles!

In the mirages of my imagination I beheld it seated on the banks of its sapphire river, that wound like a peacock's neck between its white and gilded walls. I pictured it to myself as situated in an ideal plain, while its suburbs reposed on horizontal rocks, like the immense steps of a Cyclopean amphitheatre. The pearly-gray hue of these rocks cast into relief the brilliant bloom of the clumps of oleanders which grew in their crevices. The houses had a simplicity, a harmony of line, a just-ness of proportion, which charmed at once. Separated by groves of olives and orange-trees, they bordered long streets flooded with light. Noble beings, with pure pro-files, firm, rounded necks, and olive complexions, of dig-nified and unaffected mien, walked through them—beings endowed not only with the beauty of the Greeks, but also with their love for and their comprehension of the Beautiful.

Magnificent antique ruins added to, but did not con-stitute, the beauty of the city, playing there the part of ancestral portraits.

The temperature must be mild there. In winter its hills sheltered it on the north, in summer the fountains and the breeze from the river brought it coolness. Such was the Arles of my dreams.

And I set out full of enthusiasm, intoxicated with the impatient happiness of youth. I set out alone, and my enthusiasm, without any one to moderate it, gave full play to its poetic ardor.

And I fancied I discovered marvels in the things among which I had passed my childhood, and which only presented themselves to me under a different aspect and differently grouped, but transfigured, as it were, in the light cast upon them by my imagination: "There are the Apennines, there the Caucasus!"

O deceptive intoxication of our first travels! O the danger of loving a country for that which distinguishes it from other countries and of forgetting grand and universal Nature, whose laws are everywhere manifest!

How impatient I was!

First the Loire!

But how irritating it is to travel by railroad! For a long time I suffered the tortures of Tantalus, obliged as I was to be satisfied with divining the river through the distant poplars which bordered its banks; then I caught glimpses of it through the hedges, the railway stations, and the trains standing on the road, all which made me fume; at last I was entranced by the full view of the enchanted river dominated by the sleeping châteaux on its banks.

Not even Mangin, who, his cap on his head, retailed his crayons and his puns in front of the Palace of Justice —not even Mangin himself could draw me from my dream!

This Palace of Justice seemed to me none the less, however, to resemble the Parthenon. There were there immense elms, and rainbows spanning the jets of the fountains! Gazelles (*sic*, I added in the letter I wrote to my wife) roamed at will in the garden of the prefecture.

And the sunshine! How it streamed! I thought myself already in the south!

And to think that wonders like these were to succeed one another in ever-increasing splendor until we should reach Arles!

This state of mental intoxication lasted the whole time of my stay in Medoc.

I arrived at the Château of Lagrange at the time of the vintage of 1862.

When I reached the château I found every one out visiting, with the exception of the head of the family.

I directed myself to the steward, who showed me to my room, and sent me the valet who was to attend me.

After making some changes in my toilet, I presented myself in the study of Count Duchâtel, whom I found absorbed in the perusal of some lengthy document. He received me with a somewhat brusque kindness, and with so much simplicity and cordiality of manner, that he put me immediately at my ease.

His expression was identical with that of his bust by Chapu, now in the Louvre, in the hall to which his name was given in recognition of his presentation to the Museum, of some work of art.

A broad forehead, raised eyebrows, indicating intelligence; small, bright, gray eyes with sparse lashes; a large, well-rooted aquiline nose; a mouth benevolent, although shrewd in expression, whose corners were habitually drawn up by an indulgent irony; a powerful and prominent chin, expressive of self-will; a massive head; a body strongly built and slightly obese, easy and dignified in its movements—such was the first impression I received of Count Duchâtel.

This retired statesman loved both nature and the arts; and notwithstanding his habitual intercourse with the highest society (perhaps for that very reason, for extremes meet), had in his general appearance something country-bred.

He spoke little. His knowledge of men and things often plunged him into fits of silent meditation, which he would interrupt occasionally to throw out some short and pointed remark.

He liked to indulge in a gentle raillery, blended with that sort of amiable skepticism which is often acquired in political life.

The vast Hôtel of the Rue de Varenne threw open its doors to the residents of the Faubourg Saint Germain, but Lagrange extended its hospitality to a few intimate friends only, one of those who most frequently came there as a guest being Monsieur Vitet, of the French Academy.

In the evening there were often reunions at the château, composed of the proprietors of the neighboring estates, and Madame Duchâtel sometimes gave dinners and *fêtes*.

On leaving Count Duchâtel's study, I descended to the drawing-room, and it was not long before I saw the carriages returning, containing the Duke and the Duchess of La Trémoille, a newly-married couple overflowing with spirits, a few guests, and the soul of the château, the admirable woman who was called Countess Duchâtel.

I was her compatriot, she being a native of Douai, and she laid stress upon this fact in the friendly welcome she accorded me.

She was more than a gracious lady; she was an adorable woman, and, I may say, that during the two seasons I spent at Lagrange I never for a single instant saw her when she was not occupied in contributing to the happiness or comfort of others, extending her solicitude to the poor as well as to the rich.

She was possessed of as much energy as sweetness of character, and one day during a walk she related to me with touching simplicity some tragic incidents of the Revolution of February, in which she had displayed genuine heroism.

As may be seen from a portrait of her by Winterhalter, painted at the time of her residence at the house of the Minister of the Interior, she had in her youth been superbly beautiful, with a beauty of a blonde, Flemish type, like one of Rubens' goddesses.

She was now much thinner, but. notwithstanding her years, her countenance still preserved a youthful and charming expression.

An incident related by her in a letter to me dated December 3, 1863, will give some idea of her goodness of heart. I quote the passage referring to it, and which, in the moral beauty it unconsciously reveals, is more eloquent than any words of mine could be. It is as follows :

"I have had a keen sorrow since your departure. My poor Flemish coachman, just as the surgeon who was attending him at Bordeaux thought him cured—he had written to me on the 2d that he was going to send him back—died on the 5th of last month. I went to Bordeaux and spent there in the hospital, at Alfred's bedside, two very sad days.

"Erysipelas declared itself, spread over the body, and—

"I have just learned, and I think it well to mention the fact to you, that a whitlow is always a serious thing, and should be attended to at once, especially when it is the result of a sting."

Ah, how simple is true charity! This great lady sees no special merit in leaving the society of her friends to go and spend two days at Bordeaux, in a gloomy hospital, to console her dying coachman ; and she is mindful, in writing to a friend, of pointing out the danger of

17

neglecting an ailment more serious than it is generally thought to be—always intent on being of service to others.

But when we consider her life spent among the splendors and the futilities of the great world, we may well see in this action something not far from saintliness.

I can picture to myself the close friendship that was later to unite her and her daughter-in-law, the younger Countess Duchâtel, who was to die so young, and whose remarkable life was the subject of an obituary notice which touched us deeply and awoke our sympathetic admiration, for Marie d'Harcourt had a highly endowed mind, and a soul that responded to every noble emotion.

There was no thought of her at Lagrange at this time, however. The Viscount Duchâtel, her future husband, could not have even dreamed of her, child as she then was.

Elegant and distinguished in appearance, but extremely reserved in his manner, the viscount was regarded as somewhat cold, somewhat supercilious even, by the beautiful ladies who visited the château. In reality he was not fond of society, preferring study, solitary meditation, or conversation with intimate friends.

Sometimes he would escape from the drawing-room when the merriment was at its height, taking me with him to his room to smoke a cigar there. He was at such times gay and communicative, but with an undercurrent of seriousness; for his cold exterior concealed a heart capable of the tenderest friendship  This reserve kept him from being greatly influenced by his surroundings, and while his fellow-aristocrats still cherished their illusions, more pious than rational, regarding the monarchy, he frankly attached himself to the republic, serving it first as deputy, and afterward brilliantly representing it as ambassador at Copenhagen, Brussels, and Vienna.

I do not know whether, at the time of which I speak, he had already begun to indulge in nobly-ambitious dreams, but he appeared to enjoy less than any of us the amusements going on at the château—the hunts and pleasure parties which the brilliant couple, his brother-in-law and sister, the Duke and Duchess of La Trémoille, animated by their amiable gayety.

I remember there was a pretty girl, engaged in the vintage, whom the ladies of the château called Mademoiselle de Bardouillant, from the name of her native hamlet.

She was posing for me one day, and Count Duchâtel complimenting her on her beauty, as a châtelaine of the neighborhood chanced to be passing by, the latter cast a disdainful glance, full of offensive meaning, at the young girl.

When the lady had passed, the former minister of Louis Philippe whispered to me : " She is jealous of her. Beauty, you see, constitutes the real aristocracy among women."

Meanwhile, during the whole time of my stay at Lagrange, I had never ceased for a moment to see in the distance the Promised Land, the long dreamed-of south, and, above all, Arles !

## LXXXIV.

At last I saw the true South ! I fell into an ecstasy at the sight of the first stunted olive tree that bent its puny branches before the mistral.

I was so eager to arrive at Arles that I stopped only at Toulouse, Montpellier, and Nîmes.

I reached Avignon in the evening just as twilight was beginning to fall.

In order to obtain a general view of the city at once, I proudly crossed the Rhone, the Rhone that I had never hoped to see, and whose course I had so many times followed on the map at school.

The sun had sunk behind the terraced hills on the right bank of the river, diffusing a warm glow throughout the atmosphere, and striking with his fiery arrows the white summit of the Ventoux.

The city was not yet wrapped in darkness, but, reddened by the warm light from the west, quivered in the mists that rose from the river, like the steam that arises from water into which a red-hot iron has been plunged.

Transfigured in the warm light, the palace of the popes raised on high its enormous mass, which seemed still larger from the crenelated forts at its base. The gilded Virgin of the basilica shone in the light, and, higher up, in the rose-tinted gray sky, the full moon glimmered like a host.

This wonderful picture was reflected back from the bosom of the sleeping Rhone.

Ah, how I pitied my poor Artois ! "This," I cried, "is the true land of art; here is the real magic of light and color ! Here are outlines to make a Poussin despair ! And to-morrow I shall see Arles."

And I saw thee, Arles !

On that day the mistral blew pitilessly. The city shivered in the cold and gloomy light. The Rhone exhaled fever-laden mists.

In the gray light, under a gray sky, the gray streets looked grayer still.

My soul was oppressed by a melancholy yet more

gray. The women I met were ugly, the men uglier still, and spleen took possession of me in this tomb-like city.

And I remembered with regret the tender green willows that dipped their silvery foliage in the crystal waters of the springs of the Artois.

I returned by way of Lyon. I made a *detour*, taking in St. Etienne, where I had the joy of embracing my youngest brother, Ludovic Breton, at that time a pupil in the Central School of Arts and Trades, and lately chief engineer of the submarine tunnel of the British Channel, a work which, it is to be hoped, has not been finally abandoned. The difference in our pursuits and our professions has always kept us apart, but our hearts have not for that reason been the less united.

The son of another mother, and our junior by fifteen or sixteen years, he had had no part in our childhood.

This happy day, spent in my brother's society, increased still more my desire to see my native place again.

I traversed Burgundy, completely indifferent to all I saw.

The charm was broken. And then, almost all the time the rain fell in torrents, casting a gloom over everything, and I shut my eyes in order to see again my native village and its pleasant marsh, where the alders were bleeding from their wounds.

At last I saw again, indeed, its peaceful belfry, towering above the elms. I found myself again alone in that vast white plain where I had run about when a child.

The wheat was ripening. Late carnations gently swayed their white cups. The roads, white with dust, like the crust of a good loaf, wound gracefully through the fields, scarcely distinguishable in the distance by an exquisitely delicate violet line of shadow. The short grass, soft as velvet, followed their course. Here and there fine thistles proudly raised their carmine crowns, or let their silky white hair float on the evening breeze.

An opal sky, in which floated a few golden clouds, roofed this sea of golden grain, carnations, clover, and grass.

The wide belt of the horizon quivered in the distance, broken by belfry towers, groups of pale poplars, and drooping willows.

Never before had I so fully understood the tenderness, the peace, and the humble majesty of this scene.

Penetrated by it, my soul was stirred to its inmost fibers, a pious enthusiasm moistened my eyes, and I cried remorsefully, " This is the country that I would have fled from ! "

## LXXXV.

WHAT remained in my mind of all the keen emotions awakened in it by the scenery of the South? Nothing which I could profit by, as far as my art was concerned, but enough to make me admire anew, and more enthusiastically than before, the simple sylvan beauty that surrounded me.

I tried in vain to transfer to canvas a few of the impressions received during this journey, which I had thought at the time I experienced them so fruitful. I could succeed with none of them.

I was even obliged to defer my " Vintage " till the following year, the observations I had made of the subject not having been sufficiently accurate, owing to my poetic enthusiasm at the time.

Travel renews and refreshes the spirit, but it is not well to abuse it, following the example of those tourists who glance at everything, but observe nothing profoundly.

The attraction of novelty, as we have seen, may make us admire enthusiastically things less beautiful than others, which satiety makes us flee from. And then a first impression is at the mercy of a mood, or even of the state of the stomach.

Thus, gloomy weather, and perhaps a fit of indigestion, had sufficed to render me absolutely unjust toward the city of Arles, which, when I saw it later, pleased me greatly. Let us travel, but let us have a safe retreat in which to nourish our thoughts.

----

## LXXXVI.

In the depths of my hermitage, however, after a few months' solitude, I felt an imperious necessity to revisit Paris.

Paris is the ardent generator of ideas, and the great touchstone of merit. A work of art, no matter what its reputation elsewhere, is always a little doubtful until it has undergone this test.

It is a curious fact that the moment one sets foot in Paris the mind is enlightened.

You are a painter. You take there your picture, long thought over and worked at in solitude. During its execution you have had alternations of satisfaction and of discontent. At times it seemed to you luminous and splendid, at times dull and expressionless. Which is it in reality?

No sooner have you descended from the railway-carriage than you traverse the streets of Paris. Before having seen any one, before opening the case which contains your painting, you have already judged it.

A light has entered your mind which establishes in your confused judgment the just proportions of things.

This is because Paris is the center toward which converge all the currents of human thought, and which is surrounded by an atmosphere in whose searching and impartial light the *Ego* is at once clearly defined for him who knows how to see.

A thousand diverse elements flow from all sides into this crucible, which is constantly in operation, and in which the pure metal is separated from the dross.

Elsewhere one observes ; in Paris one comprehends. Here no one loiters.  Every one walks on rapidly, thinking of his own affairs.*

It is a singular fact, too, that when I am in Paris I fancy I recognize the faces of those I meet in the streets. I do not experience this feeling in any other city.  This is because Paris reunites the various types one has seen elsewhere, and which strike one like old acquaintances, made one does not remember where.

It will be seen that each journey I made to Paris was the occasion of fresh self-examination and of useful observations, without taking into account the pleasure I felt in seeing my friends again.

---

* Paris has sometimes its aberrations, as we have lately seen, but happily they do not last long.  The birds of prey destroy one another.

## LXXXVII.

ONE of my first visits on arriving in Paris was to the *Boîte à Thé*.

This was the name given to a building at the rear of No. 70, Rue Notre-Dame-des-Champs, containing a dozen studios, and decorated on the outside with Chinese ornaments.

There Hamon, Gérôme, Toulmouche, Schutzemberger, Brion, and Lauwick worked for a longer or shorter period. My friend Jean Aubert, a follower of Hamon, and who created a whole mythology of charming infant gods and goddesses, lived a few steps away.

I have been at gay banquets with those excellent companions, at which was also present (and not always without committing some misdemeanor) the monkey Jacques, a pet of Gérôme, and who sat at the table on a seat made like a child's chair.

I should like to speak of all these clever artists, but, with the exception of one or two of the veterans of art, I have made it a rule to speak only of those who are no longer living.

I had a strong affection for Hamon, and who would not have loved this singularly unaffected man, so frankly epicurean in all his tendencies?

The name—Hamon—has an antique sound.

The man himself had something of the antique also. Even his chief defect, intemperance, had in his case a certain Attic decency. When he was drunk, his intoxication had nothing gross in it. It resembled the delirium inspired by a nobler passion.

At such times he was extremely sentimental; and I have heard that one day in the Campagna of Rome, in one of those moments of Bacchic exaltation, after a violent altercation with a friend, which on his side had ended in repentance, he sat down on a rock on the bank of the Tiber and let his tears fall into the river.

Ingenuous and frank to excess, he could not have kept a secret, even if his life had depended upon it.

In the mannerisms of his style, too, there is a great deal of *naïveté.* His affectation has a natural grace.

He was a pupil of Gleyre, the father of the Neo-Greeks.

But at the same time that he drew his inspiration from the ancients, and especially from Pompeii, it may be said that his style was that of Hamon; or, rather, he was a Greek of the decadence in exile among us, who was born after his time.

His simplicity was childlike.

His life was made up of acts of thoughtlessness, of bursts of tenderness, of little misunderstandings, of displays of disinterested benevolence, and of that unconscious goodness to which everything is pardoned, even neglect, which passes for absent-mindedness.

He had a momentary triumph with "My Absent Sister." He accepted it without astonishment and without vanity, but he was more sensitive with regard to the criticisms which were showered upon him at a time when he least looked for them.

He painted a great deal at Capri. When his pictures were finished he took them to Naples, where he would remain a few weeks to rest; and if any one asked him at such times if he were working, he would answer: "I can not work—I can not work; I am waiting for the Americans."

His style is wanting in force, but he has ingenuity, grace, and genuine tenderness. He is himself. He would have expressed himself in the same manner even if his subjects had been different.

This Breton peasant, who had begun life as a farmer's boy, as he himself took pleasure in relating, had preserved to some extent his plebeian appearance, but he had, at the same time, something of the air of an apostle or of an ancient philosopher.

He himself seemed enveloped in the cloudy veil which he cast over his painting.

His wandering gaze reached one as if through a mist.

The same vagueness seemed to pervade his conversation, which was full of unforeseen turns, and of delicate but irrelevant sallies of wit.

His mind was always occupied with some poetic dream, but he had no pretension to profundity of thought.

Art critics have striven to find some concealed meaning, some subtle intention, in the fantastic picture in which Hamon represents the shades of the great men of antiquity grouped around a *Théâtre Guignol* in the Champs-Élysées. I asked him one day what he had meant to signify by this picture. "Nothing," he answered; "I only imagine that things took place in the Elysian Fields of the ancients pretty much as they do in those of Paris."

He would stop you in the midst of a conversation to utter, without rhyme or reason, some such phrase as "O! la la! des plis!" or, "That is like Monsieur Ingres."

Monsieur Ingres haunted him. He regretted not having gone to the funeral of Flandrin, in order to have seen Monsieur Ingres weep.

Some one asked him in my presence if he had read the "Voyage Autour de ma Chambre."

He fell into a revery, remained silent for a time, and then suddenly cried : "Stay! What if I should make a journey around Monsieur Ingres?"

Not long afterward he painted "The Sorrowful Shore," where the shades of the great men of antiquity are represented walking in procession, while waiting to cross the Styx, around Monsieur Ingres, who wears a mitre on his head, and holds in his hand the obole destined for Charon.

He did not copy directly from nature, but he went into the country with his box to mix his colors, comparing them by means of his palette-knife with the objects which he wished to paint.

We were at one time in Brittany, and had just seen at the Pardon those filthy beggars with their factitious wounds, whom I have described. At the *table-d'hôte* several rich Englishmen, just about to leave the country, were chatting together. One of them said he would take with him as a souvenir a horse; another said he would take a cow. Suddenly Hamon cried: "I have an idea; I will take with me a beggar!"

There was no premeditation in these absurd sayings, which came as naturally to him as his unconscious goodness.

One of his cock-and-bull stories has become traditional:

Every one knows that one of the first measures of the Provisional Government of 1848 was the abolition of the crack companies of the National Guard and of bear-skin caps.

Just at that time, however, a number of artists had met at the School of Fine Arts to take counsel together, led by their love for the picturesque, regarding the style of head-gear they should adopt to distinguish them from other human beings. Hamon mounted the platform and proposed the bear-skin caps, then out of use; and as this provoked a general laugh he waited until silence was restored and then continued, with the greatest coolness, " The bear-skin caps, but — without the bear-skin !"

I should like to say a few words also regarding my friend Nazon, whom I visited often at that time, and who, God be thanked, is still in the enjoyment of good health ; but, as he has voluntarily retired from the scene in which we thought him destined to play an important part, and is now living in obscurity in his native town, I think it not out of place to recall him to the minds of those who knew him.

Nazon (another name which has an antique sound) resembled at that time an Etruscan, with his profile forming an almost unbroken line, and his head covered with harsh, thick locks rising above his forehead like a crest.

Absorbed in his own thoughts he walked along with great strides, his toes slightly turned in, his chest swelling out, his long nose, pointed like that of an ant-eater, emerging from the scarf wound about his neck, as if to snuff in whatever news might be circulating in the air.

For this excellent companion, who was so cordial in his manners, though he was intolerant of everything that savored of vulgarity, was an indefatigable talker, and exceedingly witty.

He had made a brilliant *début* as a painter. I remember especially a southern landscape representing a long wall with curves full of style, against which leaned a little girl, guarding a flock of turkeys—a picture possessing a powerful charm, of sober and delicate coloring, and absolutely original at the time of its appearance.

We expected him to become a great landscape-painter, and only to think that he should prefer the retirement of a country life at Montauban !

Gustave Brion was a man of average but admirably

balanced endowments. He designed with ease, and was well acquainted with the technic of his art.

He was a big boy, who greeted his friends cordially whenever he met them, although he preferred to lead a retired life. The only noise he made was when he played his guitar, or when he drew some melody from his harmonium.

He was a skillful illustrator, and worked with great ease and ingenuity.

He painted a great variety of subjects, passing from Alsatian peasants to the patriarchs of the Bible, and from Breton peasants to the mountebanks of the middle ages.

His " Reading the Bible," an austere painting of fine design, procured for him the medal of honor.

He soon left the *Boîte à Thé* for a house built for him by our friend Hugelin, his compatriot, and an architect of a great deal of taste. He surrounded himself there with curious articles of *bric-à-brac* and rare plants, spending many peaceful hours in cultivating the flowers in his conservatory and his little garden, and drinking between times the excellent beer which he imported from Strasbourg, his native place, and which he delighted to offer to his friends.

He ended by confining himself entirely to the house, and his health suffered in consequence.

He grew too stout. His speech, which had never been fluent, finally became obstructed, and we learned one day that this excellent man and skillful artist had died suddenly.

At the time of my acquaintance with him, in 1853, he occupied, with Schutzemberger, a studio at 53 Rue Notre-Dame-des-Champs, the same house in which I had lived with Delalleau.

He there painted his best pictures, those which have

the most character—"The Skaters of the Black Forest" and "Gathering Potatoes during an Inundation." Schutzemberger also painted a fine picture—"Alsatian Mowers at Daybreak." The peasants, it is evident, were painted in the open air.

Brion obtained a second medal this year, as did also Millet.

In the same house dwelt also Bonvin, who at that time painted young infantry recruits.

What a singular man this Bonvin was!

At first view he had the appearance of an ordinary workman, but one was not long in discovering in his eyes and in his ironical mouth tokens of an extreme acuteness of intellect.

He was, indeed, one of the wittiest men I have ever known, but his sallies were not always altogether harmless.

In his moments of enthusiasm he had delightful inspirations.

On the day of his marriage he said to his young bride, at the end of the wedding banquet, "Do not forget that you have entered a family honored by the sword and gown." His father had been a rustic guard at Montrouge and his mother a seamstress.

On another occasion, passing at the exhibition in front of a picture in which the artist had carried the tricks of still-life deception to excess, Bonvin perceived a goose-quill lying on the floor and, picking it up, and taking in the painting with a rapid glance, he handed the feather to the keeper of the hall, saying: "Take care of this; it must have fallen from that picture there."

On the day on which we celebrated the reception of Brion's medal the latter had drunk so deeply to his success that he left a part of his wits at the bottom of his glass.  Bonvin teased him, saying to him in portentous accents: "Distrust yourself!  Don't be too sure of your success!"  Then he took the last gold piece from Brion's waistcoat-pocket.  The latter, beginning to be weary of this pleasantry, grew angry, and Bonvin, waving the louis d'or under his nose, said to him: "You are all right, you have your friends to fall back upon; but what is to become of poor me, who have taken the last twenty-franc piece you had in your pocket from you?"

Such are the recollections I retain of Bonvin, that gifted artist, that Gaul who spent his life in studying the old Flemish painters, whose delicacy, it must be confessed, he did not succeed in imitating.  Nor did he succeed better with his copies of Lenain, whose vigorous firmness of touch he did not possess.

At that period I saw again, too, my old fellow-students of the Studio Drolling, some of whom, following the example of Baudry, had begun to make a name for themselves at the annual exhibitions.

Among these was poor Marchal, the gay jester, the friend of the most brilliant writers of the time, whom he entertained by his inexhaustible spirits and his bonmots. What delicate good-nature!  What cordial effusiveness of manner!  How did this artist, who dissipated his energies in so many ways, still find time and strength to paint?  He painted, however, and he brought to his work, it must be acknowledged, true conscientiousness, especially at the beginning of his career.  I have witnessed many of his valiant efforts.

Unhappily, this witty conversationalist, who was so original in his amusing paradoxes, could never rid himself, in his painting, of a sort of *bourgeois* taste.

Influenced by friendship, the critics of his acquaintance took no notice of this defect, and, instead of pointing it out to him, praised greatly certain pictures of his which were full of didactic and commonplace sentimentality—enthusiastic eulogies which they redoubled in the case of his picture " Penelope and Phryne."

" I think they must be all crazy," he said to me on this occasion. " Imagine that I have received more than eighty letters full of enthusiastic congratulations ! "

I remember, in fact, that this sentimental picture was received with universal acclamation by the press. The Sheep of Panurge, you know.

The reaction was terrible. Two or three years later the career of poor Marchal was ended, a result brought about by the very exaggeration of his success. The public grew tired of him. There were no more purchases for his pictures.

He resorted then to repetitions of those of his pictures which had formerly been successful.

Pecuniary embarrassment came.

One day Marchal was found, dressed in irreproachable evening costume, lifeless upon his bed. He had killed himself, having even in this last fatal act paid due regard to the proprieties, as was becoming to a gentleman.

Happily for his memory, he left behind him two meritorious pictures, the " Choral of Luther " and the " Servants' Fair."

<hr>

## LXXXVIII.

I LIKED to mount the long stairs that led to the studio of Feyen-Perrin in the Rue Mazarine ; for I saw, each time with renewed pleasure, this good friend, who was a painter of a vivid, fertile, and poetic imagination.

18

I have dwelt elsewhere upon his personal beauty and his ardent devotion to study.

He had come from the borders of the Moselle, a charming river which washes away in places its banks, like those of the Tiber, flowing through a country that recalls, at a distance, the Campagna of Rome. He had there mingled the intoxication of his youthful passions with the delight produced in his soul by the spectacle of Nature. He still kept the ardent enthusiasm and the dreamy melancholy of that time. His art was imbued with them.

The long line of his beautiful girls will be remembered, their silhouettes defined against the sea-mist or bathed in the violet or saffron vapors of twilight. Nor have we forgotten his beautiful nude women, his "Snake" and his "Milky Way," in which, notwithstanding the malady that was undermining his health, he showed constant progress, proving that he was far from having produced the best work of which he was capable.

At one time I met him frequently with his brother and earliest master, Eugène Feyen, in the Alsatian brewery of the Rue Jacob.

The last days of the empire were at hand.

I shall not mention all the persons distinguished for their intelligence who came to occupy the benches of this brewery, a center of friendly reunion where discussions on art were prolonged far into the night.

The new-comers seated themselves at first on the little table near the door, gradually approached us, and, if they were presented, ended by joining us.

More than one distinguished character of the present day made that little table the starting-point in his career; in particular, the young and eloquent advocate, who soon seemed to be making ready, in our little cænaculum, for future contests in the tribune to which he was to be called.

He pronounced before us, among other discourses, a magnificent speech on the day on which we learned of the death of Maximilian, the Emperor of Mexico; and which, in an apostrophe to Napoleon III, ended with these words: "That will be your Waterloo!"

This young advocate, this ardent patriot and earnest democrat, was the bearer of a very obscure name, Léon Gambetta.

Assuredly he did not dream at that time of the glorious monument of the Place du Carrousel.

In 1875, when he was at the height of his fame, as I was recalling to him one day, while he was smoking his after-dinner cigar, those hours spent at the brewery, he cried: "Good heavens! how many times have I been reproached with them!"

Here, too, used to come the delightful humorist Toussenel; the young poet Pierre Dupont; Achard, a cross-grained but good-natured old fellow, one of the earliest of our landscape-painters, and so conscientious in his art that he worked for three years at the same picture, painted from nature, and was in despair when he found, on returning to his subject the following spring, that an umbelliferous plant, frozen during the winter, had not sprouted again. Then there were Jules Héreau, who was soon to meet with a tragic death, before he had succeeded in accomplishing all he was capable of; and Blin, on whom we had founded so many hopes, but who died young, just after he had painted his masterpiece—a masterpiece indeed!

The Emperor Maximilian had bought from him this painting, which represented a lake, on whose bosom glided a bark among reeds and rushes, and which reflected back the sky—a marvel of pearly transparency.

Blin had given proof of fine qualities in several of his works, but this one seemed to us so superior to all the others that it was like a revelation.

Unfortunately, this picture was destroyed at the time of the devastation of the palace of the unfortunate Maximilian.

Poor Blin! On that day you died for the second time!

Among our friends of the brewery was also the eccentric Gustave Doré, that artist whose wonderfully luxuriant and fantastic imagination was like a magical forest haunted by marvelous apparitions.

When he ought to have been enjoying tranquilly the brilliant success of his crayons he was to be seen always preoccupied and often sad, though he would at times suddenly break out into fits of gayety, like a schoolboy let loose from school, doubtless seeking in this way to deaden thought, for this fertile and inexhaustible designer suffered during his whole career from an open wound, which probably caused his death—the chagrin of seeing his fellow-artists pass with indifference before his immense canvases, on which he had placed all his hopes, but which were in a style of art for which his genius was not adapted.

A great many others came to our reunions in the Rue Jacob—Nazon, Gattineau, our dear and charming Armand Silvestre, and the sculptor Carpeaux, who gave promise of rivaling Puget, a rude carver of stone, exiled in the midst of the luxuries to which an aristocratic marriage had raised him ; Carpeaux, the famous author of " Flora " and " Ugolino," and whose obsequies Valenciennes celebrated with regal magnificence.

———————

## LXXXIX.

But, among all the pupils of Drolling, Gustave Jundt was the one whom I most loved.　He it was to whom I always paid my first visit.

In his studio in the Rue d'Assas were heaped up, in picturesque confusion, a multitude of objects and costumes of the peasantry of the different countries where he had made studies—Alsace, the Black Forest, Brittany, and Auvergne—the latter hanging out of half-open trunks, the former heaped up in dusty corners among canvases, palettes, enormous pipes, and newspapers.　On a table was a mountain of letters, his entire correspondence during the past ten years, and a heap of old tubes which had been emptied and twisted up.

In the mornings I would find him still in bed in his little room, smoking his large cherry-wood pipe, and looking over the newspaper.

On seeing me he would utter a joyful exclamation, half rising up in bed, and repressing, at times, the expression of pain, caused by a sudden twinge of his rheumatism, which, however, took nothing from the effusiveness of his joyous welcome.

No sooner was he out of bed than he would go, often before he was fully dressed, to the piano, to limber his gouty fingers, singing or whistling to its accompaniment, and abandoning himself to the genuine musical inspirations that came into his head—reminiscences or improvisations, on which he bestowed a delightful charm.

He would begin spiritedly, to give vent to his gayety, and then, yielding himself up to the delightful melodies that seemed to float around him, his voice would assume accents so tender that I have never heard any virtuoso who delighted me so much.

Then he would place his pictures on the easel to show them to me, and it was necessary to be very cautious in giving an opinion of them, for each new counsel was immediately followed, at the risk of destroying in a moment the labor of a week. One should see with what rash haste he dipped his rag in the essence and rubbed his canvas with it, scraping off the color with his palette-knife, demolishing and reconstructing in the twinkling of an eye!

For those who saw him only in public, Jundt was nothing more than a gay *viveur*, with a heart as warm as the color of his long locks and his beard, whose bright gold seemed to reflect the sunshine. He was perpetually laughing—a frank, good-humored, and irresistibly contagious laugh.

He made the most daring accusations, in which he always seemed to have right on his side, with imperturbable self-possession. Some of these are still remembered.

He had an iron constitution and a prodigious appetite; he had a tendency to *embonpoint*, and, although he limped on account of his gout, his gait was full of aristocratic grace. His whole being radiated an inalterable gayety.

There was in him a blending of the faun and the grand seignior.

But what a heart of gold for those who enjoyed his friendship! How much tenderness of soul and true genius this wild gayety concealed!

I fancy I can see him now as I saw him five or six summers ago, toward the close of his life, at our reunions in Montgeron at the house of my children.

We would go to meet him. He would come toward us, limping with his gout and leaning on his cane, announcing himself from a distance by some Homeric exclamation of boisterous joy, along a little path bordered by the innumerable flowers with which he loved to enamel the turf of his sunny pictures, and which he let fall with so light a touch, and whose stems he would scratch in skillfully with the handle of his brush, all the time humming snatches of some melody.

The cloudless sky, the greenery, and the flowers, all these served to augment his joy, which would bubble over in childlike ebullitions of gayety.

And then, when he executed his grand morning symphony!

He would begin by some rural prelude, imitating the bleating of the sheep and the tinkling of the sheep-bells, and, to this accompaniment, would follow all the sounds of rural life—faint and distant lowings, loud neighings, cackling of geese, crowing of cocks, clucking of hens, yelping of dogs, braying of donkeys—all rendered with perfect truth to nature, and an indescribable accentuation which elevated this mimicry to the dignity of an art.

And one could fancy one's self drinking in the morning mists, inhaling the perfume of the new-mown hay and the odor of the dung-hill, and the rustic picture presented itself in life-like colors to the imagination.

One day when he was to dine at Montgeron with Lemoyne, that landscape-painter of the pen, Heredia, the prince of sonnetteers, and the celebrated Leconte de Lisle, Jundt took it into his head on the way to write some crambo verses, absolutely idiotic in themselves, but composed of impassioned or Scriptural words, such as love, flame, sobs, tears, Zion, Jerusalem, and the like.

As he gave them to me to read, I looked at them in consternation, asking myself if he were crazy.

"You do not appear to comprehend the beauty of those verses," he said to me, "but you will see by and by, after dinner."

And after dinner, in effect, he improvised on the piano, in a burst of inspiration, a delightful melody, which he accompanied with charming chords on those absurd words.

And Leconte de Lisle cried out, enchanted, " Nonsense verses are decidedly the best for music."

Fine verses, being themselves divine music, stand in no need of any other.

In this way Jundt flung about at random the most precious natural gifts.

And yet he could never succeed in bringing to perfection those qualities which would have made him famous as a painter.

With more precision, more correctness in drawing, and, had it not been for that modest distrust in himself which made him rub out and begin over again twenty times the same picture, he would have been a great artist.

But, notwithstanding everything, what ravishing creations sprang to life under his incorrect touch !

In his " Islets of the Rhine," what charming yellow reeds bend over the clear waters, parted by the fingers of shadowy and evanescent naiads, that gleam with silvery lights !

And his tender Marguerite, who, when the uncertain light of dawn opens the petals of her little sisters of the field, braids her golden locks over the water of a spring in the hollow trunk of a tree, reviving a symbol which had seemed hopelessly hackneyed.

And the white light of morning which glimmers over the tender spring verdure and the quivering mists, who, O sunny-haired friend—save the divine Corot—could better than thou have interpreted their intoxicating sweetness !

All this gayety concealed suffering, perhaps despair,

not dreamed of by his most intimate friends, not even by his devoted brother Théodore Jundt, an engineer at Belfort, who, though more serious than Gustave, reminds us of him—physical pain, cruel disillusions, his patriotic anguish as an Alsatian, for he could never be consoled for his lost country.

All his friends will remember the spiteful caricatures with which he covered a series of panels, on one of which was represented an' imposing effigy made up of slices of bacon, black-pudding and sausages, as well as that panorama of Alsace, with which he terminated the sketch so fondly dreamed of !

No anguish can compare with that experienced by those wildly gay natures when misfortune overtakes them !

One morning Paris was shocked by the news of his tragic death, as it had before been shocked by the news of the death of Marchal, that other Alsatian and fellow-student of Jundt.

---

## XC.

OTHER friends, venerable ones, attracted me also. I refer to the old masters who repose in the Louvre.

Their calm and assured fame is beyond the reach of the vicissitudes to which ours is subject, and, in the midst of the preoccupations which excite and fatigue our nerves, it is well from time to time to contemplate them and to question them.

I never cross the threshold of our museum without experiencing a reverential emotion.

I know this museum almost by heart, and yet it offers at each new visit a fresh field of. observation.

The impressions of art are subject to so many subtle

influences, that, according to what he has just seen or studied, the admiration of the artist is modified, if not in its intensity at least in its direction.

On one day I am more affected by the *naïve* fervor of Gothic art, on another by the pomp of the Renaissance, or by the touching homeliness of the Dutch school. But there are certain masterpieces which, for me, are placed beyond the fluctuations of judgment or of feeling.

I have made of these chosen masterpieces my brightest constellation in the heaven of the ideal.

I should place, perhaps, at their head, the Sistine Chapel and the divine marbles of Phidias, which, when I saw them in London, moved me to tears; but these I have seen only once.

The works which I can see often, and of which I can speak with more certainty, are the "Saint Anne" of Leonardo da Vinci, the "Pilgrims of Emmaüs" of Rembrandt, and the last picture of Poussin, "Apollo and Daphne," in the Louvre; the little "Waxen Head" at Lille; and the "Vocation of Saint Bavon" of Rubens, at Ghent.

I do not think art has ever produced anything more touching than the head of the "Saint Anne" of Leonardo da Vinci. No artist has every joined more profound feeling with greater correctness of design. It is ideal sweetness expressed with ideal force. Nothing there is due to chance; everything is predetermined, but each detail is rendered subordinate to the expression of the whole in a half-tint more resplendent than crude light. It trembles and glows with the radiance of the soul. It is clothed with a divine and supernatural brightness. It is the transfiguration of matter!

I love this Leonardo with all the fervor of an artist's soul.

May not the adorable "Waxen Head" in the Museum of Lille, that young virgin, the wondrous work of an unknown hand, be by Leonardo also? There is nothing to be compared to the pensive innocence of this white lily! How many times has the pure glance of her melancholy eyes come to haunt me in my solitude!

It is difficult to believe that, in these days, when travel is so easy, there could be in the superb cathedral of an important city an almost unknown masterpiece, in in my opinion the finest picture of one of the greatest painters. Yet so it is in the case of the "Vocation of Saint Bavon" of Rubens.

And, what renders this obscurity still more extraordinary, is the fact that there is in a chapel of the same cathedral an extremely well-known work, the "Paschal Lamb" of Van Eyck.

Clad in rich armor, and wearing a long purple mantle which is held up behind by a page, Saint Bavon is represented kneeling, surrounded by his court, on a massive staircase which leads to the porch of a convent.

Between the columns of this porch bishops in their episcopal robes of state incline themselves toward him, extending their hands to receive him.

The lower part of the staircase is occupied by beggars, among whom attendants are distributing the possessions of the saint. They look like a pack of hounds throwing themselves on the quarry. There are among them emaciated old men, boys in rags, and two superb beggar-women, of whom one, with uncovered bosom, discloses to view, as she rushes forward, two infants, whom she holds in her powerful arms.

To the left, near the frame, two noble ladies, the most ideal creations of the painter, of a pure and elevated type of beauty, are looking with emotion at the saint who is making the sacrifice of all his earthly splendor.

All the figures in this composition are grouped with perfect skill and naturalness.  Its coloring is incomparably rich and sober.

Here are none of those timid muscles which, in the shadows, look like raw flesh ; none of those crude blues and reds that we see in the "Virgin with the Parrot" and the "Lance-Thrust"; none of the porcelain tints of the "Christ on the Straw" and the "Unbelief of Saint Thomas"; nothing of the vulgarity of the foreshortened "Dead Christ."  Here all is life-like and natural, and beauty reigns supreme.

The coloring of a slightly amber tint is of the same quality as that of another admirable though much less important masterpiece of the same artist; I refer to the painting of Saint George, which adorns the tomb of the great genius of Antwerp, in the church of Saint Jacques.

There are in it the same warm and pearly flesh-tints, the same powerful harmonies in yellow.  But, indeed, when Rubens paints with delicacy he has no rival.

As for the "Pilgrims of Emmaüs" of Rembrandt, it is the goal of my pious pilgrimages whenever I can make them, and I never weary of contemplating it.

By what miracle does this "Christ," which, according to conventional rules, is not beautiful, awaken in the mind the highest and holiest thoughts?  Whence comes the irresistible charm breathed by this face crowned by its mild and mysterious halo?  As in the presence of Leonardo da Vinci, we here feel ourselves under the spell of a supernatural irradiation.

To learn its secret, it would be necessary to read the soul of Rembrandt.

For, however inexplicable may be the attraction of this work, we feel that it is the radiation of a pure thought; it gives proof of the supremacy of human genius over the rest of the creation; it confutes those materialists who would debase that genius to the level of the blind instinct of the brute.

But if the chief fascination of this masterpiece, the inspiration which it breathes, escapes our limited methods of analysis, what we can estimate in it is the superior harmony of the values and the tones, the pious attention of the attitudes, and the magic of the chiaroscuro. Rembrandt has created nothing more softly intense.

And, a consoling fact for those among us who are growing old, when we consider the work of the great masters, we find that their latest manner is their best.

This is true of Michael Angelo, Rubens, Leonardo da Vinci, Rembrandt, Poussin, and many others.

Contrariwise to what the Greeks used to say of their heroes, " Happy they who die young, and in full possession of their physical beauty ! " we may say, of artists especially, " Happy they who die old, in the plenitude of their mental faculties ! " They alone reach that full maturity of the powers when, having mastered the technic of their art, and freed themselves from prejudices and from vulgar passions, they see only the supreme expression of things. There is no trace of effort in their work; the means employed disappear, and the hand may tremble with impunity under the superior charm which it confers.

For the young, new efforts, dangerous exaltations, · dazzling triumphs, and resounding defeats, disillusions, prodigality, daring experiments, and the noisy trumpeting of new reputations ! For the old who have retained their vigor, the free and radiant flow of sublime inspirations concealing profound knowledge, the more profound the more it is concealed. For the old, serene visions freed from earthly trammels.

I have just spoken of Poussin. Well, compare with the "Rape of the Sabines," and other pompous paintings of his youth, the "Grapes of the Promised Land," the "Episode of Ruth and Boaz," and, above all, the last and best of his pictures, "Apollo and Daphne," which he left unfinished, and in which his failing fingers were the interpreters of one of the highest visions of art.

Oh, you who affirm that the ideal does not exist, how describe the celestial atmosphere which bathes this old man's dream, the august beauty of this epopœia, at once Olympian and pastoral, and the episodes which it unfolds?

Look at this picture, and say whether art has made much progress since it was painted.

In the deep blue sky float soft pearl-gray clouds, charmingly rose-tinted, beautifully rounded in form, and pierced here and there by golden gleams, which gather, seeming charged with electricity, on the distant peak that, behind an azure lake, bounds the horizon.

In the warm, humid atmosphere of this rich background, majestic trees, rooted among sharply outlined rocks, spread their fan-like foliage.

To the left, a nymph, enveloped in a yellow drapery, swings, half-reclining, among the branches; another nymph, crowned with oak-leaves, is seated at her feet, clasping with interlaced fingers, the branch of a tree.

A little below Apollo is looking at Daphne, whose nude figure is seen surrounded by nymphs, also nude, on the other side of the composition. Near Apollo a little Cupid, bow and arrow in hand, is taking aim at her.

Various figures are seated or recline in the foreground in attitudes of repose. A wide space affords rest to the eye in the midst of these groups, whose undulating lines lead the glance of the spectator to the left toward Apollo, and to the right toward Daphne.

The background of the picture is occupied by shepherds, dogs, and a herd of oxen, whose backs form a straight line, full of style.

How intense, peaceful, warm, and tender is the whole composition!

A soft light gilds the distances and the nymph seated on the grass, while the rest of the picture is in a half-shadow of exquisite transparency.

In this painting the contours and the colors, at once sublime and familiar, are so naturally graded, so enchantingly harmonized, that the eye, deceived by the charm, fancies it perceives in it a sort of palpitation, I might almost say a divine breathing! This palpitation, this breathing, this supernatural life, produced by the perfect equilibrium of the parts forming a complete whole, is not this the infallible sign of a genuine masterpiece?

---

## XCI.

IT will be seen how great an attraction Paris possessed for me, since it brought me in frequent contact with friends such as those I have just described.

But, if it is unwise to remain long away from Paris, it is not well, on the other hand, to live there constantly.

Do not the continual opportunities offered by the great city for the interchange of ideas interfere with their complete assimilation? Do not those constant conversations, in which each one shines or seeks to shine, occasion a useless expenditure of energy?

Might not the ardor dissipated in often sterile words, if concentrated and employed in work, produce more serious results?

Thoughts, to prove fertile, require to be concentrated, and not scattered to the winds. Condensation increases their force a hundred-fold.

The boulevard alone can develop that brilliant but superficial faculty which we call *esprit*, but the ambition of the artist should go further than this. Without the prudence of the fox, it may be said that *esprit* is dangerous in art.

I am of the opinion that historical painters would gain greatly by living occasionally in the country, in the midst of the primitive inhabitants. I think by doing so they would often obtain an insight into past ages, for, to my mind, in order to make past ages live upon the canvas, something more is needed than to rummage among heaps of documents and sneeze among the dust of old papers.

---

## XCII.

EMERGING from the whirlpool of Paris I experienced, every time I returned to Courrières, the supreme delight of the intense peace of the country, and enjoyed the solitary walks in which I could again follow the changes of Nature, and study their causes in simple subjects, in which are more plainly manifested her great and immutable laws.

At such times the thousand problems discussed in Paris with my fellow-artists returned to my mind. They presented themselves to my reason more clearly in this solitude, and I sought then to solve them.

Perhaps I would have done better to follow my natural bent, without any other care than that of seeking to attain the ideal I had formed, without vain longings or too exalted an ambition.

This is what I had done, without suspecting it, when I painted my first pictures at Courrières; this is what I strive to do, less unconsciously, now.

But how settle the account with one's conscience, exacted by a sense of responsibility?

I have always had a passion for the Beautiful.

I have always believed that the aim of art was to realize the expression of the Beautiful. I believe in the Beautiful—I feel it, I see it!

If the man in me is often a pessimist, the artist, on the contrary, is pre-eminently an optimist.

More than this, I affirm that life would seem to me absolutely miserable and contemptible if we had not continually before our eyes the enchanting splendors of the Beautiful.

In affirming this, I speak of moral as well as physical Beauty.

But what is the Beautiful? Where is it? What are its attributes?

Reason is powerless to answer this question continually propounded, and to which the response of Plato, vague though it be, is yet the best:

"Love is the only light that can guide us in a region where all is mystery."

One might add to the definition of Plato that the Beautiful is not only the *splendor of the true*, but also *its intensity*, and it is for this reason that it is to be met with even where the vulgar see only ugliness.

If I did not fear to be still more vague than Plato, I should say, The Beautiful is the *essence of Life*.

It is also the grand symphony of the World, which can be interpreted only by those who possess a profound

19

knowledge of its laws, and of the relation between discords and harmonies.

All beings provided with eyes perceive the images
of things ; only those who are artistically and poetically
endowed see them, because they alone comprehend
their *harmonic sense* in the *universal concert.*

Hence their delight and their dissatisfaction with
things concerning which the majority of people are absolutely indifferent; hence their contempt for purely
imitative art, that art which considers things only for
themselves, and seeks to deceive the eye by a patient
and contemptible mechanical process.

Art, then, has not for its end merely the imitation of
Nature.

But in what degree should Nature be imitated ?  To
what extent should the artist create?  How should he
create ?

Is it not presumption on his part to think that he
can create ?

How many questions arise to trouble his judgment !

A painter may be interesting provided he has studied
Nature sufficiently to avoid copying her expressionless
aspects, but he will touch the feelings only in so far as
he can interpret her intensities.

How is the artist to learn to recognize the essential
features of Nature which he is to depict, and the com-
monplaces which he is to avoid ?

He can only do this by elevating his soul by the contemplation of the beautiful spectacles which strike his
imagination, and by lovingly interpreting them.

For it is not enough to discern and portray the superficial character of things; it is necessary also—and
this is the most important point—to interpret their
meaning, their expression learned by putting our souls

in communication with what I shall call the *souls* of inanimate objects.

For everything in nature has a hidden, and, so to say, a moral life.

This life is mysterious, but in nowise chimerical, and only those, whether poets or artists, who are penetrated deeply with it, have the power to touch the feelings.

What is the sky to me if it does not give me the idea of infinity?

Looking at a twilight scene, it matters little that my eye should receive the impression of the view, if my spirit does not at once experience a feeling of repose, of tranquillity, and of peace. A bunch of flowers should, above all things, rejoice the eye by its freshness.

The spirit of a subject should take precedence of the letter.

Force, Elegance, Majesty, Sweetness, Splendor, Grace, Naïveté, Abundance, Simplicity, Richness, Humility—some one of these qualities, according to the genius of the painter and the nature of the subject, should strike the beholder, in every work, before he has had the time to take in the details of the scene represented.

These are the æsthetic virtues.

They are common to all the arts, which live only through them. The most skillful execution, the most accurate knowledge, can not supply their place.

They are eternal, and pass through the caprices of fashion, without losing any of their sovereign power.

They insure lasting fame, which grows with time.

Just as many beauties as there are, just so many corresponding defects are there which assume the appearance of the former, and, misleading the public, give rise to ephemeral fashions.

At the side of Beauty is Prettiness; of Grace and

Elegance, Affectation ; of Naïveté, Silliness; of Force, Heaviness ; of Majesty, Pomp; of Softness, Insipidity ; of Abundance, Prodigality; of Splendor, Tawdriness ; of Simplicity, Poverty.

The public often allow themselves to be deceived by appearances, and do not easily distinguish the false coin from the true. The crowd, led astray at first, end by ranging themselves on the side of the acknowledged critics ; and as, after all, they never know why they do so, we see them going into ecstasies before masterpieces which, at the bottom of their hearts, they still think ugly.

True art will always address itself only to a limited public.

The great quality which constitutes the artist, and which is born with him, is, then, the love of the Beautiful; that fire which thrills the soul, fertilizes it, and bestows upon it that profound and almost unconscious perception which is its result, the light of feeling.

Knowledge gives clearness, feeling surrounds this clearness with mystery, divines the Beyond, pierces the Infinite ; and it is for this reason that I have said in my verses :

. . . . L'art est la clarté<br>
Suprême rayonnant au milieu du mystère.*

---

## XCIII.

ALL these questions, suggested by my studies, crossed my mind at one time or another; and, in order to terminate this digression into the field of pure æsthetics, I will give here some pages copied from my note-books, written in 1865, and summing up the convictions on art

---

* Théodore Rousseau et le Bûcheron : Les Champs et la Mer.

which I then entertained—convictions which I may say have changed but little since that time.

Truth in art is the essence of visible truth, and this essence of truth is the Beautiful.

The Beautiful is a mystery which can be interpreted only by another mystery—inspiration.

For how, in truth, does the painter succeed in expressing the Beautiful? Is it by deliberately correcting the faults of the model who is posing for him? No; he could only make this correction by virtue of a system, and experience demonstrates that every system in art irrevocably leads to coldness, to death.

Nature, then, is not to be corrected by making it conform to a conventional type. The artist must have the intention of rendering what he sees and conceives as he sees and conceives it.

His exaltation of feeling will make him discern the line of expression, of beauty, which he will follow; and unconsciously he will diminish or eliminate the insignificant or useless details which interfere with it.

I have said "unconsciously," and I lay stress upon this point. If the artist is penetrated by his *subject*, he will see in reality, in the model that is posing for him, only those traits which adapt themselves to his thought.

Besides, it is not when he reasons best that he does best. How many times does it happen that he does not perceive his success until afterward! God created the world, and then saw that it was good.

For when a work is completed it is easy to analyze it and to explain the means by which the effect produced has been brought about. How many people fancy they have made a fine discovery, are eager to avail themselves of it, and find themselves unable to profit by it!

 .  .  .  .  .  .  .

Painters should not trouble themselves too much about execution.  I mean by this that they should have in view the representation of a sincere observation of Nature, and shun, as they would the plague, the coquetries of the brush.  Those whose aim it is to display upon canvas their skilfulness of touch can succeed in pleasing only fools.

Oh, the insipid skill of a hand which is always infallible !  Oh, the delightful unskilfulness of a hand trembling with emotion !

Truly fine execution does not parade itself; it effaces itself humbly, to give place to the image it represents.

O artists ! instruct yourselves, nourish your hearts, exalt your souls, extend your vision, and do not trouble yourselves about painting well.  The more clearly you see into the secrets of Nature, the *clearer* and more skilful will be your touch ; the more powerfully you are thrilled by feeling, the more expressive it will be !  To see, to feel, to express—all this must take place simultaneously, spontaneously.  How could one expect a cold calculation to produce the touch which should give expression to your thought, follow it unceasingly and immediately in all its inflections, in all its movements ?

The excellence of the method followed is also a quality which is to be analyzed after the work is completed, in regard to which it is well to consult the masters, because this study will enable you to penetrate more deeply into their spirit, but which must not be thought of while working.

We know how one of our most gifted artists, Decamps, allowed himself to be hampered by the fruitless study of method, to the great detriment of his work.

If, instead of confusing his touch by labored and premeditated painting, by useless rubbing out, by glairy varnishing, he had allowed it to follow his inspiration freely, how much greater he would have been !

Nothing can supply the place of spontaneity of touch, conveying, fresh and life-like, the direct expression of the feeling

How important it is to make good use of the moments of inspiration ; and how often it happens that the execution becomes heavy in seeking after a superficial and impossible perfection !

This is because fatigue is a bad counselor, and the desire for "the better" is to be distrusted which springs from too long a contemplation of one's work.

This touch, indeed, the direct expression of the feeling and the thought, must come at last, in order to avoid the necessity for retouching one's work, which would render it heavy, and deprive it of freshness and life.

A young and inexperienced painter will thoughtlessly dissipate in his sketch all the fire of his inspiration, and, when he wishes to complete his work, he will find before him an impassable gulf. The more beautiful his sketch, the heavier and more labored will be every touch that he adds to it ; and every effort which he makes to finish it will seem to remove it still further from the desired end.

The experienced artist, on the contrary, will first fix, in a life-like sketch, the emotion he wishes to interpret ; then taking his canvas, he will fill in the details without haste, and will prepare all the materials of which he will have need. He will make all the necessary studies, and will outline the masses of his painting with care.

He will know how to restrain the ardor of his enthusiasm, always ready to carry him away, in order that his sketch, made with premeditation, may in no way interfere with the work which is to follow.

He knows that it is necessary to lay the foundations of his work in this way, in order to give greater firmness to the forms, greater power and solidity to the tones, as well as to aid in the distribution of the effects; but he will do it in such a way—there being nothing to distract his attention—as will leave a free field to spontaneity of feeling, so that the touch which is to interpret it may be final.

It is necessary that everything in this sketch, the general outlines, proportions, and relative values, be rigorously predetermined. Every detail, as well as every charm of color, must be omitted.

This sketch must have, besides, contrasts sufficiently strong, accents sufficiently pronounced, to prevent the artist from being led into weakness of execution, when he shall begin his picture.

It must not be painted in the final tone, for nothing renders a painting so heavy as to place two layers of the same color one over the other.

Once the sketch is well laid ·in, and perfectly dry, let the painter attack his work boldly, and let every touch of his brush be the consequence of the feeling which animates him, and never made with the aim of producing a fine work.

.　　.　　.　　.　　.　　.　　.

The precept, " Know thyself," may be addressed with peculiar aptness to the painter. It is of the utmost importance that he should discover in what his originality consists. This is not easy, for we generally attach special importance to the qualities which Heaven has denied us. Let the artist shun this temptation, which would turn him aside from his true career.

If his nature, for instance, is energetic and robust, and he wishes to paint in a sweet and tender style, he will lose his natural qualities without acquiring those which he seeks to attain.

Figure to yourself Géricault influenced by Prudhon!

It must not be deduced from this that an artist would do wrong to draw inspiration from the various feelings which attract him; this remark applies to the character which he is best fitted to give his painting—to style, in a word.

The style is the man. Let us not forget this old saying.

The great masters will teach us to see clearly, will elevate our souls, and nourish our hearts, but let us imitate in them only their ardent study of life and all its manifestations.

If we seek to acquire the style of another, we renounce the individual style which we might have acquired. Let us keep to that which we like, that which we feel.

Let us be severe toward ourselves; but, when we are conscious of a defect in ourselves, let us seek to correct it only in so far as this may be done without injury to some precious quality: we were hard, but expressive; we may become insipid and weak.

Enlightened art critics will give us the best possible counsels, which we should accept with gratitude, but which we must follow with extreme precaution. That which they have called a defect is perhaps an energetic mode of expression peculiar to us; to lose it, therefore, would be to lessen our worth.

Nothing is more insipid than an expressionless perfection. A touch of madness is better than death.

The great masters have always sought to preserve their originality. They were naturally influenced in the beginning by their teachers, and their first works show traces of this influence; but, once acquired, their manner has continued entirely their own, and the successive variations to be observed in it are only the consequence of the changes which had taken place in themselves.

This manner reveals itself all at once from the very first essays. Education, the counsels of the teacher, the influence of fellow-students, and other causes, may turn the artist from it for a time. But, if he be really gifted, he will infallibly come back to it. His self-assertion will be at first excessive, for he will push forward toward the desired goal with that unreflecting ardor which gives to youth its rash and exclusive ignorance. His defects will be plainly perceptible, but he will attract irresistibly. Such is the power of dawning genius.

Happy period of unconscious inspiration and sudden flashes of genius!

But soon, the first surprise past, the public and the artist himself, if he be not blinded by the incense of flattery, will discover that the praise accorded to the work is not based upon a solid foundation.

The artist becomes restless. Then follows a period of doubt, of painful effort, and of discouragement.

Timidity succeeds to the first freedom of manner.

Burning to acquire what he lacks, the painter loses for a time that which he possessed

He depreciates his native qualities; and in this consists the danger. In reaching after the shadow he may lose the substance. He grows tired and discouraged. He strives after singular or subtle effects, strange novelties—in a word, he seeks the impossible.

His painting, worked up to excess, becomes feeble and expressionless, labored and heavy.

Even his early successes add to his despondency, since they have led only to this. Formerly his style was hard and coarse, it is true; but was not this better than the impotence in which he now languishes?

His efforts, however, are less futile than he imagines. They will prove useful to him, if only as experience.

One day he sees again one of his early paintings, long forgotten, and which strikes him as if it were the work of another painter. True, it is full of defects into which he would not now fall, but it exists, it lives! It has a real power, an inexplicable but irresistible charm.

"And yet I was born a painter!" he says. "Whence comes it, then, that I exhaust myself now in futile attempts, when formerly I could awaken emotion with so little effort?"

Then his eyes are opened. He sees clearly into the depths of his own nature. He has only to dare; he will dare. He will go straight forward, shaking off the borrowed burden which impedes his progress.

An enthusiasm which will not prove fruitless again takes possession of him during his sleepless vigils. His sight is restored to him, his eyes see clearly!

The voluptuous ardor, the feverish thrills which are produced by the consciousness of the creative power, have chased away the restless suffering which paralyzed his imagination. He is astonished at the spirit he displays, at the expression and the animation which forms and colors assume under his brush.

He is himself once more. What do I say? Himself, but greater, broader, purer, simpler than before!

With the faults of his youth have disappeared also, it is true, some regrettable charms, but his finer qualities have gained singularly in power.

The power which freedom and broadness of view confer, such is the supreme quality which distinguishes the final manner of the true masters.

It is feeling directed by science. It is science

warmed by feeling, force self-contained and self-conscious.

.    .    .    .    .    .    .

What we call a *study* is a fragment, a note, an indication, and can never constitute a *whole*. The objects are there for their own sakes, without any correlation which would make them form part of a general idea.

A picture, on the contrary, should be a harmonious blending of different elements, all conducing to the same end.

In a really fine composition no change can be made, nothing can be added or taken away, without disturbing the harmony of the whole. Even the most insignificant of its details must be in its own proper place and not elsewhere. There should, indeed, be nothing insignificant in it. Everything should conduce to render more expressive the sentiment of the subject.

A detail which should not be associated with the leading idea would tend to destroy the feeling of the composition.

Every subject requires an arrangement, an effect, an execution peculiar to itself ; and no general rules can be laid down for the composition of a picture.

The finest composition is not that which displays the most elegant lines, but that which expresses most clearly the spirit of the subject. No detail can be exempt from the logic imposed by the central idea of the work.

The same thing is true of color.

The most ravishing caprices of the palette would be most out of place in a composition which requires sober coloring, and *vice versa*.

The sovereign law which should govern every composition is unity. The central idea must reveal itself clearly, always, and instantaneously, whatever may be the number and importance of the subordinate ideas which accompany it.

Painters without experience often weaken the effect they wish to produce by a prodigality which multiplies uselessly the figures and the accessories of a picture.

It will not be long before they learn that, the greater the conciseness and simplicity with which a thought is interpreted, the more it gains in expressive force.

The public in general believe that a composition containing a hundred figures denotes more imagination than a composition containing only ten, but it is often the reverse of this which is true.

In a good composition the means employed, the springs, so to say, disappear to let the action and the sentiment of the scene expressed speak for themselves.

Supreme skill does not reveal itself; it knows how to conceal itself under the form of extreme simplicity.

Whatever the realists may say, there are few scenes in nature which can be copied exactly as they are.

The most horrible catastrophes often take place among surroundings which have nothing sinister in them. A joyous sunbeam may light up the death agony of a man dying of the plague. I know how art may avail itself of a contrast like this, but how often does a tragedy occur under circumstances seemingly the most commonplace!

I remember I was turning the corner of a street one day in Antwerp, when I perceived, a few steps away, a crowd of people gathered around some object which was hidden from my view.

I thought at first that they had been attracted there merely by curiosity, and the idea of a tragedy having taken place never occurred to my mind.

Drawing nearer, I saw lying on the ground before

me, apparently lifeless, a workman who had fallen from a ladder and crushed his skull against the pavement.

I was vividly impressed by the brutal realism of the occurrence itself, but not at all by the circumstances under which it had taken place.

Art, happily not having at its disposal this means of stirring the emotions, must do so by more striking methods than would be strictly correct according to true feeling and the logic of the imagination.

When I was close to the dying man I recognized expressions and details which my reason told me were characteristic of his condition, but which I had never before seen ; this recognition, however, was not immediate, and was at first confused.

It is the part of the artist to seize these elements, to group them together, or to separate them, as may be necessary, in order to bring out clearly the general idea.

Those realists who reject arrangement, and refuse to admit the necessity of selection even, deny the existence of art.

They may laugh at the rustic who said to Rousseau as he was painting an oak, "Why are you making that tree, when it is already made?"

It is none the less evident, however, that if the landscape-painter had in view only the exact reproduction of the oak, the remark of the peasant would have been perfectly just.

What Rousseau aimed at, then, was an individual interpretation which should be superior to the reality.

He did not paint the tree itself, but the expression which he lent it, the impression he received from it, and this perhaps unconsciously and impelled by his passion for the Beautiful, thinking all the time that he was making an exact copy of nature.

There are certain pictures which please at first, but

when they are out of sight leave only a faint impression on the mind; there are others, on the contrary, which leave an impression on the mind that grows stronger with time, engraves itself upon the memory, and is never again effaced from it.

One often finds it difficult to estimate the exact degree of merit possessed by a work while one is looking at it; but later, when the impression received from it shall have settled, so to say, and become classified, it will be easy to discern which are its really powerful qualities, and which are those that have only a superficial interest.

The effect a picture produces on the memory is the counter-proof of its direct effect.

In a painting, parts which are beautiful in themselves may constitute a bad whole.

To say of any work of art that it has beauties is to condemn it. This thought does not occur to one in contemplating a masterpiece.

If an accessory in a picture strikes the eye, so much the worse! A defect which did not attract the attention would be better.

When an artist, in exhibiting his picture, perceives that his visitors are struck by the beauty of a subordinate part, let him not hesitate for an instant to sacrifice it.

.    .    .    .    .    .    .

To close these extracts, taken from the note-books in which I recorded my thoughts on art in former years, I will give the conclusions I have arrived at:

The true is not material reality only.

Spirit should govern matter.

The terrestrial creation is made for the service of man, who is its king.

We all have thoughts, feelings, and passions; the

artist should not be satisfied to be the only one to play the passive part of a mirror.

------

## XCIV.

I AM now nearing the end of the task I imposed upon myself in writing these memoirs.

When I say the task I imposed upon myself, I do not mean to imply that this task has been, in the main, a painful one.

But, if it has for the most part afforded me happiness, on the other hand I have had to overcome at times a natural reluctance to recall, in retracing the past, sorrows which sadden the lives of even the happiest men.

Yet even sorrow itself, viewed from a distance, is not without a certain melancholy charm.

It is from this distance that I would contemplate the sorrows of past years ; at this distance, when the shreds of their fleece, left by the frightened flock upon the brambles, are undistinguishable from the blossoms of the heather.

I wish to preserve this illusion.

This chapter will be in this work like those little cemeteries reposing on the outskirts of villages, whose horror is concealed under a network of flowery verdure.

In bringing here the beloved beings who have had a part in these memoirs, I shall yield myself up not to anguish but to pious emotion.

It is in our hearts that we cherish the venerated memory of those we have loved and lost.

Their mortal part, committed to earth, passes into the grass and the flowers with which we adorn their graves, and under this form we still love it with that vague sentiment of universal brotherhood which unites all nature.

But the soul is not there!

This has gone to mingle with the supernatural world, to which it aspired even here below—the dreamed-of Ideal!  It sees the promised light.

And it has departed, leaving its memory in our hearts living and fresh as if it had not left us.

The sight of the grave, with all its afflicting suggestions, could add nothing to the intensity of this memory.

The chrysalis dries up pitiably on the tree to which its silken cocoon still remains attached—the dark and narrow tomb whence the splendid butterfly has taken flight toward the sun, as souls take flight toward happier spheres.

The tomb of the worm was the cradle of the butterfly.

Who does not feel, in the depths of his consciousness, that the soul has nothing in common with the darkness of the sepulchre?

Who can understand the laws which govern the invisible realms?

May we not hope for all things?

We have long since seen depart for those regions of rest, my little sister, my mother, my grandmother, and my father.

And now, in 1862, on St. Nicholas' Day, just as my wife was preparing the gay bonbons of the season which were to give Virginie so much delight (we all know with what joyful enthusiasm mothers set about these tasks), the telegraph brought us, without warning, the news of the death of Félix de Vigne.  Rheumatism of the heart had carried him off, after an illness of a few days.  I had thought, from a reassuring letter I had received, and which I had not shown to Elodie, that his malady was nothing more than a slight indisposition.

We have seen that he was making progress in his art. One of his latest pictures, "Sunday Morning in the Middle Ages," occupies a good place in the museum at Brussels. He was a Chevalier of Leopold, and on the day of his death his appointment to the post of Director of the Academy of Louvain arrived.

In 1866 we lost our little angel Louis, the son of my brother Louis, at the age of seven.

And, in 1867, thou, our beloved uncle and second father, didst in thy turn leave us !

Notwithstanding his sixty-nine years his health had appeared excellent, when he suddenly fell a victim to an unforeseen disease. It may be said of him that he had no old age, so full of enthusiasm was he still for the good and the beautiful.

It is needless for me to say how greatly he was regretted, even by many of those whose opinions he had opposed.

He had transmitted his own noble sentiments to my niece Julie, whose education he had directed, with the intention, as he said, of " making a woman of her."

He sought to cultivate in her heroism of soul. The poor child, who was of a highly-strung temperament, had need, rather, of a preceptor who should have taught her to moderate her stoical ardor.

When a child she had burned herself with a red-hot iron, in order to accustom herself to pain.

She read Plutarch, Lamartine, and Leconte de Lisle, with delight.

She had a passion for martyrs. She cherished a devotion to the memory of André Chénier that bordered on love.

Physically she resembled Charlotte Corday.

She shared every pang suffered by her country! Poor blighted flower, she soon languished under our cold sky.

They took her to the south—to the land where the orange-tree blooms.

The warm sunshine revived her for a time; they thought her saved.

She believed she was well, and ran about one day imprudently on the beach of Antibes, when a sea-breeze was blowing. There it was that she suggested to our friend, the delightful poet, Paul Arène, one of his most charming poems—"Au Bord de la Mer"—of which I shall quote a few stanzas:

> " Un matin je rêvait de Grèce
>     Près de la mer, quand sur le bord,
>   Passèrent, de l'or dans leur tresse,
>     Deux mignonnes enfants du Nord.
>
>         .     .     .     .     .
>
> " Vois là-bas frémir à la brise
>     Le rire innombrable des flots,
>   Vois cette écume qui se brise
>     Aux pointes blanches des ilots.
>
> " C'est fête en Méditerranée."
>
>         .     .     .     .     .

Alas! six months later the Mediterranean was no longer *en fête*.

There are days when its restless, rapid waves beat against the shore with the lugubrious sound of a knell!

------

## XCV.

IN 1865, after I had finished the " Day's Work Done," I was again seized with the desire to travel, and I set out for Brittany.

I was profoundly struck by Finistere, under all its aspects, maritime, rural, and religious.

The dreary moors, the granite crosses of the Calvaries * erected at the solitary cross-roads, expressing the rude fervor of the inhabitants ; the deep, dark paths where neither the light from the zenith, nor the sunbeams sifted through the leafy roof overhead sufficed to dispel the eternal gloom in which innumerable roots twisted and interlaced themselves, like knots of vipers ; the wan light of the crepuscule and of cloudy days that cast a leaden hue, like a gray tan, over the thin faces of the peasants with their fierce eyes and their long, thick hair, falling down their backs, over their stooped shoulders ; the women that looked like pictures of the Virgin, with their mitre-shaped head-dresses, their ruffs, out of which rose their slender, curved necks, and their cotton petticoats trimmed with gold or silver braid—this monastic rusticity, this mystic wildness, evoked in my mind confused and far-off recollections, more remote than any I retained of my native Artois.

And I felt that I was indeed a descendant of the Bretons.

These were the thoughts that crossed my mind when we came in full view of the square of Châteaulin, where a fair, crowded with people from the neighboring villages, was being held.  At sight of the various costumes —brown, black, yellow, red, and blue—our little Virginie cried, " O mamma, the Carnival ! "

We were, then, at Châteaulin, where we had just arrived by boat from Brest, on our way to Douarnenez.

We hired a rickety vehicle, a sort of cabriolet-carriole, with a glazed window, where we were completely protected from the rain which fell unceasingly.

---

* In Catholic countries, a hill with a chapel or cross on the top.

We soon entered the moors covered with pink heather and wrapped in vapor far as the eye could reach, a gloomy and desolate scene viewed through the rain that beat against the window-panes which rattled in their frames, and that was now beginning to make its way through the crevices.

Our little Virginie, in harmony with the weather, burst into a torrent of tears, and the only way in which I could succeed in pacifying her was by gathering bunches of broom and fox-glove for her.

In this way we passed through Kerghoat, celebrated for its *Pardon*, and through Locronan and Kerglass, two villages full of individuality, each containing a fine church.

These granite monuments, their inner walls moss-grown from the dampness, symbolize well the somber character of the faith of these people.

The Breton is, by nature, artistic.

In Brittany, more frequently than elsewhere, does the traveler meet, even in the most solitary hamlets, those rudely carved shapeless stones that exercise so mysterious a fascination over the beholder.

They may be monstrous, but they are neither vulgar nor ridiculous; their dreamy ugliness has a somber and even a menacing air.

Thrilling with the ardor of mystic visions it was that the obscure artists of an earlier age gave with unskilful touch to their works a power of expression that is seldom the result of polished art.

And nothing could be more in harmony with these desert heaths than those granite monuments of art.

Douarnenez, whose women and whose beach I had heard so highly extolled, impressed me but little at first.

At Douarnenez one misses the sunshine.

The shores of the bay, vaguely defined in the soft,

heavy, bluish mists, had an indescribably chilling effect.

And then this fog, slowly but surely inhaled, had damped the ardor of my enthusiasm. The women looked awkward in their Sunday finery. The men, with reddish-brown complexions and bluish-black costumes, swarmed in the streets, many of them drunk, or stood in groups around the doors of the taverns. Under the leaden sky all this was intensely depressing.

We alighted from our carriole at the Hôtel du Commerce, where we found Edouard Leconte, a landscape painter full of promise, who died at thirty; our charming poet André Theuriet, and Emanuel Lansyer, whose skilful pencil was the first to interpret Douarnenez.

But how different everything looked the next day when, after winding our way through a network of fetid streets permeated with a nauseating odor of sardines, we suddenly found ourselves in sight of the bay that stretched before us in its dazzling beauty!

It looked like an immense cup, carved by some Greek giant for the use of the gods.

Brown cliffs, streaked with white and pink; black cliffs, veined with gold; creeks, capes, shores—wound away far as the eye could reach, inexpressibly graceful in outline and harmonious in color.

In the background, the heath-clad hills of the Menez C'hom, pink like the peach-blossom, rose in the limpid atmosphere.

And along the beach fringed with foam stretched somber woods and golden harvests toward Locronan seated on its graceful mountain-slope, its beautiful church standing sharply out against the sky.

To the left were Cape La Chèvre with its bold buttresses, peaked cliffs, and lace-like stone-work, and

Point L'Heidé, at whose feet the unresting ocean dashes ceaselessly.

In its bed of tawny sand the sea boiled—a sea of sapphires and amethysts, through which flashed here and there a dazzling gleam of white foam, covered with a thousand barks, whose brown and red sails flapped in the wind.

From precipitous granite walls, constantly exuding moisture, flashing in the sunshine and clouding in the shade, innumerable springs gushed forth and flowed sparkling down over the sand where they wound like moiré ribbons, so clear and transparent as to be almost invisible, then disappeared, losing themselves in the sea, leaving behind them pools, motionless mirrors reflecting the sky and the brown rocks that framed them in.

Occasionally a wave would dash with force against the rocks covered with sea-weed, and hurry then swiftly back to the sea, carrying with it the pebbles of the shingly beach.

Around the quiet pools, like flights of swallows, here strongly defined in the full sunshine, there half-veiled by the clouds of dashing spray, moved groups of washer-women, *svelte* and tall, their heads covered by the white coiffe of Douarnenez, tightly drawn in on the top of the head, and with lappets like pointed wings turned up at the back, leaving the neck bare.

The population is maritime, and of various types and customs.

There are here faces with straight profiles, the forehead and chin prominent, the lips thick, the jaws square and strong, the eyes blue and with well-opened lids, the arch of the brow wide, prolonging the eyebrows to the temples—a Gallo-Roman type, dear to Michael Angelo. There is, too, the gazelle-like type, with flexible neck, that recalls the desert, oblique eyes, the pupils sparkling like black diamonds set in brilliant white enamel, delicate and sharply chiseled features and an olive-bronze complexion.

The one brings to the mind the dolmens of Celtic forests, the other the harems of the East.

Here are none of the vanities of dress ; the garments are thrown on hap-hazard—petticoats, once black, now rusty with use ; blue petticoats, discolored with the sea-air, following in an unbroken line the outlines of the form, or gathered up in front and fastened back behind, revealing the graceful outlines of the legs ; shawls, darned, patched, and ragged, swaying with every movement of the form—now thrown over the shoulders, like wings, now falling in graceful folds, swelling out and blowing about at the caprice of the breeze, or with the movements of the wearer.

Here and there young girls bent gracefully over the water, the head slightly raised, the bare arms extended as they wrung the linen, or rising and falling with the blows of the bats that clacked swiftly to the ceaseless accompaniment of the dashing of the waves.

Then there were groups of children, in rags of every color, tumbling about, and rolling over one another ; little half-naked fisher-boys, agile as monkeys ; little girls wearing their mothers' old caps hind-side foremost ; round heads covered with red, curly hair, with ruddy faces that looked at you with glorious eyes and gaping mouths.

Finally, in the midst of this scene of life, light, and clouds of humid dust, were to be seen more quiet figures—a tall girl standing in the sunshine, her weight resting on her hip, her face turned toward the sea, and lazily twisting her body and her neck, against which the breeze flapped the lappets of her cap ; while farther away gloomy-looking old women, like mummies, sitting bolt upright against the rock, in which they almost seemed to be incrusted, spun their flax like the Parcæ; and grave matrons passed and repassed ceaselessly, with erect head and straight neck, and firm and slow step, their hands on their hips, their eyes cast down, their jugs firmly balanced on their heads.

You who visit this coast—Poulmarch—after me, may find there types of ugliness. As for me, I saw none.

I expended my energy in profitless admiration of it.

It made me fall ill.

I made my studio there. I filled my note-books with sketches of it.

But I would have liked to paint everything at once—the people, the rocks, the sea, the sky, the backgrounds.

What should I give up, and why give up anything?

And I began to plan, to turn over, to mix up a hundred different compositions, always hoping to put in everything, never succeeding, and ready to begin over again the next day.

I lost my sleep on account of it, and, if I sometimes dropped asleep from fatigue, I continued to paint and design in my dream; and I again saw those wonders, whirling before me in greater confusion than ever, and I thought that I had grasped at last that sorcerer of the bay.

For was he not indeed a sorcerer, this Proteus, who changed his form and color every day; now, with blurred and softened outlines, looming gigantic through the fog, now diminishing in size and permitting the eye to distinguish his adornments of lace-like arabesques; at times dashing himself, white with anger, against the impassive rocks covered with yellow sea-weed, at times, calm as a mirror, reflecting the sky with its white clouds,

broken by the shadows of the vessels; at times sending forth dazzling lights, that flashed along the sapphire
and emerald waves to kindle furnace-like flames in the
saffron atmosphere, and then fade into the leaden gray
of night!

At last, when I had sketched my composition (and
I may say that I did not choose the best among those I
had planned), I began the picture of the "Washer-women
of the Rocks of Finistere."

As usual, the sketch had been made with perfect
ease, and I thought that the picture was going to paint
itself.

The principal group was in the sun-flecked shadow,
while sunshine flooded the background. Oh, the background! It was there that I had thought the chief
beauty of my picture was to lie; and, leaving my figures
in outline, I spent all my energies in working at the
distances, not reflecting that their effect must depend
on the firmness and the finish of the figures.

But I put off touching these figures to the last,
working desperately at the grottoes, the beach, and the
villages rising one above the other on the shore, and
which were to shimmer so poetically in the sunshine.

It was a Penelope's web. I found it impossible to
rid myself of the fixed idea that always brought me
back to the same parts of my composition, which I
worked up, rubbed out, scratched out, and outlined
again in vain.

My nerves became disordered. At times it seemed
as if my brain would burst, but I did not give up my
task. I would lie down upon the ground and wait
until the crisis had passed. Then I would resume my
work, exclaiming to myself, "I will accomplish it, or
die in the attempt!"

Finally, I was obliged to put aside this picture for

another year. It had produced a buzzing in the ears which rendered me deaf, and other nervous disturbances which at times made work impossible to me.

Decidedly this bay set at naught the pencil and the brush of the artist. Its problem was the Infinite.

---

## XCVI.

I RETURNED to the peasants with whom I had been so much struck at Châteaulin.

I saw them again on the following Sunday morning at Ploaré.

Ploaré is a village of some importance, situated on the hill between Douarnenez and Quimper.

The scenery here is superb—woods of tall pines and beeches, where squirrels leap from branch to branch; gnarled oaks; chestnuts, some of them of gigantic size; white poplars and quince-trees; here and there a rude granite farm-house, with thatched roof, surrounded by its dung-heap; then moors covered with pink heather, or golden gorse; a smiling sylvan glen, its little streamlet, and its mill hidden in the flowery brush; farther on, meadows, fields of rye, and snowy buckwheat; magnificent alleys, always shady, traversed by herds of small cows and majestic swine, and along which long lines of peasants wind picturesquely on market-days.

The church, situated at the entrance to the village, faces Douarnenez, to which it appears to belong. It is of Gothic architecture, and in the genuine Breton style, with its low porch, its slender tower, through which the light is seen, its beautiful foliage, and its fantastic gargoyles. Its gray granite walls are stained with patches of white, green, and yellow lichens.

Around the church, in its low-walled inclosure shaded by large, leafy elms, are grouped picturesquely the houses of the village that stand out in bold relief against the sea, which in the distance seems to rise above the level of the streets.

Fisher-folk and the peasants of the neighboring villages attend mass here.

Although large, the church is too small for its purpose. The faithful for whom it has no room kneel under the porch, under the trees, and along the sacred walls, against which fanatics stretch out their arms in the form of a cross, like bas reliefs, while others prostrate themselves, touching the stone with their foreheads, their rosaries in their hands, their features hidden among the masses of their straggling locks. The less devout sit on the wall of the inclosure.

At the entrance a blind man kneels in the street, bending forward, his head raised, his sightless eyes wide open, leaning on his stick with one hand and holding out his worn felt hat, in a supplicating attitude, with the other. He is pathetically beautiful with his long black locks floating over his rags of coarse gray cloth.

In a powerful voice, now with vehemence, now in droning accents, he hurries or retards his song with fanatic inflections that seem to have come down from long past ages.

It brought before my mind the beggars who clamored and stretched out their arms toward Christ on the borders of the Dead Sea.

Here, too, as in the time of Christ, dogs crouched and venders encumbered with their wares the entrance and the porch.

In the middle of the inclosure, where we are seated, the faithful sleep stretched on the grass, with their hats for pillows; they are sleeping away their too early potations without attracting the slightest attention.

For here both gossip and ridicule are unknown.

A drunken peasant on his knees, his rosary between his fingers, is praying with great fervor; but his heavy head falls first on one side and then on the other, and sleep threatens to get the better of his devotion. He ends by resting his head on the shoulder of his neighbor, who is not at all disturbed in his devotions thereby. But there comes a moment in which the ceremony requires that they shall rise. The pious drunkard, losing his support, tumbles on his back, with his feet in the air. He continues his prayer without releasing his hold on the beads of his rosary.

No one is surprised. They raise him, and set him again on his knees. He continues to mumble his *pater*, and no one has even smiled.

Such are these simple believers!

If the men among the sea-faring part of the population are less handsome than the peasants, the peasant women, on the other hand, are far from being less graceful than the fisher-women.

Many of the women of the land are ugly, heavy, and ill-shaped; I will not speak of those who are only commonplace.

Poverty and neglect of hygienic laws have here given rise to many deformities, some of them extraordinarily unusual.

I have seen here several sisters who actually made one think of the beasts of the Apocalypse, whose frightful and monstrous appearance possessed such a horrible fascination that I could not remove my eyes from them. They exercised over me a sort of spell; grotesque faces in which, incredible as it may seem, were to be recognized certain distinctive features which constitute the beauty of their race !

Perhaps gentle souls were exiled in these hideous forms !

And I thought of "Beauty and the Beast," a story that had made me shed many tears in my childhood.

The recollection of those forms and faces still disturbs me.

But there are also to be found among the peasantry women superbly beautiful, with rounded contours and fresh complexions, in contrast with interesting and devout types of stunted ugliness, such as the painters of the middle ages loved to depict.

Pallid, pathetic, unhealthy natures, resembling those unnatural flowers that grow in caves, and turn their drooping forms toward the opening where the sunshine enters.

They have the appealing, languid air of those flowers, the same aspirations toward the light; pallid virgins, consumed by a hidden flame, in whose waxen faces the eyes burn like tapers.

On their pure foreheads the band of red cloth seems to bleed like a wound, while the pink strings fall down the slender neck emerging from the ruffle that surrounds it, from the heavy mitre-shaped head-dress dotted with blue and gold spangles softened by the misty whiteness of embroidered tulle.

Then, missal in hand, there were rich farmers' wives, robust and florid, with equally high head-dresses adorned with lace through which sparkled metallic spangles, with broad faces and high cheek-bones, resembling those virgins carved and painted by the peasants, dressed in embroidered cloth of gold with flounced and embroidered aprons of shot silk, and heavy black petticoats trimmed with as many rows of silver braid as they had livres for their dowry.

And in the midst of these groups I listened absently to the sound of the mass, my mind filled with ravishing dreams, and I fancied I saw rise before me scenes of long-vanished ages.

The strains of the organ came from the church, floating in mystic harmonies among the branches of the elms, and seeming to animate everything, even to the very stones, with a supernatural life. And I fancied the saints in the porch and the gargoyles of the cornices, with their grotesque heads, breathed as if under the spell of a sorcerer, while the sisters resembling the beasts of the Apocalypse, prostrated themselves in the grass below.

And I half expected to see the Galilean come and drive away the venders and the dogs who encumbered the porch, and by the touch of his divine fingers restore sight to the poor blind man whose droning accents reached us from the road.

---

## XCVII.

BUT it is at the *Pardons* that one must see this population of the sea-coast and the country inland—at Saint Anne la Palud, at Plougastel, at Saint Wendel, at La Clarté, at Kerghoat, and many other places where these religious festivals and fairs are held.

Here is Saint Anne la Palud, with its isolated church, that, from the desert where it stands, looks out upon the sea : moors, granite rocks, a few stunted and twisted trees, two or three little farm-houses, two or three gray pools hidden in the somber oasis of brush that bends before the ever-blowing wind of the ocean. In this vast arid plain dotted by low hills and hollowed out by furrows, on a solitary hill, the well of Saint Anne, which shelters the miraculous statuette of the saint, sends forth its sacred water that first forms a pool, and then flows farther down in a slender streamlet toward the bay whose plaintive moan can be heard at regular intervals.

Occasionally the lowings of the cows mingle with this noise. These are the only sounds to be heard in this desert.

But one morning all this is changed.

As in the time of the migrations of pastoral tribes, suddenly a village of tents springs up on this naked soil, with its inns, its shops, its sheds, and its stables.

Brown or white tents of different sizes and shapes, with dark openings in their sides, shine in the sunlight.

Around are the vehicles, the donkeys, and the horses.

It is the last Sunday in August.

And from the neighboring heights, on every path, over the rocks, on the plains below which fade into the blue of the sea covered with boats—from all sides, in a word, come lines of pilgrims with banners at their head.

I have witnessed this remarkable scene, grand and variegated with a thousand costumes of somber or brilliant colors. I have seen Châteaulin all black; Pleeben all brown; Plonevez all blue; Plougastel mingling together the most vivid colors—yellows, greens, violets, and oranges—Plougastel, whose fishermen, with their superb attitudes, wear the Neapolitan caps, and whose women look like parrots with their large head-dresses raised on hoops.

I have celebrated this *Pardon* of Saint Anne in my verses. I have described these fanatics arriving at the sacred fountain and, streaming with perspiration, worn out by the long journey, pouring bowlfuls of the icy cold water down their backs under their open shirts, and down their sleeves along their raised arms.

But poetry refuses to describe those women whose blind faith extinguishes their modesty, and who dip in the miraculous water of the pool whatever part of their body may be diseased.

I have tried to paint these people of another age streaming among the tents, gathering around the dram-shops or the chapels, mingling piety and drunkenness together under the surveillance of the *gendarme*, whose bicorn seems as much out of place here as it would have seemed at the procession of *La Juive*.

But how describe all these strange beings, these beggars who gather behind the arch of the church, gesticulating, uttering groans and wild cries—shameless cries, shameless groups, maniacal contortions and balancings of hideous monsters, as nearly resembling the earth in color as the toads which hop about in the dry soil, and with here and there among the horrible filth of their rags and on their ghastly faces, like those of clowns, a red spot, which is a broken-out ulcer!

I have described the pious crowd surrounding the church. I have shown them winding like a long ribbon along the sea-shore, while the beggars, left behind, dance about, gathered together in mocking groups and, forgetting for a moment their sighs and groans, give themselves up to jokes and jeers.

I have tried to describe the innumerable groups seen through the smoke and the gathering shades of twilight assembled on the evening of the *fête* around the blazing fires kindled here and there between the tents, for the evening meal, while crowds of frolicsome urchins leap daringly through the flames. Then all these sounds die away one by one in the silence of the night, and nothing is heard but the hollow moaning of the sea.

Finally, I have painted the sun breaking through the morning mists, lighting up Locronan seated midway on the gentle slope of its mountain, and Plougastel intoning its canticle, which is echoed from the cliffs, then dies away behind the high rocks at the foot of Menez C'hom.

But, whatever be the character of the multitude that press around Saint Anne de la Palud, the scene of action is so vast that, unhappily, the interest it awakens is picturesque and historic rather than personal. The imagination is more struck than the heart.

At Kerghoat, on the contrary, a profound emotion takes possession of one to the exclusion of every other sentiment. Such was the case with me on the occasion of my first visit there.

With the exception of the people of Plougastel and a few more distant parishes, the assemblage was almost the same as at Saint Anne's.

The church of gray granite, defined against a background of dark-green foliage, and standing near an oak-grove, was, as is customary at the *Pardons*, surrounded by a triple cordon of wax-candles, the offering of the neighboring parishes. The inclosure, dotted with graves, with here and there a rusty iron cross, was overgrown with the thick, bright-green grass peculiar to cemeteries.

In the center was a Calvary.

With an image of Christ on the cross were stone images of saints, defaced by time, types whose pious deformity awakened mystic dreams, and who presented some traits of resemblance with the faithful seated on the steps of the pedestal.

The inclosure was crowded with people.

The blind man of Ploaré was stretched upon the grass in a drunken stupor. Other striking-looking beggars sang psalms near the apsis, while the prostrate crowd prayed in silence.

I have already described the different types to be

seen among this multitude—their beauties, their expressive ugliness, their strange, almost demoniac deformities ; and the pallid girls, ecstatic souls, whose eyes burned with fever, and whose waxen foreheads seemed to bleed under their red bands, like the miraculous wafers of the legends.

There, too, were to be seen Chouans, with hawk-like faces, their yellow eyes shining through their long, tangled locks.

There were the same costumes, with gold and blue spangles glittering through lace ; the same subdued reds, like the rosy hues of dawn ; the same gorgeous harmonies of color.

The multitude wore an expectant air.

The shrine of the saint was about to appear.

The tall trees cast over the scene that semi-obscurity of the woods characteristic of Celtic ceremonies.

Stormy clouds, which had gradually gathered in the heavens, deepened this obscurity. The effect of the brilliant colors was heightened by this gloom, but the pallid faces of the sickly-looking girls looked paler still in this mystic light, while the sunburned complexions of the Chouans took on a sinister gray color.

Everything breathed a sacred awe.

Suddenly in the silence the bell sounds, shrill and clear !

The multitude rise to their feet.

They press forward from all sides.

Thousands of white head-dresses crowd together among the trees, looking like a vast sea of snow, rising and falling under the stormy sky.

And the two thousand tapers in the hands of the multitude, lighted one from the other, blaze forth at once, casting around in the gloom a rosy glow, stars glowing in an earthly heaven, ardent as the souls that glow in this place of prayer.

There is a movement at the entrance.  The first banner, which they find necessary to lower passing under the arch, makes its appearance.

It is heavy, and the man who carries it staggers, borne down by its weight.  He stops, and by a violent effort which strains all his muscles lifts it up again.

A crucifix—the face of a ghostly pallor, the arms fleshless—is represented on this barbaric ensign.

The drummers beat their drums whose warlike sounds mingle with the strains of sacred psalms.

They emerge from the shadows of the dark doorway, looking like portraits of Rembrandt.  There are three of them—one with the face of an eagle, one with the face of a Christ, one with the face of a bandit.  Plan, plan, plan !  They walk on, proud and full of emotion.

Little girls, with gilt mitre-shaped head-dresses and red, embroidered frocks, pass on bearing the shrine, toward which every eye is eagerly turned.

Then come the penitents.  They walk with trembling step and bowed head, the expiatory tapers in their hands, their legs and feet bare, their open shirts displaying their hairy breasts ; their eyes, haggard and burning feverishly, shining through their tangled locks, blonde, black, or gray, that float behind them, blown, as it were, by the wind of remorse ; faces, some of them so fleshless that they already seem to belong to the charnel-house where the dead look at us from the eyeless sockets of their grinning skulls.

Their sharp, emaciated features contrast with the religious peace of this starry field, where the flames of the tapers flicker on the death-like faces of shadowy virgins, whose souls soar in ecstatic rapture toward their heavenly home, for which more than one of them waits but the first chills of autumn to depart.

## XCVIII.

It is twenty-five years since I witnessed the *Pardon* which I have just described, and which took place in 1865. The character of this religious festival has probably, along with everything else, undergone great modifications since that time.

Many causes have contributed to this, among others and chiefly, the fatal war of 1870, which called all the young men of the country to arms. Adieu, then, *brogou-craz* and long locks! And, too, the *bourgeois*, in search of sea-bathing, have invaded the scenes of these pilgrimages which were before unintruded upon by strangers.

In 1873 we were again at Douarnenez, and we spent some delightful hours on the enchanting beach which winds among the rocks at the foot of the town.

While I, in a retired nook, painted or wrote verses, Virginie played with her little companions beside her mother, who occupied herself in reading or sewing.

But while she built castles with their moats in the sand and watched the waves washing them away, she was silently observing all that was taking place around her—children bathing in the sunshine or rolling on the sand, or washer-women wielding their swift and noisy bats.

And, returning to our room, she would draw all this from memory. I have now hundreds of her sketches which are very curious, and in which her progress may be followed step by step.

At one time I was a little alarmed by the ardor she displayed in her work and, fearing the effect on her growing brain, I forbade her to work in this way from memory.

For several months I saw no more sketches.

Finding that she obeyed my command to the letter, and beginning to be uneasy lest her creative power might be weakened, I communicated my fears to my mother.

She spoke of the matter to Virginie, who confessed that she had continued to draw in secret.

And it was with great delight that I found in the bottom of her bureau-drawer a heap of drawings, varied compositions, which were no longer the scrawls of the child, but which rendered expressive scenes very clearly and altogether in the style of the paintings she has since made. She had used for her drawings every scrap of paper that came in her way—leaves torn from note-books, old copy-books, envelopes of letters, on which she drew hasty sketches with the trepidation which accompanies every forbidden act.

One day as I was sitting on a rock on the beach of Douarnenez, sketching, I saw a dark, elegantly dressed young man, who formed the center of a group, advancing toward me over the moist sand which reflected the blue light from the zenith. He walked with rapid strides, his head raised, his right arm extended, declaiming verses in that mock-heroic manner in which irony and enthusiasm are blended, as if he did not wish to be taken altogether seriously while reciting to his friends these improvisations which displayed genuine poetic fervor. This sort of mock-heroism is another form of modesty.

The exhilarating atmosphere had inspired him, and he called out to some of his companions, who had remained on the beach, " I have just found the last line of a superb sonnet ! "

I had caught, from my seat on the rocks, the words of this last line :

" En poussant de grands cris, je marchais dans le ciel ! "

" Who is this crazy actor ? " I said to myself.

On the following day I met him on the Ploaré road, in the company of several artists who were returning from an excursion into the country.  He wore a manila hat, around which was twisted a branch of honeysuckle plucked on the way.  He carried, slung over his shoulder, with the triumphant air of a conqueror, a number of mushrooms tied in a white handkerchief which was fastened to the end of his umbrella.

He was accompanied by a young lady of a Minerva type of beauty, and a charming little girl with eyes the color of black coffee, whom her nurse was carrying in her arms.

He was declaiming in the same mock-heroic fashion as on the preceding day.

Among the persons who accompanied him I perceived my friend Jundt and Moulin, the sculptor.  They asked me to call on them in the evening, at the Hôtel du Commerce, where all the members of this gay party were stopping.

I had just returned to Douarnenez, where I had hired an apartment.

Passing through Paris, I had bought at the railway-station Lemerre's "Anthologie."  I must confess, to my shame, that for the first time I read there some verses of Leconte de Lisle.

They had enchanted me.

" Le Condor," " Les Hurleurs," *L'Epée d'Angantyr*, with their magnificent rhythm, their splendor of diction, the tragic horrors of their images, their profound insight into the spiritual, their wonderful melody, resounded ceaselessly in my memory and held me captive by their spell.

·I had read there also with great delight "Les Aïeules," of Coppée, that exquisite pastoral by a Parisian, in which

I fancied I again saw the dear old Catharine of my childhood.

In the evening, then, I presented myself at the Hôtel du Commerce, as had been agreed upon. I found the party still at table.

The conversation, in which the dark young man took an active part, was animated.

Moulin made the introductions, and the pompous declaimer of the beach showed himself so simple and cordial that he won my heart at once.

We naturally spoke of poetry, and of Leconte de Lisle.

" What!" he cried, " you are a painter, and you have read and appreciate Leconte de Lisle!"

I confessed that I had only read him recently.

He was an intimate friend of the great poet, and he recited various passages from his poems to me. He repeated, too, some sonnets of his own, with whose splendid plastic and heroic form every one is now familiar.

And when I returned home, at a very late hour, I went to whisper to my wife, who had already retired: " You remember our handsome actor? He is a charming young man and an entertaining poet; his name is José Maria de Heredia."

It is to be conjectured that I, on my side, had not displeased him, for he came on the following day to see us. He inspired me with sudden confidence, and I confessed to him that I, too, made verses in secret.

He took my manuscript away with him.

He was so amiable as to take an interest in my verses, and he gave me excellent advice concerning many of their faults of inexperience. But where is the young poet (for I was young as a poet) who has not profited by the counsels of Heredia?

A close friendship soon united us. .

## XCIX.

I HAD written some verses at college in 1843, and others at Courrières in 1847, while convalescing from the illness which had interrupted my painting.

Occasionally after that I felt the impulse to write verses, and in 1864 I wrote my first sonnet, "Courrières," inspired by the plain of my native village dominated by its belfry-tower, a building whose happy proportions have been admired by all the architects who have seen it.

It bears the date 1532, and was built by Charles V.

Shortly afterward, inspired by the view of a pool sleeping in the shadow of the alders, I composed a little poem called "Le Soir," which, like the sonnet just mentioned, is included in the collection, "Les Champs et la Mer." Then my poetic ardor had cooled.

When the fatal year of 1870 arrived, I threw away my brushes and expended my energy in writing furious imprecations and wild stanzas, all of which I destroyed with the exception of two or three sonnets of a more moderate character, and which are included in the first edition of the before-mentioned work.*

When this excitement passed away, my thoughts still continued to clothe themselves occasionally in the form of poetry.

I found in this a new source of joy, and at the same time an outlet for certain aspirations which had begun to give my painting a too realistic character.

---

* At this time my brother Émile, remembering that he had been a soldier, quitted his wife and child and joined the active troops at Pas-de-Calais. He was named commandant, and at the head of his battalion was one of those who protected the retreat of Faidherbe, after the battle of Saint Quentin.

The appearance of "Les Champs et la Mer" procured me the advantage of the friendship, formed at the house of my publisher and dear friend, Alphonse Lemerre, of some of the distinguished poets who are an honor to our literature.

Then I grew more ambitious, and I was so daring as to conceive the project of writing a sort of pastoral epic.

But, before telling how this idea came to my mind, I wish to devote a few lines to an artist whom I knew and loved, who was for ten years my colleague on the jury of painting, and who was the first to encourage me to write.

I refer to Eugène Fromentin.

He was a man of singularly delicate and refined nature, of a highly-strung temperament, and both amiable and noble-minded.

Every one is familiar with his admirable qualities as a painter, and his distinguished gifts as a writer. Théophile Gautier has told me that he considered "L'Été dans le Sahara" one of the masterpieces of our literature.

How many beauties there are, too, in "L'Armée dans le Sahale," "Dominique," and "Les Maîtres d'Autrefois"!

He had made his *début* with some unpretentious little landscapes of his native place, which had attracted my attention in 1847.

I was therefore greatly surprised when I saw his first pictures of Africa, two or three years later. A complete transformation had taken place in his style, which had become absolutely independent. Those strange canvases looked at a distance like marble plaques, so confused seemed the masses formed by the groups of Arabs and camels enveloped in the rosy gray shadows of the twilight.

But the eye soon learned to separate them, and the

mystery, thus penetrated, gave rise to delightful emotions.

I remember a picture in this style, of some Arab women, running, laden with their leathern water-bottles. Oh, the delightful freshness of the first impressions of an unknown land !

Fromentin afterward became more concise, more learned ; but I have always regretted those first delightful flowers of his imagination.

Every one who knew him will remember how great were his personal attractions.

His frame was small, but perfectly well-proportioned.

From his long sojourn in Africa he had acquired a resemblance to the Arabs, but in the vivacity of his manners and in his witty eloquence he was still a Frenchman.

Amiable, cordial, and kind-hearted, intolerant of everything commonplace, upright and frank, Fromentin had gained the esteem and affection of his comrades. His black eyes, full of expression, were brilliant and soft.

I never pass before his little house in the Place Pigalle, now a restaurant, without thinking with emotion of our pleasant chats at the studio, in the company of a few congenial friends, among them my excellent friend Busson.

In 1876 I was again in Brittany, and on a beautiful summer day I was contemplating, for the hundredth time, the wonderful Bay of Douarnenez, when an acquaintance handed me his newspaper, with the remark, " Fromentin is dead."

This unexpected piece of intelligence petrified me with amazement and grief.

I had so lately left him full of life and health ! A

phlegmon, probably the result of a carbuncle, had caused his death after an illness of a few days, at La Rochelle, his native place.

And I remember that, by a singular conincidence, the same bay that now stretched before me was the subject of the poem which I had dedicated to Fromentin.

And I recalled with keen emotion the words of the delightful letter of thanks he had written me, and which I preserve among my most precious autographs.

----

## C.

I went to the fields to look for subjects and effects, and to plan new pictures, taking with me a wild little country-girl, who carried my box, and from time to time posed for me.

She was a dark, slender child, full of spirits, and agile as a goat, and she would run about, her flying locks bronzed by the sun, fascinating by the playfulness of her every movement.

She suggested to me a little poem which was the germ of Jeanne. It is in the " Chant de l'Enfance," and begins as follows :

" Bientôt Jeanne courut, pieds nus, par les chiens,"

and ending with this :

" Le logis s'éclairait d'une lueur d'aurore . . ."

When I had written these verses, I had become so interested in my little girl, that I conceived the idea of making her the heroine of a long poem. Another of my models furnished me with the subject and the *dénoûment* of the plot.

This latter was a foundling who had been brought up at Courrières, but had been claimed by her mother, who was now in comfortable circumstances. She had refused to go back to her, however, preferring to remain with her adoptive parents, and to marry the peasant whom she loved.

As for the various scenes and episodes, with the exception of a few passages referring to the origin of Jeanne, I drew them from my imagination.

I have been asked why I made her an Indian. Why, because I wished to open up a new path toward the ideal, which has always haunted my imagination.

I wished, too, to make Jeanne not only the peasant of Artois, but the primitive woman, with all her uncultivated and natural instincts, in contrast with Angèle, the tender and mystic daughter of our Christian soil.

Was I wrong in not allowing myself to be hampered by the narrow limits of a province?

Never having been in India, I consulted authentic documents bearing on the subject.

Besides, it is not my intention to defend the errors I may have committed.

What exquisite pleasure has the writing of this poem afforded me!

What can there be more delightful than to create a little world and shut one's self up in it? During four years I was absorbed in its life, mingling more with its imaginary characters than with the real world surrounding me.

The art of the poet is more intoxicating than that of the painter; for the succession of the tableaux and the thoughts, the rapidity of the images, the intensity of the sentiments, and the immateriality of the process, tend to maintain in the brain and the nervous system a perpetual and pleasing excitement.

Painting, on the contrary, employs itself in the interpretation of a simple idea by palpable means.

But how many resemblances there are between the two arts ! In both there are the same general laws of composition, of comparison, of rejection, of contrast, and of harmony.

Often, at the movement of the rhythm, I fancied my pen was designing forms, while at the same time the sonorousness of the sounds produced upon me almost the effect of color.

But, precisely because it is intoxicating, the labor of the poet is excessively fatiguing. I contracted in this way a nervous affection of the brain, accompanied by vertigoes which resembled trances and lasted for hours.

Since then the physicians have absolutely prohibited me from writing poetry. It is in order to take my revenge for this that I write these memoirs.

Prose, that one can take up and lay down at will, permits periods of repose to the mind which the linking together of the verses and the continual obsession of the rhymes render restless.

Jeanne was published by Charpentier in 1880, and was afterward included in the " Petit Bibliothèque Litéraire " of Alphonse Lemerre.

----

## CI.

In the same year (1880) I received a fresh blow in my tenderest affections.

Madame Breton and I were taking some refreshment in the Café de l'Univers. It was at the beginning of May, and we were returning from the Exposition.

We were speaking of the good De Winne, whom we were accusing of having forgotten us.

We had had no news of him lately.  He had not, as was his custom, been present at the opening of the *Salon*.  He had not even acknowledged the receipt of my poem which I had sent him.

Just as we were attributing De Winne's silence to his incorrigible laziness, we perceived our cousin Paul de Vigne, the sculptor, driving rapidly in an open carriage across the Place du Palais Royal.

We called to him gayly, and we were surprised to see .him approach us with strong marks of agitation on his countenance.

He held out to me a telegram which he had just received, containing the words : "De Winne, pneumonia ; desperate condition.   Come."

I need not describe our consternation.  We returned home.  A similar dispatch awaited us there, which was soon followed by another containing these words : "All is ended."

You know what a fraternal friendship united me to De Winne.  I set out immediately for Brussels, a prey to the most poignant anguish.

We have seen the trials he had experienced at the outset of his career.  We have seen him again in the Boulevard du Mont Parnasse.  We last saw him at the moment when I threw myself into his arms, asking his pardon for having, in an access of mental suffering, suspected his loyal friendship.  I could say much more regarding this artist, who was a great portrait-painter.

It will be remembered that he painted a biblical subject, the " Parting of Ruth and Naomi," while I was painting my first picture of " The Harvesters."

With what emotion we regarded those canvases which cheated our hopes—pallid and insignificant paintings which the public did not even glance at when they were exhibited in the *Salon* of 1853!

But Liévin de Winne shortly after painted a picture which showed what he was capable of, "The Ecstatic Vision of Saint Francis of Assisi," in which the young artist suddenly developed remarkable power, and which created a sensation at the Exhibition at Brussels, where it was exhibited in 1854.

On his return to Ghent at this epoch, he painted a "Christ on the Mount of Olives," but, his hesitations returning to him, he did not succeed in giving this picture the virile qualities of the "Saint Francis." Then he went to Holland, whence he returned dazzled with the magic light of Rembrandt. He painted, then, several brilliant portraits of a powerful composition, but marred by too yellow a tinge.

The portrait of Félix de Vigne which he made shortly afterward bears a trace of this defect, but it is a masterly work, full of life, strongly modeled, the grounds broad, and faultless in drawing.

In 1858 our artist, whose ambition it was to be a great historical painter, executed an important picture, "The Holy Women at the Tomb of Christ." He showed at this time the influence of the German painters, and especially of Schnor.

This was contrary to his own nature, which was all sincerity and simplicity. Therefore "The Holy Women" is only a passably good picture, notwithstanding the persistent labor expended on it. This did not prevent him from planning a large picture, and he fixed upon the subject, "An Orgy of the Roman Cæsar while Some Slaves Are Being Put to Death."

He spoke of this picture with a great deal of enthusiasm.

One day he procured more than twenty volumes on

the subject of Roman history, shut himself up all the evening in his study, and after all he read none of them.

It will be seen by these prepossessions that our artist would have become a historical painter had it not been that his education was neglected, owing to the misfortunes of his early youth. His imagination, powerful in reality, was always impeded by this want. He felt this, and suffered from it, but, at the age when he might still have instructed himself, he had not the necessary time to do so, for he was obliged to give all his attention to earning a livelihood.

A sprightly gayety had succeeded to Liévin's former gloom. This gayety had become the indispensable aliment of his ardent soul.

He had suffered so much that he had taken a hatred to suffering, whose specter terrified him. His heart was profoundly compassionate, but, while he would give generously and promptly to succor distress, he shrank from the sight of misery.

This was the only thing in his character that resembled selfishness.

He was at once the most neglectful and the most faithful of friends. He displayed in his friendship the most delicate thoughtfulness and the most inexplicable forgetfulness—transitory periods of oblivion in which his heart slept, suddenly to awaken full of affectionate enthusiasm.

On such occasions he would smother one in his embraces, and respond to the reproaches addressed to him .by such outrageous and apparently well-grounded charges that one ended by believing them one's self, hardly knowing whether to laugh or to cry.

But, if he sometimes succeeded in escaping pain, he was always powerless to repress the violent irritation which every species of injustice caused him.

22

As an artist he was never envious; he delighted in speaking well of his fellow-artists, but he was always pitiless toward triumphant mediocrity.

Whenever his friends asked his opinion of their work, he gave it with a frankness that sometimes bor-dered on brutality.

And what valuable counsels he gave! Never again will he give me those wise counsels; and my pictures, at the critical moment, will wait for him in vain in the village which he so often lighted by his presence—the village of Courrières, where every one was so glad to see him, and where he loved, of a Sunday, to join in the amusements of his friends the peasants, whose hands, hardened by toil, he would press so cordially between his own.

The poor, too, have mourned him.

Since the year 1861 De Winne had lived in Brussels; he had bought there the comfortable house built by Otto de Thoren, the Austrian painter, who died recently in Paris, where several fine paintings had brought him into note.

De Winne had painted the portraits of the Count and Countess of Flanders, and of King Leopold I, and his reputation was firmly established.

As a preparation for the portrait of the king, he had first painted a camaïeu, which is now in the museum in Ghent.

This work is a masterpiece; all the sagacity of the diplomat, all the intellectual power of the scholar, all the majesty of the king, are expressed in this portrait which I have seen a hundred times with ever new ad-miration.

The modeling is of extraordinary delicacy and force. What incisive and flexible touches! The traits of the illustrious old man have been, so to speak, caught on the wing and fixed on the canvas forever.  The king is there, forever living.  Holbein might have been proud to paint this camaïeu.

Parisians will remember the famous portrait of Mr. Sandfort, an American, who is represented wearing an eyeglass and holding his hat in his hand.  It was perhaps the finest portrait of the International Exposition of 1878.  Other portrait-painters have displayed more pomp, more technical skill, but not one has depicted by more legitimate means or with profounder insight the masterpiece of creation—the human being.

What first strikes one in all De Winne's portraits are an indescribable air of austerity and familiarity blended, a sweet and gentle severity, unity, variety, and that ease, that tranquil power which results from the harmony of the parts and which is the highest quality of the true artist.  Here are no miracles of composition ; here is no apparent effort.  The characters regard you calmly from the depths of their souls, and reflect what is in their souls.

Such was my opinion, such was the opinion of the jury of the International Exposition of 1878, who unanimously voted him a first medal, after eleven votes had been given him for the medal of honor, which is only accorded to important compositions.

His later portraits, some of which were interrupted by death, show that De Winne was capable of even still better things.

I have tried to characterize in a few words his other pictures, but what shall I say of those where art itself disappears, or where only the thought of the artist guides his hand, dominating matter so completely that it seems to shine with its own brightness, to show two things only, the individuality of the subject and that of the painter.

When I arrived in Brussels for the funeral I had not seen any of these latter works, with the exception of an unfinished portrait of my brother Louis, one of the most extraordinarily life-like portraits I have ever seen.

On this day, when the creative hand was still in death, and when, shaken by sobs, I hurried up the stairs which I had so often ascended, my heart beating joyfully, when, entering the studio filled still with the presence of the artist, I found myself face to face with those superb and unpretending pictures, so spiritual, yet so life-like, my grief was changed to pious ecstasy and— touching mystery !—it seemed to me as if Liévin's spirit, mingling with the spirits of those he had so faithfully portrayed, was regarding me.   I felt it still present, still in communication with mine, and in this feeling—consoling thought !—I found something like an assurance of his immortality.

## CII.

HERE my memoirs end.

I do not wish to close this book, however, without casting a glance at the Exhibition of the paintings of the present century in the Champs de Mars, which has just closed.

This Exhibition has caused hardly any modification in my opinions regarding the works I have just mentioned, and it has still further confirmed the authority of the true masters for whom I had for a long time past entertained the sincerest admiration.

But how delightful to be able to behold in a few hours all the masterpieces seen at different times, and of which each successive impression was naturally weakened by the one following it !

How instructive for the public, to be able to compare these masterpieces with one another! How quickly this comparison brings back to the right path the judgment too often led astray by the exaggerated enthusiasms of private exhibitions, and still more by the incense of the coteries!

Thus it is that from some elevated plateau one surveys at a glance the road traversed during the heat of the day.

Such a view did I obtain, not long since, from the pass of the Aspin, in the Pyrenees. And scarcely had I taken in the marvelous scene of the valley of the Arrau than the clouds that had been slowly gathering at my feet spread their thick veil over the landscape and burst in a water-spout, plunging everything into obscurity.

But soon the somber curtain opened again, and the valley was disclosed to view, more glorious than before.

Thus will time dispel the moral cloud of which the International Exposition was but the apparent cause.

French art traverses the world like those broad rivers that flow on, free and peaceful, but irresistible in their course. Let us not separate this river into little streams, which the storm might indeed swell and send noisily on their way for a time, but which in ordinary weather would flow only through barren soil.

Let there be no unprofitable dissensions, and let the light which the great Exposition of 1889 has diffused, by bringing together so many masterpieces, long continue to shine.

But, rich as this Exposition was, it would have been still more so if all the artists admitted there had been represented, like a few of the favored ones, by their best works.

For example, if we were so fortunate as to see there

the " Sacre " of David, and the " Eighteenth Brumaire "
of Bouchet, why, I ask, was a certain Jupiter with I
know not what nymph (nor do I desire to know), admitted—one of the worst works of our great artist Ingres, who, as we are aware, at times committed strange
mistakes ?

The great landscape-painter, Rousseau, was represented there by several canvases belonging to the epoch
when, confining himself too much to his own inspiration,
the puissant recluse had ended, alas! by producing
trivialities such as a prisoner in his cell might have
amused his solitude by painting.

The two or three little panels which are worthy of
him do not supply the place of his absent masterpieces.

Neither do the paintings of Daubigny, scattered at
random, give any just idea of the merits of this delightful artist.

I do not blame the committee of organization for
this.   Doubtless they had insurmountable difficulties to
contend against.

Neither did I see there the best works of Delacroix,
nor those of Gustave Moreau.

And instead of the " Lady Macbeth " of Müller, why
was not his " Appeal of the Victims of the Reign of
Terror " exhibited—a picture which was so greatly admired at Versailles, where it has since been placed ?

But to many of those who knew Charlet only from
his popular lithographs, of which, it must be confessed,
many are commonplace, his " Retreat from Moscow "
was a revelation.   They had not expected so powerful
and dramatic a scene from him.   The " Leonardo da
Vinci " of Jean Gigóux and his " Portrait of a General," life-like as a Reynolds, also awakened a great
deal of interest.

Let us salute, in passing, one of our most valiant

veterans, Jean Gigóux, who, at eighty-four, continues to paint, without relaxation, works full of tender and natural feeling, and heads of young girls, full of a touching simplicity.

Our dear Baudry was badly represented by some portraits, the greater number in his inferior manner—his best painting, "The Pearl and the Wave," having been relegated to a distance from his panel, which, like that of Bastien Lepage, was hung on a lateral wall of the chapel of Manet.

For some years past the impressionists have occupied public attention, and it is but natural that they should have been put in a conspicuous place.

Their admirers on the committee, however, restrained no doubt by the sense of responsibility entailed by their delicate functions, admitted scarcely any but their earlier pictures, those whose reputation is established, and I must confess that they did not seem to me very striking ; some of them, indeed, I thought very inferior.

But if, on the one hand, though doubtless unintentionally, the importance of Manet, the recognized leader of the impressionist school, was exaggerated, perhaps, on the other, those who call themselves his followers were hardly done justice to.

Remembering former ridicule they feared to expose themselves to this again. But the public does not now laugh at those things ; and, besides, ridicule no longer kills in Paris.

They had wished to throw wide the doors to innovators, and they hesitated at the names of those who might have made good their claim to that title ; or rather, as I said before, they have admitted only their least characteristic works.

I can not believe that posterity will recognize a leader in Manet, who is rather a mediocre pupil of Goya and

Velasquez, and, later, of the Japanese school, while I remember to have seen some interesting and striking efforts in the midst of those fantastically iridescent landscapes that one seems to look at through the stopper of a decanter, or those pictures that seem as if made by machinery for birthday presents for grandpapas—those cows with wonderful horns, those boatmen overlaid with saffron, paddling in water the color of washing-blue (I do not here refer to Manet); in the midst of this St.-Vitus'-dance of Nature in the paroxysm of an hysterical attack, I remember, as I said, to have seen in some private exhibitions some works of this school whose strangeness attracted me—white lakes quivering in opalescent lights, where real breezes blow from the silvery sky and bend the yellow reeds—charming pictures, in which familiar graces are presented under a fresh aspect.

Since the honor was accorded to the impressionists of admitting them to the Blue Dome, why not have chosen, at least, some of their poetic essays?

At the present day more words are invented than things—in art, at least.

Are not all who seek the Ideal in the Real, impressionists?

But cliques have always sought to monopolize the exclusive use of the best things—including the finest of the red carnations.

By *impressionism* may perhaps be meant the confused impressions of neurosis, for impression in its true sense is eternal!

It is the whole of art!

At other epochs it was called inspiration, the divine fire. By Topper it was called a sixth sense, and by Boileau himself a hidden power.

There is a saying so true as to be a commonplace :

"There is nothing new under the sun!" Not even Manet.

It has been said that this artist delivered the French school of painting from the sauces of the Bolognese kitchen ; it must be in jest that this stereotyped phrase is repeated in turn to every novice, for the French school of art has long ceased to be influenced by that of Bologna.

He made war upon shadow, it has also been said. Another jest! Was Prudhomme right, then, when he said that *shadow is one of the imperfections of painting ?*

Answer, O Rembrandt, magician who shinest in the darkness!

But Prudhomme, without suspecting it, meant black and false shadows; and the friend to whom he spoke would not have complained of the cigar he had blamed the painter for having placed under the nose in his portrait if the shadow had been true, for he would not then have seen this shadow any more than he sees the shadows in Nature.

And, for my part, I would say to many of those young painters who, through a horror of false shadows, fall into a dull and leaden coloring worse than the Bolognese sauce : Paint shadows that the *bourgeois* will not see.

I would give the same advice with respect to those famous violet tints in the shadows which Prudhomme has ridiculed, and with reason, in the work of certain impressionist painters. If those violet tints seem to him exaggerated, it is not because they are violet; they might without detriment be still more so. It is because they are out of harmony, because they are not in accord with the contiguous tones. If harmony of coloring were preserved, an arm, a leg, a head, lighted from the blue heavens, would seem to Prudhomme the natural color of flesh, although a logical brush would mingle with its coloring a tinge of true violet.

What I mean by atmosphere is the play of ambient reflections under the broad sky ; not that white, even light in which the *values* are altogether absent.

Harmony, that magician, can make use of all tones, the most intense and the most discordant, by bringing them into accord and transfiguring them in its enchanting orchestration.

How many pretended impressionists have introduced only the discords of reflections !

But let us come to the painters of whom we have yet to speak.

Bastien Lepage will leave a lasting fame. This young artist, cut down in the flush of his promise, was a true investigator.

How conscientious was his work !

He made his *début* with a masterpiece, the " Portrait of my Grandfather." Touching familiarity, simple and accurate drawing, admirable truth of tone, strong and fine harmony, just relation of the figure to the background—all are there.

But why did he in his pictures attach equal importance to all the details, even the insignificant ones, without sufficiently considering their relative values ? But if what we call the envelope is wanting, how many true touches are there !

And how can we sufficiently admire the marvelous little panel in which he has immortalized his brother Émile !

France, in Bastien Lepage, has lost her Holbein.

If Rousseau, Delacroix, Baudry, and Daubigny were not represented by their best works, at least we may say that the finest pictures of Troyon sustain well the fame of this animal painter.

The pictures of Millet, too, have been chosen from among the masterpieces which, realizing more than the superficial aspects of things, evoke dreams of simple rural life.

There were in the Exhibition " The Gleaners," " The Man with the Hoe," " The Sheep-fold," and a less well-known landscape, of an impressive charm, where rise hills covered with austere verdure, and impenetrable hedges border the meadows along the roadside, while the warm rays of a clouded sun shine through the misty atmosphere—a picture rendered still more moving by a sort of conscious unskilfulness full of childlike candor.

There were those humble farm-houses which exhaled a thousand rural effluences in the peaceful surroundings of familiar lowings and sunburnt plains tawny with dust and the emanations of the wheat.

And the Corots, the incomparable Corots, so resplendent with ideal beauty that they transport one to heaven, so true to Nature that in seeing them one fancies one is looking through an open window upon Nature's self !

These pictures awakened universal admiration.

Why were you not there to witness it, good Father Corot, as you were called by your contemporaries? And, indeed, who could be more paternal than this great painter, who never married, and who at first sight looked like a worthy farmer, with his wide trousers and his ample waistcoat buttoned to the chin ?  What good-nature, but what brilliancy also, and what intelligence in his gentle glance !  What a clear, serene forehead !  What love, what charity did that mobile mouth express, the lips pressed together at times and the corners turning down slightly !  For his was not the commonplace amiability which keeps the mouths of many superficially good-natured people stretched in a continual smile.

And this man, so modest in his tastes, who addressed

grateful apostrophes to his dear *little pipe*, this frugal epicurean who went into raptures over the savoriness of a simple *pot-au-feu* or a fat pullet, this man so ingenuous and so little vain, had a just appreciation of his high value as an artist.

He would have witnessed tranquilly and without astonishment the triumph he obtained at the Exposition of 1889. This does not mean that he had ever expected it; no, he had been too long neglected by the public to have any faith in its justice. And yet his life was a continual overflow of pure joy, nourished by the spectacle of Nature, which he adored.

I seem to see him now in the studio of the Rue Paradis-Poissonnière, when he showed me one of his new pictures, saying: "Look at that sky, you little villain; how it shines of itself! You can see nothing else for it!" And afterward, at Douai, at the house of our fellow-artist Robaut, and at Arras, at the house of his faithful friend Dutilleux, who had also a keen and delicate feeling for Nature. And that day when, making a study of the fortifications of the city, I dared to remark to the great painter that one of his *values* seemed to me a little pale, and he took his black hat, and comparing it with the corresponding value in the subject of his sketch, said to me, "See if it is too pale."

And as I objected that he was not going to paint his hat in the study, he answered, "He is right, the little fellow!"

Such was the candor of this excellent man and great artist.

He did me the distinguished honor of coming to see me at Courrières in 1860. I went to meet him. We walked through the woods and the plains, indulging all the way in expressions of childlike delight.

The merest nothing, a bud freshly opened, the tender

shoot of a plant, was sufficient to launch him into poetry, and what poetry !

Our circumstances were still somewhat straitened.
There was no luxury at the table of my uncle, whose
guest he was.　But we knew his fondness for a tender
and succulent leg of mutton, cooked to a turn, a good
juicy pullet, and strong coffee ; all these we gave him, and,
besides, a bottle of old Romanee Conti from the cellar.

During the whole time of his stay he enchanted us
with his gayety and good-humor.

In the midst of our gayety, however, a thoughtful
look suddenly crossed his face.　He had observed in
my wife, who for nine months had nursed our Virginie,
unmistakable signs of exhaustion, and he urged the
necessity of weaning the child without delay, adding
that it was high time to do so; then, turning to me
with a severe expression, which I had never before seen
on his face, he said, " Can you not see this, too?"
None of us had observed it.

My wife followed his advice, and the proof of the
necessity for doing so was that she was seriously ill for
several months afterward, and I feared for a time that I
was going to lose her.

Heaven only knows how much I owe our great
painter for his friendly advice !

Corot, who was the first to depict poetically atmosphere and the infinite depths of the sky, is perhaps the
most original genius of our modern school of art, although he has drawn his inspiration from Claude Lorraine, and still more from Poussin.

He is the purest, the most tender, the most fascinating, the most spiritual, the most animated, and, although
his unity gives an appearance of sameness to his works,
in reality one of the most versatile of our contemporary
painters.

Each of his landscapes is a hymn of serene purity, where everything, however, lives, rejoices, loves, and palpitates.

He has expressed in natural surroundings, earthly realities and the ideals of Olympus and of Eden, preserving naturalness and simplicity, even in the subtle refinements of taste. Genius made of dawn and spring-time! Eternal sunshine, that age has not been able to chill! A child in the freshness of his enthusiasm; a thinker in the sureness of his profound knowledge!

We say the divine Mozart; we may also say the divine Corot, for he is the Mozart of painting! And with all this he has the good-natured simplicity of a country squire.

Paris may well be proud of having given him birth.

O France, who hast produced such artists, glory to thee!

Glory to thee, also, for having thrown open the vastest arena to the noblest combats of human genius!

O my country! Thou, for whom we have wept, believing thee lost, when thou wast bleeding from every pore, behold, thou hast just given the most astonishing proof of life in creating this immense beehive, where, from all the confines of the earth, have come countless swarms of industrious bees, whose pacific humming has drowned the vain noise of warlike clarions!

I have lived to see this miracle, and I thank Heaven for it. France will not stop here, and my daughter will one day say to her dear husband, the hearts of both filled with pious emotion at the sight of some new wonder sprung from the genius of our beloved country, what I have so often repeated, "Would that our fathers could see this!"

THE END.